## Praise for Shirley Wells

"This book has everything to make a good mystery.... Fans of mystery and suspense will enjoy this read."
—*Night Owl Reviews* on *Presumed Dead*

"The interrelationships between the people in the town are almost as intriguing as the mystery itself and the author lets readers piece together images of Dawson's Clough in bits and snatches. The setting gave the story a brooding mood which matched Dylan Scott's character well indeed."
—*All About Books* on *Presumed Dead*

"*Dead Silent* is an engrossing and spellbinding mystery that is full of surprises. With a wide variety of startling twists and turns, Shirley Wells brings *Dead Silent* to a stunning and unanticipated conclusion that is guaranteed to shock her readers."
—*The Readers Roundtable*

"I really enjoy reading this series, as so far the mysteries have been so well crafted that I'm never entirely sure what will happen next, or where the case will take us to."
—*BookChickCity.com* on *Dead Silent*

"I'm yet to completely figure out a Dylan Scott mystery. There are always plenty of ingenious twists and turns that lead me down the primrose path.... Dylan ranks in my top five mystery series. I already want to read the next one."
—*ManicReaders.com* on *Dead Calm*

## Also available from Shirley Wells and Carina Press

# SHIRLEY WELLS

# Dead Simple

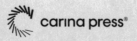

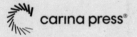 carina press®

ISBN-13: 978-0-373-00276-4

Dead Simple

Copyright © 2015 by Shirley Wells

Recycling programs
for this product may
not exist in your area.

Dear Reader,

I'm extremely fortunate to have the best job in the world. Being an author means receiving lovely letters from readers, having lots of writerly friends, knowing that when the words refuse to flow, I can take off to the hills with the dogs or enjoy a particularly long coffee break—well, you get the picture. Trust me, it's the best job in the world, and it means I spend time with my favorite private investigator, Dylan Scott.

In the course of his work, Dylan meets good guys and bad guys. Good guys might meet him in the pub, even buy him a pint. The bad guys, however, like to lure him to a place where they can do some serious damage. In *Dead Simple*, Dylan meets a bad guy at an old abandoned mill, a mill that only existed in my imagination—until I saw the front cover. *Awesome* is a word that seems to be thrown about at random these days, but it's the only one I can think of to describe the team that produce the covers for my Dylan Scott novels.

I love this cover and the way it shows Dylan walking toward that mill in his quest for justice. That's what *Dead Simple* is about—Dylan's determination to find justice for a simple soul who once helped him.

I hope you enjoy reading *Dead Simple* as much as I enjoyed writing it. I can be found at shirleywells.com, so please let me know, or just drop by for a chat.

Happy reading!

*Shirley Wells*

To my amazing family.
Love you all.

# Dead
## Simple

## Acknowledgments

I'm indebted to everyone at Carina Press for their hard work, dedication and professionalism. Special thanks must go to my awesome editor, Deb Nemeth, who takes my stories and makes them shine.

Finally, my undying gratitude goes to you, the reader, for allowing me to have the best job in the world.

# ONE

As Dylan stared at his ringing phone, it struck him that indecisiveness had taken a real hold. These days, the only snap decisions he made were about whether he wanted another whisky. Usually, yes. The phone continued to ring and he continued the inner debate. If he answered, Frank would want to know how he was doing. On the other hand, if he ignored it, Frank would call the landline and Dylan's mother would answer it. Either way, he'd have to speak to him.

He hit the button. "Hi, Frank. How are things with you?"

"Can't complain. Well, I could, but I won't. How are *you* doing?"

"I'm good, thanks."

*Good* wasn't a particularly truthful description. *Falling apart* would be more accurate. It was what people wanted to hear though. And Frank—ex-Detective Chief Inspector Willoughby—especially wanted to hear it. When Dylan had been a member of the police force, and Frank had been his boss, Frank had made his thoughts on "soft fucking southerners" well known. Perhaps Frank had been right. Maybe Dylan *was* soft. God knows, he ought to be doing better than this. He should have more purpose in life than turning down jobs because the thought of them bored him rigid. He should be doing more than reaching for the whisky bottle every night too.

"And how are you *really* doing?" Frank asked.

"I'm okay. Just catching up on some paperwork while everyone else watches TV." The closest he'd come to paperwork was picking at the label on the whisky bottle.

"Luke and Freya okay?"

"They're great, thanks. Luke was miffed because he's no longer eligible for the Under-16 football team, and is now over the moon because he's got a place in the Under-18 side. He'll be playing for the Gunners yet. Freya doesn't stop talking. She's either talking or asleep. But yeah, they're both great, thanks."

"Good. And your mother?"

"Stoned. Crazy. The usual."

Frank laughed. "You'd be lost without her."

Sad, but true.

Life was supposed to begin at forty, but Dylan's had disintegrated. As a widower, living with his mother, a sixteen-year-old and a two-year-old—

A widower. Widowers were old men who spent the day wearing slippers and who struggled to iron a shirt or boil an egg. Okay, so he wasn't very good with an iron, but he could boil an egg and he didn't even possess a pair of slippers. He was far too young to be a widower though. Too young and far too ill-equipped.

"So how's life in the frozen north?" he asked, keen for a change of subject. It was cold in London so God alone knew how bleak and inhospitable it was in Lancashire.

"That's what I'm calling about. Do you remember Stephen Greenwood?"

"Of course." Dylan had met Stevie, a tragic figure, on his first case in Dawson's Clough. "What's he been up to? Stealing supermarket trolleys?"

"He hasn't been up to a lot. He's dead."

"Dead? But he was only—"

"Murdered."

"No." Stevie, nicknamed Simple Stevie by some of the crueller locals, was the most harmless person one could meet. He wouldn't hurt a soul. "Who'd want to kill Stevie? What the hell happened?"

"The poor bugger was stabbed in his own home. Other than that, I don't know much. No sign of a forced entry, no prints, no murder weapon, no motive, certainly no suspects—nothing."

"When was this?"

"Tuesday. House-to-house inquiries and a search for the weapon or anything else hasn't turned up anything. There's a new detective chief inspector in charge and I can't say that me and him see eye to eye, so I'm struggling to get any information at all."

"Really? What happened to your cult hero status?"

Frank snorted at that. "It doesn't seem to be counting for much right now."

Poor Frank had been forced to retire on health grounds, but he'd been so respected that he'd never had trouble borrowing a file or getting the inside information on cases. To be left on the outside would hurt.

"I'm sure you've still got plenty of friends at the nick," Dylan said.

"Hmm. Sadly, none of them are working this case. I'll let you know if I manage to hear anything though."

"Do that, Frank. Thanks."

They talked of other things, and they reminisced as they always did, and when he ended the call, Dylan switched on his computer and searched for news on Stevie's murder. There was nothing that Frank hadn't told him though. Even the local newspaper hadn't managed to invent anything interesting.

Stevie's body had been found on Wednesday morning, time of death was estimated to be between eight and eleven o'clock the previous night, but other than that, the reporter could only talk about the scale of the operation and the determination of the police to bring Stevie's killer to justice.

Yeah, right. Cuts being made to the force were so drastic that they'd soon need a whip-round for a new pair of handcuffs. No way did they have the resources to launch a huge investigation. And, of course, Stevie was a nobody. His file would soon be gathering dust.

The door to his den swung open. "My, aren't you a little ray of sunshine," his mother said. "A face like that could send the cream sour."

She looked like a relic from the sixties. Slim and grey-haired, she wore her own body weight in beads, bangles and chains. Her long skirt couldn't decide if it was blue, red or purple and her jumper could compete with any rainbow. She didn't have a joint in her hand— her drug-taking had taken a back seat since she'd moved in with him and the kids—but she always looked stoned. For all that, she never failed to make him smile and, as Frank had said, he'd be lost without her.

"It's my thinking expression."

"Then I trust you're thinking about the dent you're making in that whisky." She nodded in a disapproving way at the bottle. Before he could comment, she added, "I always thought it a pity that you didn't inherit my good looks."

"Have you just come to insult me?" he asked, and she smiled.

"Nope. Luke's on the phone to the girlfriend so I thought I'd give him some peace."

"You're kidding. I thought your greatest pleasure was eavesdropping on his love life."

"It is, but he's getting wise to it. I've decided to back off a bit. If he thinks we're not interested, he might tell us about her."

"I wouldn't count on it."

"He's got a photo of her on his phone. Have you seen it?"

"No."

"Nor have I. Officially, at least. I had a sneaky look when he was in the shower."

"You did what? That's terrible."

"I know," she agreed. "I'm a bad, bad grandmother."

"How can you live with yourself?"

"Oh, I get by. She's very pretty, you know. She'd easily pass for eighteen. Perhaps she is eighteen. Has he said anything about her to you?"

"No. And unlike you, I don't pry."

"Ooh, hark at Goody Two-shoes." She hooted with laughter.

Dylan knew she'd really come to tell him that hiding out in his den—the room he'd grabbed for himself after Bev died—wasn't an option on a Sunday night. He got to his feet and, reluctantly, left the whisky bottle behind as he followed her into the sitting room where Luke had finished his phone call and was watching highlights of the day's football matches.

Bozo, the dog they'd adopted, was sleeping for once. It was rare to see the animal without something—a shoe, a shirt, a ball—in his mouth.

"I've told Charlie she can come round here on Saturday to watch the football." Luke kept his gaze firmly on the TV screen as he spoke. "Her mum and dad have got decorators in so—" He shrugged and left the sentence unfinished.

As no one answered—Dylan and his mother were too surprised to speak—he added, "That's okay, isn't it?"

"Of course," Dylan said. "Does Charlotte—Charlie—like football?"

"Of course. She plays for the school. It's only girls' football, but still."

"A girl who understands the offside rule?" Dylan said. "I'm impressed."

"Yeah, well." Luke clearly preferred to concentrate on the TV.

Dylan glanced at his mother who was trying, and failing, to keep the excitement from her expression. She'd been dying to meet Luke's girlfriend ever since she'd known of her existence. Dylan almost felt sorry for the two lovebirds.

He was pleased for Luke though. He'd wondered how his kids would cope with the loss of their mother but their ability to bounce back never failed to amaze him. Freya was too young to understand fully, but he'd thought Luke's world would fall apart. Yet his son had surprised him. Luke was down-to-earth, sensible and— remarkably resilient. He laughed, he had fun and he believed they were doing well.

Outwardly, Dylan knew they *were* doing well. It was inwardly that he was struggling. Perhaps he needed to take a leaf out of his son's book.

He wasn't too bad around people but, when he was alone, the guilt and anger crept up on him...

When Luke and his mother went to bed, he returned

to his den and poured himself another whisky. He'd promised himself he'd cut down after Christmas, but January had finally rolled into February and he'd done nothing about it. He would cut down though. He'd give the matter serious thought tomorrow.

He thought of the jobs he might do this week. None were pressing, and all were boring, so he could raise little enthusiasm. People thought a private investigator's lot was an exciting one. They had no idea that the vast majority of time was spent in front of a computer sorting out tedious insurance claims or checking up on errant spouses.

Many people had boring jobs though, so he wasn't alone in that. He was like the millions of others who worked simply to provide for their families. And at least he was his own boss. Life would be very different if he were still a member of the police.

Thanks to politics within the force, and thanks to a known criminal who'd claimed—wrongly—that Dylan had used excessive force during an arrest, he'd been kicked off the force in disgrace and spent a few months in prison for his trouble. Oh yes, when the force opted to show Joe Public that complaints about its officers were taken seriously, it did so in style.

Still, no use going over and over that. Sod 'em. Being his own boss had many advantages. He could break all the rules he wanted, within reason, and that suited him. Unlike the police who had to put a halt to investigations because they didn't have the resources, Dylan could dig away for as long as he liked. Not that he had resources, as his bank manager would be only too pleased to confirm, but in theory he could do as he liked.

Stevie's murder was a prime example. Dylan would

bet his life the killer would get away with it because police wouldn't have the necessary resources. And that was wrong on so many levels.

If anyone more harmless than Stevie had walked the planet, Dylan hadn't met them.

Stevie's mother had been killed when he was five years old. She'd been holding Stevie's hand as she'd walked him to school. A car had mounted the pavement and hit her, dragging her along the road. Poor Stevie had been dragged with her.

Apart from a limp and a deformed hand, Stevie's physical injuries were barely noticeable. The mental scars never healed though. He'd been looked after by his father and grandmother, and then, presumably because it was too much like hard work, placed into care. And he'd walked. Years ago, doctors had told him that he must walk, and that such a tragedy wouldn't happen again, and Stevie had been walking ever since. Occasionally, he'd stolen trolleys from the supermarkets and pushed those along the streets of Dawson's Clough.

It was unthinkable that someone could want Stevie dead. He'd never harmed anyone. Not to Dylan's knowledge anyway.

Getting conversation out of Stevie had been an art form. If you asked him a question, you'd be given a yes or no if you were lucky. If a more detailed response was called for, you'd have a long wait.

He remembered asking Stevie about a suspect he'd needed information on. Stevie had told him how this person had been cruel, how he'd dropped a cat from a bridge. The cat had broken two legs and it had been left to Stevie to care for the animal. Dylan had pictured the two damaged creatures together. Fearing the answer, he'd asked Stevie how long the animal had lived, and he'd laughed when Stevie had said eleven years. Stevie would have spent his last penny on that cat. He'd hated cruelty in any form. And now someone had decided that Stevie must die.

It was wrong. Bloody wrong.

Stevie was a few years younger than Dylan, but in his short life he'd known nothing but tragedy. There was no one to fight Stevie's corner, either. He had no family, no friends that Dylan knew of, a police force working under tight financial constraints—there was no one.

Life wasn't fair and, with that sad fact uppermost, Dylan went to bed. That proved a waste of time because, an hour later, he was sitting in the kitchen nursing a coffee. He would have preferred whisky but he really did need to cut down. He returned to his bed, confident he'd sleep, and then lay awake for another couple of hours.

All he could think about was the first time he met Stevie and the shambles his own life had been back then. Recently released from prison after his spectacular fall from grace in the eyes of the police force, Dylan had been living alone because Bev had thrown him out. A drunkard and a bloody loser, she'd called him. Life had gone from bad to worse because his mother had decided to move in with him. He'd registered as an investigator and reluctantly taken on his first job in Dawson's Clough.

It was that case, solved with help from Stevie, that had brought him back to the real world, a much better world. He'd realised that life as an investigator wasn't too bad. In fact, it was pretty good—no rule book and no answering to his superiors.

Far more important though, that case had helped him patch up his marriage. If he hadn't taken the job in

Dawson's Clough, solved the case and taken back his self-esteem, there was no knowing how low he would have sunk. He wouldn't have had those last few years with Bev. They'd been such good years too.

He owed Stevie for a hell of a lot more than either of them had realised.

On that thought, he finally dozed off.

When morning arrived, he was dog tired. He also knew that he was returning to Dawson's Clough.

His accountant would have a coronary if he knew. He'd remind Dylan that his swanky office had to be paid for. His accountant wouldn't know though.

There would be some money coming in because Bobby would be working. He'd taken on an assistant after Bev died because he'd known he couldn't afford to turn clients away as clearly as he'd known he wasn't up to doing the damn work.

Why he'd taken on a female assistant, he wouldn't understand until he took his dying breath. Bobby—she'd warned him in no uncertain terms that no one called her Roberta—was five feet three inches of determination. Twenty-eight years old, she'd been a police constable but had decided she needed more of a challenge. She bossed him around in the same way she'd been bossing around her two brothers all her life, but she worked tirelessly, and for that Dylan was eternally grateful.

Anyway, he'd worry about the finances later. For now, he had to return to Dawson's Clough.

Someone had to find justice for Stevie and, if that person had to be him, so be it.

# TWO

As DYLAN DROVE along the motorway toward Raw-tenstall, he experienced a strange sensation of coming home. The hills of east Lancashire were a familiar sight, and this morning they looked particularly stunning. A weak sun was doing its best, a rare occurrence in this part of the world, but a few patches of snow still lay on the peaks.

He remembered the first case he'd worked in the area, and how alien Lancashire had seemed back then. The accent had been too harsh, the voices too loud for his southern ear. The way people waved their hands around as they spoke, a hangover from the days when workers had shouted to make themselves heard over the heavy machinery in the cotton mills, had taken him by surprise too. Yet he'd soon discovered that northerners were, for the most part, friendlier and more trusting than their southern counterparts. They weren't afraid to talk to strangers, and their openness was refreshing. Or perhaps they were simply nosy. Either way, what you saw was what you got.

The cotton mills were long silent, but a few tall chimneys still dominated the towns' skylines. Some had been converted to luxury apartments, others had been left to chance their luck with the vagaries of the elements.

He drove over the hills and dropped down into Dawson's Clough. It wasn't raining, which made a refreshing change, and the pavements were crowded with people rushing from shop to office to coffee bar and making the most of their lunch break.

Dylan drove on to Market Street, the road that ran through the middle of the town, and to the Pennine Hotel. Even the familiar sight of the hotel was welcome. A stone building, erected in 1865 if you believed the sign above the main entrance, it managed to look somewhat aloof and grand from the car park.

He grabbed his bags from the car, locked the Morgan and strode inside. "Good grief."

"Hello, Mr. Scott. Yes, we've had a facelift since you were last here. We had to close for four months."

Dylan had seen the receptionist before but couldn't remember her name. "It looks good."

"Rewired and re-plumbed, new carpets throughout, painted from top to bottom, new lift installed—"

"Can I still afford to stay here?"

She smiled at that. "You can at this time of year. It's dead."

He filled in the form, giving his name, address and the Morgan's registration number. In return, he was handed the card for Room 24. "Thanks."

Unlike the old lift that had panicked many a passenger with its creaks and groans, this one moved swiftly and silently before depositing him right opposite his room.

The key card opened the door immediately and he stepped into a warm room. This was totally different to his first stay at the hotel. All he remembered of that was the cold, and the way he'd tramped the streets of Dawson's Clough, returned to his room and pulled on more clothes. He'd needed to drag the chair to the lukewarm radiator and sit and hug the thing, he recalled. This was far more comfortable.

He'd phoned Frank this morning to tell him he was returning to the area and, as he'd expected, Frank had suggested he stay at his place. It was tempting, and would be much less expensive, but he needed to be on the streets and Frank's home was too far out of town. Besides, he didn't want company.

It was nearing two o'clock and he decided he might as well start at the beginning.

He left the hotel and headed along the streets to find the apartment Stevie had called home for the last two years. The address Frank had given him, Anderson Street, was in a rundown, tired-looking area of town. A gusting wind blew litter along the gutter as he walked. Waste bins, stuffed full, spilled burger wrappers and empty cans onto the pavement. The newsagent's window was boarded up. Used chewing gum and dog shit littered the paths.

Perhaps he shouldn't be too surprised. The recession had seen many people lose their jobs, and the north of the U.K. had been hit especially hard. When people lost jobs, they often lost their sense of pride too.

He found the address and stood on the pavement outside to look up at the three-storey building. There were six apartments on each floor and balconies ran along the exterior of the upper storeys.

It was easy to see which was Stevie's flat because tatty police tape fluttered around the door to bar entry. A window was boarded up. Stevie would have hated that. His previous home had been spotless.

Dylan walked through the building's main entrance. An out-of-order notice stuck to lift doors informed people that they'd have to take the stairs. Dylan did so and was soon standing outside Stevie's door. He ducked under the police tape and, always proud of his breaking-and-entering skills, had the door unlocked within two minutes.

The door squeaked as he pushed it open and he stepped into a narrow hallway. Vinyl flooring was covered in dirty boot prints, probably belonging to coppers.

Dylan went straight into the kitchen. Everything in the room had been dusted for prints and the place was a mess, but what drew the eye was the large patch of dried blood on the floor and the red splashes on the wall. He took a dozen or so photos with his phone's camera, then stood at the sink to stare out at the buildings opposite. Most were business premises—a hairdresser's, an Indian takeaway, betting office, newsagent—and looked to have accommodation above.

He left the sad kitchen and stepped into the small sitting room. This room was too bare for even the most aggressive of coppers. It possessed a two-seater leather sofa, a wooden coffee table and a small TV. And that was it.

Stevie had never been one for gathering possessions. His old flat had been equally sparsely furnished. Spotlessly clean, but sparsely furnished.

He had a quick look in the minuscule bathroom and found a white towel, toothbrush and mug, and enough pills and potions to stock a pharmacist's.

He slipped the toothbrush into a sterile bag and put it in his pocket.

The only bedroom was—well, it was different. One complete wall was hidden by a stack of cardboard boxes of uniform size—about eighteen by eighteen by eighteen inches—most of which had been roughly opened. Against the other wall was a narrow single bed. The small wardrobe held a few clothes and a couple of pairs of shoes. An instant photo print machine sat on a table at the foot of the bed.

The sight made Dylan smile. It seemed that Stevie had given up collecting newspaper cuttings and moved on to digital photography. Either way, there would have been little happening in Dawson's Clough that escaped his notice. It was thanks in part to Stevie's collection of old newspaper clippings that Dylan had solved his very first case.

He opened the nearest cardboard box and, sure enough, it was crammed full of six-by-four-inch photos. There were hundreds. Thousands. A quick flick through told him that some were out of focus and all were date-stamped.

There was no sign of a camera though.

Ten minutes later, having learned nothing more about Stevie's life—or more important, his death—Dylan decided he'd better leave. He grabbed one of the cardboard boxes and locked the flat.

"Shit." He'd just ducked under the police tape when a uniformed copper appeared on the balcony. "Shit."

Dylan pinned his most innocent smile in place and began stamping his feet. "It's a cold one today."

The copper, who looked no older than Luke, nodded. "Can I help you, sir?"

"What? Oh, no, thanks. No, I'm waiting for a mate." He nodded at the neighbouring flat. "Should have been here by now but—" he shrugged, "—I'm trying to keep my feet warm."

The copper looked at the box.

"Full of old books," Dylan said, "so I'll be glad to get inside. Here—" he nodded at Stevie's flat, "—have you found out who did that bloke in yet?"

"The investigation's still ongoing."

"Any suspects?"

"We're following several leads. Now then—" He broke off as a young woman appeared on the landing and strode toward the flat adjoining Stevie's. "Looks like your *mate's* here, sir."

*Shit.*

"About time too." He strode up to the woman, and gave her his most pleading look. "I've got those books. Can we get inside? It's freezing out here."

"Hello, Lizzie," the copper greeted her. "Do you know this gentleman?"

She looked from him to Dylan and back to the copper. "Of course I bloody well know him. And no, he's not a customer. He's not the type to go for the cut-price whore, is he? Hey, don't forget, Plodders, the offer still stands. I'll give you an even bigger discount. And another thing—" She threw an accusing finger at the tape around Stevie's door. "When are you getting rid of that? It puts folk off. Bloody disgusting, it is. You should be out catching the bugger who did that instead of picking on me and my friends."

Without giving the officer time to respond to her tirade, she unlocked the door to her flat, pushed it open and stood back to let Dylan enter. He could have kissed her. Except—

She was tall, probably around the five ten mark, and slim. Her hair was an attractive red colour. Her face was caked in makeup that did little to hide the large red stain, presumably a birthmark, that covered the left side.

She was wearing black boots, short denim skirt and denim jacket.

"Right, mate." She leaned back against the closed door. "You've got ten seconds to tell me who you are. You're lucky that I don't like coppers or you'd be on your bloody bike. Having said that, I don't like bloody muggers, rapists or killers, either. So which are you?"

"None of those. It's a long story, but—"

"Five seconds."

"I'm an old friend—acquaintance of Stevie's. I was inside doing a bit of snooping. As it's against the law, I told that copper I was waiting for a mate. I don't think he believed me. Anyway, then you showed up. Thanks. I appreciate it."

Doubt flickered in her eyes. "How come a bloke like you was a friend of Stevie's?"

She deserved the truth, but he didn't want people knowing he was a private investigator. Not yet. "I worked up here a few years back and Stevie helped me."

"He did?" She looked even more doubtful.

"As surprising as it sounds, yes. I used to buy him breakfast at Asda, and he'd tell me stuff I needed to know—in words of one syllable, obviously."

She smiled at the latter. "He wasn't a great talker, was he? Poor bugger. Are you going to put that box down? It looks heavy."

"It is. Thanks." He put the box on flooring that was the same as in Stevie's flat. "Sorry about this. As soon as that copper's gone, I'll be on my way."

She marched off, presumably into the sitting room. "He's still hanging around, the nosy bugger," she called out. "I suppose you may as well have a drink while you're here. I'm having one, and as you're a friend of

Stevie's—" She crossed in front of him and into the kitchen. Dylan followed.

"I haven't got much in." She opened the fridge, took out two cans of cheap beer and handed one to Dylan. "It's this or nothing. Unless you want a cup of coffee, but there's no milk."

"Beer's great. Thanks." Cheap canned beer was better than no beer. "Really, I appreciate this. And I'm sorry I put you on the spot like that."

"S'alright. So why are you here? Are you trying to find out who killed Stevie? Let's face it, the lazy-arse coppers won't. They're too busy picking on the rest of us to get the real bloody criminals. It's like Plodders out there." She flicked a thumb to indicate where the police officer was probably standing. "Twice he's dragged me and my girlfriends in, and twice he's had to let us go. Bloody ridiculous. We're not doing anyone any harm, are we? Christ, offering some bloke a cheap blow job will land you in a cell and yet muggers, rapists and bloody killers can walk the streets without question. Bloody ridiculous."

She had a valid point there. "Did you know Stevie well?"

"No, not really. Who did? I used to call on him quite often, usually when I ran out of milk or coffee, but I can't say I knew much about him. I talked, he listened. Christ, we were a right bloody pair together. You couldn't get a word out of Stevie, and everyone reckons I'm either talking or sleeping. That's not quite true, because I don't talk when I'm working—unless they're into that sort of stuff, of course—but I'll admit that I can rattle on a bit."

"Really?" Dylan asked deadpan, and she laughed.

photo that had been taped to a water heater and handed it over. "That's Al. Stevie took it. It made him laugh."

The picture showed a tall, skinny man, probably about thirty. His jeans had fallen round his ankles.

"I fetched him when I saw that Stevie hadn't taken his wheelie bin in. They empty them early, even before Stevie got up, and he always put it round the back before he went out. I hammered on his door a few times, thinking perhaps he wasn't well, and panicked when I couldn't get an answer. I went and grabbed Al. I thought he could smash the door in. He couldn't—he's not as tough as he looks—but he smashed the kitchen window. He thought Stevie might still be alive but they reckon he'd been killed the night before."

"You didn't hear anything that night? See anyone unusual?"

"No, I was out. Working. They said there was no sign of a break-in, but how would they know that? Al smashed the kitchen window but you wouldn't think they'd take his word for it, would you? Still, why would anyone need to break in? Stevie was way too trusting for his own good. He would have let anyone in." She let out her breath on a sigh. "It always happens to the nice people, doesn't it?"

"Not always, Lizzie, but I know what you mean."

He drank the last mouthful of beer—it had tasted pretty good considering—and peered out the window. "It looks like that copper's gone now. I'll leave you in peace."

She strode past him to the living room and looked out at the balcony and the street below. "Looks like it."

"Thanks for letting me in, and thanks for the beer. I owe you one."

"You're welcome."

He thought for a moment, decided it didn't matter if people knew he was an investigator, and handed over his card. "If you see or hear anything, will you give me a call?"

"A P.I.? Oh. I will, yeah."

She walked with him to the front door, waited until he'd picked up the box of photos, and then opened the door. "Good luck, Dylan Scott. Stevie would be happy to know you were here."

He was halfway along the balcony, about to head for the steps, when Lizzie shouted after him. "Hey, you should try talking to Rachel. Rachel King."

"Where will I find her?"

"She'll either be working, sleeping or off her head on heroin. She lives at the bottom of the street, above the kebab shop. Believe it or not, this is the quiet end of Anderson Street. Our mini red-light district starts by the pub and ends at the canal. If I see her, I'll tell her you're looking for her. She probably knew Stevie a bit better than me."

# THREE

AN INSISTENT RINGING dragged Rachel from a sleep in which she'd been dreaming about being chased along a never-ending tunnel. Part of her was relieved to wake. The other part wondered who the hell could be ringing her doorbell with such enthusiasm.

She dragged herself out of bed, reached for her dressing gown and caught sight of her reflection. She looked like a witch. Long blond hair stuck out at every angle, and dark smudges beneath her eyes were a mix of lack of sleep and mascara that she hadn't had the energy to remove last night. She didn't much care, though. With her dressing gown tied tight around her, she reached for a cigarette and lit it.

The bell rang again. "I'm coming. Bloody hell."

She walked along the hall and pressed the button on the intercom. "Yeah?"

"Rachel King? I'm a friend of Stevie's. Stevie Greenwood. Lizzie said I should have a word with you. Can I come up?"

The chap spoke too fast and nothing registered other than Stevie's and Lizzie's names. She hit the button to open the door and then heard his footsteps on the stairs. She pulled open the door and saw a dark-haired bloke, probably about forty, carrying a heavy-looking cardboard box and taking the stairs two at a time.

"Hi, Rachel." He was out of breath. "I'm Dylan Scott. Can I have a word with you about Stevie?"

"Stevie?"

"Stevie Greenwood." He nodded. "You knew him, I gather. That's what Lizzie said anyway."

"Oh, yeah." She was still half-asleep. And hungover.

"Can I come in?"

She shrugged and wandered to the kitchen, leaving him to put the box on the floor and close the door behind him. He followed.

"I'll go and get dressed," she said. "What time is it anyway?"

"Half past three. I'm sorry if I've come at an inconvenient time. Shall I make you a coffee or something?" He looked around the kitchen as if expecting to see a gleaming coffee machine. He'd be lucky.

"Sure." She took a drag on her cigarette and left him to it.

Her bedroom was a mess. Like her. She pulled on clean underwear, a pair of jeans that had been tossed on the carpet a week or so ago and a pink sweater that smelled of curry. Her head protested as she yanked a brush through her tangled hair. She always had a headache. Always. It was probably the methadone. Or the drink.

She lit another cigarette and returned to the kitchen where—God, she couldn't believe this—a cup of strong, steaming black coffee waited for her.

"Sorry, but you're out of milk," he said.

"I don't drink milk." She'd always loved the smell of coffee. It reminded her of her childhood, of happier days when her mum had worked in a posh coffee bar and they'd lived above it. The place had always smelled of coffee. Sometimes, when the shop was closed and their mum was cleaning up, she and Gemma had sat on tall stools with a cappuccino and a muffin each. "So what did you want? Did you say you're a friend of Lizzie's?"

He leaned against the sink, hands in the pockets of black jeans. "I'm a friend of Stevie Greenwood's. I've just met Lizzie and she gave me your name and address. I'm a private investigator and I'm trying to find out what happened to Stevie."

He didn't look like an investigator. She'd never met one before though so she had no clear idea what they looked like. He certainly didn't look like those she'd seen on TV. Nor did he look like a friend of Stevie's. He looked as if he belonged in a different world, a better world, a world where people stopped at coffee bars, like the one her mum had managed, and made plans for the weekend.

"Did you know Stevie well?" he asked.

"Probably as well as anyone else. But no. He kept himself to himself."

He smiled at that. "I know. He wasn't a great talker, was he?"

"No." But she'd liked him. He'd been kind to her.

She couldn't remember the last time anyone other than a punter had been in her flat, and it felt odd. Perhaps she was more like Stevie than she'd thought because she didn't know how to deal with strangers—the non-paying sort at least. Yet, this chap looked nice enough. Friendly even.

"I've lived here a year," she explained. "Came from Manchester. About nine months ago, I got beat up by a bloke who decided he enjoyed the rough stuff but didn't enjoy paying for the privilege. Stevie found me down by the canal. He didn't know me from Adam, but he took me back to his place and let me have a bath and clean myself up. He made me coffee too."

Dylan Scott didn't seem surprised by this. "Stevie was very kind."

"He was." She flicked cigarette ash into the sink. Her hands were shaking, but that was probably the methadone too. "It was another three months before I saw him again. I shared this place with my sister and, one night, I came home and found Gemma—" Her voice broke and she cursed herself. "She was dead. The police say she died of an overdose, but she didn't."

"Oh?"

"No. She was using, we both were. I'm not now, though," she added. "I'm on a recovery program."

"Methadone?"

"Yeah."

He nodded as if he'd expected no less. Perhaps he thought it explained the state she was in and the way she couldn't stop shaking. "So what do you think happened to Gemma?"

"I don't know." She took a long pull on her cigarette. There were times, and this was one, when she longed to curl into a little ball and howl for Gemma. She would never stop missing her. Never stop hurting. "Someone had been here, though. In the flat."

He didn't say anything.

"She was lying in the bath." Now she'd started talking, she couldn't stop. "Dead. Cold. Drowned. The police reckoned she'd overdosed because—well, just because. But I found a receipt from that posh flower shop down the road. It was lying on the floor, just inside the door." She pointed toward the door. "When I gave it to the police, they said she must have bought herself flowers. As if. Neither of us could afford to chuck away forty quid on a bunch of flowers. If we'd had any spare money, we'd have bought—I don't know, food or something. Someone had definitely been here."

"Do you still have the receipt?" he asked.

"No, the police took it away."

"Was there a credit card number or anything on it?"

"No. Apart from the name of the shop, and the price, there was nothing. Oh, and the date. September the fourteenth. The day I found her. No way did she buy those flowers though. In any case, what would she have done with them? There wasn't so much as a bloody dandelion here."

"Fingerprints? Anything like that? Presumably the police checked for prints."

"Oh, yeah. They certainly did, and they found zilch. I was told Gemma must have cleaned the flat before she died."

"Is that likely?"

"I'd have been less surprised if they'd told me she'd been shopping on Mars. She was worse than me and you can see the state the place is in now. It was an even bigger tip when Gemma was here."

"What was she like in the days leading up to it? Did she seem different? Did she mention anyone? Someone she was seeing perhaps? Someone she was meeting?"

"Nah. Oh, there was one bloke." Rachel was surprised by the memory. She hadn't thought about him, not since Gemma had first mentioned him. "About a fortnight before she died, she told me about some bloke who'd paid her a lot of money. She was pretty. Seriously pretty. Here, come with me."

She carried her coffee into the sitting room and immediately felt embarrassed. Funny how she hadn't noticed the mess until now. This bloke looked out of place in such surroundings and it made her see the overflowing ashtray, the empty beer cans and vodka bottle, the dirty plate and rotting apple core.

"Sorry," she said. "I was going to clean it up. I must have overslept. Late night, you see."

"That's okay."

It would have to be.

She picked up the photo that was propped against the TV and handed it to him. "This is Gemma."

"Good God."

Rachel smiled and nodded. "I know."

"Why was she working as a prostitute in Dawson's Clough? She could have made a fortune as a Marilyn Monroe lookalike."

"Yeah. She did. That's what I was going to tell you about. We didn't often bring men here, but if we did, the other knew to keep out the way. I got a message from her one night and had to stay out. All bleedin' night. I was bloody mad when I finally got home, I can tell you. Anyway, it turned out she'd been picked up by this rich bloke and he'd paid four hundred quid for the whole night. She'd got the wig on, and was doing her Marilyn thing—she'd sing 'Happy Birthday'—when he picked her up. Four hundred quid though."

He handed back the photo. "Who was he?"

"She said he was creepy, that's all I know. In this line of work, we don't ask for names let alone addresses. And if blokes do tell you their name, they're lying more often than not."

"You're sure she didn't say anything else about him?"

"We were too busy spending the daft sod's money and hoping he'd become a regular." She shook off the memories. "But no, Gemma was the same as ever before she died. And no way did she OD."

She propped the photo against the TV. "Stevie gave me the picture. He took it in the pub the Christmas before she died. And that's what I was saying. He brought me the photo a couple of days after she died and I got to calling at his flat sometimes. It was depressing being here. It still is. His place was—nicer. We'd talk. At least, I'd talk and he'd listen. Either way, he used to make me feel better."

"Any idea who might have wanted him dead?"

"It could have been anyone. All the lost causes end up in this part of town. Or the vulnerable, as people prefer to call us. Like I said, I'm on a recovery program, but before, I would have killed for a fix. It's the drug. That's what it does to you. If he had a tenner in his back pocket, anyone would have done him in."

"Hmm."

"Your sort don't understand. It's as if people like us are invisible. No one likes to see the mess we're in so they pretend we don't exist. We soon start wondering if we do. No one sees us, no one cares—" There was no point talking about it. He wouldn't—couldn't—understand.

"Was Stevie invisible?"

"Pretty much, yeah. Either that or he was a joke. He'd lived here all his life and people called him Simple Stevie. They enjoyed making fun of him."

"When was the last time you saw him?"

"Two nights before he died." Half the time, she couldn't remember what she'd done an hour ago. That was the methadone. That night, though, was clear in her mind. "I don't know why I called on him, but it was early, about half past six, so I went there before I went out to work. I was working on Canal Street and it was a cold, wet night. I suppose I was putting it off as long as I could."

He nodded as if he understood. How could he? He wore a wedding ring, and she could picture his smart home, his pretty wife and probably a couple of kids. His would be an easy life.

"He made me a cup of tea," she said. "Then, without speaking, he got up, went out and came back with fish and chips for us both." She smiled at the memory. "I would have eaten them out of the paper, but he got plates and cutlery."

"I remember buying him fish and chips when he was at his last flat," he said. "He produced plates and cutlery then too. And his flat was spotless."

"It always was." Again, she felt embarrassed by the state of her home. "Anyway, we ate those and then I went out to try to earn some money. It was the last time I saw him."

"I don't suppose he mentioned anyone or anything out of the ordinary?"

"No. He hardly said a word. He was the same as he always was." A drum was pounding in her head now. She needed to lie down and sleep it off. "You won't find out what happened to him. No one talks round here."

"We'll see about that."

His answer surprised her. "Who's paying you?"

"No one. This is personal." He gave her a smile. "Thanks for talking to me, Rachel. I'll leave you in peace now."

"Er, right. I'll clear up a bit." When she'd had some sleep.

"Will you get in touch if you think of anything else?"
He gave her a card. "I'm staying at the Pennine Hotel
if you can't reach me by phone."

How she'd love a night in the Pennine. Even an hour
or two would do. That would be long enough to have a
leisurely soak in a hot bath, wrap a huge, clean towel
around herself and then lie on the bed and—and just be.
She'd never been inside the place and wasn't likely to.

She shoved his card in the pocket of her dressing
gown and nodded.

"Thanks," he said.

She followed him into the hall, watched him pick up
the cardboard box and leave. It was unlikely she'd see
him again. He didn't belong in this world. Men like him
belonged at the Pennine Hotel.

# FOUR

DYLAN WAS GLAD to reach his hotel room and drop the box of photos on the bed. It weighed a ton.

His room was warm and felt cosy after Rachel's shabby accommodation, and with a cup of coffee to hand he grabbed a pile of photos and skimmed through them. It took less than five minutes to wonder why he'd bothered, and less than two to wonder why Stevie had bothered. The pictures weren't technically good. In fact, it was difficult to know what Stevie had been aiming for. Most were of the streets, and a few landmarks were recognisable, like the corner of the town hall and the steps leading up to the library, but most were simply random images that looked as if Stevie had simply pressed the shutter without bothering with the viewfinder.

Many pictures had been taken recently. One taken the week before Christmas showed the tree in the square, and it was possible to make out a poster advertising the annual Christmas market. In the midst of those was a picture of daffodils in the park that had been taken last April. There was no order to the photos, or none that he could make out. They certainly weren't in chronological order and didn't appear to be arranged by subject. Like Stevie himself, they were haphazard and confusing.

Realising he was getting nowhere, he left the photos scattered on the bed and took a shower. He'd arranged to meet Frank at eight o'clock, which gave him a couple of hours to chat with the residents of Stevie's building, assuming no coppers were hanging around...

There were no coppers, but no residents either. Or no residents prepared to answer his knock at the door.

Finally, an elderly man peered around the door he'd opened a couple of inches. He was wearing slippers. And a tracksuit. A cigarette dangled from dirty, nicotine-stained fingers. "Who sent you?"

"No one," Dylan said. "I'm an old friend of Stevie Greenwood's. Did you know him?"

"Saw him about. Why?"

"The night he was killed—did you see anything? Hear anything?"

"No. I keep myself to myself. It's a pity more don't do the same. Who are you anyway?" Old eyes were suspicious. "The filth asked us questions. Not the filth, are you?"

"No. Just a friend of Stevie's."

"I never heard nothing." He went to close the door. Dylan stopped him.

"I've spoken to Lizzie." He nodded in the direction of Lizzie's flat. "She found him, I gather. Her and Al. Do you know Al?"

"I do. More's the pity."

"Which is his flat?"

"Next door." He nodded to his left.

"I've tried there, but there's no answer. Any idea where he might be?"

"No." Again, he tried to close the door and, this time, Dylan let him.

He spent the next twenty minutes hammering on doors and peering through windows. Nothing. Sod it, he'd grab a bite to eat and get to the pub early. It seemed forever since he'd been inside the Dog and Fox and he was looking forward to reacquainting himself.

AT A FEW minutes after seven, Dylan pushed open the door of the Dog and Fox—and inhaled. Even the smell, a mix of log fires and good beers, was familiar. How he wished this pub was on his doorstep.

He didn't recognise any of the staff, but the service was as quick and friendly as ever, and he was soon sitting at a table in front of a crackling log fire with a pint of his favourite beer, Black Sheep, in front of him.

He'd phoned home, but he might as well not have bothered. Luke was out, and his mother had been in the process of reading Freya a bedtime story. They were managing perfectly well without him so there was no need for him to feel guilty about being in Dawson's Clough. In all honesty, it wasn't the being here that made him feel guilty, it was the relief with which he'd driven away from his responsibilities. His kids were more precious to him than life itself but he couldn't deny that a little peace was welcome. Even more welcome was being able to sit in a pub, surrounded by grownups, and know that he could get totally legless if he so chose.

He'd settled down with his second pint when Frank arrived. Looking every inch a copper, despite having retired several years ago, Frank surveyed the room and used hand signals to ask if Dylan wanted a drink. Satisfied that Dylan's glass was almost full, Frank bought himself a pint and carried it over to Dylan's table.

"Good to see you, Dylan. You're looking well."

"You, too, Frank."

"So how are you doing?" Frank sat opposite him and took a slug of beer. "How are you *really* doing, I mean?"

"Oh—" Dylan usually told people he was doing great, and an honest answer took him a few moments. "I'm doing okay." But he didn't want to talk about himself. "Actually, although it pains me to say this, it's good to be back in the north."

Frank smiled, somewhat smugly Dylan thought. "It gets in your blood, this place. The hills, the people, the buildings—"

"The rain."

"A little rain's fine. Even you soft southerners will cope." Frank leaned back in his chair. "What time did you get here?"

"Lunchtime. I went straight to Stevie's flat and had a look round." At Frank's frown, he explained, "The door was unlocked."

"Yeah, yeah."

"There was nothing much to see," Dylan said, "but Stevie had taken up photography. There were literally thousands of photos in boxes. I've borrowed a boxful."

"Borrowed? I'll forget you said that."

Dylan often thought Frank was a bigger stickler for the rules since he'd retired than when he'd worked on the force.

"Then I met Stevie's neighbour, Lizzie. She seemed all right, and it was her and another chap in the building who found the body. She couldn't tell me a lot though. She was out working at the time in question."

"A hooker?"

"Yes."

Frank nodded. "All the no-hopers end up in that building."

"It's not just that building. It's the whole area. She gave me the name of another working girl who she thought might have known Stevie better, so I paid her a visit. Rachel King."

"That name rings a bell. Got her. Her mother—or her sister—maybe even her daughter—died of an overdose. I can't remember, but it's sure to be in the local rag. Quite recently."

"Her sister. And it was six months ago."

"Probably. So this Rachel is another crackhead?" Frank asked.

"She's trying to clean herself up. Methadone. But she doesn't believe her sister OD'd."

Frank rolled his eyes at that. "From what I remember reading, her body was pumped full of enough heroin to slay an elephant."

"Rachel found a receipt from a nearby florist's on the floor. Two junkies spending forty quid on flowers? Come on, Frank, that's not likely, is it?"

"I don't remember hearing about that."

"The coppers have the receipt. Apparently, they believe Gemma bought them herself. So what did she do with them? Donate them to the hospital? Give them to a friend and then trot off and inject herself with a deadly dose? There were no flowers at the flat."

"Who knows? Not me. What I do know, and what you need to remember is that addicts don't make reliable witnesses."

Dylan didn't need reminding, but given the state of the area, and the way the local authority shoved the vulnerable into a pile where few would see them, he'd have an enormous task on his hands if he wanted to find a reliable witness.

"Other than that, I didn't learn much. Stevie's life, according to Lizzie and Rachel, was a quiet one. He walked the streets, he took photos, he ate and slept. Maybe he took photos of something he shouldn't have. Or someone."

"Like who or what?"

"No idea. And searching through thousands of photos—" Dylan shuddered at the prospect. "He'd taken a photo of Rachel's sister, Gemma. She was a looker, despite her drug problems. A ringer for Marilyn Monroe."

Frank snorted doubtfully.

"I saw the evidence," Dylan told him. "Believe me, I wouldn't have kicked her out of bed. Anyway, a couple of weeks before she supposedly OD'd, some bloke had paid her four hundred quid for a whole night of bliss."

"Mad sod."

"Rich sod." Dylan drank his beer. "Maybe the sort of rich sod who'd spend forty quid on flowers."

Frank made a steeple beneath his chin with his hands. "Dylan, it's great to see you up here. It's even better to see you niggling away at things with your old enthusiasm. But don't get carried away. Stevie's murder was most likely a random thing. There are enough addicts living within a hundred yards of him who'd sell their grandmother for a fix. There's little hope of finding out what really happened to him. As for Gemma King, autopsy reports don't lie. She was a user. She died of an overdose. It seems to me—"

"That I'm wasting my time?" Dylan smiled. "That's what I do best, Frank. Let me get us another drink."

As Dylan stood at the bar waiting for their drinks to be poured, he acknowledged that Frank was probably right. But if he didn't waste his time, who would? Nothing had been stolen from Stevie's flat, as far as they knew, simply because he had nothing to steal. Maybe he'd had a tenner in his back pocket. Maybe someone knew he'd cashed his benefits cheque that morning and decided to relieve him of the cash. Either way, it was unlikely that the culprit would be found. As the killer had walked into the flat, it might be reasonable to assume he was known to Stevie. On the other hand, Stevie would have let anyone in.

He carried their drinks back to the table.

"It *is* what you do best," Frank said, carrying on their conversation, "but you need to eat. Your kids need to eat too. No one will pay you for this. No one will care. You can't carry on like a modern-day Robin Hood."

Dylan refused to think about the finances. They'd get by. Besides, he'd checked his emails before coming here and, among the eight from Bobby was one telling him that, finally, a fairly large account had been settled. It would keep them going for a while.

"I'm curious, that's all, Frank. I'd bet my life that someone knows something about Stevie's murder. All I have to do is find that person and get them to talk. And then there's Gemma. Who went to her flat and dropped that receipt? What happened to the flowers? Who paid four hundred quid for a night of sex with her?"

Frank smiled knowingly, but he had no answers.

"Something Rachel said made me stop and think. According to her, everyone in that area becomes invisible. She's right too. The dregs of society get shoved away in a little corner of the town and forgotten. It's not right. Someone has to look out for them."

"And that someone has to be you?"

"Who else is there?" He was sounding way too noble. The crux of it was that he was enjoying being back in Dawson's Clough. Or, more accurate, he was enjoying being away from his responsibilities and the memories.

"I did manage a look at Stevie's autopsy report," Frank said.

"And?"

"He was stabbed seventeen times. Chest, arms and neck."

"So either it was a frenzied attack or it was the work of an amateur."

Frank nodded. "The knife was thought to have a five-inch blade."

"Small and easy to conceal."

"Yep. He bled to death but it would have taken a while. There was nothing neat about it."

Dylan ran his finger along the rim of his pint glass. "Perhaps you could sneak a look at Gemma's file when you're next catching up with your friends."

"Ha. I have very few friends left at the nick. They've either retired or been transferred."

"You're still the hero."

"I don't know about that. I'll see what I can do though."

"Thanks. You're a star." Dylan took a swig of beer and thought how civilised this was. His favourite beer, his favourite pub, good company—it was exactly how life should be. "What happened to Stevie's camera, Frank? Any idea?"

"Yes, it's locked away in the evidence room. There wasn't a single picture on it. We can only assume he took photos, printed them out, immediately deleted them from the camera and memory card, then took more."

"And it's considered evidence because?"

"There were a couple of partial prints on it."

"That's interesting."

Frank chuckled. "Not really. Maybe he forgot it and someone handed it to him. Maybe someone took a photo of him. One belonged to the woman who owns the Sportsman pub. The other's unidentified so far. But if you think that's interesting, you really are clutching at straws."

# FIVE

EVEN AT NINE-THIRTY in the morning, Forget-me-nots was enjoying a brisk trade. The florist's wasn't in the most upmarket of areas but it was within five hundred yards of the crematorium.

"Flowers for the living," Bev had said. "There's no point putting flowers on my grave, is there? I won't be able to enjoy them…"

He'd bought flowers for her birthdays, their wedding anniversaries, Valentine's Days and for Easter so he shouldn't be taken aback by the price of the things. He always was though, and he'd learned long ago that no sane man bought red roses. They were a complete rip-off.

Here, it was possible to buy every flower known to man. Every colour was represented. Large photos on one wall showed intricate wreaths at extortionate prices. Another wall displayed photos of wedding bouquets. Flowers for every occasion were promised. Teddies with It's a Boy or It's a Girl emblazoned across their chests could be bought along with congratulatory helium balloons and handmade greetings cards.

As Dylan inspected the various offers, the shop emptied until it was just him and the young female assistant.

"Can I help you, sir? Are you looking for something in particular? A special occasion perhaps?"

She was slim and tiny with short dark hair and large brown eyes.

"No, nothing like that. Sorry. I'm after information."

"Oh?" She looked confused and out of her depth.

"Yes. Nothing to worry about, but I was wondering if it's possible to find out who bought flowers on a particular day." He looked around the shop. "There's no CCTV, is there?"

"Oh, no, nothing like that."

There never was when you needed it.

"So if people pay cash," he said, "there would be no way of tracing them."

"Of course not. Unless they had the flowers delivered. Then we'd have the customer and the recipient's address."

"But if someone walked in and paid forty pounds for flowers, there would be no way of knowing?"

"None at all. Forty pounds is the standard price for a hand-tied bouquet so there would be several of those sold every day. Why do you need to know?"

Before he could answer, a burly bald-headed man emerged from a room at the back. "Is there a problem?"

"No," she said quickly.

"I'm after information," Dylan said, giving him a smile that wasn't returned, "and this young lady has been most helpful."

"What sort of information?"

"I'm a private investigator," Dylan explained, "and I was hoping to find out who paid forty pounds in cash for flowers on the fourteenth of September."

His eyes had widened in surprise and then narrowed to tiny suspicious slits. "Why d'you want to know that?"

"The receipt was found in a young girl's flat. I gather it's not possible to trace that person?"

"Of course it's not. Good God, people buy flowers

for all sorts of reasons. And even in this day and age, some people still pay in cash, thank God."

"I appreciate that. I don't suppose anyone would remember someone paying cash on that day?"

"Of course not. And even if they did, they wouldn't shout their mouth off." He gave the young assistant a fierce glare. "They'd soon be out of a job if they did. Say a married man comes in to buy flowers for his girlfriend, he's not going to appreciate the whole bloody world knowing, is he? I'd soon be losing trade."

"I suppose you would."

"Is there something you'd like to buy? Because I've got a business to run."

"No, that's it, thanks. I'll be on my way."

"Good." The owner stomped away to the back room.

"Thanks for your help." Dylan gave the assistant a reassuring smile, took his business card from his pocket and handed it to her. "Bye."

THE SPORTSMAN WAS the type of pub Dylan loathed. A big barn of a place, it was cold and soulless. Two TV screens, one on a table near the bar and one the size of a small country hanging on a wall, were showing horse racing. The sound was muted, presumably because it couldn't hope to compete with the eighties hits blasting out from an ancient music system. On the plus side, the beer was cheap.

Surprisingly, given that it was only a little after midday on a Tuesday, trade was okay. Four men were playing darts, a couple were enjoying a game of pool, and three, like Dylan, were sitting at the bar. Presumably none of them had jobs.

The barmaid was a shrewlike creature. Dylan would

put her at about forty, maybe a little older. She was slim and nervy-looking, with bleached blond hair and heavy makeup that did little to enhance narrow eyes, and an overlong pointed nose. Fingernails like talons were painted a shocking pink and every finger bore a ring. She didn't possess much in the way of cleavage but what she did was on show.

"I don't think I've been in here before," Dylan said, striking up a conversation when she wasn't busy.

"I thought I hadn't seen you. We haven't been here too long." She paused to do the mental calculation. "Eight months now. It was June when we took it over."

"So you own it?"

"Me and my husband, yes. We've come up here from the Midlands. We had a pub near Solihull, the Pheasant, but there was a fire. A bad one. The place had to be pulled down."

"I hope you were insured."

"Oh, yes. That's how we came to buy this place. We fancied a change of scene."

"It looks as if you're doing okay now."

"We can't complain. We're handy for the nightclub so the evening trade is good. What about you? Are you local?"

"No. I've worked up here before, though, so I know the town well."

"What work would that be?" He put his empty glass on the bar and she picked it up. "A refill?"

"Please." He handed her a five-pound note. "I'm a private investigator."

"Oh?"

"Yes, I'm looking into a murder case. Stephen Greenwood. You must have heard about it. Did you know him?"

Unless he was mistaken, his words had startled her.

"Not really." She put his full glass in front of him and counted out his change. "There you go. So where are you from?" It seemed she was reluctant to talk about Stevie.

"I'm up from London. I expected this to be Stevie's local. It's the nearest pub to his home, after all." It was directly opposite Rachel King's flat.

Before she could answer, a customer sitting nearby sidled up to Dylan. "Is that Stevie Greenwood you're talking about?"

"Yes. Did you know him?"

The chap was short, overweight and middle-aged. Despite the grubby I Love California sweatshirt covering his considerable girth, Dylan would bet he'd never strayed far from Dawson's Clough.

"We all knew Simple Stevie. Your favourite customer, wasn't he, Ruby?" He grinned at the landlady and received a glare for his trouble.

"He was fine." She looked a little sheepish as she added for Dylan's benefit, "He sometimes drank here."

"Only when he was feeling brave." The stranger was still chuckling. "You should have heard what Ruby threatened him with."

Another glare was fired in his direction. "It was his camera," she said. "He'd shove it in people's faces and make a damn nuisance of himself. It drove customers away. Who can blame them for going somewhere else? Not me. When you come out for a quiet drink, you don't expect to get a nutter pointing a camera in your face."

"He was harmless enough," the chap said.

"He was if you weren't relying on trade, yes." The phone rang and she turned away to answer it.

"Can I buy you a drink?" Dylan asked his new friend.

"Thanks. I'll have a pint of John Smith's, please. That's decent of you. I'm Tony, by the way."

They had to wait while Ruby took her phone call. From the half of the conversation he could hear, Dylan guessed that someone employed by Ruby was calling in sick. Ruby didn't sound pleased. She didn't look the sort who was easily pleased though.

As she ended the call, she was joined behind the bar by a smiling, rosy-cheeked, bald-headed landlord. Greetings were exchanged all round and Dylan soon realised that Bill was far more popular with the drinkers than his wife.

"We were talking about Ruby's favourite customer, Bill," Tony said.

"Oh? Who's that then?"

"Stephen Greenwood."

"Oh." A shadow crossed the landlord's face. "He was all right, wasn't he, Ruby?"

"Hmm."

"The last time I saw him in here," Tony said, "Ruby was threatening to ram his camera down his throat. I don't think he came in again."

"For God's sake," Ruby muttered, irritation in every wrinkle. "He was welcome to drink in here. I told him to stop taking pictures of everyone, that's all. No one liked it." She gave her husband a glare. "Someone had to say something to him and you weren't going to. It's hard enough for us to make a living as it is without the likes of him driving customers away."

"Of course he didn't come in again," Bill said. "The poor bugger was dead, wasn't he?"

At least it explained the presence of Ruby's fingerprint on Stevie's camera. "When was the last time he was in?" Dylan asked.

"A couple of nights before he was done in," Tony said.

"It wasn't." Ruby sighed. "It was before then."

"He was killed last Tuesday night, and he was in here on the Saturday before. Three nights before he was done in." Tony was in the mood to argue. "I remember it well because this place was packed out. Loads of folk were heading off to Catch-22 and the pool game was on. We were playing the Black Bull."

"Have it your way." Ruby's tone was grudging to say the least.

"He'd got his camera with him," Tony said, "and Ruby confiscated it. When he tried to order another drink, she really laid into him. She sent him away and we never saw him in here again."

"That's not my fault." Ruby picked up a bulging leather handbag from behind the bar and headed for the stairs to the private accommodation above the pub. "You're on your own, Bill," she said. "That good-for-nothing Anne's sick again. I said she was trouble the minute I clapped eyes on her."

"It's okay. I'll manage."

"We shouldn't have to manage though. People don't realise the hours we put in to keep this place running, and we can do without flighty bits like Anne picking and choosing her hours."

"I'll manage," Bill said again. "You go and have a rest."

The atmosphere immediately improved when Ruby closed the door behind her. Customers and landlord alike looked more relaxed.

Bill gave Dylan a long appraising look. "I haven't seen you around before."

"No. I'm just visiting the Clough." He put out his hand. "Dylan Scott."

"Bill Wilson." Hands were duly shaken.

"I was explaining to Ruby that I'm a private investigator and also an old friend of Stevie Greenwood's."

"Ah. No one seems to know anything about what happened to him."

"You don't think Ruby did him in then?" Tony said, chuckling to himself.

"That's not funny, Tony." Bill picked up a glass and polished it. "You know she went to the police? Oh, yes," he said at their surprised expressions. "They were appealing for information and especially asking about his camera because they'd found fingerprints on it. Well, as she'd confiscated his camera to stop him annoying the customers, she had to go along and explain. She only kept it half an hour or so, just until he finished his drink and was ready to go home, but those fingerprints could have been hers so she had to talk to them. Nothing else she could do, was there? She wouldn't have rested otherwise. Neither of us would. Anyway, she went along and explained, had her fingerprints taken and that was the end of that." He gave Tony a stern look. "It's still not a joking matter though."

"Come on, Bill. I was only having a laugh."

"And I'm saying it's no laughing matter," Bill said.

"All right, all right."

"Who did he talk to when he came in?" Dylan asked.

Both Bill and Tony looked at him as if he were insane.

"That's just it," Bill said. "He'd hardly say a word. He'd ask for his drink and then start taking photos of everyone and everything. Ruby's right, people didn't like it."

"Everyone knew him," Tony said. "Christ, he was

like an old landmark in the Clough. And everyone would say hello to him. You'd rarely get an acknowledgement though. He lived in his own little dreamworld."

Dylan knew they were right. Getting a word out of Stevie had always been almost impossible.

"Hey, doff your caps, lads. Royalty's about," Tony said.

Dylan followed his gaze. Three windows, the bottom half stained glass and the top clear, gave a good view of the street outside. A man who looked totally out of place in this area was striding along the pavement with his head held high and a fixed smile on his face.

"Royalty?" Dylan asked.

"That, believe it or not, is our next member of parliament. At least, that's what he's hoping for. Haven't seen or heard anything of him until recently but, with an election coming up, he's like a bad smell under your nose. That's probably a dozen times I've seen him round here in the last couple of months."

"He's about a lot more often than that," Bill said. "I'll see him probably once a week. He lives out in the sticks on the edge of town, but occasionally he comes round here to see how the other half live. Or his voters, as he likes to call us."

"Ha, that's what he'd like to think." Tony turned back to face the bar when the man in question was out of sight. "No bloody Tory will ever get my vote. He sits in his bloody fancy house with his fields around him and expects us to believe he has a clue about real life. Tosser."

"He's all right," Bill said.

"What's his name?" Dylan asked.

"Jeremy Brent." Bill was busy polishing a glass.

"From what I've heard, his is a rags-to-riches story. He was born a few streets from here—"

"I didn't know that." Tony looked doubtful. "Where did the posh accent come from then?"

"His dad made a fortune apparently. He worked for a bookmaker and when the owner of it died, he had no family so he left the business to Jeremy's dad. I'm not sure how honest a bloke he was, but he certainly believed in speculating to accumulate. He invented some sort of gambling machine and made a mint. When our Jeremy was about ten, his life was transformed. The family suddenly had money and he was sent to some posh boarding school." Bill shrugged. "Jeremy reckons he's never lost touch with the working man and went into politics to do his bit for him."

"So why would he be a bloody Tory?" Tony asked. "What have they ever done for the working man?"

Bill grinned. "It's far too early for discussing politics. I'm only saying that Jeremy's okay. Another reason he's often seen round here is that his mother, God rest her soul, was cremated just round the corner. You should have seen the size of the wreath he put on her plot at Christmas. That cost him a pretty penny, no doubt about it. I reckon he keeps Forget-me-nots in business. He still goes to the church here too. He's a Catholic."

"He's a bloody Tory," Tony said. "That's reason enough to dislike the bloke in my book."

"If he manages to clean up this part of town—" Bill began, but Tony soon cut him off.

"But he won't. He's just grovelling round us for votes. Besides, this part of town is getting cleaned up. It's nowhere near as bad as it used to be."

"The new nightclub's helped, I suppose. Anyone

who's anyone goes there so we see some really flash cars being driven down here."

Tony laughed at that. "The celebrities visit, a lot of the footballers, but they don't hang around. Who would? Hey—" He nudged Dylan's arm. "Talking of celebrities, your friend Stevie reckoned he had a ticket for this weekend's fundraiser. I can't see it myself, but that's what he claimed. Mr. Jeremy Brent will be there and most of the football team. I can imagine Stevie in his posh suit for that, can you?"

"Did he say where he got the ticket from?" Dylan asked.

"Nope. I asked, jokingly, if he'd got a ticket and he said yes. I just laughed at him. That's about as likely as Lionel Messi nipping in here for a swift pint."

Stevie was many things, but Dylan wouldn't expect him to lie. It wasn't in his simple nature. If he said he had a ticket for the fundraiser, he had a ticket.

"I wouldn't have minded going myself and seeing how the other half live," Tony said, "but it's been sold out for ages. Chris Elliott, our local hero, will be there. He's getting some award or other."

"Yeah?" Dylan was impressed. "There are rumours that he'll be playing for Arsenal next season."

"He'll definitely be going somewhere," Tony said. "What a talent that lad is. He's already had an England call-up."

Bill, clearly not interested in football, was busy polishing glasses so it was left to Dylan to discuss England's chances of ever having a world-class football team.

He was more interested in Stevie's ticket to the fundraiser though. If he'd said he had one, he had one.

# SIX

AL HAD BEEN through every inch of this flat, first when Stevie had been alive and again this afternoon. He stood in the sitting room, thinking, but it was no use. There was nothing here and no hiding places.

Police had taken away the tape this morning. They'd checked that the building was secure, and then vanished. They wouldn't be back. Al's patience had been rewarded.

According to Lizzie though, some private detective was snooping around. That didn't sound likely. Who cared about Stevie? No, it made no sense. It was probably one of her tall stories. She could gossip for bloody England and, half the time, none of it was true.

When she'd burst into Al's flat to tell him she was worried about Stevie, she'd been stuttering and stammering like an idiot at the drama of it all. When she wasn't working, she was watching stupid bloody soaps on TV and believing every word. Of course, on realising Stevie was dead, she'd got hysterical. Tears had poured down her face for hours, but Al guessed she'd enjoy spreading the gossip across the town.

Al knew every inch of Stevie's flat, but he still couldn't find what he was looking for. He'd broken in many times and helped himself to the odd tenner. Nothing that would be noticed, of course. There was no point causing trouble. Stevie had always kept his cash in a

cereal box in the top cupboard so it had been easy to
take the odd note without anyone knowing. Not that
Stevie had ever had much cash. No bugger round here
had a lot.

So where was this bloody ticket Stevie had been
given?

It was Lizzie who'd said he had one and, when Al
hadn't believed her, Stevie had taken it from the back
pocket of his jeans and waved it in the air.

It hadn't been in his back pocket when they'd taken
Stevie's body away. Al had checked. He wasn't stupid.
All Stevie had been carrying was thirty quid, which Al
had transferred to his own pocket. Stevie would have
no use for it where he was going. Oh, and he'd had that
bloody camera of his in his coat pocket. Al had thought
about taking that, he might have got a few quid for it,
but it had been too difficult what with the police turning up so fast.

Where in fuck's name was this bloody ticket?

He'd searched every cupboard, every item of cloth-
ing Stevie had owned, under the mattress—it was nowhere to be found.

The letterbox clattered as the free newspaper was
pushed through, and Al put a hand to his chest to calm
his racing heartbeat. He kicked the newspaper out of
the way.

It was a bit spooky to see Stevie's unsmiling face
staring up at him from the front page. Worse, it looked
as if Stevie was watching him. Christ, Al would be as
crazy as Lizzie if he didn't pull himself together.

He went into the bathroom and took every item
out of the cabinet. There were boxes of pills, but he'd
checked those before and knew they contained nothing

that could be sold on. There were two spare toilet rolls and he checked inside the cardboard tubes—nothing. Back in the kitchen, he rechecked every cereal box, coffee jar, saucepan, mug—

A scratching noise startled him. It was coming from the front door. Bloody hell, someone was breaking in.

Al lifted the nearest weapon to hand, a heavy frying pan, and held it aloft. Who the hell could it be? At least it wasn't coppers coming back because they'd use the keys they presumably still had.

The front door opened and closed.

Al held his breath, the frying pan above his head ready for action.

All he saw was the blur of a figure, the back of a head. Dark hair. Tall.

Al wasted no time. He brought the frying pan crashing down on the back of that head, saw the figure crumple to the floor, and ran.

# SEVEN

As THERE WAS a frying pan on the floor beside him when he came to, Dylan assumed that was responsible for the throbbing pain in his head. He put up a hand and checked for blood, but there was nothing. It hurt like hell though.

It had to be a first. Person breaking and entering gets whacked on the head by person breaking and entering.

By the time the room stopped spinning and he was able to stagger to his feet, there was no sign of anyone. He stepped outside, but the balcony and stairs outside the flat were deserted.

He'd broken in to see if he could find Stevie's ticket for the prestigious fundraiser, but that wouldn't be of interest to anyone else. Whoever had attacked him must have been looking for something though.

As he walked through Stevie's flat, he wished he hadn't had those pints at the Sportsman. He was feeling decidedly queasy.

He tried to forget about the blow to the head, not easy when his skull was protesting so loudly, and concentrate on finding Stevie's ticket. It was unlikely to be hidden. Why would Stevie bother to do that? It had to be in plain sight. And as Stevie was so averse to possessions, it shouldn't take long to find it.

Ten minutes later, he hadn't found a single piece of paperwork. How strange was that? Everyone had electricity bills lying around. Stevie was neat and tidy so junk mail would have gone straight into the recycling bin, but he must have had bills and receipts. Everyone did. There was no calendar on view either which was surprising. How had Stevie kept track of what must have been frequent medical appointments? On his previous look round the flat, Dylan had seen dozens of pills and lotions. Surely, Stevie must have seen a doctor regularly.

And another thing—when Dylan had first met him, Stevie had been obsessed with newspaper cuttings. Surely, after spending years—decades—collecting clippings, he wouldn't have simply thrown them away when he got his camera. Or perhaps he'd had no choice but to get rid of them when he'd been moved into this smaller flat. His last home had had two bedrooms and was almost twice the size of this one.

There was nowhere to store anything in the flat, just a small cabinet in the bathroom, a couple of kitchen cupboards hanging on the wall, and a walk-in one where an old coat, vacuum cleaner and ironing board were stored. Obviously, there was no loft space and no cellar.

He stood in the walk-in cupboard. It was an odd shape, sloping steeply at the back. Stuff had been thrown in the cupboard haphazardly which wasn't Stevie's way. Perhaps the police were responsible. Or perhaps the person who'd whacked Dylan over the head had been looking for something. No, that didn't make sense. Stevie hadn't owned anything of value.

Dylan pulled out the ironing board, a small camping stove and a vacuum cleaner, and it became obvious that the sloping wall was in fact a sheet of plasterboard that was simply leaning there. He pulled it away and found three large cardboard boxes and a single large

brown envelope that was stuffed with paper. Along with
a rent book, TV licence and other assorted receipts was
a card in its own envelope requesting the company of
the bearer to a fundraising event at the town hall on
Friday night.

His delight at finding the ticket was lessened considerably by four words printed in the bottom left-hand
corner. *Dress code: Black tie.*

*Sod it.*

Dylan pocketed the ticket. He hadn't even brought an
old suit with him, he abhorred the things, and he loathed
these fancy affairs where people were obliged to dress
up. However, he wanted to go along so he'd have to hire
a suit and spend the evening trussed up like a chicken.
Bev had always said he looked like James Bond when
he dressed for black tie events, but she'd never said
*which* James Bond.

The main thing was that he had the ticket. Mission
accomplished.

The cardboard boxes contained fairly recent newspaper clippings. Dylan scanned them quickly but found
nothing of interest. Lots featured the football team's
young star, Chris Elliott. A few articles told of Jeremy
Brent's determination to do his bit for the people of this
corner of Lancashire. Nothing interested Dylan so he
put the clippings back in their boxes and returned the
cupboard to its former haphazard state.

He left Stevie's flat as he'd found it and ventured
outside. It was time to hire a suit. And swallow some
painkillers.

# EIGHT

ATTENDING THE FUNDRAISER was probably as big a waste of time as Dylan's week had been. On Wednesday, he'd still been suffering the effects of the whack to his head and had spent most of the day alternating between looking through Stevie's photos and checking out the signs and dangers of concussion. He'd felt worse on Wednesday than he had after the initial impact but, thankfully, after swallowing a dozen painkillers, he'd been more or less back to normal on Thursday. That day, too, had been a waste of time though. He'd managed to speak to all the residents in Stevie's building apart from the elusive Al. "He'll bugger off for days at a time," he'd been told. "Bloody good riddance too."

Everyone knew Stevie, by sight if nothing else, but no one had seen or heard anything that might offer clues as to his killer's identity. Dylan had spoken to more people, business owners on Anderson Street mostly, but again, no one knew—or owned up to knowing—anything.

Being here at the fundraiser promised yet more time wasting. Stevie wouldn't have bothered attending. It wasn't his thing at all. Neither was it Dylan's. As far as he could tell, it involved sitting at a table with smartly dressed strangers and making small talk. This hell would be followed by listening to several tedious speeches, seeing the town's rising football star be presented with an award, bidding on items to raise more funds for the local hospice, and making yet more small talk.

Not everyone on Dylan's table was a stranger. Looking as if he'd been born to attend black tie bashes was Frank.

Dylan had spoken to Frank on Wednesday and told him of the trouble he'd had finding Stevie's ticket. Frank had laughed. "You should have mentioned it and I could have saved you a blow to the head. I've got a spare. I support it every year by buying a couple of tickets, but I didn't intend to go. Perhaps I will…"

So here they sat, drinking wine and making small talk with two businessmen and their wives, and two nurses who were representing the hospice. The businessmen had egos the size of Lancashire.

"How come Stevie got a ticket?" Frank asked.

"I'd love to know that. He'll either have found it or been given it. There's no way he'd have bought one. No way he would have come either. He might not have been the brightest bloke on the planet, but he had more sense than to put himself through this." Dylan looked around the crowded town hall. "I expect he found it. Then again, maybe someone in this room gave it to him."

"It wasn't me," Frank said, "so that narrows it down to one in one hundred and ninety-nine. One hundred and ninety-eight because you didn't give it to him either." Serious, he added, "Think logically. Only a complete idiot would give Stevie a ticket. They'd know he wouldn't turn up."

"The world's full of complete idiots, Frank. When the speeches are done and dusted, and everyone's had a drink or two, I'll ask around and see what I can find out."

Meanwhile, as the tedious conversations carried on around him, he watched people.

He recognised Jeremy Brent because he'd done an online search for him. Fifty years old, Brent was a tall, distinguished-looking chap. Confident too. Smooth.

The only other people he recognised were footballers. Dylan followed Arsenal so was only clued up on the Premier League and European teams, but he knew that Dawson's Clough, mostly thanks to the talent of Chris Elliott, were storming up the league and hoping to gain promotion to the Premier League.

He recognised Elliott, of course, but had thought him taller. Elliot was five feet ten, the same height as Dylan. He wasn't anything special to look at, but every female in the room seemed unable to drag their gaze from him. Talent was a powerful aphrodisiac. Or perhaps the million-pound sponsorship deal he'd recently signed with an energy drinks company was the attraction. He looked about sixteen but was twenty-one. He'd recently scraped into the England Under-21 team with a month to spare. The spiky hairstyle, bleached almost white at the ends, probably cost him a fortune, but at least the tattoos that covered most of his body were hidden beneath his suit this evening.

He drove an Audi R8 Spyder with a personalised number plate and Dylan shuddered to think how much the insurance on that would be. The car itself cost over a hundred grand.

To his mind, it was madness paying twenty-one-year-olds such huge salaries and throwing sponsorship deals at them. Money was ruining the beautiful game too.

The food was finally eaten—there hadn't been much but it had taken hours—and the speeches began. A woman spoke of her role in ensuring the local hospice continued to provide the high quality of care that everyone would want for their loved ones in their final days.

Dylan shut himself off and inspected the old interior of the building instead. He loathed thinking of hospitals and hospices, and he especially loathed thinking of the dreaded disease that had sunk its claws into Bev. Far better to admire the high domed ceiling of the town hall.

Jeremy Brent was next to stand at the top table in front of the microphone. He held a sheaf of papers in his hands. "You'll be delighted to know that I intend to keep my speech short." He waved the pages in the air and smiled as laughter rippled around the hall.

The tired old joke made Dylan stifle a groan. Brent put down the papers and spoke passionately about his hopes and dreams for the town of Dawson's Clough. He sounded sincere, but there wasn't a politician born who Dylan would trust as far as he could throw an elephant. Without exception, they made grand promises before elections and then vanished, never to be seen again, until the next election rolled round. Besides, these days, politicians didn't need policies or beliefs, they simply needed to be able to deliver a good speech, as Brent undoubtedly could. He soon had the audience hanging on his every word. Vote for him, and he'd make sure investment was poured into the area, providing more jobs, improved services and a vastly superior rail network.

*Yeah, yeah.*

Everyone's best friend by now, Brent presented a Player of the Year trophy to Elliott and then left the young lad to make an acceptance speech.

Elliott began by thanking everyone at the football club from the board, to the manager, and then the groundsmen for giving him such a perfect playing surface. He thanked the fans for cheering him on each week and offering their tremendous support, even when he wasn't playing at his best.

Dylan had thought Elliott might find it daunting to stand up and talk to a couple of hundred people, but he was a confident young man and had no trouble at all.

"Last, and most important of all, I'd like to thank my parents, Trevor and Daphne Elliott." He waved his arms, persuading his parents to stand. They did, briefly, and both looked fit to burst with pride as everyone in the room stood to applaud them.

"You can't choose your parents," Elliott said as the applause died down, "although I can claim that, unlike most people, my parents chose me and that makes me feel very special. The gods were smiling down on me the day my parents adopted me and I know without doubt that, if they hadn't been smiling on me, I wouldn't be here. My dad, a good footballer himself, encouraged me and spent hours kicking a ball around with me. My mum—well, she doesn't even understand the rules—" ripples of laughter ran around the hall, "—but she is a brilliant chauffeur, and I thank her for all the miles she did so that I could get to training. Without the encouragement, belief and self-sacrifice of my parents, I wouldn't be standing here tonight to receive this award. Thank you." Elliott held the glass award aloft in tribute to his parents and strode back to his table to much applause.

Frank nudged Dylan's arm. "It's not often you find a footballer who can string a sentence together."

"Too true. I'm impressed. I still think it's ridiculous

he should be worrying about how to spend his millions at his age though."

"At least we don't have that problem," Frank said.

"I'm counting my blessings."

Tables were finally being cleared, seating was placed around the outside of the room, and the auction began. Items available to bid on ranged from a Caribbean cruise donated by the local travel agent to a pair of football boots, worn and signed by none other than Elliott.

When the auction was over, people began to mingle.

"I need to get Elliott's autograph," Dylan told Frank, eying the queue for the footballer.

"And I need to get a drink. I'll get you a whisky, shall I? Or would you prefer brandy?"

"Whisky sounds perfect. Perhaps I'll come over to the bar with you and let the queue die down."

Elliott was sitting at a table in the corner of the large room, signing photos of himself in exchange for a donation to the hospice funds. He was very much in demand too. Young women wanted to talk to him and convince him they were perfect girlfriend or wife material. Men simply wanted to get close to him in the hope that some of his talent would rub off on them. Credit where it was due, Elliott's smile didn't slip for a moment. He looked happy enough to be under the spotlight.

"He seems a really nice lad," Frank said.

"Yes, he does."

A band was setting up on the small stage and Dylan dreaded to think what music they'd be treated to. Hits from the Victorian era judging by the age of the musicians.

"I'll go and get that autograph," Dylan said.

He joined the end of the short queue and, when a

couple stood behind him, he let them go first. Finally, it was his turn to be in the presence of the man tipped to be the next Lionel Messi.

Elliott looked a little weary but the smile was still broad. "Who's it for?" he asked, picking up a photo to sign.

"My son, Luke," Dylan said. "He, too, dreams of playing for Arsenal. That's where the journalists believe you're heading. Any truth in the rumours?"

"Take no notice of rumours," Elliot said. "I love to play football, that's all. Everything else I leave to my agent."

He handed Dylan the photo on which he'd written *Keep fit, train hard and live your dream, Luke. Best wishes, Chris Elliott.*

"Thanks." Dylan was impressed and a little moved by the inscription. "He'll be thrilled with this."

"I hope so." Elliott smiled and got to his feet. His signing stint was over.

"I'm a gatecrasher here," Dylan said, eager to prolong the conversation. "A friend of mine had a ticket. Stevie Greenwood. I don't suppose you knew him, did you?"

Elliott's eyes widened in surprise. "Hey, I gave him—" He looked as if he regretted the statement, but it was too late to retract the half-sentence.

"You gave him a ticket?"

"Yes." Elliott really did regret admitting as much.

"Why?"

"I met him briefly. Very briefly. I didn't even know his name." He shrugged and offered up a smile that looked forced. "I felt sorry for him. Thinking about it, it was a pretty stupid thing to do, but it was all I had on

me at the time. I didn't even have any photos to sign."
Elliott was talking too fast. "I didn't know him. Like I
said, I didn't even know his name, but I recognised his
face in the paper afterwards so I know what happened
to him. It's awful."

Before Dylan could ask for dates and times, an ener-
getic-looking man in his thirties slapped a hand on Elliott's shoulder. "Chris, you're needed. A quick photo."

Elliott looked relieved at the interruption. "My
agent," he told Dylan. "He says jump and I ask how
high. Anyway, it was nice to meet you. All the best to
your son."

"Thanks. And thanks again for the signature."

Elliott was whisked away by his agent, leaving Dylan
clutching the signed photo. He wandered back to the
bar where Frank had refills waiting.

"Thanks." He took a swig of whisky and handed
Frank the photo.

"Wow. You'll be in Luke's good books for at least
a week."

"I know. I must get him on car-washing duty before
his gratitude wears off." Dylan put the photo in his
pocket. "Here's something odd though. Stevie got his
ticket for tonight's bash from none other than Elliott.
That seems as likely as the pope giving crack cocaine
to nuns. Elliott claims he gave Stevie the ticket because
he felt sorry for him."

Frank pulled a doubtful face at that. "How come he
knew Stevie?"

"That's just it. He didn't. They met briefly, Elliott
felt sorry for him and gave him the ticket. He didn't
even know Stevie's name until he read about his murder in the local rag."

"But why give a bloke like Stevie a ticket for a black tie bash?"

"That's what I can't figure. A tin of baked beans, yes. A ticket for this, no."

"Perhaps Elliott believes everyone lives at functions like this. Maybe he doesn't realise how the other half live."

"Possible." But, if that were case, why would he feel sorry for Stevie? Perhaps it was Stevie's limp that had elicited sympathy. No footballer would be comfortable looking at that without wincing. Most would think twice about going in for hard tackles.

One of the things Dylan had always liked about Dawson's Clough was the fact that you could talk to people and know that what you saw was what you got. Yet, it wasn't. In this town, experience had taught him that nothing was ever as simple as it seemed.

"It's time we mingled," Frank said.

"Yes, I want to see if I can get Elliott on his own again. I'm damned if I can understand why he gave Stevie a ticket to this god-awful affair."

Elliott was in great demand though. The town's aspiring member of parliament wanted to talk to him, and then his agent was rushing him from one person to another, mostly journalists at a guess. The price of fame...

Dylan was on his way to chat to Elliott's proud parents when a girl, a drunk girl, spilled her drink all over his sleeve.

"God, I'm sorry."

"It's nothing. Really."

She took a tissue from a small bag she was carrying and dabbed at the moisture. All that did was leave tiny pieces of white fluff stuck to his sleeve. "Sorry."

She was late teens, he'd guess, or maybe even early twenties, and very slim. Skinny almost. A mass of dark hair fell around her face and tumbled down her back. Her eyes were a very dark green.

"It's fine," he said. "Really. The hire company will never notice."

"It's hired? Oh, no."

He laughed at the expression on her face. "Truly, it's fine. It serves them right for charging such ridiculous prices." He patted his damp arm. "As I seem to be wearing most of your drink, let me get you another."

"I shouldn't really. But hey, why not? Thanks. It might stave off the boredom."

"What brings you here?" he asked as they walked toward the bar.

"My parents and my superstar brother." She nodded in the direction of Elliott, who was currently surrounded by a gaggle of journalists.

"Chris Elliott's your brother? What a nice lad he is. He signed a photo for my son."

"Oh, he's wonderful. The best thing that's happened to the world since bread came sliced."

"Don't you get on well?"

"We get along wonderfully well. He's the best brother anyone could wish for, and I love him more than anyone else in the whole world. Sometimes, though, it's hard living in his shadow."

Now he thought about it, she did look lonely. Young, lost, vulnerable—and lonely.

He bought their drinks and they moved away from the crowd to stand by a tall table next to a potted palm.

"I don't envy your brother," Dylan said. "I mean, I'd love to be good enough to play football for England, it's every young boy's dream, but I'd hate all the media interest. It must be hard for him being the centre of attention all the time."

"I often tell him that if he hadn't made it as a footballer, he should have been an actor." She laughed. "If the public only knew what he's really like. Still, there are advantages to his fame and fortune. I get to crash at his place tonight and, as he doesn't have a game tomorrow, he's promised to take me out."

"That's nice."

"Yeah."

"Your parents must be very proud of you both," he said.

"Nope." Her smile was sad. "They're proud of Chris, but I've been a disappointment from the moment I was born."

"I'm sure that's not true."

"To be honest, I think any child would have been. They tried for years and years for a baby, but nothing happened. That's why they adopted Chris. The same week that he came home, Mum realised she was pregnant with me. By then, I was an inconvenience, a distraction from the miracle that was Chris."

Dylan was horrified to see a sheen of tears glistening. She was drunk, true, and that wouldn't help, but she was obviously very hurt by what she saw as her parents' neglect.

"What about you?" she asked, making an effort to be ultra-cheery. "Where's your wife? No, don't tell me. I love matching up spouses. It's a game I often play. How about that one? The tall one with the red dress talking to that bald bloke."

"She's dead."

"What? Oh—God, me and my big mouth. How come?"

"Cancer."

"That's rough." She put a hand on his arm. "I'm really sorry."

Dylan felt the familiar painful clenching of his gut. It *was* rough and, damn it, it refused to get any easier. People said time healed but, in his experience, that was a load of bollocks.

It was strange though. When Bev had first been diagnosed with cancer, he hadn't been able to think about the word let alone utter it. No, the c-word had been absent from all conversations. "This hospital stuff," they'd called it. Now, though, it was much easier to tell people that the dreaded disease had claimed her life than tell the truth. The truth was far too horrifying to talk about.

"She was far prettier than the woman in the red dress too," he said lightly.

"Not that you're biased. That woman does look gorgeous though, doesn't she?" She sounded wistful.

The tall, slim, dark-haired woman had long painted fingernails, immaculate hair, a false smile and cold features. "She's not a patch on you."

Her eyes widened in surprise. "Are you flirting with me?"

"I hope not. My son's almost your age." The idea made him laugh though. "I don't even know your name."

"Jo."

"Josephine? Joanna?"

"Jo. It might say Joanne on my birth certificate, but I refuse to answer to that. It sounds like something from the dark ages. Who are you?"

"Dylan. Dylan Scott." He put out his hand and, smiling, she shook it.

"And if you're flirting with me to get to Chris, you're out of luck. I'm wise to that by now." The shadows flitted across her face again. "That's what everyone does, you know. My last two boyfriends—" She shook her head in disgust. "Both of them were only trying to get to Chris. God knows why. What do they think will happen? Do they imagine that, if they talk to him, they'll turn into great footballers? Do they think they'll get all the girls fawning over them instead? That they'll wake up and find a flash car parked in their garages? They make me sick."

Dylan had hoped that Jo might be his route to Elliott, but he decided to forget that for the moment. There was no rush.

"Not that I'm accusing you of that," she said quickly.

"Good."

"Did you love your wife?" She was either frowning with curiosity as she spoke or struggling to bring him into focus. He suspected the latter.

"I couldn't have loved her more," he said solemnly. "Unless David Beckham had been her brother, of course."

Laughing, she punched him on the arm.

"At least you get to crash at your brother's place tonight," he said. "I bet he has a really nice home."

"Yeah, and it has every gadget imaginable."

"On Millionaire's Row?"

"Where else?"

Millionaire's Row was the locals' nickname for the top end of Manchester Road. Houses there were status symbols. Some had swimming pools, some had their own gyms, and all had tall gates and excellent security systems.

He'd soon find out which was Elliott's home. It would be the one where the Audi R8 Spyder lived.

"So what about you?" he asked. "What do you like to do?"

"Apart from get drunk?" she asked, a little shamefaced. "I'm at uni. I want to be a doctor."

"Really? Hey, that's great."

"It will be if I get through it. I'm hoping to be a surgeon one day."

"Brains *and* beauty. I'm impressed."

The laughter died on her lips as she spotted her parents making straight for them.

Reluctantly, Jo made introductions and hands were shaken. Neither Trevor nor Daphne were curious about him. Perhaps they were in too much of a rush.

"Chris has gone home," Daphne said, "so we're heading off now."

"Did he sneak out?" Jo sounded horrified.

"Of course not. Several people are leaving, and he's done all that he was asked to do. He said you'd be getting a taxi to his house, yes?"

"I don't have much choice, do I?"

"Do you have enough money, love?" Trevor Elliott dug in his pocket, pulled out a couple of twenty-pound notes and put them in her hand. "That'll pay for the taxi."

"And watch what you're doing," Daphne said. "Don't go getting Chris into any scrapes, will you?"

"Mum, he's big enough to take care of himself."

"Yes, but you have a habit of doing some silly things and getting Chris involved."

"I'll make sure he behaves."

"Good." Daphne air-kissed her daughter and turned on her heel.

"Take care, love." Trevor hugged Jo tight. "It's been lovely to see you. Have some fun tomorrow, eh?"

She smiled. "We will. Night, Dad."

Trevor and Daphne were stopped three times on their way out of the building, but eventually they were gone.

"Your dad seems a nice chap," Dylan said, and Jo gave a despairing laugh.

"Is that a polite way of saying my mum's a cow?"

"No, of course not." Yet he hadn't warmed to Daphne Elliott. It wasn't only that she'd had no interest in him, in her daughter or anything other than making sure her son was protected. There was more to it than that. She'd been cold, almost unpleasant.

Jo drained her glass. "I may as well go and call a taxi. It's been good talking to you."

"Just glad to stave off the boredom for a few minutes. There should be taxis outside."

He waited while she collected a small jacket and then they stepped out into a deluge. It was lashing down.

"Stand under cover," Dylan said.

There were no taxis in sight, but they only had a couple of minutes to wait before one pulled up outside the town hall. Dylan rushed up to claim it and Jo staggered none too steadily down the steps and jumped in.

"Thanks," she said, shaking off water droplets. "Be seeing you. 143, Manchester Road, please." She closed the door and the taxi drove off into the night.

Number 143. Dylan would check it out.

HALF AN HOUR LATER, having said his goodnights to Frank, Dylan stood on the town hall's steps waiting for a taxi. As there were none around, presumably because everyone had decided to leave at the same time, he opted to go back inside and have another drink.

The bar was a long curving affair staffed by energetic, smartly dressed students. There were currently five young barmen and three drinkers. Four when Dylan joined them.

When he had his drink in his hand, he walked to the centre of the bar and sat on a stool next to a man who looked to be in his early sixties and who was staring into the bottom of an empty whisky glass. A brown leather bag was slung over his shoulder.

"If you're wanting a taxi," Dylan said, "I'd give it a few minutes. There aren't any about at the moment."

"It's okay, I'm walking." He lifted his empty glass. "I'm in no rush though."

The young barman had soon poured him a double whisky with ice.

"It seems to have been a successful evening," Dylan said. "They should have made a good sum for the hospice."

"They should. And let's hope it gets to the hospice and doesn't go straight into the pockets of the big noises organising it. Still, what do I care?" He tapped his bag. "My story's written and sent in so it's job done for me."

"You're a reporter?"

"Dave Edwards. *Chronicle*. Two years off retirement and it can't come quickly enough."

"Oh?"

"The job's not like it was years back." Edwards savoured his whisky. "These days, we're so afraid of hurting someone's feelings—or, more important, waking up to a libel action—that we only publish waffle. There's

nothing interesting you can say about a night like tonight, but it'll make the front page because nothing else
happens in the Clough. It'll be a couple of paragraphs,
and a dozen photos because people want pictures, not
news, and it'll fill most of the paper."

"I wouldn't say nothing happens in the Clough,"
Dylan said. "There's the murder of Stevie Greenwood
for a start."

"True, but I've done that to death. No pun intended.
When you let some junkie into your house, getting
stabbed is always a strong possibility. That's it. End
of story. There are only so many angles you can give
that. Police are following several leads, blah, blah. Police are appealing for anyone with information to contact them, blah, blah."

"Is that what happened? You think he let a junkie
into his house?"

"Give me another theory."

Dylan only wished he could.

"Greenwood had nothing worth stealing," the disillusioned hack said, "but your average junkie isn't looking
for anything valuable. They're not in touch with reality
enough to think of valuables. All they want is a tenner,
or a fiver. Even some loose change will do. They'll kill
their own grandmother for a few pence to put toward
their next fix."

Jeremy Brent walked past. He was shrugging on a
grey woollen overcoat but paused to wave a regal hand
to those at the bar.

"He's another of the untouchables," Edwards said as
Brent and another man disappeared through the impressive doorway. "I'd love to print all I know about that

two-faced bastard, but I'd be in front of a judge before you could say 'Read all about it.'"

"Oh?" Journalists, disillusioned or not, were a mine of information. "Here, let me get you another drink. Whisky on the rocks, is it?"

"That's generous. Thank you." Edwards downed the dregs of his drink and put the empty glass on the bar. "Sorry, I didn't catch your name."

"Dylan Scott. I'm an old acquaintance of Stevie Greenwood."

"Is that so?" Finally, Edwards looked vaguely interested. Vaguely.

Dylan bought their drinks. He had no idea what time the bar would close, but the staff looked in no hurry to leave.

"You're not a fan of Jeremy Brent then?" Dylan asked.

"Nope. I'm not a fan of any Tory. What about you?"

"I don't know the bloke. Tonight was the first time I'd seen him. But I know what you mean about the Tories." It was always best to agree with someone if you wanted them to talk.

"Brent's worse than most. He'd sell his soul to the devil for an extra vote. He'll promise the earth and do nothing but line his own pockets. They're all the same."

Dylan nodded his agreement.

"He's been lucky so far," Edwards said, "but, one of these days, his perfect little world will come crashing down around his ears. I just hope I live long enough to see him banged up in a prison cell where he belongs."

"Prison? What's he been up to then?"

"Like I say, I can't print it. If nothing's proven, a

man's innocent, and God help anyone who says otherwise."

Dylan knew that only too well. During his time on the police force, he'd seen many a crook deemed innocent. Getting a strong enough case to convict someone was getting harder and harder.

"Years ago," Edwards said, leaning in close, "a girl accused him of indecent assault. Of course, it was all nicely tidied up when she, for some reason known only to herself, dropped all charges. Two years later, another girl made the same accusation. She claimed she'd been beaten up and raped by him. The week before it went to court, she was conveniently killed in a car accident and the accusation must never be mentioned again."

"Are you saying he was responsible for a fatal car accident?"

"No." Edwards swirled amber liquid around his glass. "I wouldn't put such a thing past him, but no, I think it really was an accident. It was bloody convenient timing for him though."

"Perhaps he was innocent."

"And perhaps you're a Martian." Edwards took an ice cube from his glass and sucked on it, setting Dylan's teeth on edge. "He can afford to visit high-class prostitutes down in London, but I've heard—" Edwards looked around to make sure no one else was within earshot. "I've heard he's operating a bit closer to home."

"He's visiting prostitutes in the Clough?"

Edwards nodded. "Rumour has it that he drives round quite often checking out what's on offer. Now, I don't care what men get up to in their spare time. That's their business. Each to their own, I say. But I do object to blokes like him standing up and telling us how great they are, giving us the squeaky-clean churchgoing family-man image and then cheating on those of us who are supposed to vote for them. And cheating on their wives too, of course. Like I say, though, I can't print a bad word about him."

Edwards crunched on that ice cube. "Men like him always have someone with them—an advisor, a PR man, a bodyguard, a driver—someone like that. Those people are paid well to provide alibis and keep their mouths shut."

"Who was that chap who just left with Brent?" Dylan asked.

"His secretary." Edwards swallowed what was left of the ice cube, much to Dylan's relief. "Anyone who wants to speak to Brent has to go through his secretary and they might, just might, be granted an audience with the great man."

"I suppose anyone in the public eye needs someone like that."

"Maybe. In Chris Elliott's case, I can understand it. The lad's only twenty-one and, although he might know a lot about football, he can't be expected to do all the public stuff. His agent will be making a fortune out of him so I can see the need to make sure he says and does the right thing. Now that he's got this lucrative sponsorship deal, they won't want him putting a foot wrong."

"He seems a nice young man."

"Yes, I think so. I don't have much to do with him, but our sports reporter speaks highly of him. He always has time to speak to the press, and that's more than you can say about a lot of folk."

Edwards swallowed the last of his whisky, stood up and grabbed the edge of the bar to steady himself for a moment. "I'm heading home now, but I'll get you a drink in before I go."

"Don't worry about that," Dylan said. "I'll be leaving myself in a minute. I'm staying in the Clough for a while so I'll probably see you around."

"Probably. Good night then."

Dylan watched Edwards sway out of the room. Then he finished his own drink and left the town hall.

There were no taxis around so he decided to take the not-so-scenic route home and see what was happening in Anderson Street.

All seemed quiet at Stevie's flat. Dylan watched the place for a few minutes but thought it unlikely anyone was breaking in—again. The only movement on the street came from litter that blew along the gutter. Everywhere looked tired and neglected. A black cat dived beneath a car to hide from him. One of the few streetlights flickered wearily. A couple of cars passed him, but Dawson's Clough was settling down for the night.

He walked on to the canal where the air seemed colder and where a light drizzle began to fall.

A young woman was leaning against the bridge, shivering as she pulled on a cigarette. She looked hopeful as Dylan approached. Seeing her up close, he was surprised to see that she looked no more than eighteen. He was even more surprised to notice that she was attractive despite her underdressed style. Attractive hookers in Dawson's Clough should have been something of a rarity, but Rachel was a looker and her sister had been something else. This girl matched them. Hair that looked naturally blond formed a neat curtain down her back and she had a figure that said she ate well and exercised properly as opposed to the more usual half-starved look that most of the working girls possessed.

She ground out her cigarette with a high-heeled boot. "You looking for someone? Or something?"

"I am, actually. You haven't seen Jeremy Brent, have you? I hear he's sometimes seen around here."

She was so surprised that she took an involuntary step back. "Bloody hell, he's not likely to be walking around the canal, is he?"

"You know him then?"

"Everyone knows him, don't they?"

"I suppose they do. You haven't seen him? He might be driving around. I've heard he does that sometimes."

"Dunno about that." She was lying. "Who are you anyway?"

"Just a man looking for Jeremy Brent. Who are you?"

"Fiona. Why are you asking me about him? Why do you think I'd know anything?"

She wrapped her arms around herself and tapped her feet on the cold concrete. Chewing on her bottom lip, she gave off the air of someone who was very nervous.

"I'll pay for anything you can tell me."

She looked up and down the path as if expecting to see Brent materialise. "How much?"

"What can you tell me?"

She gave all directions another close scrutiny and dropped her voice to a whisper. "He sometimes comes round here, but he'd kill me if he found out I told you so."

"He won't. I promise you that." Dylan took notes from his wallet and she almost drooled at the sight of them. He didn't blame her. He might be able to give her enough to go home for the night instead of hang-

ing around the canal plying her trade. "A good customer, is he?"

She shrugged. "He pays well."

"He's popular then?"

"Not really. He's a funny bugger. Like I say, he pays
well. Half of him seems to like the idea of slumming
it round here, but the other half would kill anyone who
whispered a word about what he was up to. I haven't
seen him for months. At one time, he used to ask for
me. Christ, the stupid fucker even brought me flowers
and champagne as if we were friends. What the bloody
hell would I do with them, eh?" She shook her head at
Brent's stupidity. "It didn't last long. I assume he found
someone else. Look, I don't know anything. Like I said,
I haven't seen him for months. Perhaps he doesn't come
round here anymore."

Dylan handed over sixty pounds and her face relaxed
a little. "Thanks."

"I'd keep away from him if I were you, Fiona. He
might pay well, but he's not worth it."

Not if Edwards was to be believed…

# NINE

"You can take the food through now." Ruby gave Anne a shove in the direction of the bar. "Don't do what you did last week and put all the sandwiches in one area and the sausage rolls in another. Put chicken legs, sausage rolls and sandwiches on the long table and—"

"Relax," Anne said. "I know what I'm doing."

"You didn't last week!"

Ruby had had plenty of experience of bar staff, but she'd never had to deal with one as conceited and arrogant as Anne. As a past Miss Lancashire, Anne was happy to believe that her looks and her figure would see her through life. Bill reckoned she was good for trade and Ruby supposed, grudgingly, that he was right. When Anne was pulling pints, men would usually stay for another drink instead of going home to their wives. She was flirty by nature and the men were daft enough to lap it up.

Before going into the bar to check on Anne, Ruby went upstairs to apply fresh lipstick and put on a bit of jewellery. She scowled at the wrinkles staring back at her from the mirror. In a good light, as opposed to the soft lighting in her bedroom, they looked even worse. No amount of makeup covered the frown lines. She tried to stop herself frowning, but there was precious little to smile about.

When she walked into the bar, the usual Saturday

night noise assaulted her ears. The place was heaving with youngsters who often called at the Sportsman before heading off to the nearby nightclub. For most, the cheap drinks and free food was the attraction. For others, the main appeal was the fact that several of the football players, with or without their wives or girlfriends, visited.

Aided by Oscar, a keen young student, Bill was pouring drinks and making nice with the customers. Everyone liked Bill. The perfect landlord. A genial host.

He was suited to the pub trade whereas Ruby hated everything about it. People had no idea of the long hours involved. Everyone seemed to think that you only worked when the place was open. How wrong they were. There was stock to be ordered, pumps to be cleaned, barrels to be changed, cleaners to be supervised, dozens of laws to be obeyed, food to be provided, smoking areas to be maintained and cleaned—it was relentless. Seven days a week.

It wasn't only the pub trade that she disliked. Ruby hated everything about Lancashire. She'd been born and raised on the south coast and a move to the Midlands had been enough of a culture shock for her. She'd adjusted though, fairly quickly in fact, but after eight months in Lancashire, she knew she'd never get used to the bloody awful weather—it seemed that every day dawned grey and wet—or the people. Northerners were too loud and pushy for her liking.

Some days, she wished she could burn this pub to the ground.

Still, she shouldn't have to endure it for much longer. She *couldn't* endure it for much longer.

She lifted the hatch, went behind the bar and put on

her best smile as she stood alongside Bill and Oscar to cater to the customers' whims. Oscar was a quick worker, but Bill took time to chat to every customer. She merely poured drinks, took the money and gave out change. It was difficult to make conversation over the noise anyway.

It wasn't that she was particularly standoffish, it was more that she liked to daydream as she worked. Her hands might be pouring drinks, but her mind was miles away. In her head, she was running along the shoreline in Cornwall. Funny to look back at her childhood and remember how she'd longed to escape the small fishing village. Mind, she'd never longed to come north to Lancashire. Her dreams had always centred on a life in London and she'd been clever enough to know that the thing most likely to get her there was education. She'd studied hard, had been rewarded by a place at University College London and had looked forward to living in the vibrant City and studying modern languages for the next three years.

Life in London had been everything she'd dreamed it might be. She'd loved the pace of the City and had soon made new friends. Life had been good. For seven months.

She stifled a sigh and returned her thoughts to the present. There were drinks to be served, bar staff to be watched and Bill to be avoided. Oh, he might be laughing heartily with the customers, but she knew he was in a bad mood. She also knew she'd suffer the brunt of it.

Saturday nights often saw the football players arriving, although she had no idea why they chose the Sportsman. They certainly didn't need to consider the price of the drinks. Overpaid prima donnas. The recently opened nightclub, Catch-22, was nearby and she supposed the Sportsman made a handy meeting place before going to that far more trendy and outrageously expensive establishment.

Ruby had no interest in football whatsoever. She never had seen the point in grown men kicking a ball around and she never would. Last year, she and Bill had taken a holiday to Barcelona and Bill had decided they couldn't visit without taking in a game of football and seeing Messi. Ruby had at least recognised the name of the world-famous player. They duly arrived with thousands of spectators only to be greeted with the news that the great man was injured and would be taking no part in the game.

She recognised those who played for the local team, but only because they sometimes drank in the pub and only because they'd been pointed out to her. They weren't great drinkers. In fact, several of them stuck to soft drinks.

A quick glance at her watch had her looking up at the clock above the bar to check that it hadn't stopped. It was only nine-thirty. Time was dragging. Still, within the hour, the bar would be almost empty and Ruby couldn't wait.

Tony was in his usual seat at the bar. He wasn't drinking as much as usual, probably because he was too busy ogling all the flesh on display. Every Saturday night, the town's female population donned the shortest dresses they could find, and tottered to the club on ridiculously high heels. It was a wonder they didn't go down with hypothermia.

"I was hoping Chris Elliott would be in tonight," Tony said, taking a pause from drooling at female flesh.

"He rarely comes in." On the rare occasions that he did, he had one glass of mineral water and then left. "If you want to find him, I'd try Catch-22. He's sure to be there."

Tony laughed. "I'm a bit too long in the tooth for clubbing, Ruby."

"Me too. Are you having another drink or are you going to sit and nurse that empty glass all night?"

"I'll have one more for the road. Same again, please."

The end was in sight. Two people decided it was time to head for Catch-22 and, like lemmings, the rest tipped back their drinks and followed. In under five minutes, the Sportsman was quiet. Only four customers remained.

There was no need for Ruby to hang around. Bill, Oscar and Anne could manage if a miracle occurred and more customers arrived. She could go to bed and, hopefully, be asleep before Bill came up.

She was planning her escape when Bill nudged her arm. "No sign of the boy wonder then."

"Sorry?"

"You know who I mean." The smile, still in place for the benefit of any customers who might be watching, seemed sinister to Ruby.

"Oh, yes. I mean, no. I didn't see him. I overheard someone say something about him getting a knock during the game today."

"That's crap because they haven't had a game today."

"Oh." She hadn't known that. "Perhaps he's resting then. Anyway, talking about rest, I think I'll go up."

Without waiting for a response, she said goodnight to Oscar and took the stairs to their private accommodation.

She had plenty of time, Bill wouldn't be up for an hour or so yet, but she still removed her makeup as quickly as she could. Ten minutes later, she climbed into bed and switched off the light.

Misery settled around her. She hated her life and she hated the person she'd become. It was impossible to remember the last time she'd laughed, really laughed. Oh, she might smile now and again for the sake of appearances, although even that was rare, but she couldn't remember the last time she'd laughed.

She'd laugh if one of her lottery tickets came good. She bought a dozen each week and spent hours planning how she'd spend her winnings. Not that it took much planning. She'd be straight on a plane to—well, the destination wasn't important and she changed her mind on a weekly basis—but there would be sunshine and tranquillity. Italy appealed to her. As did Spain. She'd check into a hotel before buying herself a house in a small village where no one would ever find her.

A customer had told her she was statistically more likely to be struck by lightning than win the lottery, but she didn't care. Her escape wasn't reliant on a lottery win. She had other plans.

# TEN

DYLAN WAS STRETCHED out on his bed, a full glass of whisky at his side and a mountain of guilt on his shoulders. He'd achieved nothing today, other than bruised knuckles from hammering on Al's door several times. There was still no sign of the bloke. Dylan should have saved his energy and gone home to see his kids instead. He might have if he hadn't had so much to drink at last night's fundraiser. It wasn't as if anyone was missing him, though. He'd had a quick chat with them earlier and, although Luke had been delighted to hear he'd be home on Friday night, he clearly had other things on his mind. How the hell had Dylan got old enough to have a son who, if he wasn't thinking about football, was wondering how he could get his girlfriend into bed?

The problem with phoning home these days was that, even though he always rang Luke's mobile, after a quick chat with his kids he always ended up stuck with his mother.

"Hark at Methuselah," she said, cackling with laughter when he'd made the mistake of asking her how he'd got so old. "Age is just a number."

A familiar tinkling sound caught his attention. "What's that noise?"

"I can't hear anything."

Dylan could. "Where are you?"

"Standing in your hallway. I've given it a fresh lick of paint."

"What?"

"Let's face it, you and paintbrushes don't go together, do they? It was looking tired and grubby."

"I'd been thinking about doing that." He should be grateful. He *was* grateful. She was right in that he hated anything that smacked of do-it-yourself.

"Then I've saved you a job."

The tinkling sound faded. Perhaps it was a dodgy phone line. "Anyway, I'd better go, Mum."

"Why? What are you finding to do at this time on a Saturday night?"

"I have a stack of paperwork to look through before morning…"

For *paperwork* read *photos*. He was looking at each and every one methodically and Stevie could win awards for the worst snaps ever taken. It was like some sort of puzzle. A pair of legs would be captured in one scene and Dylan would spend an age trying to figure out if the legs belonged to the person in another picture he found.

Around thirty photos had been taken in the Sportsman pub. A glowering Ruby was easily recognisable as was a smiling Bill. The rest were candid shots of customers Dylan didn't know.

Most of the photos were street scenes. One young copper must have posed for Stevie because he was smiling straight at the camera.

A couple were arty shots. Arty by accident rather than design, he suspected. One was of a long row of supermarket trolleys and one showed a streetlamp shining on a puddle below.

If Dylan had known what he was looking for, this job might have been easier. But he didn't have a clue. Maybe there was nothing to be found. It seemed odd though that, no sooner had Stevie bought a camera, he was murdered. Ruby had complained about him shoving the thing in customers' faces. Dylan would bet good money that Stevie had captured something he wasn't supposed to.

But what?

The first thing he needed to do was put the photos in order. It was odd that Stevie hadn't done that. When Stevie had collected newspaper clippings, he'd stored them neatly in chronological order. Perhaps someone, coppers maybe, had rifled through these photos and left them in this mess.

He went back through the pile he'd just inspected and gave the one of the streetlamp a closer look. Part of a street sign had been captured and he'd bet it read Anderson Street. The blurring wasn't a deliberate effect at all. The photo was out of focus because Stevie had pointed his camera through his kitchen window.

So what?

"So nothing."

There were hundreds of photos of cars. Hundreds. Perhaps it was little surprise that Stevie had a fascination with the things, given the circumstances of his mother's death and his own injury.

Dylan looked at rows of stationary traffic. He saw dozens of car parks with the cars trapped neatly in bays marked out with white lines.

Another streetlamp—

Correction. Another photo of the same streetlamp, and this photo was interesting enough to increase his pulse rate a little. It was possible to make out more of the street sign and it was definitely Anderson Street. Although this picture was also a little blurred, it was filled with life. A taxi bearing the DC Taxi's logo and phone number was disappearing out of the frame. A man wearing a long, dark coat, the collar turned up to ward off the night air, was about to cross the road in the direction of Stevie's flat. He was holding something behind his back because it was possible to see a blur of white at waist height.

What made it so interesting was the very slim possibility that the man in question was Jeremy Brent. It was equally possible that the something behind his back was a bunch of flowers.

What was certain, assuming Stevie had set the date correctly on his camera, was that it had been taken on September the fourteenth, the night Gemma King died.

# ELEVEN

DYLAN SWORE THAT if it wasn't raining in Dawson's Clough, it was snowing. To be fair, he hadn't seen much rain since he'd arrived, just an irritating drizzle, but he woke up on Sunday morning to see snow flurries swirling around the hotel.

For him, the main attraction of staying at the Pennine was the breakfasts. Every morning, he ordered a full English, and every morning he was surprised by the plate that was placed in front of him. Bacon, sausages, eggs, tomatoes—all cooked exactly as he liked them. His coffee cup was refilled without him even noticing. He could easily get used to hotel life.

Bev would tell him he'd get fat and lazy. But Bev wasn't here so it didn't matter if he put on a few pounds.

He called Bobby while he ate to check that everything was running smoothly in his absence.

"It's going a whole lot better than smoothly," she said. "We've got a new client. A celebrity no less."

"Oh?"

"It's only Heather bloody Basingstoke. I couldn't believe it. What about that then?"

"Not *the* Heather Basingstoke."

There was a pause. "You've never heard of her, have you?"

"I haven't. Sorry."

"Honestly, Dylan, anyone would think you lived in

a cave. She does the TV weather. Tall, blonde, stick-thin bimbo."

"Oh, that Heather Basingstoke." He was none the wiser. "What brought her to us?"

"She believes she's got a stalker. Brilliant, eh? It's probably wishful thinking on her part, but I've promised to do a bit of surveillance and see if anyone's following her. She's been to the police, but as she has no evidence, and as no threats have been made, they're not doing anything. I'll email you later and keep you updated. Otherwise, nothing much is happening..."

Dylan ended the call, finished his breakfast and stepped outside.

A heavy grey sky threatened six feet of the white stuff before the day was over. Still, he had nowhere to be and nothing to do. If the weather did its worst, he'd simply go back to the hotel.

Aware of the extra sausages he'd eaten, he walked a little more briskly than usual. He should take up running again—that had been his mantra for years—but he hadn't even jogged since the morning Bev—

He pushed the thoughts away. There was no point dwelling on that. Bev was dead and life went on. Albeit in a slower, sadder, more pointless way.

What he needed to do was concentrate on Stevie and find his killer. Everyone, even junkies hunting a quick fix, left clues in their wake. Stevie's killer was walking the streets, a free man, and Dylan vowed to do all in his power to rectify that.

He was heading toward Anderson Street and found himself walking past the crematorium. Without conscious thought, he walked inside and into the peaceful garden of rest. He immediately wished he hadn't.

People were tending plots, arranging flowers or merely standing in quiet contemplation. Some were probably talking to the dead. Dylan wished he could visit Bev's grave—no cremation for her—and have a good chinwag, but he couldn't. He did talk to her, usually when he'd had a few drinks which, thinking about it, would annoy the hell out of her, but never at her graveside. He had no idea where she was, but he couldn't believe in heaven and he sure as hell couldn't believe she was in that cold, wet earth.

He shuddered, turned around and walked out of the crematorium's grounds. The bloody place gave him the creeps.

The snow was settling where a gusting wind blew it. Pavements were still clear, but he couldn't imagine that lasting long.

He was surprised to see a man walking out of the florist's. It hadn't occurred to him that the shop would be open on a Sunday morning but, given the proximity to the crematorium, and the way people felt better if they put flowers on a loved one's grave, he supposed it made sound economic sense.

The window display was more or less the same as the last time he'd visited, but he pretended to pay it close attention while peering inside. A young woman, one he hadn't seen before, was serving an elderly couple. The burly, bald-headed owner was nowhere in sight, but he'd probably appear the second Dylan stepped through the door.

Still, nothing ventured…

Dylan looked around while the young woman continued to serve the elderly couple. She looked no more than eighteen and she appeared a little flustered.

"I won't keep you a minute," she said.

"There's no rush," Dylan said. "I'll have a look round while I wait."

The couple she was dealing with, the man at least, was querying the price of the flowers, and Dylan sympathised. He'd never seen the point to flowers because they were always dead within a week. When he'd handed them over to Bev, she'd had to hunt around for something suitable to put them in and, naturally, despite being able to supply a small country with clutter, they didn't possess such a thing. Then the stems were too long. And then they died.

Man and woman left the shop clutching a small bunch of flowers. Dylan hadn't caught how much they'd been charged, but he'd guess it was a ridiculous figure.

"Sorry about that," the assistant said.

"Don't worry about it. Are you on your own today?"

"Yes. The owner should have been here with me, but he phoned last night to say he'd done his back in."

Excellent news.

"Are you busy on Sundays?" he asked.

"Very. Everyone visits family and friends in hospitals or goes to the crematorium to clean up the graves. Sunday's the day for things like that, isn't it?"

"I suppose it is."

"So what can I do for you?" she asked.

"I'm after something a little different for a very special lady." He wasn't frightening her off by mentioning he was a P.I. "A friend recommended this shop. Jeremy Brent. He tells me he's a regular customer."

"He is." She was smiling as she spoke. "Your friend's always buying flowers for his wife. You should have seen the flowers he bought for her birthday back in August. They were really special. We had a bit of a panic ordering the right roses, but we sorted it. He said she loved them. Well, she would. Who wouldn't?"

"I think I might have seen them. I was up here in— oh, no, I'm getting confused. It was September. In fact, I can even tell you the date. September the fourteenth."

"Hey, that's my birthday." She blushed with embarrassment and Dylan wondered if she was even eighteen.

"Really? Were you working that day?"

"I was. Believe me, I'll never forget it. It was a nightmare from the moment I woke up." She frowned as she thought back to that day. "Your friend came in that day, but he didn't buy anything special. He bought the normal hand-tied arrangement. Perhaps he bought the flowers you saw from somewhere else."

"That sounds unlikely. The flowers looked special to me, but I'm no expert."

"Ah."

"What was so awful about that day?" he asked.

"Oh, stuff." She sighed. "It was a naff birthday all round. My boyfriend had dumped me the night before—"

"Ouch."

"Yeah. That wasn't a nice thing to do, was it? I thought of phoning in sick, but then I thought I'd be better off keeping myself busy. I hadn't been here more than an hour when I dropped a vase and cut my hand. There was blood everywhere and I had to go to the hospital for stitches. I came back here because I needed to collect my stuff, and I expected our boss to tell me to go home. He didn't. To be fair, we were really busy and I suppose it was only a cut hand. Then your friend Mr. Brent came in and he told me off for—" She blushed again. "I'm sure he didn't mean it, but it hurt to move my hand, and I messed up the ribbon on his bouquet. He was right to complain. It was my stupid fault."

"Good grief. What a day."

"Like I said, it was a nightmare. Still, it could have been a lot worse. On the way out that night, I caught the bus that comes along Anderson Street and there was a bit of a delay because an ambulance was blocking the road. We heard the next day that a girl had died. That put everything in perspective."

"I remember reading about that. Gemma King, I think her name was."

"It was. Poor girl."

"Did you know her?"

"I didn't, no. I won't forget her though. There was me moaning about a naff birthday and there was her—she couldn't moan about anything, could she?"

"No."

A woman came into the shop and Dylan guessed their chat was over. Still, he'd found out, surprisingly easily, what he'd wanted to know.

"I'll have the normal hand-tied bouquet then, please. Similar to the one Jeremy bought on your birthday."

A few minutes later, she handed him his bouquet and, when he paid, she tucked the receipt into the flowers. Dylan left the shop with a wallet that was forty pounds lighter.

Damn it, the snow was even heavier now. He walked on quickly, with the wind blowing litter around his feet, until he was outside the kebab shop. He rang the bell for Rachel King's flat.

"Yeah?" She sounded more awake this morning.

"Hi, it's Dylan. Dylan Scott. We met—"

"Oh, yeah. Come on up, if you want."

"Thanks."

It was slightly warmer inside the building, but the stairwell had a depressing damp smell to it.

She had the door open when he reached it. Her hair had been brushed and she was wearing a little makeup.

"Hi," he said. "I was passing—here, you may as well have these."

She looked at the flowers as if they might explode in her face. "Why?"

"I paid a visit to the florist's and I felt obliged to buy these."

"Why give them to me?" Her hands were clasped behind her back.

"I couldn't think of anyone else."

"What about your wife? Wouldn't she like them?"

God almighty, why did everyone assume he had a wife? He didn't think he'd looked particularly married when Bev had been alive, and he certainly didn't now. He must look a floundering mess.

"I'm not married. Widowed. She died." She didn't look as if she believed him. "Look, can I leave them here? You can chuck them in the bin if you don't want them."

"They're beautiful," she said.

"They're supposed to be similar to the ones Jeremy Brent bought the day Gemma died."

Her eyes narrowed in confusion. "Do you want to come in?" She finally took the flowers from him and walked down the hallway to the kitchen. "What's that Brent bloke got to do with anything?"

"I heard he was seeing working girls in this area. I also heard someone say he must be keeping the florist's in business. Apparently, he bought flowers the day Gemma died. Now, who those flowers were for and what he did with them is anyone's guess, but I know he's been with girls in the area, I know he pays well, and I know he's given one girl flowers and champagne."

"You reckon it was him who paid Gemma that four hundred quid?" She dropped down onto a stool. "Jesus. You reckon that receipt I found came from him? You reckon he was here? In this flat?"

"I don't know." He wished he did. "Are you sure Gemma didn't give you any clues as to the man's identity, the one who paid her the four hundred?"

"Nothing. She said he was a bit creepy, but that's nothing new. Creepy we can do, especially if they pay well. Perhaps it *was* Brent. Perhaps she didn't know him. I've only heard of him recently. He's in the paper every week at the moment for something or other. Jesus," she said again.

She was shaking. Dylan wasn't sure if it was the methadone or thinking about her sister. He knew from painful experience that thinking about dead loved ones was enough to give anyone the shakes.

"If she'd known the bloke," she said, "she would have told me. We looked out for each other. We didn't have secrets."

"It could have been someone else. It's a bit of a co-incidence though."

"Yeah." Sadness settled around her like a dark cloak. "I don't suppose we'll ever know what really happened to her."

"It's unlikely. I'm sorry, that must be tough."

"Yeah." She shrugged it off. "What about your wife then? Is she really dead? What happened to her?"

"Cancer." The word flew out of his mouth with the usual shocking ease. "Have you seen Brent around here? Have you heard any of the other girls mention him?"

"No." She thought for a moment. "But one of the girls, Fiona, used to see a bloke who was a bit posh. I saw her once, getting into the back of a huge, expensive-looking car. She wouldn't talk about him, though. In fact, she got pretty snappy if anyone mentioned him. I reckon she was too scared to talk about him. That might have been him."

"Hmm." He'd already spoken to Fiona. That was Brent all right. "I don't suppose you've heard anything about Stevie?"

"Nothing. You usually hear rumours flying around the street, but I haven't heard anything. It's as if the poor bugger never existed. What about you? Have you heard anything?"

"Not a lot." Nothing would be more accurate. "But I will."

She nodded, as if she didn't doubt it. Dylan admired her confidence.

"You've tidied up since the last time I was here." She'd tidied herself up, too, but he didn't say so.

"Yeah. I'm going to Manchester tomorrow to see a bloke about a job. Well, it's not a real job. I'm going to see about selling the *Big Issue in the North*."

"Hey, that's great. Good for you. I don't know much about it, but you buy the magazine for a pound and sell it for two pounds, right?"

"Yeah. They give you five free magazines and then you're on your own. There are quite a few rules and regulations though. You can only sell on your own pitch, and you have to wear one of those bib things and an official badge. I don't know. I'll see what happens. I thought you had to be homeless, but you don't. People in vulnerable housing, like this, and people who can't earn an income any other way can sell it too."

"That's brilliant. Good luck. I hope it goes well."

She looked embarrassed. "Thanks."

Dylan made his way to the front door. He had things to do.

"Thanks for the flowers," she said.

"You're welcome."

"Your wife—" She broke off as if she regretted speaking, but her gaze was thoughtful. "She didn't really die of cancer, did she?"

Her insight took him completely by surprise. "No, she didn't. Let me know how you get on with that job interview, okay?"

"I will. Be seeing you."

He ran down the steps and was glad to get outside where the snow was falling more steadily now. It had already covered the pavements although passing traffic kept the road clear.

How did she know Bev hadn't died of cancer? And why the hell couldn't he talk about it calmly and sensibly? Probably because the guilt always threatened to overwhelm him when he thought about it. He should never have left her alone to go out running that morning. Christ, he'd had enough warnings from that crazy bastard—

He strode along the snow-covered pavement and concentrated on anything but Bev until he reached the building he wanted.

Five minutes later, he was knocking on Al's door

again. Nothing. God knows why the council provided him with a home. He sure as hell wasn't using it.

He gave up, took the stairs and was soon inside Stevie's flat.

There was nothing to see, nothing of interest, but he spent a good fifteen minutes checking it out. He'd soon know the contents of Stevie's flat better than his own home. It was a waste of time because he'd done the same when looking for that ticket, but he kept thinking, or hoping, that he'd overlooked something. He hadn't.

He grabbed what he'd come for, another box of photos, and managed to leave the flat without getting smacked on the head for his trouble. He needed to return with his car and grab the rest of the photos before the council, or whoever was responsible, cleared out the flat and destroyed Stevie's possessions.

It was a relief to return to his hotel room and drop the heavy box on the bed. He was getting his breath back when Frank phoned.

"I've managed a look at Gemma King's postmortem report," he said, getting straight to the point. "You won't like it, because it's too conclusive."

"Oh?"

"She OD'd from a lethal combination of heroin, alcohol and codeine. There's no doubt."

He was right, Dylan *didn't* like it. It was too neat. "I'm almost certain that Jeremy Brent was in her flat that night," he said.

Frank whistled. "You are joking, I hope."

"Nope. He's visited local prostitutes and he's taken them flowers. Tosser. He bought flowers from the right shop on the right day too. That seems too much of a coincidence to me, Frank."

"Brent visiting street girls? You can't be serious."

"I'm deadly serious."

There was a moment's silence as Frank allowed this startling piece of news on one of the town's good guys to sink in. "And you have proof?" he asked at last. "Real evidence that would stand up in court?"

"Nope."

"Okay, perhaps he was there. Perhaps he had great sex with her. I don't know. What I do know is that she died from a lethal combination of—"

"Heroin, alcohol and codeine. Yeah, I know. It's a coincidence, though. Even you have to admit that. And her sister's convinced she didn't die from an overdose."

"Of course her sister's convinced. Who wants to admit that a loved one was stupid enough to throw a life away?" Frank took a breath. "Maybe Brent is seeing prostitutes, but there's no point digging into his life. Everything will be squeaky clean. You know it will."

"Maybe."

"But you're going to dig anyway?"

"Of course."

Frank sighed. "Do you fancy a pint later?"

"Sounds perfect." Dylan glanced out the window to the car park below. "Assuming we're not snowed in."

# TWELVE

CHRIS WAS THE last to leave the training ground on Monday morning. He always was. Apart from the gaffer's car, the place was deserted.

It was only two o'clock, but it felt much later. The sky, still full of snow, was a leaden grey.

He fastened his seatbelt, fired the Audi's engine and was about to pull out of the car park when his phone rang. It was Paige so he killed the engine and answered it.

"Hi, you." She sounded breathless. "I was going to call earlier, but you wouldn't believe the morning I've had. Truly, the gods are against me. It started badly because there was a really creepy guy on the Tube. I swear he was following me. He leered at me."

Chris had to smile. Paige was a mix of walking disaster and drama queen. He'd known her all his life—at least, it seemed that way. She'd been his sister's best friend for ever and their home was as familiar to her as her own.

"Anyway," she rushed on in typical Paige style before he could answer, "can you get me two decent tickets for the Queens Park Rangers game? I needed a favour and I promised. You know how it is."

"I know how it is. Send me a text tomorrow to remind me, and I'll get them organised."

"Thanks. You are lovely, you know."

"I know," he said, and she laughed.

"Are we still on for the weekend?" she asked.

"Yes." He was about to say more, but it could wait until he saw her. "I'll meet you at the station on Friday night, okay?"

"I'll call you," she said. "I'm in Birmingham on Friday for a human interest story on IVF treatment. I got lumbered with that because I owed someone else a favour. I couldn't give a toss about IVF, but I'll have to go through the motions. Assuming I get it wrapped up nice and early, I'll be with you late afternoon."

"Okay. And you can tell me all about your leering stalker."

She laughed. "I will. God, he was horrid. He couldn't take his eyes off my boobs. Anyway, I've got to dash. I'll see you on Friday. And I'll send you a reminder about those tickets. Bye."

Chris drove out of the car park. The roads were clear, but the pavements were still thick with snow. There were few pedestrians about, and those that were walked slowly and carefully, some choosing to risk oncoming traffic rather than the treacherous paths.

He was soon home. Not that this huge house ever felt like home. When it was full of friends or family, it was fine, but he hadn't yet grown used to rattling around on his own in it.

He drove through the gates and watched through his rear-view mirror as they closed behind him. His own luxury prison.

As he was intending to go out later, he left the Audi on the drive. A familiar sensation of being watched made his spine tingle as he walked to the front door but, although he stopped and looked around, no journalists leapt out of the shrubbery pointing cameras at him. There was no one there. He was becoming paranoid and it had to stop.

He let himself into the house, threw his bag on the floor and went straight to the kitchen to fix himself a coffee. While he waited for the machine to deliver, he switched on some music.

Until recently, he'd enjoyed his own company. Now, he counted the minutes until people visited. Matt would be here tomorrow, and Paige would be here for the weekend. It was fine.

He wasn't worried about Paige's leering Tube companion because he'd taken too many journeys on public transport with her. While other people chatted or lost themselves in a book, Paige decided that each passenger was a psychopath. She had far too vivid an imagination.

His footsteps echoed on the wooden floor as he paced his living room. More rugs were needed to absorb the sound. It was too loud, too irritating.

A photo near the TV showed him and Paige standing in front of the Eiffel Tower. His arm was resting on her shoulders and she was laughing at the person behind the camera. Her red hair—she insisted it was titian—fell around her face in huge curls, and he often wondered how his sister's leggy friend had grown into such a beauty. She could easily have been a model. She knew it, too, and wasn't averse to using her looks to her advantage. A journalist, she was always hunting for the story that would bring her worldwide acclaim.

He walked over to the drawers, opened the top one and pulled out the small velvet-covered box. Black seemed all wrong for a box holding a thing of such beauty. It was a colour associated with mourning rather than celebration.

He flicked open the lid, and the diamond caught what little daylight was left and reflected it back at him.

For years, he'd known how Paige would react to anything—usually with a great deal of drama—but he had no idea if she'd be prepared to wear his ring. As a piece of jewellery, she'd love it, he knew that, but would she wear it?

He snapped the box shut and returned it to the drawer. He'd find out at the weekend.

Memories of his sister swamped him when he went upstairs to run a bath. As a child, Jo had been convinced that monsters lurked in the wardrobes. Countless times, Chris had woken in the middle of the night to the sounds of Jo's terrified screams coming from the next room. Back then, he'd told her how ridiculous she was being but now, when Jo had outgrown her fears years ago, he had exactly the same terrors. No matter how much he tried to pull himself together, he couldn't shake off the feeling that someone was watching him. Someone with sinister intent.

A long soak in the bath relaxed him a little. Matt would be here tomorrow and, by then, everything would feel much better.

He dressed, came downstairs and deliberately ignored the shadows that seemed to move in the garden. Darkness came early at this time of the year, and he was grateful to pull down the blinds and shut it out.

The buzzer at the gate startled him as it shattered the silence. He was tempted to ignore it and, when he heard the whining voice on the intercom, he wished he had.

"Hello, Chris. I thought we could have a quick chat."

Bloody Ruby. He'd been wondering when she'd show her ugly face again. He wished that tatty little pub she ran would fall to the ground and bury her in the rubble.

"I'm really busy—"

"That's unfortunate, because I need two minutes of your time. I'm sure you can spare me that, can't you?"

"Sorry, Ruby, can we make it another time?"

"No." Her voice was clipped. "Two minutes, Chris. I've got all night. I can wait here until you can make time for me. Of course, people might start asking questions if they saw me standing outside your gate."

*Fuck her.* She was brash enough and stubborn enough to stand there all night, he had no doubt on that score.

"Fine. Come up to the house." He pushed the button to open the gates, marched to the front door and yanked it open.

"Two minutes," he said when she stood, a little breathless, in front of him. She was dressed for the cold in knee-length boots, a fake fur coat and black leather gloves.

"Aren't you going to invite me inside?"

"No. Say what you have to say and then leave. As I said, I'm very busy."

"Tut-tut. If people knew how rude you were, they'd soon revise their opinion. Mind you, if people knew—"

"What do you want, Ruby?" The icy wind was making him shiver and, against his better judgement, he nodded for her to step into the hallway.

He closed the door behind her, but didn't invite her further into his private domain.

"What do you want?" he asked.

"This is lovely, isn't it?"

"Yes. Your two minutes is almost up."

"It's not me, Chris, you know that." She removed her gloves, and her long painted fingernails made him think of vicious birds that swooped down from the sky and sank their evil talons into unsuspecting prey. "It's Bill. He insists that you and I come to some sort of arrangement."

"I've paid you, Ruby, and you won't get a penny more. There is no more. You can tell that to your husband. I'm sick of repeating myself, but neither of you will get another penny out of me. There will be no arrangement."

"That's just it, I have told him. I've told him over and over again. But then he read about that million-pound sponsorship deal you got and—" She shrugged and left the sentence unfinished.

"That's nothing but paper talk." It wasn't, but what would Ruby know about anything?

"That's what I said, but you know what he's like. Like a terrier with a bone is my Bill."

He didn't know what Bill was like as all he'd seen was the smiling, jovial man behind the bar at the Sportsman. He couldn't believe Bill was as low, as despicable and as loathsome as the woman standing before him.

"Let's face it," she said, "if it weren't for me, you wouldn't be living here in your flash house, would you? You wouldn't have that big car sitting on the drive. And no company on the planet would be giving you a million pounds."

He wanted to scream at her. He wanted to grab her by the throat and choke the last breath from her body. "Blackmail is an ugly word. Almost as ugly as you. Now, either you leave or I call the police. What's it going to be?"

She laughed at that, a humourless laugh that bounced off the hall's walls. "Oh, I can imagine you calling the police. I'm sure we could all have a nice cosy chat when they turned up, couldn't we? My, we could tell them some tales." The smile slid off her face. "You're bluffing and we both know it."

"Am I?"

"Of course you are. It's not worth it, Chris. It's not as if we're being greedy, is it? All we want is a couple of thousand. A couple of thousand pounds is like pocket money to you, isn't it? It doesn't even make a dent in your nice million-pound windfall."

"And how long would two thousand pounds last you?"

"That would be the last you'd hear from me."

"So this is the deal? You're telling me that if I give you two thousand pounds, I'll never hear from you again?"

"That's it."

An inner voice told him he was mad for even listening to her. He could give her every penny he had and she still wouldn't be satisfied. People like her never were. Once they got their talons into their prey—

"It's up to you," she said. "Give me two thousand pounds or call the police. That has to be your decision. I can't guide you."

He'd have to give her the cash. It wouldn't end there, but at least it would keep her quiet long enough for him to decide what the hell to do about her.

"I don't have that much cash in the house," he said.

"That's okay. Tomorrow will be fine." She smiled again. "You're a good boy, Chris. A credit to your parents. They must be so proud of you."

"I'll meet you at the entrance to the park at four o'clock tomorrow with the cash."

"I'll look forward to it." She looked around the hallway again. "This really is nice. You've got excellent taste."

"I've done nothing to it." He pulled open the door, letting in a blast of cold air. "Goodbye."

"I'll see you tomorrow, Chris. Have a lovely evening, won't you?"

He didn't answer and she walked away from the house. His eyes didn't leave her until the gates closed behind her and she tottered carefully along the icy pavements.

He hoped she broke her blasted neck.

# THIRTEEN

BETWEEN MONDAY NIGHT and Tuesday morning, the snow melted and then the resulting slush froze to leave a lethal carpet of ice on the pavements.

Dylan walked, with difficulty, to Dutton Street where everyone's favourite aspiring member of parliament, Jeremy Brent, was due to open the newly refurbished library. During the half-hour walk, which usually took five minutes, Dylan lost count of the times he heard people complaining about the council's inability to deal with the icy conditions. Where was the grit? they wanted to know. How many people would end up in the accident emergency department of the local hospital with broken ankles or wrists?

The council's highways department had been busy outside the soon-to-be-opened library, which was just as well because the large crowd that had gathered outside contained a lot of elderly people. A Tuesday morning seemed a strange time to open a library, but perhaps it was the only time Brent was available. Or perhaps the library preferred to provide people with tea, coffee and biscuits rather than offer cheese and wine that an evening function might have demanded.

A lone photographer was in attendance, and standing next to him was Dave Edwards. Dylan wandered over and watched Edwards get a couple of quotes from two elderly women about what the library would mean to them.

"I just hope it's full of books and not silly computers," one of the women said. "A library card should be a passport to everywhere. It shouldn't be a meeting place for gum-chewing, noisy teenagers."

*A passport to everywhere.* Bev would have approved wholeheartedly of the woman's choice of words. She, too, had been a staunch believer in public libraries.

Edwards didn't look quite as impressed as he took the woman's name for inclusion of her quote in the local rag.

Dylan wandered over and Edwards looked up at him, frowning. "Ah, it's—" Recognition had dawned, but not Dylan's name.

"Dylan Scott. We met at the town hall on Friday night."

"Got you. What brings you here?"

"A couple of things. Did I mention that I'm a private investigator?" He knew he hadn't.

"I thought you were a friend of Stevie Greenwood's." Edwards looked suspicious.

"I am. That's why I'm in the Clough. I'm trying to find out what happened to him. But there's another matter—" He dug in his pocket, pulled out the photo Stevie had taken, and showed it to Edwards. "Does this remind you of anyone?"

Edwards held the photo at arm's length. He obviously needed glasses. "Where was it taken?"

"I can't say for sure, but my bet is that it's the streetlight outside Stevie's flat on Anderson Street."

"Hmm. It's a bad photo, obviously, but I'd say the

chap bears an uncanny resemblance to my favourite Tory, Jeremy Brent."

"Exactly what I thought."

"So what?" Edwards asked.

"So—" Dylan broke off, unsure how much to tell Edwards. "Look, this is strictly off the record, okay? If I learn anything positive, you'll be the first to know but, meanwhile, nothing goes to print. Okay?"

"Okay." Edwards looked interested, though, and Dylan knew the word of a journalist counted for nothing.

"This was taken—" he pointed at the date stamp, "—on the night that a prostitute, Gemma King, overdosed on heroin. Her sister, who lived with her, found a receipt from the local florist's at the flat. No flowers. Just a receipt. Now, you told me that Brent visits the local prostitutes. I was talking to one of the girls and heard that he occasionally takes them flowers."

Edwards let out a soft, low whistle. "I remember the Gemma King story. Tell you what, if you give me the photo, I'll put it through our scanner and see if I can mess about with it and get a clearer image."

Dylan hesitated. The last thing he wanted was an enhanced copy of this photo splashed across the *Chronicle*'s front page.

"You can trust me," Edwards said. "I'm not stupid enough to print any story that would put Brent on his guard. But I'd love to print one when there's enough evidence to put the bastard away. I'll see what I can do with the photo and then return it to you. You have my word on that."

Still Dylan hesitated. Yes, he'd love a clearer image. Only his mistrust of journalists held him back.

A hush fell over the crowd as a dark car pulled up, stopped on double yellow lines and disgorged its passengers.

Dylan looked from Brent to his photo. It was impossible to say for sure if they were one and the same. He handed the photo to Edwards and fished in his pocket for a business card. "Call me, okay?"

Edwards pocketed the photo and gave Dylan his own card. "I'll get back to you as soon as I can." He returned to the photographer's side.

Brent, all smiles for the waiting crowd, apologised for the weather, made a short speech, declared the new library open, walked inside the building, closely followed by his secretary, and greeted everyone who followed.

Once inside, Brent talked. And talked. He was passionate about libraries, he said, just as he was passionate about local schools, hospitals and public transport in the area. The man with the golden voice was wooing his audience with ease. He was also checking his watch every five minutes and Dylan wondered if he was bored, which was understandable, or if he had another appointment looming.

Dylan helped himself to coffee and biscuits, and passed time by inspecting the books on display. A line of computers sat along one wall and, nearby, a circle of chairs surrounded shiny new toys for children. It would be difficult to find a quiet spot for reading or research in this building.

Edwards and his photographer soon left and the crowd began to thin out.

Dylan hung around until he saw Brent alone, gulping down a coffee.

"Mr. Brent? I wonder if I could have a word, please."

Brent smiled to show off perfect white teeth. "Of course. What can I do for you?"

"It's a personal matter."

"Oh?"

"Yes, it's about a young girl, Gemma King. As you'll know, she overdosed about six months ago—"

"Sorry, but I haven't heard about this. The name means nothing to me."

"Really? Oh, I'm surprised. I thought you kept up-to-date on all local matters."

"I try, of course. I'm sorry, but that slipped by. She overdosed, you say? Such a tragic waste."

"Indeed. The thing is, you knew her."

"What?" The smooth smile slipped a little. "No, you're mistaken. As I said, the name means nothing to me. What makes you think I might have known her?"

"You definitely knew her. She was a prostitute who lived on Anderson Street with her sister."

Brent checked his watch again and shook his head. "I know the area, of course, but I'm afraid her name means nothing to me. Sorry. Look, I'm afraid I'll have to cut this chat short. I'm due elsewhere and my car will be waiting."

"In that case, perhaps we could meet up at a more convenient time," Dylan said.

"I'm not sure what it is you want from me."

"Just some information about Gemma."

"But I've told you, I've never heard the name before. Sorry, but I have to go." The smile was restored. "There's no peace for the wicked, as they say."

Never a truer word.

"Good talking to you, Mr., um—"

"Scott. Dylan Scott. Private investigator."

His words killed Brent's smile. A million questions were visible in Brent's eyes, but he didn't utter a single one. "Right. Well, good speaking to you, Mr. Scott, but I must go. Goodbye."

"I'll see you again soon."

Brent headed off with his secretary. They'd almost reached the door when Brent said something to his secretary that was enough to have the man spinning round to take a good long look at Dylan. It wasn't the friendliest of looks either.

# FOURTEEN

CHRIS CALLED HIMSELF all sorts of a fool as he gazed at the brown envelope sitting on the passenger seat. It wasn't the money that irked him. Ruby was right in that two grand was nothing to him. People believed all footballers were overpaid and perhaps they were right. Without any add-ons from sponsorship deals or appearances, he earned twenty-six grand a week. It was a lot of money. What people didn't understand though was that his career was such a fragile thing. He could break a leg on Saturday and never play again. Unlikely, as rehabilitation programs were so successful these days, but he knew several players who'd never regained form after a serious injury. Even if he managed to avoid injury, once he hit thirty he'd be looking at the end of his career. Footballers might get paid well, but it was only for a short time.

At least that evil witch Ruby wasn't affecting his form. He was on top of his game and intended to stay there. Thankfully, once he was on the pitch, or even the training ground, nothing but the game registered. Ruby might not have existed.

She did damn well exist, though.

He started up the Audi, checked the dashboard clock and drove slowly toward the park.

He wasn't a malicious person, but he'd never disliked anyone as much as he disliked Ruby. Bill, her husband, seemed a kind, jovial man, exactly the right sort of bloke to run a successful pub, but perhaps Ruby was right, and perhaps it was him pulling the strings. Chris didn't know. He only knew that he loathed Ruby with every breath in his body.

He wished she were dead.

To think this was her final demand was ridiculous. When she'd spent the two grand, which wouldn't take long, she'd be back for more. She saw him as her personal bank account, one with no limit, and he was foolish enough to let her.

What was the alternative though? She was right in that the newspapers would pay a lot for her story. He could go to the police, but what could they do? They might issue a restraining order so that she couldn't go anywhere near him, but that wasn't enough. It wasn't nearly enough.

Traffic was moving slowly, but he reached the park's entrance at two minutes to four. As he'd guessed, there was no one in sight other than Ruby. He'd chosen to meet her here because the park was rarely used, especially in this weather, making it unlikely that anyone would see him. Not that it mattered if they did, he supposed.

He stopped the car, grabbed the envelope and got out. The sight of her, standing beneath an umbrella to ward off the sleet, made his stomach clench with loathing.

After a quick look round to make sure no one was watching, he handed her the envelope. She put it in a large black bag. "You're a good boy, Chris."

"That's it. That's the last you'll get from me. If I hear from you again, I'm going straight to the police. My mother's a successful barrister. You know that, do you?"

"Who doesn't?" She patted his arm. "Don't get so worked up. Stress is really bad for you. I've told Bill that this is the last time. He understands. I'm sure he won't want any more from you."

"He can want what he likes, but he won't fucking get."

"Now, now. There's no need for language like that."

"There's every need. You disgust me." He turned back to his car.

The fact that he'd been childish enough to mention his mother's profession infuriated him even more than Ruby if that were possible. He was twenty-one years old and he no longer needed his mother to fight his battles for him.

"Aren't you going to offer me a lift?" Ruby asked. "You're not going to make me walk in this, are you?"

He couldn't bring himself to answer. Without a backward glance, he jumped in the Audi, fired the engine and drove off. It took five minutes for him to realise he was heading in the wrong direction.

At the next roundabout, he did a U-turn and took the road for home.

The dark and the cold did nothing to improve his mood. Only the sight of Matt's car, the one Chris had bought him, cheered him. Even the house, lit up like a Christmas tree, looked welcoming. Matt would make him forget Ruby and her sickening demands. They'd relax, have a few laughs, and everything would look brighter. Besides, Ruby wasn't the cleverest person around. Perhaps he could take her at her word. Maybe he'd never have to see or hear from her again.

Matt was in the kitchen with the ever-present phone stuck to his ear. He'd lost weight lately and the tight black jeans he wore emphasised the fact, as did the black cashmere sweater stretched across his chest.

He smiled and put up his hand in greeting but continued to talk rapidly and authoritatively to the person on the other end.

Chris supposed they were equally driven by their chosen professions. No modern-day footballer reached the top without devoting every second of their life to keeping fit. Fifty years ago, it wasn't unusual to see top players enjoying a couple of pints and a few cigarettes. These days, a player's life was ruled by science and nutrition experts.

Matt, too, lived for his work. He had his own film company and was currently trying to raise interest in a controversial project about immigration and the homeless. Driven he most definitely was. Successful he wasn't. Not yet. Even at this hour, a half-empty bottle of wine sat on the counter.

As he spoke to his caller, Matt paced, he ran his fingers through thick dark hair, he chewed on his bottom lip as he listened—he looked ten years older than Chris instead of four, and so tense.

"Chill," Chris murmured when there was a lull in Matt's conversation, and Matt smiled at him and shrugged.

Chris was a fine one to talk. He was the one constantly imagining he was being watched by some evil force.

Knowing the conversation could last a while, he went into the living room and took that black velvet-covered box from the drawer. Before they did or said anything, he needed to tell Matt his plans. He slipped the box into his pocket.

When he returned to the kitchen, Matt was refilling his wineglass and wrapping up the conversation.

Chris took the box from his pocket and set it on the counter. Matt saw it, slowly guessed at its significance and became even more determined to end his call.

When he finally did, he put his phone on the counter. "Sorry, it's been nonstop today. So what's this? Or can I guess?" He flipped open the box and gazed, expressionless, at the ring. "Very nice. Very pricey too."

"I haven't mentioned it to her yet, but she's coming up this weekend so I'll ask her then. What do you think?"

Matt picked up his glass and swallowed some wine. "You know what I think."

Chris supposed he did. They'd talked about it often enough. "What do you think she'll say?"

Matt finally smiled and the tension seemed to fall from his face. "She'll say yes, she'll plan an enormous star-studded party to celebrate, she'll grab your credit card and shop for England and, most important in her eyes, she'll milk the story for all it's worth."

Chris laughed with relief. "That sounds like Paige. I hope you're right. I hope she says yes."

"She will. Don't worry." Matt took a wrap of heroin from his pocket. "I suggest we celebrate in advance…"

# FIFTEEN

DYLAN FOLLOWED BRENT out of the library and spent most of the day tracking him, but it was impossible to get near the man. He made sure Brent knew he was being watched though. It would put him on his guard but, hopefully, it would also make him sweat a bit. Brent could deny it all he liked, but Dylan was convinced he'd known Gemma King *and* visited her the night she died.

That evening, as Brent was ensconced in his very attractive home with his perfect family, Dylan went on another mission.

He was two minutes away from Elliott's home when his phone rang. He didn't recognise the number but he stopped the car to answer it.

"Dave Edwards, *Chronicle*."

It amused Dylan the way Edwards couldn't say his name without mentioning the local newspaper. "Hi, Dave. Do you have anything for me?"

"Where are you?"

"I'm in the Clough. On Manchester Road."

"Tell you what, I can be in the Park View in ten minutes. Is that any good to you? I want to return your photo."

"Okay. I'll see you there."

The Park View was probably Edwards's local as it was close to the *Chronicle*'s offices. It took Dylan almost fifteen minutes to get there and he walked inside to see Edwards nursing a large whisky. Dylan went to the bar, bought himself a pint of beer, and joined Edwards at a table in the centre of the room.

The pub was quiet. It was one of those that didn't know if it was pub or restaurant and was making a poor job of being either. It also deemed it necessary to have live music or karaoke on every night, and a couple of men were carrying speakers, drums and guitars into the room. Dylan hoped this would be a short chat because he loathed the acts that pubs like this called entertainment. They were either tribute bands, bad ones, or they covered all the cheesy hits that everyone knew and hated.

"So," he said. "What do you have?"

Edwards placed a large brown envelope on the table. When Dylan opened it, he found an enlarged portion of the photo he'd given Edwards. He'd been right. It was definitely Brent.

"This is great," he said, and Edwards nodded.

"I had to mess around with the contrast and the colour balance, but it's him, isn't it?" He didn't wait for Dylan to confirm this. "Of course it's him."

There were more enlarged sections of the photo and it was clear to see, peeping out from behind Brent's back, flowers. It proved that Brent had been in Anderson Street, carrying flowers, on the night Gemma died. The night her sister found a florist's receipt.

"Can I keep these?" Dylan asked.

"Of course. The original's there too. I'll expect you to let me know if you get something on Brent though."

"Believe me, you'll be the first to know." He wasn't about to dash Edwards's hopes, but he knew the photos proved nothing that would stand up in a court of law.

But if Brent was involved in Gemma's death, and if he'd known that Stevie had photographic evidence of sorts—

Part of Dylan found it difficult to imagine the clever, smooth-talking Brent as Stevie's killer. On the other hand, it was easy to see Brent as a man who would do anything to protect his glossy reputation. Brent wouldn't have got his own hands dirty though. He would have paid a professional. And a professional wouldn't have made such a mess of the job. Stevie's murder had been very amateurish.

"What else do you have on Brent?" Dylan asked. "You mentioned stuff from his past. I've looked on the net and haven't found much of interest."

"You won't. Nothing was ever published apart from a paragraph here and there. I'll dig those paragraphs out for you."

"Thanks."

"Seeing Brent sent down would make my retirement so much sweeter. It really would. I've never liked the bloke. I've never trusted him, either, and I never will." Edwards sighed. "He's clever though. He'll always have someone covering his tracks. Bastard." He drank the last of his whisky. "It's time I headed home. Call me when you have something. I'll do the same, of course. Night."

"Night."

Dylan watched him go, then finished his pint and left the Park View just as the band issued a warning sound check.

He drove back the way he'd come and went to Elliott's home. Lights were on at number 143, but there was no sign of the Audi. Perhaps it was in the garage. There was enough room for five in there.

He pressed the button on the panel at the side of the tall iron gates. He was about to press it again when a male voice said, "Yes?"

"Chris Elliott?"

"Yes."

"Dylan Scott. We met at the fundraiser. I wondered if I might have a quick word with you, please."

There was a long pause. "About what?"

Dylan didn't want to scare him off. "It's nothing serious. If you could spare a couple of minutes, I'd be very grateful."

"Okay, but I'm about to go out so it really will have to be a couple of minutes."

The gates whirred open and by the time Dylan had walked up the drive, Elliott was holding the front door open.

"Oh, hello. Sorry, I didn't recognise the name. Your son's the budding footballer, right?"

"That's right, yes." Dylan was surprised he'd remembered. "Thanks for seeing me. I appreciate it. You must be busy."

"Like I said, you've only just caught me. I have to go out in a minute. Come inside."

Dylan followed him into a kitchen that was bigger than the entire ground floor of his own house. It was vast, and along with every shiny kitchen appliance ever invented, it boasted an enviable sound system. Classical music, a piece Dylan didn't recognise, was playing at an acceptably low level.

Elliott wasn't alone. A man, probably a few years older than Elliott, was leaning against the counter with a glass of red wine in his hand.

"Sorry, I didn't mean to intrude." Dylan looked at the stranger. "Dylan Scott. I met Chris on Friday night."

He smiled expectantly and, eventually, Elliott introduced his companion. "This is Matt, a friend. He's staying with me for a couple of days. So what can I do for you?"

"Did I mention that I was a private investigator?"

"No." Elliott looked wary now, as if he regretted letting Dylan in. "I thought you were a friend of that chap who was murdered, Stephen Greenwood."

"I am. Was. That's why I'm here. I'm trying to find out what happened to him, and I'm getting nowhere. You mentioned giving him a ticket to that fundraiser and I wondered if you could tell me about that."

"There's nothing to tell you, I'm afraid." Elliott paced the considerable length of the kitchen with his hands deep in the pockets of black jeans. "I'd seen him about the town, of course. Once seen, never forgotten really. The limp, the camera—" He picked up a set of car keys and played with them like worry beads. "I didn't even know his name until I saw it in the newspaper."

"Where was he when you spoke to him? When you gave him the ticket?"

Elliott was a long time answering. It was as if he'd needed to prepare his words and present them carefully. "We were at that pub. The one near Catch-22."

"The Sportsman?"

"That's the one," Matt said, taking Dylan by surprise. "A bloody awful place, but everyone gathers there before heading on to Catch-22."

"You were both there?"

"Yes," Matt said. "For my sins, Chris dragged me along."

"And you were going on to the club?"

"Yes." They both spoke together.

"What was Stevie doing?"

"He was having a drink. He had his camera with him." Elliott wasn't comfortable with the memories. He put the car keys on the counter and shoved his hands back in his pockets. "I'd had a couple of drinks, if you must know. More than a couple if I'm honest."

"A lot more than a couple," Matt said with a laugh.

Elliott wasn't smiling. "Stevie took a photo of me when I was looking far from my best, and I asked him to delete it. The press would love it if they knew I'd been found drunk in that place. Found drunk anywhere, of course. Anyway, your friend Stevie was fine about it. He was more than happy to delete the photo, and I was grateful to him. I didn't have much cash on me, and anyway, I thought he might have been a bit insulted if I offered him any. But I wanted to say thank you and so I gave him a ticket to the fundraiser. I thought he'd sell it or something. Perhaps it was stupid of me."

"Chris should know better," Matt said, still finding the situation amusing. "He rarely drinks, so half a glass of beer has him falling all over the place."

Dylan gave them both what he hoped was an encouraging smile. "Ah, that makes sense. I was curious. You had no need to worry about Stevie, though. He wasn't a gossip. He wasn't even a talker. Your secret would have been safe with him."

"Yes, I know," Elliott said. "I suppose I panicked a bit. But he was fine about it."

"And that was how long before he was killed?"

"A couple of days." Elliott moistened dry lips. "It

was the Saturday night. He was killed on the Tuesday. I never saw him again after that night."

"Who else saw you? Other than Stevie?"

"A lot of people, obviously. Everyone at the pub and everyone at the club. But I'd sobered up a bit. As far as I know, only Stevie saw me staggering around."

"That's all right then. Your secret's safe enough." He smiled to show he was joking. "I was curious about the ticket, that's all, but now you've explained, it all makes sense."

Elliott looked relieved. So did Matt. Dylan would love to know what they were hiding.

There was a photo stuck to a huge freezer that showed Elliott with his arm around two girls. One was his sister, Jo.

"I met Jo at the fundraiser," Dylan said, nodding at the picture. "She's planning to be a surgeon, I gather."

"Yes." Elliott was happy to be on easier ground. "She's the brains of the family. Mum is too, of course. She's a barrister. A formidable one."

"Really? Jo has a lot to live up to then, what with her mum a barrister and her brother a hotshot footballer. What about your father? I suppose he's a rocket scientist."

Elliott chuckled at that. "He's an architect. He'd really like to be designing big cathedrals, like that awful thing in Barcelona, the one that looks like it was built by a five-year-old—"

"The Sagrada Famillia? Gaudi's?"

"That's the one."

Dylan had to smile. Gaudi would be turning in his grave at the description. He remembered visiting Barcelona with Bev and deciding that getting to the top of the unfinished cathedral was a must. Bev had been fine, but Dylan didn't have a particularly good head for heights and all he'd been able to think about was the health and safety regulations in Spain—or, more accurate, the lack of them. The place had resembled a building site and there hadn't been so much as a hard hat in sight.

"Poor Dad has to be content with designing offices and the like. Pretty boring really."

"Ah." Dylan smiled sympathetically. "Do you have another sister? The girl in the photo?"

"No, that's Paige. My girlfriend and Jo's best friend."

"And I thought you were young, free and single. I fear you're going to break a lot of girls' hearts when that's common knowledge." He was damn sure it wasn't common knowledge.

"I'm sure they'll get over it," Elliott said lightly.

"I expect you're right. You think it's best to keep it quiet for now, do you?"

"It's no great secret, although the time's never seemed right to go public. Paige is a journalist and lives down in London so getting together is a bit difficult. Actually, I'm hoping we'll go public next week. Watch this space."

"I will. Good luck with it all. And thanks for your time. I'd better not keep you or you'll be late for your appointment. Thanks again for the signed photo. I haven't been home since the fundraiser so Luke hasn't seen it yet, but he'll be thrilled, really thrilled."

"It was nothing." Elliott began ushering him toward the door. "Goodnight then."

"Goodnight. Nice to meet you, Matt."

"Likewise," Matt said.

Dylan walked back to his car and heard the clunk of those tall iron gates closing behind him.

He sat in his car and watched the house. Lights came on and went off. Nine o'clock came and went. As did ten o'clock. At a little before eleven, the house was in darkness.

Perhaps Elliott had decided not to go out after all. Or perhaps, and this was more likely, he'd never intended to. Dylan couldn't blame him for telling that particular lie. He often said the same if he received unwelcome callers.

Elliott had been hiding something though, and Dylan would give a lot to know what that something was.

# SIXTEEN

DYLAN WASTED MUCH of the morning. After a breakfast that had been far too leisurely, he'd spent a couple
of hours in his hotel room looking through Stevie's
photos and putting them in order. The final shot Stevie
had taken, or the most recent Dylan had found, was of
the tall iron gates opening into the crematorium. That
was more apt than Stevie had known. Dylan found a
great shot of a scowling Ruby taken in the Sportsman. A
close-up, it showed every wrinkle. She would have been
far from amused if she'd seen that one. There wasn't
a glimpse of a drunken footballer in any of the shots.
There was nothing that grabbed his interest.

He needed to do something constructive so he left
the hotel, jumped in his car and drove to Brent's house.
It was on the outskirts of town and although it wasn't in
the same price range as Elliott's, it had far more character and more land. At a guess, Dylan would say it had
been built with local stone in the nineteenth century. A
couple of ponies grazed in a muddy field to the left of
the house. If the land belonged to Brent, the ponies were
probably ridden by his children. No tall gates guarded
the property so it would be easy enough to walk up to
the front door.

There was little point though because Brent wouldn't
speak to him, and Dylan didn't intend to cause a scene
in front of his wife and children. On the other hand,

with his wife within earshot, Brent was more likely to agree to a meeting, especially if Dylan dropped the *prostitute* word into the conversation.

He was about to get out of his car when the Brent family walked out the front door. Brent was carrying a suitcase, his wife was checking the contents of her handbag, and his two sons had a backpack each. Brent dropped the suitcase near the garage, went inside and reversed his car onto the drive. He jumped out and helped the children stow the luggage. There was no minder—or secretary, as Brent preferred to call him—in sight.

The family piled in the car, and Brent drove off. Dylan followed.

It soon became obvious they were heading to Manchester Airport. Damn it. He didn't want Brent leaving town.

Once they reached the airport, Dylan was pleased to see Brent head for the short stay car park. Dylan followed and parked the Morgan, making sure there were a couple of dozen vehicles between it and Brent's car. A 1956 Morgan in Daytona Yellow was probably the worst car in the world for surveillance work, but it was Dylan's pride and joy so it was going nowhere. He had to be careful, that was all.

Brent carried the suitcase, and his wife called out directions to their children who were striding toward the terminal with their backpacks.

Once inside the building, Dylan bought himself a newspaper and kept it in front of his face as he watched the family. Mrs. Brent bought a couple of paperbacks, and the children bought magazines and chocolate.

The check-in process was slow, but Dylan managed

to get close enough to read the labels that were attached to the suitcase. The destination was Edinburgh.

Hugs and kisses were soon given out. Mrs. Brent and the children headed for the departures lounge and Brent returned to his car.

Dylan followed him, all the way back to his home in Dawson's Clough.

Darkness was already descending and spring seemed a long way off. At least it wasn't snowing or raining though, and that made a pleasant change in this part of the country, but it was cold and dismal.

Dylan sat in his car, watching the house. Nothing stirred. No one arrived, and Brent didn't go anywhere.

After an hour, Dylan decided it was time for a chat.

He walked along the considerable driveway and rapped the iron knocker against a solid oak door.

A smiling Brent opened the door, but the smile slipped when he recognised Dylan.

"So, we meet again," Brent said. "And again, I have nothing to tell you."

"I'm here to jog your memory," Dylan said. "It's about Gemma King. But you know that, don't you?"

Brent gave an exasperated laugh. "Yes, but I told you, I don't know the woman. I've never heard of her. A prostitute, you said? I wouldn't know any of those girls, would I? I mean, why would I?"

The longer Dylan remained silent, the more Brent talked.

"Look, I'm sorry, but you've had a wasted journey, Mr.—"

"Scott. Dylan Scott."

"Well, Mr. Scott, you're wasting your time with me.

I'm sorry, but I can't help you." He tried to close the door but Dylan blocked it with his foot.

"As I said, I'm here to jog your memory. I have photographic evidence, you see."

Shock had Brent's eyebrows beetling together. "What?"

"Yes, that's the point. I have a photo that clearly proves you *did* know her."

"Let's see it."

"I don't have it with me." The photo was in Dylan's pocket, but if he showed it to Brent, Brent would quickly decide he was raving mad and he'd probably be right. It showed Brent walking along Anderson Street with a bunch of flowers. So what? It didn't prove anything, and it certainly didn't prove that Brent had known Gemma. "It's safe enough, don't worry about that."

"When was the photo taken? And by whom?"

"It was taken the night that Gemma died. And it was taken by Stevie Greenwood—you know the name, I'm sure."

"Of course I know the name. The poor chap was murdered." Brent looked out of his depth. He needed time to assess the situation and Dylan wasn't giving him that time. "Okay. You'd better come in for a moment and we'll straighten this out."

"Thanks."

Inside, the house was even more impressive. It was crammed with original features, like the old beams and the exposed stonework. Stone floors were covered with thick colourful rugs. Mrs. Brent, if she was responsible, had style. It was a beautiful home.

Dylan was taken into a study that was warm and cosy. An oak desk sat in the centre of the room, and a log-burning stove welcomed two leather armchairs to its warmth.

"Sit down," Brent said, indicating one of the chairs.

"Thanks."

Brent took a breath. "You'll have to tell me about this photo because I'm at a total loss. I simply can't place the poor woman."

"You'd recognise her easily enough," Dylan said. "She looked like Marilyn Monroe. Had the wig and the dress—a very beautiful woman."

"And this photo you have?"

Anyone else, when hearing that a Dawson's Clough hooker could look like Marilyn, would be disbelieving. The Clough wasn't known for drop-dead-gorgeous hookers.

"I have a couple. One shows you going to Gemma's flat, the one she shared with her sister. The other shows the flowers quite clearly. You dropped the receipt, did you know that? I'm not sure if the media printed that or not." He knew damn well they hadn't. "Her sister found the receipt and the police took it as evidence. Presumably they checked it for prints. And presumably they found none or they'd have been knocking on your door before now."

Brent was so pale that Dylan feared for his health. He might not like the bloke, and he sure as hell didn't want to see him get away with murder, but he didn't want him having a coronary.

"I wouldn't worry," Dylan said, "because you probably didn't touch the receipt. I bought flowers from Forget-me-nots too. I was served by the same girl who served you. When you pay, she tucks the receipt in the flowers. It struck me as an odd thing to do at the time because it would be easy to hand over the flowers with the receipt still with them. But I expect that's what happened to you. You will have forgotten to put the receipt in your wallet, and it will have fallen out of the bouquet without you even touching it."

"What do you want?" Brent's voice was slightly above a whisper.

"The truth would make a refreshing change."

"You want money, is that it? You're blackmailing me, aren't you? I give you money and you give me the photo. Meanwhile, you'll have made copies—"

"I don't want money."

Brent didn't look reassured. He looked scared to death. "So what *do* you want?"

"I told you. I want the truth."

"Where are the photos?"

"They're safe enough. I have one set and as added insurance, I gave copies to a journalist."

Brent put his head in his hands. He looked as if he were about to burst into tears.

"Okay," he said at last, "but I did nothing wrong. I did know the girl—I didn't know her real name, and she didn't know mine. She was a looker, you're right about that. Few men would be able to resist her when she was dressed up like Marilyn Monroe. I'm afraid I couldn't. I'm not proud of that fact, obviously. I'm a married man, a very happily married man." He sucked in a ragged breath. "I saw her twice, that's all. And I paid well for the privilege. I'd arranged to see her the night she died."

He was swallowing convulsively and Dylan still feared for his health.

"It was to be the last time," Brent said. "A man in

my position—a happily married, family man—couldn't meet a prostitute. The idea was ludicrous. So I vowed that it would be the last time." He tried for a smile and failed miserably. "I bought her flowers to soften the blow. I'm sure she didn't have feelings for me, but as I said, I paid well and I knew she'd miss that. I got to her flat and—and the door was open. I walked inside, called her name and received no answer. I found her lying in the bath. She was dead."

Dylan said nothing. His face, he hoped, was devoid of all expression.

"She was dead," Brent said again, his voice rising. "The stupid little fool was already dead."

"You checked for a pulse?"

"What? Yes, of course I did. I'm telling you, she was dead. It was too late for anyone to do anything."

"So you called an ambulance and then—?"

"How could I?" Brent scoffed.

"Quite easily," Dylan said. "You pick up your phone and hit 999. It works every time."

"Don't be absurd. I couldn't, could I? Not a man in my position. If I'd got involved, my career and my life would have been over. That wouldn't have helped anyone, would it? She was dead," he said again, as if he thought Dylan couldn't grasp this important fact. "There was nothing I could do."

"So you cleaned the flat—removing all traces of fingerprints?"

Brent had the grace to look a little ashamed. "I'd only touched the door handle."

"And then you scarpered?"

"Yes."

Dylan left the comfort of the leather armchair and

walked over to the window. A couple of exterior lights
lit the front driveway, but there was nothing to see.

"It's an interesting story," he said, turning around.
And sod it, he couldn't disprove it.

"It's the truth."

"Is it? Maybe you'd tired of her and decided she had
to be silenced." Which wouldn't account for the heroin,
alcohol and codeine in her system. It would be hard for
someone to administer such a lethal dose. "Maybe you
then found out that Stevie Greenwood had taken a photo
that put you in Anderson Street at the time in question.
Maybe you decided he had to be silenced too."

"What? Are you completely mad?"

"Just throwing out ideas."

"I had nothing to do with his murder, you have to believe me. I told you, that girl was already dead. As for
Greenwood, I have no idea what you're talking about.
I didn't know he'd taken photos. I didn't know anything about him."

"Okay." Dylan gave him a warm smile. "Thanks for
your time, I appreciate it. I'll be off now."

"What about the photos?"

"I told you, they're safe enough."

"But you can give them to me. I've told you the truth.
You have to destroy them."

"If you've told me the truth, there's no need to destroy them, is there?" Another warm smile. "Thanks
again. I'll see myself out."

"Hang on a minute." Brent's voice was hard and cold.
"You can't come into my home, throw out all sorts of
crazy accusations and walk out again."

"I think you'll find that I can."

"You won't get away with this—"

Dylan carried on walking until he was outside. As he strolled back to his car, he could hear Brent still spluttering about those photos. The photos that were a figment of Dylan's imagination.

As he drove back to his hotel, he didn't know whether to believe Brent's story. He certainly wasn't falling for all that romantic bollocks about being unable to resist the Marilyn lookalike. Fiona looked nothing like any celebrity, alive or dead, and he'd taken her flowers too.

For the moment, Brent could spend time worrying about his reputation. It wouldn't harm him. On the contrary, it would be character building.

# SEVENTEEN

DYLAN PUSHED OPEN his front door and did a double take. For a moment, he thought he'd walked into the wrong house, but that was wishful thinking. "Holy bloody crap."

The sound of his voice had Luke dashing into the hall. "Hey, Dad. You're home early."

Bozo came rushing up and leapt at Dylan's face as if they hadn't seen each other for eight years rather than eight days. Judging by the muddy paw prints he left on Dylan's shirt, he'd been digging in the garden again.

Dylan ruffled his son's hair. He hadn't missed the house with all its dark memories, but he'd missed his kids more than he'd imagined possible. Originally, he'd planned to come home tomorrow but, as he was still thinking about his chat with Brent and didn't have much of a plan in mind, he'd decided to come early.

"What the hell's this?"

"Oh, yeah." Luke snorted. "Vicky thought it needed a bit of colour."

"Daddy!" Freya launched herself through the door and headed at top speed for Dylan. He managed to scoop her into his arms before she fell flat on her face. When she concentrated, Freya was a good walker, and she was certainly an expert climber, but everything had to be done at top speed and she was an accident waiting to happen. She was wearing a pretty pink dress that belied her tomboy nature. A stair-gate did nothing to deter her, she simply climbed over the things. It would be trees next...

"Hi, gorgeous." He buried his face in her blond curls.

She clapped her hands together in rapture then pointed to the ceiling. "Pretty."

*Pretty bloody awful.*

"Do you like the lights?" he asked her, and she clapped her hands together again.

"Pretty, pretty, pretty."

The excitement brought the ageing hippy that Dylan was forced to call Mother into the hall. "Hello, love. You're back then."

She didn't looked stoned, which was a plus, but the clothes she wore—long purple skirt, red T-shirt and orange waistcoat—would have been more suited to a seventies music festival in a sunny field.

"So it would seem."

"What do you think?" She gestured to what had once been a spacious hallway and which now resembled a living nightmare.

"There are young, impressionable children present so I'd better not say."

She tutted. "I knew you wouldn't like it. How did you get so boring, Dylan? Freya loves it."

"Freya loves ice cream with sausages."

"Sausages," Freya said, as if to confirm this.

Crisscrossing the ceiling were several strings of flashing white lights. Between these, red lanterns hung down. Two of those blasted feather things that his mother called dream catchers were placed at a height that meant any man of average build would end up risking strangulation. Walls that had once been a muted, tasteful cream were now sunshine yellow.

Still carrying Freya, he walked into the kitchen, with Bozo trotting behind him, and looked around. Everything looked as it should and he began to relax a little.

"What possessed you?" he asked, and his mother laughed.

"I decided the place needed cheering up. Do you want a coffee?"

"Please."

The house did need cheering up, but feathers, lanterns and flashing lights weren't going to do it. There should have been plenty of good memories but somehow, the bad memories were too overpowering.

Dylan was beginning to hate this house.

"What's new?" he asked, shaking off his thoughts.

His mother and Luke both started talking at once. Freya raced across the kitchen and fell head first. She was so used to this, she didn't bother to cry.

As they chatted, he began to feel the tension leave him. They'd been fine and perfectly happy without him. The guilt lessened.

"Luke, I've got something for you," he said. "It's in the car."

He battled his way through the hallway and fetched his bags and computer from his car.

Like a magician pulling a rabbit from a hat, Dylan produced the signed photo and handed it over. Luke's face lit up, just as Dylan had known it would.

"Wow. Just wow! Did you meet him? What's he like? He's not very tall, is he? Is he signing for Arsenal next season?"

"Yes. Very nice. Not particularly. And he denied all rumours. Anything else?"

Luke grinned. "What did he say?"

"He said he loves playing football and he leaves everything else—and that includes thinking about the club he'll be playing for next season—to his agent. I gather he finds it a bit hard work being in the spotlight surrounded by photographers all the time."

"Wow. Hey, wait till I tell Charlie." Luke raced off to phone his girlfriend in private. Few girls would be impressed by a signed photo of Dawson Clough's talented striker, but Charlotte would.

"As you're home," Dylan's mother said, "I think I'll go out and have a smoke." She exhaled with anticipated pleasure.

"You don't have to get stoned just because I'm here."

"No, but it makes you so much easier to deal with." Cackling at her own joke, she left him alone with Freya.

He scooped up his daughter as she was about to risk concussion by diving headlong across the kitchen floor. "So what do you have to say for yourself, sweetheart?"

She pointed in the vague direction of the hall. "Pretty."

"I suppose you're too young to understand but, one of these days, you'll come to realise that your grandmother is certifiable. What you mean is pretty horrible, right?"

"Pretty horrible." She gurgled with laughter. "Sausages and ice cream?" she asked hopefully and Dylan laughed.

"Maybe. Who knows? It's more likely to be nut cutlets with yoghurt but, as I said, your grandmother's certifiable. There's no knowing what she's been cooking."

When evening rolled round and the kids were in bed,

he sat in the kitchen to enjoy a small glass of whisky. His mother had ventured out into the cold night air to smoke a joint. Rather her than him.

He absently threw the tennis ball that Bozo dropped on his lap. The dog was easily pleased and Dylan envied the animal's simple view of life. Given food and a bed, and someone to throw a ball, Bozo wasn't just happy, he was delirious.

His mother walked inside and stood by the radiator hugging herself. "Roll on summer. That's if we get one this year."

She filled the kettle and switched it on. "Why the long face?"

"Sorry?"

"You look as if you've lost a million pounds and found a penny. What's wrong?"

"I'm fine. It's the face I was born with, and that's your fault."

"You could always move, you know, if this house is too bad. There's nothing keeping you here. Nothing keeping you in London either. Why not ring the changes and give yourself a fresh start?"

"Ring the changes?" He didn't believe what he'd heard. "I've had enough changes, thanks very much."

She made one of her herbal concoctions and sat at the table to drink it. "Even without—well, you know. Even if that hadn't happened, Bev wouldn't be here now."

"I know." He didn't want to talk about it. Or think about it.

"You still have a lot to be thankful for. Bev left you with two wonderful children—"

"I know that too." He *seriously* didn't want to talk about it.

"If the house is getting you down—"

"The house isn't getting me down." It was. As ridiculous as it sounded, given that it was nothing more than bricks and mortar, the place seemed to have taken on a depressing character of its own. "Well, maybe a little. It hits me every time I walk through the door. I hate it."

"Then move. This was always Bev's house. Live somewhere that you can make your own."

"Run away, you mean?"

"You can't run from it. You can change things though."

"We'll see." He refilled his glass. "So what plans do you have for the week? More redecorating?"

"I don't know yet. I'll have to give it some thought. What about you? How are you getting on in the frozen north?"

He was relieved to be on safer ground. It was far easier to talk about murder and speculate on the secrets being hidden in Dawson's Clough than face up to any problems in his own life.

When his phone rang, he glanced at the display and wasn't surprised to see that Brent was calling him for the fourth time today. He ignored it, waited until a message had been left, and listened to that.

"Dylan? Jeremy here again. You're a difficult man to tie down. Anyway, give me a call, will you? Any time. I'd like a quick chat."

Good to know they were suddenly on first-name terms. Good to know Brent was panicking too...

# EIGHTEEN

CHRIS PUT PAIGE'S luggage in the car and wondered why she couldn't grasp the concept of travelling light. She was only staying with him for the weekend, yet she'd brought enough clothes—if the bags were full of clothes—to keep her going for at least a fortnight.

"Is the kitchen sink coming by carrier?" he asked, and she laughed.

"I haven't brought much stuff." When they were inside the car, she added, "It's just that I'm in Birmingham again on Monday and staying the night there."

"For this story you're doing?"

"Yes. It's a pain in the arse, and I may need to do a bit of work on it over the weekend but, apart from that, I'm all yours. You can wine and dine me in the manner to which I long to be accustomed."

"It'll be a quiet night tonight," he warned. "I've got a game tomorrow."

"I know. We can hit the town in style tomorrow night though. Mind you, we'll need to have sobered up by Sunday morning. Your mum's coming up. Did she tell you?"

"What? No, she didn't." Chris tapped irritated fingers on the steering wheel. "Why's she suddenly decided on that?"

"She said you've been difficult to tie down lately so she's coming to check up on you." Paige grinned at him. "She thought you'd been ignoring her calls. Really, Chris, shame on you."

"I haven't." He saw her disbelieving glance. "Okay, I might have missed a couple. You know what she's like though."

"Yeah."

Traffic was beginning to build up as people tried to get from work to home in the shortest possible time. Friday afternoons were always busy.

Chris supposed his mother's planned visit wasn't too big a deal. He just wished she'd let him know. He hated being taken for granted. For all she knew, he might have something planned for Sunday. He did have something planned because he wanted to treat Paige, but he could have been doing any of a number of things. He shouldn't complain about his mother, he knew that, but he did resent the way she thought he was always available for her.

"Is Dad coming with her?" he asked.

"I assume so, but I don't know. She didn't say and I didn't ask. All she said was that she'd see us on Sunday, and she added that she hadn't been able to let you know yet because you kept ignoring her calls."

"And my answer machine isn't working?"

"You know she hates leaving messages."

"She hates leaving messages for me. She leaves them all the time for other people."

"Ah, but you're the special one."

"Ha."

His earliest memory was of being told he was special and it had always been a standing joke between him, Jo and Paige. Jo resented it, he knew that, and he didn't blame her. He often tried to convince her that there were distinct disadvantages to the accolade. Being wrapped in cotton wool and never being allowed to live his own life was the main one.

They were about five minutes from home when it started snowing again. Chris doubted it would come to anything because they'd already had several light falls during the day and very little had settled.

"So tell me about your stalker," he said.

"What?"

"The bloke on the Tube who was ogling your boobs."

"Oh, him." She spluttered with laughter. "I'd forgotten about him. I'm delighted to report that I haven't seen him since. But God, he was horrid. He was wearing a grubby suit, one that had gone all shiny, he had thinning hair that he'd combed over to try to hide the fact that he was almost bald, and he leered at me. I did my best to ignore him, but I could see his reflection in the window and he didn't take his eyes off me for the entire journey. Yuck. I tried to take a photo of him but—did I tell you I'd got a new phone? I love it, fantastic screen, but I hadn't got the hang of the camera by then."

Chris smiled as she talked at her usual pace, flitting from one subject to the next with ease. She was a great journalist, and Chris often thought she'd make a lot more sense if only she could edit her thoughts before they left her mouth. A coherent conversation with Paige was difficult to say the least.

When he stopped the car outside the house, Paige let out a contented sigh. "Here at last. The first thing I'm going to do is have the longest soak in the hottest bath you can imagine. Oh, and then I promised to phone Jo."

"Don't take too long. There's something I need to talk to you about."

She frowned. "That sounds ominous."

"Not at all." He got out of the car and grabbed her luggage.

"Is everything all right?" she asked.

"Everything's great." He unlocked the front door and stepped back to let her enter. "Enjoy your bath, have a quick chat with Jo—by quick I mean no longer than your usual hour—and then we'll talk." He patted her backside to hurry her along.

When he'd carried her bags upstairs, he left her to have a bath.

It still rankled that his mother was visiting. He'd wanted to have some fun with Paige this weekend, not listen to his mother asking fifty questions about how he was. She analysed every expression, every word— and always came up with a negative. Convincing her he was fine was bloody hard work.

Still, he'd forget about her until Sunday. Right now, everything was good and he planned to enjoy the evening. He had a tough game tomorrow and he wanted to relax tonight.

He drank a quick coffee, then stretched out on the sofa and closed his eyes.

Sleep must have claimed him because the next thing he knew, Paige was looking down at him. "Do you need a nap, old man?"

He looked at his watch. "I thought you were going to phone Jo."

"I tried. She's obviously taking tips from her brother and ignoring her phone."

He smiled at that. "You know as well as I do that there's nothing Jo loves more than a good gossip. If she's not answering, she's out of earshot."

"Yeah, I know." She pushed his legs off the sofa and sat beside him. "What did you want to talk about?"

"This." He went to the drawer and took out the black velvet-covered box. He'd been worrying about this moment since he'd bought the ring, almost a fortnight ago, but now, strangely, he felt calm. He flicked open the lid to reveal the diamond nestling in its silk, but he wasn't given chance to speak.

Paige shrieked and leapt to her feet. Her hands flew to her face and then she laughed. "Oh, my freakin' God! That is the most bloody awesome ring I have ever seen. Holy shit, will you look at that diamond."

"I thought you'd like it." He smiled at the expressions flitting across her face. She was like a child at Christmas. "Anything less wouldn't be suitable for my fiancée, would it?"

"It certainly wouldn't. Bloody hell, Chris." She gave another excited squeal.

"So what do you say? Do you—?"

"What do I say?" she repeated in amazement. "I say yes, yes, yes. Holy shit, I say yes." She threw her arms around his neck and squeezed him tight. "Does Jo know?"

"Nope. Matt does, he saw the ring, but he's the only one." Chris slipped the ring onto the third finger of her left hand.

"Look at the state I'm in," she said, laughing at herself. "We've talked about it enough, so it's not as if it's a complete surprise, but I can't stop shaking. Does your mum know?"

"No. I told you, only Matt knows."

"What will she say?"

"She'll be thrilled, you know she will."

"Yes. Yes, of course she will. Okay, I need to write the story. We'll have the news break on Monday, shall we? What about Tuesday night? I'll come back for that, shall I? It would be the perfect photo opportunity."

He'd forgotten about Tuesday's bash at the club. The team was doing a question and answer session with the fans. Half a dozen players would be there, himself included, and after the session, they'd be signing shirts, boots, books and photos. It was supposed to bring fans and players together and create a sense of unity at the football club.

"That would be good," he said.

"I'll be here. Hey, I wouldn't be surprised if your mum doesn't stay for that. And Jo, maybe she'll come too. It'll be a great night." She hugged him again and dashed off to get her phone. "I need to tell Jo. Then I must work on the story…"

This time, Jo answered her phone. Although Chris was in the kitchen looking through the fridge for something to eat, he couldn't help hearing snippets of the conversation, Paige's side of it at least. "I know, I know…wait till you see the ring, oh, hang on, I'll send you a pic…this bloody camera…I know, I know…"

Despite Paige's excited chatter, Chris could guess at his sister's reaction to the news. She wouldn't be happy.

# NINETEEN

When Jeremy arrived at Manchester Airport on Sunday evening, it was to discover that the damn plane hadn't even taken off from Edinburgh. According to the information board, it had been delayed because of fog in Scotland, but would be taking off in ten minutes. The flight only took an hour, but it was still an hour he had to waste at the airport.

Every damn thing Jeremy touched at the moment was falling apart. His life was out of his control, and he hated it.

He took his phone from his jacket pocket and punched in Dylan Scott's number. It went straight to voicemail. Did the bloke ever answer the damn thing?

"Hi, Dylan. Jeremy here. Sorry about this, but I may be a little late. I'm meeting my family from the airport and the plane's been delayed. I should be there by nine but, if not, I'll call you again."

He tried Claire's number, but that went to voicemail too. Presumably, hopefully, she was sitting on the plane and had switched off her phone.

Pacing up and down was making him even more tense so he bought himself a newspaper and a coffee and forced himself to sit still at a table that offered a good view of the information board. The coffee was too strong though and he couldn't concentrate on the newsprint.

No matter how many times he tried to tell himself there was nothing to worry about, he continued to worry. It was crazy. It was also unlike him. Everyone had their price and Scott would be no exception.

The problem was he knew so little about the man. He was a private investigator—Jeremy knew this to be true because he'd looked him up on the internet. His office boasted an extremely swanky address in London. He was also an ex-copper—a bad copper. Jeremy didn't know why he'd been dismissed from the police force in disgrace, something to do with beating some chap up during an arrest, but it didn't matter. The important thing was that Scott wasn't averse to breaking a few rules. Other than that, and the fact that he never answered his damn phone, Jeremy knew nothing about him.

There were always ways to get to people, though. Everyone had secrets, everyone had a vulnerable spot, and everyone, especially bent coppers, had their price. All Jeremy had to do was find out Scott's price.

He'd have to do it without saying too much too because Scott probably recorded all conversations. Jeremy wished he'd thought of that when Scott was in his home, but he'd been too shocked to know that photos existed that he hadn't been able to think straight. He'd been too shocked to deny being in that blasted girl's revolting flat too.

It was unlike him. Jeremy had always prided himself on being able to think on his feet. He'd had enough practice over the years.

He'd gone over and over that damn conversation in his head so many times that, now, he wasn't sure what he'd imagined saying and what he'd actually said. Damn it. He'd owned up to wiping his prints from everything.

Perhaps Scott hadn't recorded their conversation.

Tonight's meeting would be very different. Jeremy was on his guard and would be very careful about what he said. More important, he'd get hold of those damn photos.

That girl, Gemma King as he'd discovered her name was, had been nothing but trouble since the moment he'd clapped eyes on her. Stunning to look at and, despite her youth, way too skilled at driving a man insane, but trouble.

Jeremy couldn't love Claire more and, apart from a few hookers, he'd never wanted to be unfaithful. The hookers didn't count, for God's sake. It was just sex. Good sex.

How many men could have the sort of sex they wanted with their wives? None. Claire would have been horrified if he'd asked her to do the things that Gemma King and her sort did.

Sex with Claire was good. They'd been married for over twenty years, yet the sex was still good. It simply wasn't—exciting. Married sex never was. There was too much emotion involved, and too much respect.

Handing over money changed all that. If a man was paying, he was entitled to get what he wanted. If he spent his working week in control of all around him, he could become a slave for a few hours. If he was dominated at home, he could pay to knock some hooker around. Everything was on the menu. There were no limits.

Jeremy was a good man, he worked fucking hard, so why shouldn't he spend a few hours with a whore? Why shouldn't some little slut dress up like Marilyn fucking Monroe for him? Why shouldn't he be able to lie on his back and feel the warmth on his body as she pissed on him? Why shouldn't he be able to tie her up and slap her about a bit? He paid for the privilege and girls like that were always willing. Where was the fucking harm?

Things were different in London. He had less time and couldn't look around so he paid more and got less. Girls in the City, at least the girls he'd had, set boundaries. The local girls were different.

Finally, after what seemed like hours, but was in fact a few minutes over the hour, the plane landed.

Jeremy stood by the door and watched as the passengers filed through. He spotted his family at the exact moment they saw him. Their faces lit up—his sons' and his wife's. He loved them. They loved him. And he'd make damn sure that Scott didn't cause any trouble. If there was so much as a sniff of gossip—

"Did you have a good time?" he asked, hugging Claire to him and taking her suitcase from her.

"Ace," Freddie said.

"I wish we could go again tomorrow," Harry said.

"It was hectic." Claire was laughing as she slipped her arm through his. "My parents had the whole itinerary planned and we didn't stop for a moment. It was good, though."

"How are they?"

"The same as usual," she said. "Happy, totally devoted to each other, determined to spoil your sons rotten, full of energy."

He laughed. "Good. Come on then, let's get you home. I have a meeting, I'm afraid, so I'll have to go straight out, but it shouldn't take more than an hour…"

AT A LITTLE after nine o'clock, Jeremy walked into the Dog and Fox, which was Scott's choice of meeting place. Jeremy wasn't a pub person, he preferred his club or perhaps a restaurant, but this one was better than he'd feared. It was quite homely thanks to the logs blazing in two fireplaces. Clean too.

Scott was easy to spot. He was sitting in a corner at the far end of the room, a pint of beer in front of him, his legs stretched out in a pose of complete relaxation.

With his best smile in place, Jeremy strode over to his table. "Good to see you, Dylan. Sorry I'm late. Now, what can I get you?"

"Thanks. I'll have a pint of Black Sheep, please."

Jeremy wasn't a great beer drinker—he wasn't a great drinker at all—but he decided to have the same.

If the barmaid recognised him, and he saw no reason why she wouldn't, she didn't comment. She served him quickly and efficiently.

Jeremy carried their drinks to the table and sat opposite Scott, which meant he had his back to the room.

"I don't think I've been here before," he said.

"It's my favourite pub." Scott lifted his glass. "Cheers."

"Good health, Dylan."

They both savoured their drinks and Jeremy wondered how long it would be before Scott got to the point. He decided to hurry things along.

"Have you brought the photos with you?" he asked.

"I haven't, no. Would you believe it? I couldn't find them. Oh, they're safe enough, don't worry about that, and as I said, a journalist friend of mine has copies, but I couldn't put my hands on them this evening."

Would he believe it? No, he damn well wouldn't. Scott was lying. He'd never had any intention of bringing them.

"Let's not play games," Jeremy said. "What do you want from me?"

"Me? This meeting was at your request, not mine."

"Yes, but it's obvious what I want. I want the photos. I also want to know what you plan to do with them. Not that I'm worried. I mean, who cares if I visited a prostitute? If it were to come out, my wife would be extremely hurt, and that's the only thing that worries me. Women, they don't understand, do they?"

"Rarely."

"You're married, are you?"

"Widowed. Cancer."

"Oh, I'm sorry to hear that. Please accept my sincere condolences. She must have been very young."

"Yes." Scott traced a line in the condensation on his glass.

"I'm willing to buy those photos from you, I told you that," Jeremy said. "I don't have anything to hide, but I wouldn't like my wife to get hurt. She doesn't deserve it."

"No," Scott said.

The bloke was totally relaxed. He was bloody hard work too.

"We're none of us saints, are we?" Jeremy said. "I'll bet you've done things you're not proud of. Of course you have. You used to be a police officer, I gather."

Scott smiled. "You've been checking up on me."

Jeremy shrugged. "I had a quick look. You were dismissed from the force, weren't you?"

"I was. All down to politics. And you'd know all about that. I was trying to arrest a known criminal and he was having none of it. When I finally did, he accused me of using excessive force."

Christ, was that all? There was nothing there that Jeremy could use against him.

"I violated the poor chap's human rights, you see," Scott said. "I was punished, I spent a few months in prison, and now I'm a private investigator. There's not a lot you can pin on me, I'm afraid."

"I suppose you're recording this conversation?"

"No." Scott looked genuinely surprised and Jeremy decided he believed him.

"What about our last little chat? Did you record that?"

"No." That smile again. "I might have if I'd thought you'd confess to Gemma King's or Stevie Greenwood's murders, but I know you're far too clever for that."

"What? For God's sake, I had nothing to do with—"

"The thing is, I'm not interested in how you treat your wife, or how you treat your prostitutes. I don't care how well you pay them or how many times you buy them flowers or champagne. As I said, all I want is the truth."

"Then you don't care about the photos, do you? How much? Name your price."

"You don't get it, do you? I don't have a price."

"Everyone has a price."

"In your world maybe. Not in mine."

"Ten thousand pounds." Jeremy must be mad. "I'll buy those photos from you for ten thousand. As I said, I don't want to see my wife upset."

"They're not for sale."

"Twenty thousand."

Smiling, Scott shook his head. "You've had plenty of time to think since our last chat so perhaps you've come up with some ideas. For instance, who do you think murdered Stevie Greenwood?"

Jeremy's grip was so tight on his pint glass it was liable to smash. "I have no idea. Why would I know?"

"If you'd known he'd taken the photos—"

"I might have offered him fifty quid for them. But I didn't know. I never saw him. I never spoke to the man. Look, my only crime—and it's not really a crime—is that I visited a prostitute a couple of times. As to the rest of it, you're barking up the wrong tree. Now, you said I could see those photos—"

"And you will. All in good time." Scott emptied his glass and stood up. "Now, if there's nothing else you can tell me, I think I'll head back to my hotel."

"But the photos? What about them?"

"Don't worry, I'll keep them safe. Be seeing you, Jeremy. Oh, and if you come up with any more theories, give me a call, will you?"

He strode off, leaving Jeremy with a raging temper and an almost full glass of beer.

Who the hell did Scott think he was? Did he think he was the only one who could play dirty?

*Think again, Scott.*

He took his phone from his pocket and, with fingers shaking with fury, scrolled through his list of contacts and hit a number.

"It's me," he said, too angry to go through the social niceties. "I need as much dirt as you can dig up on a private investigator called Dylan Scott. And I need it fast."

# TWENTY

DYLAN SUPPOSED THAT only the smaller football clubs could get away with events like this. If Arsenal or Chelsea invited fans to the club to meet a few of the players, fifty thousand people would turn up. Here in Dawson's Clough, he'd bet around two or three hundred had come to talk to their heroes.

Fans' ages ranged from eight to eighty, a real mixed bunch.

Players had taken questions from the audience for about an hour and then tables and chairs had been cleared to create a free-for-all. Fans chatted to the players, bought drinks or snacks from the bar, and generally had a good time.

Dylan had only come to see Elliott. He was convinced he was hiding something.

Needless to say, the fans made a beeline for him, but he seemed comfortable in the limelight. His agent, his parents, his sister and his brand-new fiancée were all sticking close to him.

The evening edition of the *Chronicle* had been taken up with news of his engagement to Paige, but neither the newspaper's photos nor the one Dylan had seen at Elliott's house did her justice. Tall, slim and elegant, with long red hair, she belonged on the pages of the celebrity magazines that Bev used to devour.

Daphne Elliott couldn't drag her gaze from her son.

Even when her daughter said something to her, she only had eyes for Elliott.

When she was alone, although still watching Elliott, Dylan wandered over to her.

"You must be very proud of Chris," he said. "Not only a talented footballer, but such a nice person. He signed a photo for my son who's another budding footballer, and we've had a chat since."

"We're immensely proud of him," she said.

"And now you have an engagement to celebrate. I haven't spoken to the bride-to-be, but they seem made for each other."

"Oh, they are. They've been friends all their lives."

"I heard she was your daughter's best friend, am I right?"

"Yes. That's right."

"That will be nice for Jo."

"Yes." She looked down her nose at him, as if calling her daughter by such a familiar name wasn't allowed. All the same, she had nothing to say about Jo. No interest in her.

"I met Jo at the fundraiser," he said. "Brains and beauty. You must be equally proud of her."

"Jo? Oh, yes." She gave him a smile that would have frozen milk. "Excuse me."

She wandered over to Elliott and said something that made him frown.

As yet, Elliott and his new fiancée had spent hardly any time together. Paige had been laughing with Jo most of the time. Oddly, Jo hadn't looked as happy as her friend.

Dylan got himself a drink and wandered over to where the two girls were deep in conversation.

"We meet again," he said, smiling at Jo. He was about to explain that they'd met at the fundraiser, but she clearly hadn't been so drunk that she'd forgotten.

"Hi, there, Dylan. How are you? Have any drunken young women thrown their drinks over you?"

"Not yet, but I live in hope." He liked Jo. Her brother seemed nice enough, although Dylan was convinced he was putting on some sort of act, Daphne Elliott was downright cold and unpleasant, but Jo seemed genuine.

He switched his smile to Paige. "Congratulations. Chris is a very lucky man."

"So I keep telling him." She laughed and put out her left hand to show off the diamond that sparkled beneath the lights.

"That's a beautiful ring."

"I know, I know. Half of me is terrified of losing it. It's insured, of course, but even so."

"I'm sure you won't. Have you set a date yet?"

"Not yet," she said. "We're in no rush."

Dylan nodded at the wisdom of that decision. "You're both very young."

"Young and in love," she agreed which, for some reason, made her and Jo laugh, although Jo's laughter wasn't quite so enthusiastic.

"It must be quite something," he said, "to be best friends for so many years and end up as sisters-in-law."

"It's brilliant." Paige squeezed Jo's arm, and, again, Jo's smiling response lacked real warmth.

"Oops, got to go." Paige skipped off in answer to her future mother-in-law's beckoning.

"Your parents must be thrilled about the engagement," he said, and Jo nodded.

"They certainly are."

"You must be too," he said.

"Of course. Hey, this is better than that awful do at the town hall, isn't it? Well, it must be. I'm sober."

"That was a bit stuffy, wasn't it? This is great though. It's good to see the football club getting involved with the community."

"It is. They do lots of things—hospital visits at Christmas, training sessions with schoolchildren, that sort of stuff. It's a friendly little club."

They chatted about her university course, the awful weather in Lancashire and the failings of the government, and she was soon laughing and joking as she had when they'd met at the fundraiser. It seemed the one cloud on her horizon was her brother's engagement. Perhaps she was feeling left out. It was obvious that her parents, her mother at least, only had eyes for Chris. Now, with a wedding to plan, Jo probably felt as if she'd become invisible.

Jo went to catch up with her brother, and Dylan met up with Dave Edwards *Chronicle*, as he thought of him.

"I keep meaning to print out that stuff on Brent," Edwards said, "and I will. I've been a bit busy, but I'll sort it out tomorrow. As I said, it's not much, but it'll give you a flavour of the man."

"Thanks. Drop it off at the Pennine if you can't reach me."

Dylan had expected Brent to be here this evening, but there had been no sign of him. Perhaps people here were too low down on the social ladder for him to waste his time. Or maybe he was busy panicking about Dylan's nonexistent photos. He hoped it was the latter. Let the bloke stew.

Dylan was on the way to the bar to buy himself a

drink when he saw Jo and Paige, their heads bent, talking earnestly as they headed outside toward the small balcony set aside for smokers.

Curious, he followed.

Jo pulled open the door and held it for Paige to step outside in front of her. "I still say it's madness. You know what Mum's like. She's probably already convinced herself that you're actually going to marry him."

"Of course she hasn't. Stop worrying. She knows it's just for show."

The door closed behind them.

Dylan couldn't follow. Well, he could but there would be no point. They'd gone outside, he guessed, to talk in private. All conversation would end when they spotted him.

All the same he was curious. Why did Elliott and Paige need an engagement that was only for show?

# TWENTY-ONE

THE PHONE CALL came on Wednesday afternoon. Chris had driven Paige and Jo to the station and returned to a house that mocked him with its silence. He'd switched on music, an old Coldplay album that Matt had left behind, and was in the process of making a coffee when the call came.

When he saw the caller's ID, his stomach turned over with a sickening flip. He was too scared to ignore it. Almost too scared to answer it too. He hit the button and greeted her with a curt "Yes?"

"Hello, Chris," Ruby said. "How are you?"

"Forgive me if I'm wrong, but didn't you promise to stay the hell out of my life?"

"There's no need for that attitude. There's been a change of plan, and I need to talk to you."

"What change of plan? What the hell does it have to do with me?"

"I'll explain all when I see you. Hey, I'm sorry. I didn't congratulate you on your engagement. She looks a lovely girl. Paige, is it? What a pretty name. And what a ring. That diamond is huge. She's a very lucky young lady."

"I paid you, Ruby. That's it. We have nothing more to say to each other." He was so angry, he could have sat on the kitchen floor and wept.

"Oh, but I've plenty to say to you. Now, when will it

be convenient? I'll come to your house, shall I? You'll be pleased to hear what I've got to tell you, I promise. I'm going away, you see."

Going away? Dare he hope?

"Listen, I don't want to talk over the phone," she said. "It's so impersonal, isn't it? Don't worry, I'll come after dark. No one will see me. I only want to say goodbye."

Wild, glorious hope flared. If she wanted to say goodbye, if she was going away, a long way away—

"Okay. Seven o'clock," he said.

"See you then." She cut the connection.

Chris wished he'd never laid eyes on the hateful woman but perhaps it would all work out. If they said goodbye, they could end this on polite terms and forget about each other.

It would be fine. He'd thought of mentioning her to his mother because, as a barrister, she had connections and would know exactly what he could do, but perhaps there would be no need. Ruby was going away. He'd never have to see her again.

When she arrived at a little after seven that evening, he even managed a smile as he invited her inside. The sight of her didn't make him feel quite so sick this evening. In fact, he almost felt sorry for her. There was something sad and pathetic about the way she looked. It wasn't the tired, worn shoes or the revolting fake fur coat, or the way she desperately tried to look classy and merely looked ridiculous. It was the defeated expression she always wore as if life had beaten her. Perhaps it was foolish of him but he often thought that life had treated her badly and that, deep down, she wasn't such a bad person.

"I feel like royalty," she said. "I wasn't expecting to come inside. It's so cold again though, isn't it?"

"Yes."

This evening, feeling generous, he took her into the kitchen.

"Goodness, look at this. It's like something out of those magazines I read when I'm in the dentist's." She circled the room, taking in every appliance. "Do you cook?"

"No. Not really. I grill the odd steak, that's all." He was feeling more generous, but he still wanted this over. She was probably too warm in her coat but he refused to suggest she take it off. If he made her too welcome, he'd never be rid of her. "You say you're going away?"

"Yes. I grew up in Cornwall, as you know, and I miss the sea. I'm leaving Bill."

"Really?" That did surprise him.

"Yes. Our marriage—ooh, hark at me. Here's me about to have a good old moan about my marriage, and here's you on the verge of getting married. I don't suppose you've set a date yet, have you?"

"Not yet, no."

"I thought not. Well, I won't put the damper on things by telling you that marriage is hard work. Very hard work. Still, I suppose it might be different for you. I expect you'll have one of these modern marriages. It'll be a marriage of convenience for you, won't it?"

Chris shrugged, not wanting to talk about it. He was more interested in her plans. "So where are you going?"

"Italy. Or Spain. I haven't decided yet."

"Really? That's wonderful." He almost punched the air. "They're both lovely countries."

"Yes. A bit of sunshine will be welcome."

"Of course."

"The thing is—well, two things really," she said, her gaze on her worn old shoes. "First, I wanted to say goodbye. I know we never quite hit it off, and I'm sorry about that. My fault, I suppose. And Bill's. But I do wish you well."

"Thank you."

"The second thing is a bit more tricky. You see, it costs a lot of money to up sticks and live abroad."

He might have known she wanted more money.

"I suppose it does," he said, and he was aware that his voice had cooled considerably.

Thinking about it though, it would be worth a couple of thousand to be finally rid of her. If she was in Italy or Spain, he wouldn't have to see her and she wouldn't be able to turn up on his doorstep whenever the whim took her.

"How much do you want?" he asked.

"A million pounds."

Chris opened his mouth but was so shocked that he couldn't force out any words.

"It's a lot, I know," she said, as if she were discussing the weather. "I've had a long think, though, and I think I'm worth that." She seemed to stand taller and she looked a lot less beaten by life. "With that amount, I could pack up, fly to Italy, book into a hotel for a few days or weeks until I'd found a little house by the sea—"

"Are you mad?" he managed to ask. "I can't—I don't have—"

"That's just it, Chris. You can and you do."

"But I don't. For God's sake, this is fucking ridiculous."

She tutted at his language.

"I don't have that sort of money," he said, his jaw clenched so tight it was painful. "You have no idea how life works, do you? You see some story in the newspaper that says I've got a million-pound sponsorship deal—"

"Oh, yes. Energy drinks, isn't it?"

"And you imagine they hand me a cheque for a million pounds that I put in my bank account. You have no fucking idea. The deal is over three years. My agent has his cut. I simply do not have a spare million pounds sitting around."

"I'm not expecting you to write me a cheque this minute."

"I can't write you a cheque for that amount today, tomorrow, next week or next fucking month. Get real, Ruby!"

She put her hands in her coat pocket. "Okay, never mind. Don't you worry about it. I'll have a chat to the newspaper people and see if they're feeling more generous."

"You bitch. You conniving fucking bitch. You'll get nowhere, can't you see that? I've already taken legal advice about you. My mother's a barrister, I told you that."

She laughed softly. "Then she'll know, as I do, that the newspapers will need proof before they print my story. I have that proof, you know I do. Thanks to that nice Mr. Greenwood, I have all the proof I need."

He grabbed the lapels of her disgusting coat and balled the fur tight against her throat. "I wish I'd never laid eyes on you, you evil old witch. I could kill you. I really could."

"I can see why you might feel a bit annoyed—"

"Annoyed? I'm well past fucking annoyed, Ruby. You're the most evil, money-grabbing, life-wrecking bitch I've ever known. You can't be happy and you won't allow anyone else to be. Take a good long hard look at yourself and you might realise why happiness doesn't come knocking on your door. Take, take, fucking take. That's all you know."

He let her go, reluctantly, and she took a step back from him. "I'll phone you tomorrow, shall I? When you've had time to think about things."

"I don't need time to think about anything. Why can't you understand that I don't have that sort of money?"

"Maybe you don't. You could get it though." She gave him a smile as if they were the best of friends. "Have a think about it. It's your choice, Chris. If you don't want to help, I'm sure the newspapers will. Anyway, it's cold outside so you stop in here and I'll let myself out. Take care of yourself, won't you?"

She turned on her heel, looking far less beaten by life than when she'd arrived, and let herself out of the house.

"Now what the fuck do I do?" Chris asked the empty house.

## TWENTY-TWO

OF ALL THE people Dylan might have expected to see arrive at and leave Elliott's home, Ruby wasn't one of them. More surprising was that Elliott must have been expecting her because she hadn't had to explain who she was to the intercom at the gate. She'd hit the button and the gates had swung open without her uttering a word.

She'd been inside the house for less than five minutes so it had been a very brief call.

Why the devil would Ruby be visiting Elliott?

Dylan fired the Morgan's engine and drove the hundred yards or so down the road until he drew level with her. He opened the window and leaned across the passenger seat. "Can I offer you a lift, Ruby?"

She was surprised to see him. A little flustered too. "Oh, it's you. No, thanks. Well, yes. Okay. Why not? It's a cold one tonight, isn't it?"

"Down to freezing again," he said, as he pushed open the door. "Get in."

"Thank you." She was wearing a fur coat that had a distinct smell of wet dog.

"Where are you going?"

"Home. Back to the pub. But drop me anywhere that's convenient. Thank you."

"I'll take you home. I think I'll nip in to the Sportsman for a quick one." He drove off and stopped for a red light. "So where have you been on such a cold night?"

"Oh, just out for a walk."

"Really? Not spying on the rich and famous then? Someone told me they all live along here."

"I believe a lot do, yes."

"Chris Elliott does, I know that," Dylan said.

"Does he? Probably. Several of the footballers do."

"I suppose they do." At the green light, Dylan took a right turn. "He seems a nice lad, doesn't he?"

"I wouldn't know. I don't know him." She was twisting a fur cuff as she spoke.

"I can't say I know him well," Dylan said, before she had the chance to change the subject. "I spoke to him at the fundraiser though and he seemed really nice. Sensible and level-headed. Have you never spoken to him?"

"Not that I recall. I might have if he's called at the pub. I can't remember." She pulled her coat tighter around her and managed to get tangled in the seatbelt. "This is a nice car, isn't it? Lovely colour. What sort is it?"

"An old Morgan. A classic. I like it."

"Where did you say you were staying? The Pennine Hotel was it? It's lovely there, isn't it?"

She was definitely flustered. Usually, she was far too miserable to bother with polite conversation.

"Very comfortable. Do you like walking, Ruby?"

"Me? Not especially. Why do you ask?"

"Just curious. You wouldn't catch me walking anywhere on a night like this. If I wasn't taking the car, I'd fork out for a taxi."

"I would usually but I felt like getting some fresh air tonight."

Or, more likely, she didn't want a taxi driver knowing where she was going. Just as she didn't want Dylan to know where she'd been.

When he drove into the pub's car park, she fumbled with her seatbelt and had the door open before he'd switched off the engine.

"Thanks for the lift." She slammed the door, tottered across the car park and went through a door at the back of the building marked Private.

Dylan walked into the main bar where a young chap was serving drinks.

"Are you on your own?" Dylan asked him as he poured Dylan's pint.

"For the moment. Bill will be down in—" he glanced at the clock above the bar, "—twenty minutes. I think I'll cope with the rush," he added with a wry smile.

The pub was empty apart from Dylan and two young girls giggling in the corner.

He discovered the young man's name was Oscar. And that's all he did learn. After knocking back his pint, he left the Sportsman no wiser but a lot more curious than when he'd entered.

He drove out of the Sportsman's car park and headed back to Manchester Road. As Ruby was keeping quiet, he'd have to see if he could have another chat with Elliott. He could pass on Luke's thanks for the signed photo if nothing else.

He parked close to Elliott's house, walked up to those tall gates and pressed the button on the intercom. It was a little after eight-thirty.

"Yes?" Elliott didn't sound too pleased at the intrusion.

"Chris? It's Dylan. Dylan Scott. I wondered if I could have a quick word with you, please."

Elliott's voice, when it finally came through the intercom, was flat and resigned. "Yes. Why not? Come on up."

His expression when he opened the front door to

Dylan was much the same. He was frowning, and he looked tense. He also looked young. Very young.

"Come in," he said. "What can I do for you?"

"Thanks."

Elliott was wearing black jeans and a white T-shirt that looked as if it had been made to measure. People who kept themselves fit though, and Elliott was a real athlete, were always good advertisements for the clothes they wore.

They went to the kitchen where, again, nothing was out of place. There was no clutter, no cups or plates waiting to be washed, no bread crumbs on the counter.

"First," Dylan said, "I must thank you again for the signed photo. Luke was thrilled with your words. Really thrilled. That was good of you."

It was too. Elliott could easily have signed a hundred photos "Best wishes, Chris Elliott." The personal touch was appreciated.

"I'm glad he liked it."

"Are you okay?" Dylan asked. He looked a breath away from passing out.

"Fine. Yes, thanks. A bad day, that's all."

"Did Ruby have anything to do with it?"

Elliott's head flew up in surprise.

"I was out this way and saw her leaving," Dylan explained. "I felt obliged to offer her a lift."

Elliott nodded but didn't comment.

"She denied all knowledge of knowing you. Claimed she'd been out for a walk."

"I wish to hell she didn't know me." Elliott raked his fingers through his hair as if he wanted to yank it from his head. He looked barely any older than Luke. "Anyway, what can I do for you? I'm sure you didn't come all the way out here to thank me for a photo that you've already thanked me for."

Dylan smiled at that. "You're right. I didn't."

Elliott's house was warm and exceptionally quiet. In Dylan's home, there was always noise. Two kids and a dog made most of it, but even when they weren't there, pipes creaked, the central heating boiler coughed and spluttered, the kitchen clock ticked and the fridge hummed. Here, there was complete silence.

"As I told you, I'm looking into the murder of Stevie Greenwood," Dylan said. "It seems that everything I hear leads me to the same people. You're one of those people simply because you met Stevie and gave him the ticket for the fundraiser. And now I'm curious why Ruby was here and why she denied knowing you. I could be completely wrong, of course, but I think it has to do with the ticket you gave Stevie, and the photo he took of you in Ruby's pub."

Elliott didn't say anything. He picked up the kettle, filled it and switched it on. At least that made a little noise as it heated the water.

"Can I talk to you in confidence?" Elliott asked at last.

"Of course."

"It won't go any further? My mother's a barrister, you know, so she knows the law backwards."

He really did seem young. And frightened.

"It won't go any further," Dylan said. "You can trust me."

"Okay." Elliott reached his decision. "Sit down. Do you want a coffee? It'll have to be instant, I'm afraid."

"Instant's fine." It was what he usually had. His own coffee machine hadn't been touched since Bev had died.

Elliott made their coffee. Dylan would bet he didn't

really want one, it was just something for him to do while he rehearsed whatever it was he planned to say. He spilled water on the counter and mopped it up with a tea towel.

When he'd put coffee in front of Dylan, he cradled a mug in his hands and sat opposite.

"I told you about the photo your friend Stevie took, right?"

Dylan nodded.

"As you know, we were in Ruby's pub. I was drunk, very drunk. Stevie took the photo—he was always doing that and it could be a little unnerving. He never said anything to anyone, he simply wandered around taking photos. He never thought to ask or anything like that."

He wouldn't. Stevie hadn't uttered a word unless he'd been forced into it.

"We—Matt really—asked him to delete the photo because it wouldn't do for me to be seen out drinking. Matt was explaining to him that he shouldn't have taken it without asking permission, and then Ruby came in. We were in that small back room."

Dylan had a fairly good idea of what was coming. "Go on."

"So Ruby wanted to know what was going on. She grabbed Stevie's camera and went off with it. She said she wasn't having him taking photos of her customers and would give it back to him when he left. We thought it was fine. We'd make sure that, when Stevie left, that photo of me would be deleted. And that's what happened. Except—"

"Except Ruby has the photo and is blackmailing you?"

Elliott looked at him in surprise. "Yes. There are four photos and she's threatening to sell them to the newspapers."

"I'm not surprised." Ruby appeared the type of person who might enjoy a spot of blackmail. Mean. Malicious. "But it's no big deal, is it? Let's face it, you won't be the first footballer to see themselves in the paper after a night on the town. It might be frowned upon, but no worse than that."

"I've got a sponsorship deal—"

"Ah, yes. With the energy drinks company." Elliott had a point. They wouldn't want their golden boy to be seen drinking anything alcoholic, or anything other than their product come to that.

"Yes."

"Have you paid her?"

"Yes."

"And she keeps coming back for more? She would. That's what blackmailers do."

"There's more." Elliott went to take a drink of his coffee, but clearly couldn't face it and put his mug on the counter. "I know Ruby. I've known her for almost two years."

"Oh? So you knew her before she moved to Dawson's Clough?"

"Yes."

"She and her husband had a pub in the Midlands, didn't they? It burned down, I seem to recall."

"That's right."

"And then she moved to the Clough. That's interesting. Are you telling me she came up here because of you?"

"Yes. You see—" Elliott broke off. His lips were moving but no sound came out. "Ruby isn't just a landlady at that awful pub. She's—she's my mother. My birth mother."

# TWENTY-THREE

DYLAN HAD LEFT an hour ago, and all Chris had done since was lie on the sofa trying to listen to his music. He wasn't hearing anything though, other than the erratic thump of his own heartbeat.

Dylan didn't think it was the end of the world. He talked about the law, and the fact that Ruby was the criminal. He said that, even if she sold the photo to the newspapers, nothing bad would happen. Yes, he might lose the energy drinks sponsorship deal, but that would be all. Other deals would come along, he'd said.

It was easy for him to talk. He didn't know the half of it.

Before Dylan arrived, he'd been a breath away from calling his mother and telling her about Ruby's demands. He'd told her about the incident with Stevie Greenwood and his photos, but, as far as she knew, the photos had been deleted and that was the end of it. He hadn't mentioned Ruby's involvement. Hell, she didn't even know Ruby was living in Dawson's Clough.

Chris cursed whatever stupidity had ever made him curious about Ruby. All his life, he'd wondered about his real mother and father. Few days had passed when he hadn't thought about the young woman who'd been forced to give him up for adoption. It had never occurred to him that his mother had *wanted* to give him up. No, he'd simply pictured a woman who grieved for him every day.

It wasn't as if he'd lacked anything in his life. His mum and dad had been great, loving and supportive, and he'd lived with the best sister ever. He'd never thought of them as anything other than his family.

His parents had given him the sugar-coated version of how his mother, a young girl, hadn't been able to raise a child—

Why the hell had he wasted a thought on Ruby?

His head had been filled with romantic notions of a sad woman—a young girl—who'd been forced by her parents to give up her child for adoption. He'd pictured her, pretty and blond, thinking about her baby every day. When his birthdays had rolled round, he'd imagined her wishing she could share the day with him. He'd even pictured her writing in birthday cards that she couldn't send him.

Along with these romantic notions was a tinge of anger. Why hadn't she fought harder to keep him? Why hadn't she defied her parents and refused to be separated from her own flesh and blood?

Perhaps it was the anger that had made him want to boast a little. He'd wanted to show her that, despite being dumped as a child, he'd done well for himself and would soon be a household name.

What a bloody fool he'd been.

Despite all the nightmare stories he'd heard about kids who found their adoption records and then began to search for their birth parents, Chris had found the whole process fairly easy. He'd applied for the records the day after his eighteenth birthday and, a year later, almost to the day, Ruby had agreed to meet him.

He could remember everything about that day—the way it had started snowing without warning, the amount of time it took him to decide whether he should dress casually or smart, if he ought to take her a gift—

He'd taken her flowers. That had been his mother's suggestion. Daphne hadn't approved of his meeting Ruby, she hadn't understood the point, but she hadn't stood in his way. How Chris wished she had.

They'd had tea in a quaint little shop in the West End and Ruby had looked totally out of place.

They'd talked in an uncomfortable, stilted way as strangers do. He was able to tell her about his career and it came as a shock to him to realise that she had no knowledge of or interest in football. If he'd told her he was a road sweeper, she would have been just as interested. Or disinterested.

She told him how she'd left a small fishing village in Cornwall to live her dream in London. As she hadn't known who his father was, she couldn't tell him about him. She seemed more intent on complaining how her unplanned pregnancy had ruined her life. It didn't occur to her that it was her own fault.

All in all, the meeting was a huge disappointment. Chris's childhood dreams were smashed to smithereens during that hour. It was obvious that, over the years, she hadn't spared him a second thought. So much for those birthday cards he'd imagined her writing and keeping.

She hadn't even been able to understand why he'd wanted to meet her. They were strangers.

At the time, she'd been living in the Midlands and she'd complained so much about the cost of the train ticket to meet him, Chris had paid for it.

He'd walked to the station with her and watched her climb aboard with her flowers.

Then, with the snow falling even more heavily, he'd walked very slowly home. Instead of gaining a mother, or a friend, he'd simply lost his illusions.

His mother and Jo had wanted to know everything about her, but Chris hadn't been able to talk about her. "She was fine," was all he said. "It was good to see her, but I don't suppose we'll meet again."

As far as Daphne was concerned, that was that. Neither she nor Chris had mentioned Ruby's name again.

The first letter came three weeks later. A begging letter. Could he spare her a few pounds…

He'd been paying the bloody woman ever since.

# TWENTY-FOUR

DYLAN HAD ARRANGED to meet Frank for lunch, and he was grateful to mull things over with his ex-boss while enjoying a very acceptable steak. Pub food always tasted better than that served in fancy restaurants. Steak, chips and vegetables washed down with a decent bottle of red wine. Few things could beat that.

"Stevie's murder," he said, "was a messy job, right?"

"And then some," Frank agreed.

"Amateurish even."

"Yep."

"Could have been committed by a woman in fact," Dylan said.

"It could." Frank chewed on a piece of his steak. "Do you have anyone in mind?"

"Ruby Wilson. Landlady at the Sportsman."

Frank searched his memory. "I know the pub, but I don't know much about her. She and her husband took the place over fairly recently, didn't they? I gather trade's started looking up since that god-awful night-club was opened."

Dylan smiled at the description. "Catch-22. It's *the* place to go apparently."

"It's *the* place to fall out of at five in the morning. So tell me about Ruby."

"I was told this in confidence."

Frank nodded. "Spill all. You know it'll go no further."

Dylan did know. When he promised people that things they said would be treated with the strictest confidence, he didn't include Frank in that, just as he'd never included Bev.

"This is the version I've heard. Three nights before he was killed, Stevie was in the Sportsman annoying people by taking photos of them. He did that a lot apparently. Elliott and a friend of his, Matt, were in there and Stevie took a photo—three or four photos actually—of Elliott looking the worse for wear. Elliott didn't want his whiter-than-white reputation damaged, and he especially didn't want to lose his million-pound sponsorship deal by having the world know he was drunk, so he asked Stevie to delete the pictures. Before Stevie could oblige, however, Ruby turned up and confiscated Stevie's camera. She told him he could have it back when he'd finished his drink and was on his way out. She eventually returned the camera, the photos had been deleted and Elliott thought that was the end of it. But being a damn lot cleverer than she looks, Ruby kept the photos. She's now blackmailing Elliott."

"Is she indeed." Frank took an appreciate sip of red wine. "And that's gospel, is it?"

"No. That's the story Elliott gave me."

"You believe him?"

Dylan thought for a moment. "Possibly. Probably. She strikes me as a nasty piece of work. There's more though. It seems that the not-so-lovely Ruby is Elliott's birth mother. She followed him up here from the Midlands, apparently, and seems to look upon him as her own personal gold mine."

Frank let out a soft whistle.

"And there's probably even more to it than that,"

Dylan said. "I'm sure Elliott is hiding something, but I don't know what. He's got himself engaged to his childhood sweetheart, but that's not all it's cracked up to be. It's all for show."

Frank chewed on his food for a minute. "There's a flaw in your having Ruby as chief suspect," he said. "Why, when she'd deleted his photos, did she need to kill him?"

"Perhaps she thought he might talk. If the story of Elliott being drunk got out before she had a chance to use the photos, it would steal her thunder. I don't know," Dylan admitted, "but I feel sure that Stevie's photos were responsible for his murder."

"Or it could be that he let a random junkie into his house and was killed for some loose change," Frank pointed out.

"No. That's too easy." Or perhaps it wasn't. Perhaps Dylan was looking for things that simply didn't exist. "And Ruby's not my only suspect. There's Jeremy Brent too. I'm pleased to say he's stewing nicely because he thinks I have photographic evidence to prove he entered Gemma King's flat carrying flowers."

Frank's eyebrows rose. "And do you?"

"No. But I do have a photo that shows he was in Anderson Street on the night she died. And he does have a bunch of flowers in his hand."

"Ah." Frank smiled at that.

"It's enough. When I told him about the photos, he admitted to being in her flat. Not only that, he said he'd wiped the place clean of prints."

"You're kidding me."

"Nope. He claims she was already dead when he arrived."

"Brent is visiting local prostitutes? Bloody hell, is nothing sacred?"

"Makes you wonder what else Mr. Squeaky Clean does in his spare time, doesn't it? It makes me wonder anyway. Perhaps he knew Stevie had taken photos of him. Perhaps he thought he should silence Stevie for good."

"Bloody hell, Dylan."

"Then, of course, there's Elliott. Perhaps he's bluffing. Maybe Stevie refused to delete the photos, although that doesn't sound like the Stevie I knew. But perhaps the story Elliott's given me is a load of bollocks and *he* decided Stevie must be silenced."

Frank put down his knife and fork and dabbed his mouth with a napkin. "What exactly in all this is fact and not some piece of fiction you've invented?"

"I have proof that Brent was in Anderson Street, carrying flowers, on the night Gemma died. I also saw Ruby go to Elliott's house. Other than that, sweet fuck all."

"It's not a lot."

"That's the understatement of the decade."

"So what are you planning to do next?"

"I'm going to have a chat with Ruby and see what she comes up with. So far, she denies all knowledge of knowing Elliott. She thinks she might have spoken to him when he's called at the Sportsman but she's not sure."

"Pah. Elliott's a celebrity in these parts. Anyone would know if they'd spoken to him or not."

"Quite. She's usually on her own in the bar between five and six so I'll call in then."

Frank topped up their glasses and emptied the bottle.

"I managed a word with the senior investigating officer. Unlike you, they don't have a single suspect. They're also busy with other things."

"They would be." This didn't come as a surprise to Dylan. They'd decide Stevie's murder had been an unfortunate random act and put the file aside to gather dust.

Dylan couldn't let any of it gather dust. He wouldn't rest until he knew exactly what had happened in Stevie's flat that night...

When they left the pub, Frank went home and Dylan returned to his hotel room to spend ten minutes catching up on real work, the work that paid bills. Bobby could handle most of it, but there were clients' calls he needed to return, and emails to answer. Instead of ten minutes, he spent an hour at it. He spoke to Bobby to satisfy himself that everything was running smoothly without him, and then he escaped to take a walk and think.

So intent was he on trying to separate fact from fiction, he'd walked all the way to the railway station without conscious thought. A few snowflakes were falling and he hadn't even noticed those.

He was about to turn around and head toward the Sportsman when he spotted Rachel King. She was standing outside the station's main entrance, wearing a bib that told the world she was an official *Big Issue in the North* seller, and holding a pile of the magazines.

Dylan wandered over to her. "Hey, look at you. Congratulations on getting the job. How's trade?"

"It's okay." She sounded doubtful. "I thought this would be a good pitch. I mean, it's busy, right? The trouble is that people are either in a hurry to get out of the station and go home, or they're racing in to catch their trains. Most of them don't even notice me."

"I'm sure it will be better when the weather improves. People are more inclined to linger if the sun's shining."

"Maybe."

"You'd better give me a copy then." He fished in his pocket for a five-pound note.

"You don't have to."

"I know. And that's not the way to sell your magazines."

She smiled and looked more relaxed. "I'm not very good at it yet. Here." She handed him a magazine.

"Thanks. Keep the change," Dylan said.

"Really?"

"Really."

"You're the day's best customer. Thanks." The smile faded a little and she chewed on her bottom lip. "I'm still not sure if this job's right for me. I could make a lot more cash working the streets."

"This is a hell of a lot safer."

"I suppose so. It's bloody cold though."

"It'll be bloody cold on Canal Street at midnight."

She laughed softly and hugged her magazines to her. "I know. It's just that I'm not very good at this."

"You'll be fine. Give it time."

Snow was falling heavier now. She was right, it *was* bloody cold.

"How are you getting on?" she asked. "Have you found out anything about Stevie Greenwood's death?"

"Not really, no." There was no point giving her the few little gems he had learned, just as there was no point telling her that Brent had admitted to being in her flat and claimed that Gemma was already dead when he arrived. "As for your sister, I think you have to accept that Gemma died from an overdose."

She traced a pattern on the ground with a heavy black boot but didn't say anything.

"It's hard, I know," Dylan said, "but they found a lot of heroin, alcohol and codeine in her system."

"Yeah."

"There were no signs of a struggle. No one could have pumped that lot into her body without her putting up a fight."

She shrugged.

"I'm sorry," he said.

She nodded, then looked up at him. "What about you? How did your wife really die?"

He brushed snow from his shoulder. The stuff was settling on the pavements now. The wind was increasing too.

"She had cancer," he said at last. "It was terminal."

"And?"

"She was murdered. Shot. A sicko was out to get me and my family, and he managed to get to her."

"Shit!"

"Yeah. Anyway, it's time I was off." He rolled up the magazine and stuffed it in his pocket. "Stay warm, and keep away from Canal Street, okay?"

"I will. Be seeing you. Thanks for buying a magazine."

He strode off, oblivious to the snow or the cold. It was a full five minutes before he remembered he was going to the Sportsman to see Ruby. He cut through the indoor market, and was soon stepping inside the pub.

The warmth was welcome, as was the noise of the

TV for once. Any distraction that helped him stop thinking about Bev was welcome.

Bill and Ruby were both serving—at least, Bill was serving and Ruby was flicking through a newspaper—but within ten minutes or so, Bill would hopefully go and check out the cellar.

Dylan ordered his pint and tried to get warm. His bones were chilled.

"We're supposed to be getting heavy snow tonight and into tomorrow," Bill said. "That's what they reckon, but you can't take much notice of them."

"I wouldn't be surprised," Dylan said.

Ruby was reading her daily horoscope. Dylan would like to know what the future had in store for her too, but he wouldn't waste time with astrology.

Flashing orange lights lit up the interior as gritting trucks went along the street.

"That's a good sign," Bill said. "When they grit the roads, we never get snow. It's when they don't bother that we wake up to a foot of the stuff."

Dylan was on his second pint when Bill left Ruby to manage the bar while he went and checked the stock in the cellar. Two customers came in and, when Ruby had served them, Dylan edged closer to her.

"Ruby, I've thought of something that you might be able to help me with."

"Oh?" It was impossible to decide if her expression was wary or if she simply disliked the idea of helping anyone.

"A couple of nights before he was killed, I was talking to Stevie and he said something about a photo he'd taken of Elliott. It didn't strike me till just now, but I've realised he was talking about this pub. He took the photo of Elliott in this bar. Would you know anything about that?"

"No."

There was a surprise. Not.

"Are you sure? You don't remember taking his camera from him until he left?"

"No."

Dylan leaned in to whisper. "I gather Elliott had had a couple of drinks too many."

"What?" A malicious smile curved her lips. "Greenwood said he was drunk? Elliott? I don't know how that happened because he only has a bottle of mineral water on the rare occasions he comes in here."

"Really? That's odd, I could have sworn Stevie said he was drunk. Perhaps it was something else. Some other reason Elliott didn't want to be photographed."

"Perhaps it was. I know something, you shouldn't take notice of anything Greenwood ever said. I realise he was a friend of yours, but even you have to admit he was a few pence short of a shilling." She tapped her head for emphasis. "He wasn't right in the head, was he?"

"He was a bit slow," Dylan agreed.

"Very slow." She gave a cruel laugh at the description. "Perhaps he was so thick he thought they were drunk."

"They?"

She clearly regretted the error. "Chris Elliott and whoever he was with. Sorry, I don't remember Greenwood taking a photo of anything. Like I've told you, he was always shoving that damn camera in people's faces—we lost trade because of that—but I don't recall anything specific."

"That's odd."

"Not really. A lot of people walk through these doors, especially when they're going on to Catch-22. I can't be expected to remember all of them. You want to try this job sometime. It's hard work."

Dylan looked around at the almost empty pub. "I suppose it must be."

"I don't know what Greenwood was telling you," she said, "even he probably didn't know, but I can't imagine Elliott was drunk."

Ruby's shoulders sagged with relief as a young couple walked into the bar. She even managed a smile as she served them.

One thing was certain, she remembered the incident clearly. But had Elliott been drunk? Dylan had thought all along he was hiding something, and he'd also thought it no big deal that Elliott might be snapped while drunk.

So if he hadn't been drunk, what had he been doing that he hadn't wanted the world to know about?

The only person who might have given him an honest answer to that question was dead. And Stevie was even quieter in death than he had been in life.

# TWENTY-FIVE

CHRIS WATCHED MATT refill his wineglass. He wished he could join him and find the oblivion he craved. Unfortunately, he had an early morning training session so needed to abstain.

"You look wrecked," Matt said.

He felt wrecked.

"There's no point worrying about it, is there?" Matt went on. "What good will that do?"

"None whatsoever, but tell me what else I can do." Chris knew he sounded snappy, but he felt bloody snappy. He didn't know which way to turn, and Ruby and her sickening demands refused to leave his mind for a second.

"You can talk to your mother," Matt said for at least the tenth time. "Why don't we pay her a visit? You've got a day off so, after your training session tomorrow, we can drive down there and pick her brain. I'm sure she'll know what to do. I expect you can take out a court injunction or something."

"Or something? You don't have a clue, Matt."

"Of course I don't. Neither of us has a clue, which is why we need to speak to someone who knows the legal ins and outs of a case like this. I bet your mother could sort it."

"If it goes through the court, or goes anywhere official, it'll get out. You know it will."

Chris had three choices, or three that he could think of. One, he could pay Ruby her million pounds. Except he didn't have a million and, even if he did, she'd soon be back for more. Two, he could ignore her. Which would mean that she'd sell her story to the media, and his reputation and his future would be in shreds. Three, he could tell his mother, who would probably want to take out court orders or some such thing. Chris didn't have a clue how the law worked when it came to blackmailers, but he'd bet his life that anything official would get leaked to the papers and his future would still be in tatters.

What a bloody mess. Whichever way he looked at it, he was in a no-win situation.

He went to the kitchen window and pulled back the blind to look out at the darkness. Courtesy of the outside light, he could see that the snow was still falling. It was about an inch deep right now.

If it kept up, they'd be training indoors tomorrow. He didn't mind either way. When he was training, pushing his body to its limit, his head cleared and he forgot all about Ruby.

"Of all the women in the world, why did Ruby turn out to be my mother?" he asked.

"You got lucky."

Chris felt the beginnings of a smile, but it vanished before it formed properly.

"Worse, why did I have to be so stupid as to get in touch with her?"

"You know what they say about hindsight? It's twenty-twenty vision. What's done is done. We need to deal with the current situation and I say we talk to your mum."

"We?"

"Yes. We're in this together, Chris. You know I'll do anything I can to help. I hate that bloody woman for doing this to you."

Chris sighed. "I know. Thanks."

Matt took a long swallow of wine. "If it were me, I'd speak to your mother first. But if she can't come up with anything, I'd ignore Ruby. I'd let her sell her story to the papers. You're engaged to the lovely Paige, and you're a superstar. Who's going to believe Ruby?"

"Probably no one until she produces those bloody photos."

"We can say we were drunk. Tell the world we were having a laugh for the camera."

Chris had already thought of that. He'd thought of everything. "It wouldn't work. The press would be watching me for every slip. They're already doing it with other players. They're desperate to find a player like me to fill their bloody pages. It's not just the press either. Teammates, fans—the whole bloody world would be watching and wondering."

"Let them wonder."

Chris hadn't been able to eat earlier, but he was suddenly hungry. He looked in the fridge but nothing appealed to him. In the end, he grabbed a banana and ate that.

He poured himself a coffee, knowing the caffeine would have him buzzing for hours, and sat to drink it. He couldn't keep pacing round the kitchen, and he couldn't keep worrying.

"Perhaps you're right," he said. "Maybe my mother can come up with a solution."

Matt visibly relaxed. "I'm sure she can. We'll talk

to her and see what she says and, if she doesn't have an answer, we'll think again. I'll do whatever it takes to get that bloody woman off your back, you know I will."

Chris nodded. "Thanks, Matt. I appreciate it. And I'm sorry I'm so tense. I don't mean to take it out on you."

"I know. Phone your mum and tell her we'll be there tomorrow evening."

Chris took his phone from his pocket. His mother was sure to know what to do to silence Ruby for good. Ruby had, in effect, stolen those photos. She'd confiscated Stevie Greenwood's camera and then, without his permission, downloaded the contents onto her own computer. That had to be against the law.

"Hey, Mum, how are you?"

"All the better for hearing from you. I've had a long, long day and am sitting with a well-deserved gin and tonic. What about you, darling? What are you up to?"

"Matt's here and we're just chilling. Listen, Mum, we have to come to London tomorrow so I was wondering if we can stay at your place for the night."

"Of course. Oh, that will be wonderful. It's been ages since you've spent a night here. We'll all go out to dinner, shall we? I'll book a table."

"Sounds great. Actually, I could do with picking your brain about something, too, so that will give us a chance to chat."

There was a pause, just as he'd known there would be.

"Is everything all right?" she asked.

"Everything's fine."

"You're sure? Jo hasn't been getting you into any scrapes, has she?"

Poor Jo always got the blame for everything. "Of course not. Everything's fine. I'd better go, Mum, but we'll see you tomorrow."

"I'm looking forward to it already," she said.

When they ended the call, Chris felt slightly more relaxed. He didn't relish explaining all to his mother, but it was possible she would come up with something feasible and that life could return to normal.

Perhaps, after all, they could turn the tables on Ruby.

# TWENTY-SIX

IT WAS A little before seven o'clock when Dylan was woken by his phone. He reached for it only to succeed in knocking the bedside lamp, TV remote and key card to the floor along with his phone.

Wide awake, and panicking that his mother was calling about one of the kids, he groped under the bed for his phone and saw the flashing icon that told him a message had been left.

He hit the button and drew in a relieved breath as he heard the somewhat monotonous tone of his caller.

"Dave Edwards *Chronicle*." Dylan smiled as the three words came out together.

"Sorry about the delay in getting back to you, but I've made up a file about Brent. Apart from a couple of things that did go to print—nothing of interest, obviously—I've kept a lot of notes over the years. I've compiled them and printed them out for you. I was going to suggest I drop them in at the Pennine Hotel on my way to the office, but perhaps you're not there. Give me a call, will you?"

Dylan immediately returned his call.

"Dave, sorry I missed you. I am at the Pennine so call in. I'll buy you breakfast, if you've got time."

"Yeah? Brilliant. I'm on my way."

"I'll meet you in the dining room when I've showered and dressed."

"Oh. Sorry, did I wake you?"

"Yes, but it's fine. See you in about ten minutes."

Dylan made himself a coffee and left it to cool while he took a quick shower. He dressed in his usual jeans and shirt and peered out the window as he drank.

Daylight hadn't put in an appearance yet, but the hotel's lights showed that someone had been up and about early because the snow had been cleared from the car park. It was piled up like small mountains in the corners. Three or four inches must have fallen overnight.

Dylan grabbed his phone and wallet, and walked down the stairs to the dining room. Taking the stairs made him feel good—but only when he was descending. He preferred to do his lazy bastard trick and take the lift back up.

Edwards was already sitting at a table when Dylan walked in, and he stood to greet him.

"Sorry I woke you," he said.

"Don't worry about it."

"Late night?"

"Fairly."

A late night and a fruitless one. He'd been watching Elliott's house for hours and he'd seen nothing. Something insisted on niggling at Dylan, some instinct told him he'd missed something, but he couldn't think what. Elliott's friend Matt had been there and they'd stayed in all evening. The kitchen and living room lights had been on, as had the one that lit the staircase. At one point, Elliott had peered through the kitchen window into the darkness. Perhaps he'd heard a noise, perhaps he was expecting someone or maybe he'd just been looking at the snow. Either way, he'd had no visitors. At a little after midnight, all downstairs lights had been extinguished and a bedroom light had come on. Ten minutes later, the house had been in complete darkness and Dylan had returned to his hotel room.

God knows why he thought he'd missed something. Nothing had happened. There had been nothing to miss.

"So what have you got for me?" he asked as they looked at the menus.

Dylan rarely bothered with the menu as he always had a full English breakfast with as much coffee as he could drink.

"Here." Edwards opened a slim leather briefcase and pulled out a dog-eared file inside which were half a dozen sheets of typed paper. "It's not a lot, but I've made notes over the years about everything that raised my suspicions about Brent."

The waitress took their orders—two full English breakfasts—and poured a coffee for Dylan, and tea and a glass of orange juice for Edwards.

Dylan read through Edwards's notes as he ate. He was disappointed. There were dates and times, but nothing Dylan didn't already know. Brent had been accused of rape and sexual harassment on two occasions. One accuser had died in a car accident before the case went to court and the second had dropped charges. It proved sod all. There seemed to be nothing suspicious about the car accident. On the contrary, the girl had lost control of her vehicle and ploughed into the central reservation on the motorway.

On the other hand, Dylan couldn't help thinking that anyone who had sex with Brent tended to wind up dead.

"The girl who dropped charges," Dylan said, "claims she made up the story. Perhaps she did."

"Perhaps she was warned to drop them."

"Perhaps," Dylan agreed. "Have you spoken to her?"

"Once. She was very convincing."

Dylan took a swig of coffee. "So really, there's nothing to implicate Brent in any criminal activity?"

He wished it could be different because he'd taken a dislike to Brent, but there was nothing to prove he'd had anything to do with Gemma King's death. He could have helped her fill her body with lethal doses of heroin, alcohol and codeine if she'd been threatening to damage his reputation or tell his family what he was up to, but no court in the land would find evidence of that. He could admit to seeing her a few times, he could admit to being in her flat the night she died—but there was nothing to suggest he'd helped her on her journey toward those pearly gates.

In the same way, Brent could have suspected Stevie knew more than he should have and could have stabbed him to death to ensure his silence. If he'd gone to Stevie's flat with the intention of killing him, he'd have worn gloves to save himself the hassle of wiping his prints off everything.

Or perhaps Brent was as innocent as he claimed. Either way, there was no proof.

It was disheartening to say the least, but thousands of crimes remained unsolved every year. Why had Dylan thought he'd succeed in finding Stevie's killer when the police had failed?

He could uncover lies at every turn—something he was good at—but he couldn't find a single shred of evidence.

Damn it, though, Stevie's death had to be connected with his penchant for photography. And the photos

Dylan most wanted to see were in the Sportsman on Ruby's computer.

He'd thought about this long and hard and, on the face of it, breaking into the Sportsman was madness. Bill and Ruby rarely left the building. When they did, they had staff manning the pub.

If he broke in during the night though, when they were both asleep—

"Men like that," Edwards said, disturbing Dylan's line of thought, "think they're above the law. They believe they can live the life they choose without a thought for anyone else. And if something goes wrong, they'll do whatever it takes to protect themselves."

Dylan knew he had a point. "Including murder?"

"If that's what it takes, yes." Edwards finished his tea. "I don't suppose you've found out anything interesting?"

"Nothing that would stand up in a court of law."

"That's the crux of it. Brent is untouchable."

"Maybe."

"Thanks for breakfast," Edwards said. "It's time I was at the office. Lots to do. You can keep the file. It might come in useful."

"Thanks. And if I hear anything, I'll let you know."

Dylan watched him leave and thought about his choice of word. He was wrong. No one was untouchable. Not even Brent.

Dylan had another coffee before leaving the dining room, and he was in the lift, almost at his floor, when he realised what had been odd about last night. When Elliott's fiancée had been staying at the house, two upstairs lights had come on and then gone off within minutes of each other. Last night, when Elliott and Matt had been alone in the house, the ground-floor lights had been extinguished and only one light had come on upstairs.

It wasn't the most earth-shattering of thoughts, but it was mildly interesting. Which probably only showed how little progress he was making in this sodding northern town where nothing was ever what it seemed.

# TWENTY-SEVEN

CHRIS HAD BEEN dreading this. As soon as he walked into his old home, he knew he'd made a big mistake. He was almost twenty-one, far too old to run to Mummy when the going got rough, and besides, she'd only get angry.

"Darling, this is wonderful." His mother hugged him tight, squeezing the breath from him. "I can't tell you how good it is to see you."

Before he could respond, she touched Matt's arm. "Hello, Matt. How are you?"

Perhaps only Chris noticed how her voice cooled before greeting Matt. Matt either didn't notice or didn't care, probably the latter. "I'm good, Daphne, thanks. How are you? And Trevor?"

"We're fine, thank you." Dismissing Matt, she rubbed her hands together. "Now, what can I get you? Tea? Coffee? Something to eat? You must be starving after the long drive."

"We're good, Mum." Chris couldn't face food right now and he was dreading sitting in whatever restaurant she'd booked. "We stopped for a snack on the way."

"I'd like a coffee if it's not too much trouble," Matt said, and Chris wanted to hit him.

"None at all." Daphne was almost at the kitchen when she turned. "I've been working in the drawing room so it's warmer in there. I'll bring in Matt's coffee and we'll have a chat. You said you wanted to pick my brains, Chris, yes?"

He swallowed. "Yes."

It was indeed warm in the drawing room. Too warm.

The table was covered with papers that she'd been working on. It was a sight Chris had seen countless times. Everything in the room was the same as it had been for years. The carpet was a little worn, but as it was the only one he could remember being in the room, that wasn't surprising. The antique furniture was lovingly cared for. Chris's father would have liked a more modern look but this room was definitely Daphne's. It was homely and cosy, and Chris had always liked it.

They sat on the sofa, like two schoolboys waiting to be reprimanded by a stern headmaster.

Matt patted Chris's thigh. "It'll be fine. Her bark's a lot worse than her bite."

"Maybe, but her bite can still be pretty painful."

They were still smiling when Daphne entered carrying a small tray on which sat Matt's coffee, milk jug, sugar bowl and a few thin chocolates.

"Thank you," Matt said.

She sat opposite them in the high-backed chair. "You look tired, darling."

"I'm fine, Mum." He wasn't. Lack of sleep had him exhausted.

"If you say so. Your father and Jo will be dining with us this evening, by the way. I've booked the table for seven-thirty. But, as we're alone, perhaps you'd like to have that chat, Chris. I assume Matt's privy to it?"

"Of course," Chris said.

"It was my idea to talk over the problem with you," Matt said. "Neither of us knows too much about the law."

Daphne's eyes narrowed. "The law?"

Chris cleared his throat. "I have a problem, Mum."

"Go on," Daphne said.

"It's to do with Ruby."

"Ruby?" The colour drained from her face in an instant. "The Ruby who gave you up for adoption? What on earth does she have to do with anything?"

Chris cleared his throat again, but it didn't help. His voice still sounded as if he'd been chewing razor blades. "I told you about our meeting—"

"Of course."

He hoped she wasn't going to interrupt him every few seconds or he'd never get the words out.

"Are you going to see her again? Is that it?" Daphne asked.

"I have seen her," Chris said. "After our first meeting, she contacted me. She gave me a sob story and I gave her some money."

Daphne was furious. Chris could see her anger etched in every fine facial line. Dark, almost black eyes dominated her pale face. Lips were compressed into a tight thin line. "Then you're a fool, Chris."

"Generous and kind-hearted perhaps," Matt suggested, and he received a scowl for his trouble.

"There's something else I didn't tell you." Now that he'd started, Chris was determined to tell his story. "She moved to Dawson's Clough about eight months ago."

Daphne was on her feet, arms wrapped tight around her slender body. "Why? What's she doing up there? She followed you, didn't she?"

"Well—yes."

"How many times have you seen her? Why didn't you tell me? How could you, Chris?"

"I've hardly seen her, thank God. And you know why I didn't tell you. It hurts you. I know it does. I wish I'd never bothered to trace her in the first place. I don't know why I did."

"I can't believe she had the audacity to follow you. All these years, she's never given a damn. Now she decides it's perfectly all right to follow you across the country."

"It was okay at first," Chris said. "I did give her a bit of money, but it was okay. Anyway, I told you about that night in the pub when that chap took our photo—"

"That little oik! How dare he? I expect he got some kick out of—"

"He didn't, Mum. He was a bit—simple, I suppose. But he was harmless enough. He gave us no trouble."

"That's not the point," Daphne said. "He should know better than to photograph people without their permission. And if he didn't know better, he shouldn't be allowed out on his own until he did."

"He was fine. Very good about it all. And the poor chap's dead now, so don't call him an oik. That's not very nice, is it?"

"It's not very nice to take photographs of all and sundry. But you're right. The man's dead and one shouldn't speak ill."

She had the grace to look contrite but Chris knew it wouldn't last.

"The pub we were in at the time, the Sportsman, is Ruby's. She owns it along with her husband."

"You went into that woman's pub?" Daphne's words came slowly. "Knowing she owned it, you went there? To see her?"

"No, of course not. A group of us were there. It's

a general meeting place for everyone going on to the club."

"And she was there?"

"Yes," Chris said. "Matt and I were in a small back room—"

"I'm sure you were." Daphne's tone was as clipped as it always was when Matt was involved in a discussion.

"We were asking Stevie Greenwood to delete the photos he'd taken when she came in. She was angry with him and confiscated his camera. She told him he could have it back when he'd finished his drink."

Daphne had closed the blinds against the increasing darkness, but she was still staring at the window. "Go on, go on."

"When she returned his camera," Chris said, a pulse throbbing in his throat, "she said she'd deleted the photos. But she kept them for herself. She's—she's blackmailing me. She wants a million pounds—"

"What?" Daphne's screech made both Chris and Matt jump.

Chris's voice was shaking and there was damn all he could do about it. "She wants a million pounds. I've told her I don't have that sort of money, but she says she'll sell the photos to the newspapers if I don't pay up."

Papers fluttered from the table to the floor as Daphne strode past. "You idiots. You stupid, stupid idiots."

Matt shot Chris a quick glance when she had her back to them. It was a reassuring, sympathetic look that said everything would calm down in a moment. Chris hoped he was right because his mother was close to screaming pitch.

She whirled round. "So when you told me about that

horrid—about that man taking the photos, why didn't you mention Ruby?"

"I've explained that, Mum. I didn't want to upset you."

"You lied," she said. "How could you do that? What other lies have you told? The photos—you said they showed you with Matt." She pulled in a sharp, disgusted breath. "What exactly were you doing?"

"We were kissing," Matt said. "That's all. There was no one about and—"

"There clearly *was* someone about."

"Well, yes, but we didn't know he'd walked in until the flash from his camera went off."

Chris opened his mouth to speak, but he wasn't given the chance.

"Shut up, both of you." Daphne looked from one to the other of them and shook her head. "I can't believe you could be so stupid. I really can't."

"It's not as—"

"Shut the hell up, Chris!" Daphne strode to the door and yanked it open. "As I said, I've booked a table for seven-thirty. Thanks to you idiots, we're all going to have a wonderfully pleasant evening, aren't we?"

She strode out of the room, gave the door a vicious slam and was heard running up the stairs.

"That went even worse than I expected," Chris said.

"It'll be fine," Matt said. "She'll calm down. She'll come up with something, you know she will. We'll be exceptionally charming to her during dinner and all will be forgiven."

Chris wasn't so sure. When something upset Daphne, everyone had to suffer, and it seemed to Chris that all he'd done during the past couple of years was upset her.

# TWENTY-EIGHT

JEREMY JUMPED IN the back of the car. He had to attend a meeting with locals who were objecting to proposed plans for a large wind farm. Jeremy was pro-wind farms. At least, that was what everyone had to be told. Personally, he couldn't give a flying toss either way.

He waited until his secretary joined him.

"So," Jeremy said when he was confident the driver couldn't overhear them, "what have you got on Scott?"

"Nothing that's going to excite you, I'm afraid." Alistair switched on his netbook. "His dismissal from the police force gained him a lot of sympathy. Many people—including senior members of the police force—agree that he was used as a scapegoat. He served five months in prison, was dismissed from the force, and then registered as a private investigator."

"Everyone has secrets," Jeremy said.

"Perhaps, but Scott's are well-hidden."

"There's nothing to suggest he's taken a few backhanders for services rendered?"

"No, nothing like that. He gets by and that's about the best you can say about his financial situation. The bulk of his work involves investigating insurance scams and that sort of thing. He's up here looking into Stephen Greenwood's murder for personal reasons. No one's paying him. To all intents and purposes, he's a good guy looking for justice."

"He's an interfering bastard who's snooping into my fucking private life!"

The car joined a long queue of traffic at the temporary lights. The roadworks weren't close to being completed and the town's drivers had to look forward to at least another five weeks of this chaos.

"Family?" Jeremy asked.

"I told you about his dead wife. Nothing there, just tragedy. His mother moved in with him and his two children when his wife died. His son is a teenager and his daughter two years old. His family life is squeaky clean."

"No one's life is that squeaky clean." Jeremy's anger was only increasing. The private investigator he'd hired to look into Scott's life was supposedly one of the best, yet he'd come up with nothing Jeremy could use. "What about his friends?"

"One is ex-Detective Chief Inspector Frank Willoughby and there's nothing secretive about *his* past. Far from it. He's considered something of a hero in these parts."

Jeremy nodded. "I know the name."

"Scott's also friendly with another copper, one Detective Sergeant Pike. They worked together when Scott was on the force. He's happily married, devoted to his family and the job. No whiff of a scandal there either."

The car was still stuck in the queue of traffic. The driver had suggested they allow extra time for the roadworks and it was proving a wise decision.

"Okay," Jeremy said, "if we can't discover Scott's secrets, we'll think of something else. We'll believe he's whiter than white with no skeletons rattling around, and we'll go the other way. We need to know what he values most. There must be something he wouldn't want to lose."

Alistair sat straighter in his seat to look at him. "How do you mean?"

"I mean exactly that. What would Scott hate to lose the most?"

"I don't know what—"

"Family, I suppose. His son, perhaps? Or his daughter?"

"Jeremy, you can't be serious."

"Oh, believe me, I'm deadly serious. No one, but no one, is about to wreck my life, Alistair."

Scott was happy to threaten Jeremy's reputation and his future, so why shouldn't Jeremy threaten the things Scott held dear? There was no reason at all.

Tit for tat. An eye for an eye. It was the way of the world.

# TWENTY-NINE

"WHAT'S IN THE BOX?"

"Hello, Mum, nice to see you too. I've been busy, thanks. You?" Dylan put the box on the kitchen table. He would have left it in the hallway, where he tended to dump most things, but it was even more cluttered than when he'd last been home. A couple of stone pixies had arrived during the week and taken up residence either side of the door.

"Ha. Lovely to see you, Dylan. We've missed you terribly. I've no idea how we've managed to survive so long without your shining wit and charm. So what's in the box?"

"Photos. Thousands of photos." He'd wanted to come home and see his family, but he'd also wanted to do something useful, so he'd brought the last box of Stevie's photos with him.

"Lovely. Can I look through them?"

"Help yourself, although they're not exactly inspiring. Do you remember those holiday snaps you brought back from that cruise? About three hundred snaps of an empty sea? They're even worse than those."

She chuckled. "They summed up my holiday perfectly. All I saw was the sea. Except when we were in port and then I was too busy to take photos."

"Where are the kids?" he asked. "Have you sold them?"

"Yep. Fifty pence each. A bargain." She switched

on the kettle, beads and bangles jingling as she moved. "Freya's asleep, having raced round like a lunatic all day, and Luke will be here any time now. They've taken Bozo for a walk."

"They?"

"Yes, Charlie's been here for the third time this week. Bozo's getting some good long walks lately." She smiled wistfully. "I think it's serious. Young love is a wonderful thing, isn't it?"

"Damned if I can remember." He took off his jacket and slung it over the back of the chair. It was good to be home, even if it looked more like Disneyland every time he saw it. "So what's she like?"

"Lovely. She's perfect for Luke. Very polite. Sensible. They should be here any minute so you'll see for yourself."

The drive down from Lancashire had been stop-start and, after over four hours sitting in a car, he needed to shower and change. He couldn't meet the love of Luke's life in this crumpled state.

He carried his bag up the stairs and dropped it on his bed. He'd sort out his laundry later. Actually, he'd said that last time he was home and he had a horrible feeling he had one clean shirt left. His mother waited on the kids as if they were royalty, but she'd decided long ago that he was more than capable of operating the washing machine. He was, he just forgot.

Showered, dressed and feeling far more human, he was about to go down the stairs when his mother called him. He followed her voice to her bedroom and took an involuntary step back.

He couldn't remember looking inside the room since she'd moved in with him and the kids, almost a year ago, but it had certainly changed. Back then, it had been a quiet, sunny room with walls, he was fairly sure, that were a pale yellow. It sure as hell hadn't reeked of marijuana, either.

Apart from the telltale smell, it was like no room he'd ever seen. How she managed the obstacle course from door to bed, he had no idea.

A spooky black mannequin sporting a velvet beret and draped in thousands—probably millions—of beads stood next to the window. Necklaces and bracelets hung from it in a tangle and every colour of bead imaginable was there. How could one woman possess so much jewellery? None of it was of any value—the lot could probably be bought for a fiver—but he doubted she'd live long enough to wear it all. Looking at her now though, perhaps she would. She was wearing her own body weight in necklaces.

"What's wrong?" she asked.

"You. This." He gestured to the room at large and tried to decide what the very worst thing about it was. He couldn't. "You don't find it a tad—cluttered? And weird?"

"No. I want to be surrounded by things I like."

A large crystal ball sat on the dressing table. She could easily hire a tent, do her Madam Rosa impression and charge people for reading their fortunes. Let's face it, his mother wasn't the only crazy person around.

A water feature sat on a low table near the bed. The water trickled down over three stones into a well. "What's that for?"

"It's not *for* anything. I happen to like it. Anyway, the sound of moving water is one of the most relaxing things in the world."

"Ha. You're the most relaxed person I know."

"Then it's obviously doing its job."

The back wall was a dark blood red. Small red lights, switched off thankfully, were strung around the other, paler walls. A dream catcher, as his mother called the things, was suspended above the door.

"You'll give Freya nightmares if she sees this," he said.

She snorted with laughter. "Freya loves it. Especially this." She gave a twirling crystal mobile a light stroke and it spun around, casting shadows over the walls.

Not for the first time, Dylan hoped his daughter wasn't going to take after her grandmother. He appreciated his mother's help more than she'd ever know, and certainly more than he told her, but he didn't want Freya growing up to be a dope-smoking hippy.

"So what did you want me for?" he asked.

"This chair." She ran a hand over the back of a green leather armchair. "I need it moved over to the window and it's too heavy. It needs two of us to lift it."

"There's no room by the window."

"There will be if I move Pierre."

"Please don't tell me—" He broke off as his worst suspicions were confirmed. The sinister mannequin had indeed been named Pierre. "You really are crazy."

"So you keep telling me."

"And you spend far too much time with my kids."

"I know." She laughed, her usual carefree sound. "But I fear they'll still grow up to be as dull as you, Dylan. Now then, let me put Pierre over here."

Pierre was duly moved and Dylan dragged the chair, which was a hell of a lot heavier than it looked, to its new position by the window.

"Much better," she said. "Thanks."

As they got downstairs, Luke and Charlotte arrived with Bozo panting beside them.

"Hey, Dad!" Luke gave Dylan a high-five. "How long have you been here? Oh, sorry, this is Charlie. Charlie, this is my dad."

Thinking about it later, Dylan wasn't sure if they shook hands, or what they actually said. He was too taken aback by Charlotte to take any of it in. She was totally different to the girl he'd expected. More intelligent, sensible and calm. Tall and slim, with long blond hair that was tied back in a ponytail, she looked older than sixteen. Wiser too.

He remembered her saying how sorry she was about Bev, and he remembered the painful wrench in his gut when he thought how much Bev would have liked her but, other than that, the initial meeting passed in a blur.

"How long have you been here?" Luke asked again.

"About half an hour. And before I forget, you and I need to have a serious talk about your grandmother. You do realise that she should be in an institution, don't you?"

Luke grinned. "Yeah. I tell everyone at school that she's the coolest granny ever."

"Ha. When I'm celebrating my hundredth birthday and showing off my telegram from the Queen, you may call me *granny*. Utter that word before then and you're dog meat. Got that?"

"Yes, Vicky," Luke said with a wink for Dylan.

Instead of giving Dylan the usual frenzied greeting, Bozo was emptying the water bowl.

"We've been playing Frisbee with him," Charlotte said, smiling fondly at the dog. "He's run for miles."

"So have we," Luke said. "We're starving. Is there anything to eat?"

"There will be in half an hour."

Vicky took off for the kitchen to cook up a healthy but probably tasteless meal, and Dylan spent time with Luke and Charlotte. When Freya woke up, they made her giggle uncontrollably—which was the easiest task in the world.

If Dylan wished Bev could meet Charlotte, he also wished she could see her beautiful daughter.

Later, he and Luke took Charlotte home and Dylan met her parents. Her father, a builder, had his own company and her mother was a librarian. They were a decent, friendly, welcoming couple and Dylan knew that Bev would have approved wholeheartedly.

When Luke and Freya were in bed, Dylan poured himself a drink and sat on the sofa, with his feet on the coffee table, and watched the news on TV. Nothing much had happened, which wasn't a bad thing.

His mother opened the box containing Stevie's photos and looked through them.

"You're right. They're not very good," she said. "For all that, they're interesting in a strange sort of way."

Dylan knew exactly what she meant. They were awful and yet, once you'd started looking, you couldn't stop.

"I need to put them in chronological order," he said, "so don't mix them up too much."

"I won't. So why did he print them all?" she asked. "That must have cost a lot."

"I've no idea. For the same reason he collected newspaper cuttings, I suppose. He must have wanted a permanent reminder. Although why you'd want a reminder of half a park bench is beyond me. He wasn't the brightest bloke to walk the planet though, poor sod."

Thinking about it, Dylan had no idea why Stevie had even bought a camera. He hadn't been a gadget or a technology type of person. He'd been a simple soul who walked, enjoyed the occasional drink and read the local newspaper from cover to cover.

He'd been such an uncomplicated man, one of Dawson Clough's landmarks almost, that it was impossible to think that someone could have wanted him dead. But perhaps they hadn't. Maybe the popular idea that his death had been a random act was correct. If some junkie had gone to Stevie's flat to rob him—

They wouldn't have stabbed him several times. There would have been no need. One knife wound maybe, enough to disable him, but there would have been no need to plunge that knife into his body time and time again.

"Good grief, Dylan. For a minute, I thought Marilyn Monroe had been walking the streets."

"Whoa. Where?"

He grabbed the photo from her. Sure enough, it showed Gemma King walking along the street with a man. Even more interesting perhaps was the fact that, assuming the date and time stamp was correct, it had been taken the day she died. Taken before Brent had visited her flat.

Dylan recognised her companion, but it took a moment to place him. Once he did, a dozen questions came to mind.

It was Al. The junkie who lived in the ground-floor flat. The man who, along with Lizzie Trickett, had found Stevie's body. The same man Dylan had been trying to talk to since the day he'd arrived in Dawson's Clough.

# THIRTY

When Dylan drove out of London, having called at his office to make sure it was still standing and that Bobby was coping, the sun was shining. It was cold but bright. The first snowflakes started falling as he drove along the M66 and, by the time he arrived in Dawson's Clough, a couple of inches of the stuff lay on the ground. Weather-wise, the north-south divide never failed to amaze him. It was like visiting a different country.

On the journey, he'd tried to come up with a plan but he still didn't know where to start. He needed to talk to Al and find out what he'd been doing with Gemma King on the night she died. A chat with Elliott about the real reason Ruby was blackmailing him was high on his agenda, and he wanted to see the photos Ruby had for himself.

He began by walking to Anderson Street and hammering on Al's door. There was no answer—surprise, surprise—and Al's neighbours had no idea where he was.

"You never know what he's up to," the elderly chap in the adjoining flat said. "If he's gone on a bender, we don't see him for days. None of my business anyway. Like I told you the other day, I keep myself to myself."

Dylan thanked him and decided to see if Lizzie was at home. Before knocking on her door, he peered through Stevie's kitchen window. The flat had been emptied and was now a bare shell, presumably waiting for someone else to be housed there. It was a sad sight, one that made it seem as if all traces of Stevie had been erased.

He knocked on Lizzie's door and was pleased, and surprised, when she answered.

"Hey," she said, "it's—wait a minute, I'll get it. Scott? Dylan Scott?"

"That's me. How are you doing, Lizzie?"

"I'm good, ta. Are you coming in?"

"Thanks." He followed her along the hallway and into the kitchen. "I was looking for your friend Al. I don't suppose you know where he is, do you?"

"No idea, and he's no friend of mine. He's off his head most of the time. Christ, we're all out of it now and again, that's life, but he totally loses it for days at a time."

"Ah, I thought he was a friend. You fetched him when you were worried about Stevie, didn't you?"

"Yeah, but he was the last person I tried. Every other bugger was out or not answering. I was scared, and I couldn't have got inside Stevie's flat on my own. Al was the only person around. That don't mean he's a friend though. It just means he's better than no bugger. What do you want him for anyway?"

"It's to do with Gemma King."

Lizzie frowned. "She's dead. OD'd."

"I know. It's just that he was with her on the day she died and I wanted a word with him about that."

"Was he? Bloody hell, you'd think she'd have had more sense. Still, he pays up, I'll say that for him, and it's more than can be said for a lot round here. I've only been with him half a dozen times, that's when he's been desperate enough to put up with the cut-price whore. He looks the type who could get a bit nasty, and folk say he's got a temper on him, but I've never seen it. Mind, having said that, he hit some poor bugger on the head the other night. Could have killed him for all he knew. He was telling me he'd got into Stevie's flat—"

"What for?" It was Al who'd whacked him over the head with that bloody frying pan?

"Stevie reckoned he had a ticket to some posh do at the town hall. If anyone else had said that, I wouldn't have believed them, but Stevie didn't tell lies. It took him all his time to tell the truth so telling a lie would have been beyond him. Anyway, Al was determined to find it. He reckoned he could sell it for thirty quid, easy. He didn't find it though, or so he told me, but while he was looking, some bloke walked into the flat. It was probably a copper, wasn't it? Who else would have been there? So what does Al do? He smashed the poor bugger over the head with a saucepan or something and legged it. I tell you, Dylan, he's off his head most of the time."

If and when Dylan ever got hold of Al, he'd have a very serious word with him. Ironic to think they'd both broken in to Stevie's flat to look for the same thing, but bloody annoying to know that the little sod had almost fractured his skull. It was still bruised now.

"If you see Al, will you let me know?" Dylan couldn't remember if he'd given her his card or not, but it didn't matter because she was sure to have lost it. He handed her another.

"I've already got one of these," she said, surprising him. "I kept it because I've never met a P.I. before. Yeah, I'll send you a text if I see him."

"Thanks."

He tried Al's door again, but there was no response. After leaving the cheerless Anderson Street, he walked into town and bought himself a coffee in the hope it would fire his brain cells into action. What he really needed was some germ of an idea as to how he might break into the Sportsman and find Ruby's computer. He wasn't sure it could be done.

With a bucket-sized mug of coffee in front of him, he mentally ran through the layout of the pub. The plus point was that Bill and Ruby didn't own a dog to guard the premises. The bad points were the heavy bolts on the doors. The building was alarmed but, with luck, Dylan should manage to disable that.

It might be possible to gain access to the toilets through a small window at the back of the premises. Might. That window was hellish small and he wasn't sure he'd get through it. If he got stuck and had to call the fire service to rescue him, he'd have some explaining to do.

The alternative to breaking in, of course, was not leaving. He could walk in during opening hours and hide somewhere at throwing-out time. A cupboard outside the toilets housed brooms, mops and assorted cleaning paraphernalia, and it was unlikely to be opened until the cleaner arrived to do her thing in the morning. He could hide in there. Possibly. Then all he had to do was find Ruby's computer.

There was a huge gulf between imagination and reality. In his imagination, he'd found the computer and, lying next to it, a knife with a five-inch blade wrapped in a bloodstained cloth. Ah, if only life was so simple.

The reality was that he had a plan, though, and for the moment, it was the best he could come up with.

With that settled, he finished his drink, stepped out of the coffee bar into what soon became an icy blizzard and decided to walk out to Manchester Road and see if Elliott was about.

He wasn't. There was no sign of his car and no answer at the gate.

There was a coffee bar nearby, but he couldn't face more coffee. He walked the length of Manchester Road, wondering about the residents who hid behind their tall security gates. He also wondered about Ruby.

Stevie would have let her into his flat so it was feasible that she could have stabbed him several times. Surely, he would have fought back though. He would have been able to overpower Ruby, wouldn't he?

Bill was a different matter, of course. Bill was big and strong, he was used to moving heavy beer barrels around—

He was also the smiling, genial host. Even killers smiled now and again though.

And what about the elusive Al? How badly had he wanted that ticket? Not enough to kill for, surely to God. At best, he'd have sold the thing for thirty quid. Even an addict wouldn't stoop that low.

Elliott's Audi drove past and Dylan turned around and walked back along the road to his house.

When he reached the gates, the Audi was parked on the drive. A thin layer of snow had already settled on its roof.

Dylan hit the button to the side of those tall gates and was rewarded almost immediately when Elliott answered with a weary-sounding "Yes?"

"Chris? It's Dylan. Dylan Scott. Sorry to bother you again—I know I'm becoming a nuisance—but I'd like a word. It's quite important."

"About what?"

"About Ruby."

"Okay. Come on up."

Dylan's "Thanks" was lost in the whirring of the gates.

He walked up the steep and slippery drive and was brushing snow from his shoulders as Elliott opened the door.

"Thanks for seeing me, Chris. I appreciate it."

Elliott walked toward a huge sitting room Dylan hadn't seen before. Well-polished wooden floors gleamed between expensive rugs. Almost one entire wall was floor-to-ceiling glass. A couple of leather sofas and three armchairs promised comfort. A state-of-the-art audio and visual system was a reminder of exactly how much Elliott earned for playing the game he loved.

"What's Ruby said?" Elliott asked.

"Nothing. She denies all knowledge of you."

Elliott pulled a face at that. He still looked little older than Luke. "So what do you want to talk to me about?"

"The photos Stevie took. Ruby grabbed those photos for her own gain, and within a couple of days, Stevie was dead. Silenced, presumably. Now, who stood to benefit from his murder? Ruby. If he was dead, he couldn't tell the world what he'd seen, could he? And if he couldn't tell the world, the only other person who could cash in on your secret was Ruby."

Elliott was so pale that Dylan wouldn't have been surprised to see him throw up over the beautiful wooden floor.

"You think—" Elliott couldn't speak. He was swallowing rapidly.

"I don't know, but it's a possibility."

"He's dead because of me?"

"No. Not at all. But he may be dead because someone thought they could profit."

"Oh, God." Elliott sank onto a sofa made from the softest leather Dylan had ever seen.

"I'd like to know exactly what those photos show," Dylan said.

"What? But I've already told you."

"Yes, and I'm sorry, but I don't believe you. For one thing, it's very difficult to prove someone's alcoholic intake. You could be staggering, you could be throwing up or dancing on a table, but a quick snap of any of those things won't prove a person is drunk. Also, being drunk, even for a footballer who's signed a contract with a healthy energy drinks company, isn't such a big deal."

The colour had come back to Elliott's face. A lot of colour.

"I happen to know that your engagement to Paige is only for show," Dylan said.

"Who the hell told you that?"

"No one. I overheard Paige and Jo talking."

"For God's sake." Elliott was on his feet now, a bundle of nervous energy.

"Look, I'm on your side." Dylan wanted to calm him down. He needed a rational explanation. He needed the truth. "I haven't seen the photos, but I'm willing to bet they show that you're gay. Am I right?"

Elliott shook his head and put his hands to his face to cover eyes that had filled with tears.

"So what's the big deal?" Dylan asked. "We're in the twenty-first century, not the first. Who cares?"

Elliott spun around to face him, his eyes red. "Who cares? Just about everyone in the football world, that's who. Managers, teammates, fans, media—they all care. If this gets out, I'm finished. Only a month or so ago, there was a big thing in the papers about outing one of the Premier League players. Everyone's still dying to know who it is—and why it never happened. And it didn't matter that it never happened because the papers sold millions of copies just because of the speculation."

Dylan didn't know why, he'd never really thought about it until now, but it was true that homophobia was alive and well in the football world.

"There must be dozens of gay footballers in the—"

"Name one," Elliott snapped.

Dylan couldn't. The only player that came to mind was the world-famous Justin Fashanu. He'd been famous for two things, being the world's first openly gay footballer and taking his own life. Sadly, few people remembered his talent for the game. There was no point mentioning Fashanu though. He wasn't a good example.

"There are a couple who play in the lower leagues," Elliott said, "and that's it. No one else would dare own up to it. Oh, they have campaigns designed to stamp out homophobia in football, but nothing changes. I don't think it ever will."

"I'm sure it is changing."

"It's not." There was no doubt in Elliott's mind. "Even racism is still rife. Some of the comments the black players get are unbelievable. If a black player doesn't hear a monkey chant or have a banana—real or inflatable—

thrown at him during a match, he's had a good day. Believe me, if this gets out, I'm finished."

"You wouldn't be."

"Of course I would. The first thing to go would be any sponsorship deals. They want the so-called macho men advertising their products. The next thing would be my hopes of making the England squad. I'd be dropped. The chants from the terraces would be—" He dragged in a shaky breath. "When this gets out, I'm finished." He threw up his hands and a solitary tear slid down his cheek.

"That's why you've faked an engagement to Paige?"

Elliott dried his face. "Yes. Matt thought—well, we both thought it was a good idea. I'm not using Paige. We talked about it long and hard, and we both stand to benefit from the arrangement. She's being paid well for being my fake fiancée. But Matt and I thought we could bluff it out. If Ruby got those photos published, we could say we were messing around for a dare or something."

"Why can't you do that?"

"Because people would be forever wondering and asking questions. Journalists would watch our every move."

He was right, of course.

"So what are you doing about it?" Dylan asked.

Elliott shrugged. "I'm stalling. I've had to tell my mother—she's a barrister, you know."

"You mentioned it."

"Matt wants to have a word with Ruby and appeal to her better nature. Like that would do any good. She doesn't have a better nature. She's a cruel, malicious old bitch."

Dylan nodded. Anyone who could do this to their own flesh and blood was lower than low.

"My mother's getting some paperwork drawn up and I'm waiting to hear from her," Elliott said. "If I have to pay Ruby, I'll have to pay her. Not the million pounds she's demanding, though. Nowhere near that amount. And legal documents will have to be drawn up. It won't be easy."

It would be easier if Ruby was behind bars for the murder of Stevie.

"Has she ever mentioned Stevie Greenwood to you?" he asked, and Elliott shook his head.

"Never."

"What did she say when she returned his camera to him?"

"Nothing really. She told him she'd deleted the photos in case he forgot, called him a pain in the arse and then told him he wouldn't be served if he ever went to the pub with his camera again." Elliott thought back to the night in question. "He didn't seem to take offence. Perhaps he was used to people being rude to him. He nodded, said yes when she asked him if he understood, and then left the pub. I never saw him again, and Ruby's never mentioned him to me."

"Okay." Dylan sat on the edge of the leather sofa. "What's Ruby said about the photos? Where are they? On her computer at the pub? In a safe somewhere? The bank maybe?"

Elliott took a dark blue handkerchief from his pocket and blew his nose. "I don't know. All I know is that she has them. She downloaded them to her computer and that's all I know."

"So if you had the photos—"

"But that's just it. I can't get the bloody photos without paying her a load of money. Money I don't have. And even if I did have them, there's no guarantee that she wouldn't tell the world."

"Without evidence it wouldn't matter. You could laugh that off. You're engaged to a stunningly beautiful young woman. Who'd believe her?"

Elliott shook his head, a picture of despair. "She'd keep copies."

He was right about that.

"How does Matt feel about all this?" Dylan asked.

"He's as angry as me. For my sake, not his own. He wouldn't care if the whole world knew, but he knows what it would do to me and my career. He's supportive. He'll do whatever it takes to help me out of this fucking mess."

"And Paige?"

"She's furious. Obviously. She's a respected journalist, for God's sake, and if news breaks that her engagement to me and the story she told the world is fake, it could destroy her career. No one would believe a word she printed."

"And I suppose there's the money aspect too," Dylan said. "You mentioned something about paying her well to pose as your fiancée."

Elliott shrugged that off.

"What about Bill?" Dylan asked. "What's he said about any of it?"

"I've only ever spoken to him in passing. I have no idea if he knows the sort of woman his wife is or not. She claims she's leaving him. When I've paid up, she says she'll go to Italy or Spain or somewhere." He blew his nose again. "I don't know what to do. Every time I open a bloody newspaper, I expect to see myself making headlines."

"No, you're safe enough. Ruby will believe she can make more money out of you than the press."

"I hope you're right. I hope I can stall her long enough to figure out what the hell to do about her."

"You will. And it really isn't the end of the world, you know. So what if the photos are published in the papers? You and Matt can bluff it out and laugh it off. You'd marry Paige and it would soon be yesterday's news."

"But it wouldn't. Every move I made would be watched. Every word I said would be analysed to death. It would never be yesterday's news. It would be a disaster."

It wouldn't. Well, not necessarily. Perhaps Elliott was too young to see it though. And perhaps he wasn't strong enough to stand up to the media, the fans and the football world in general.

Elliott was young. He was a celebrity. Image would be everything to him.

# THIRTY-ONE

DYLAN HAD PLANNED to visit the Sportsman after leaving Elliott's house, but he made a detour via Anderson Street. Despite the photo Stevie had taken of Al with his jeans round his ankles, he was beginning to think the bloke was a figment of everyone's imagination.

He hammered on the door and was taken aback when a bleary-eyed, swaying Al opened it a fraction. "Who the fuck are you?"

"I'm the person you almost killed with a frying pan. I want a word with you, sunshine."

Al tried to slam the door, but Dylan was too quick—and too sober—for him. He pushed his way inside what had to be the filthiest home he'd ever seen. Half a dozen black bags filled with rubbish waited to be taken away. Empty beer cans were strewn along the length of the hallway. A couple of cigarettes had been stubbed out on the floor.

Al looked equally unkempt. His dark hair was long, lank and greasy, and his teeth, those he had, were a revolting shade of nicotine yellow. It would have been possible to grow potatoes beneath his fingernails, and black jeans and grey hoody clearly weren't on speaking terms with a washing machine.

"Aw, you shouldn't have bothered cleaning the place up for me," Dylan said.

Al looked at him as if he were insane. "You can fuck off."

"I will. But first—" Dylan grabbed him by the throat and slammed him hard against the wall. "First, you can tell me why you knocked me senseless with a frying pan."

"What? I don't know what you're talking about."

"Stevie's flat. You broke in. That's against the law, did you know that?"

Dylan tightened his grip and Al coughed and spluttered.

"I can't breathe."

"You can breathe enough. Talk."

"I didn't know it was you, did I? I thought—" He dragged in a lungful of breath. "I thought it was someone out to get me. It was self-defence."

"What were you doing there?"

"What's it to you?"

"You can either tell me, sunshine, or we'll go down to the local nick and you can explain to a few coppers. Your choice."

"Aw, fuck. It was nothing, right? I was in there looking for some ticket he said he had, that's all. It was no use to him, was it? Someone else could have made use of it."

"So you broke in to steal that?"

"The door was open."

"Like hell it was. Then what happened?"

"You walked in. Except I didn't know it was you, did I? How the fuck could I? I don't even know who you are." His eyes narrowed. "You're that detective that everyone's talking about, right?"

"What are they saying?"

"Just that you're sniffing around."

The flat, the hallway at least, went beyond filthy. A film of grease clung to the walls and the smell was a mix of damp, cooking oil and cat pee. Dylan would be glad to escape into the bracing Dawson's Clough air.

A large ginger cat, presumably an incontinent one, wandered into the hall, spat at Dylan, arched its back and raced back to where it had come from.

Dylan released his grip on Al's throat and gave him a shove against the wall.

"You nearly fucking choked me." Al ran a sorrowful hand around his neck.

"I might finish the job yet. Tell me about Gemma King."

"What is this? Fucking twenty questions?"

"How's your throat?"

"Okay, okay. Gemma King. She's dead. Died of an overdose. It was always likely to happen."

"Why was it always likely to happen?" Dylan asked.

"Because she couldn't handle it, that's why. She'd had her stomach pumped half a dozen times."

"Oh?"

"Well, twice anyway. You can check it out at the hospital. Twice they had to get an ambulance to her."

Dylan hadn't known that. Rachel should have mentioned it.

"You were with her on the day she died—"

"Who told you that?"

"Who's asking the questions?"

"So I was with her the day she died. So what? I was often with her. She was okay. Nice tits. Good legs too. Sometimes, when she needed a fix, she didn't charge much."

Al was enough to make the most optimistic of people despair for the sake of the world. He was probably under thirty—it was difficult to tell—and yet he was a complete waste of space. No pride, no self-respect, no aspirations—nothing.

"Tell me about the day she died. Where did you go? What did you do?"

"I fucking screwed her. What do you think I did?"

"Where?"

"At her place." He looked into Dylan's impatient face and sighed. "We took a bit of heroin, we screwed, I paid her and I left. And that's it. She chucked me out, said she was going to have a bath. She'd already popped a few painkillers and she'd got a bottle of vodka. She could sometimes go a couple of days without a drink, but when she had a bottle, it was gone in no time."

"You told the police all this, did you?"

"What was the point?"

"How did you find out she was dead?"

"Someone told me the next day. It was Lizzie. Lives next door to Stevie's place."

"Okay. So let's talk about Stevie. Where were you the night he died?"

"What? I was here."

"Alone?"

"Yes."

"Did you see anyone about? Hear anything?"

"No."

"So tell me how you found out he was dead," Dylan said. "From the beginning."

Al sighed. "That crazy Lizzie came hammering on my door. Shouting and fucking screaming she was because she thought something had happened to him. So we goes round to his flat and, because she was so worried, we tried to break in. I smashed the kitchen window. He was dead. Blood everywhere. Lizzie phoned the cops. And that's it."

At least that agreed with Lizzie's story.

"Okay." Dylan opened the door, grateful to let some fresh, clean air into the hallway. "I'll see myself out."

"Too fucking right you will." Al's bravado had returned. "And don't bother coming back."

"I can't promise that. I may yet do you for assault. Or attempted burglary. Maybe breaking and entering or using illegal substances. It's a job to know where to start with someone like you, Al."

Dylan stepped outside, closed the door behind him and walked along Anderson Street.

His phone had trilled a couple of times to alert him to a message, and he took it from his pocket to read it. The number was unknown, the text read: "You have something I want. I have something you want." A photo was attached and Dylan's heart seemed to stop beating before suddenly galloping off at an erratic pace as he gazed at it.

The photo was dark, and the background gave no clue as to where it had been taken, but it was definitely Luke.

# THIRTY-TWO

"ANY WORD FROM Golden Bollocks yet?" Bill was checking that the soft drinks cabinet was well stocked in readiness for the evening.

"Not yet." Ruby pulled on her coat and grabbed her handbag. "I'm going to see him now."

"Then make sure you're persuasive." Bill straightened up, closed the cabinet and picked up a glass to polish. "A hundred grand's nothing to him, is it? Why won't he hand it over? Perhaps I should talk to him. You don't seem to be doing a very good job."

"I can handle him," Ruby said.

If she'd merely asked Chris for a hundred grand, as Bill thought, perhaps he would have paid up by now. It wasn't nearly enough though. She wanted the million and she didn't intend to settle for anything less. He owed her that much.

If she'd been allowed to live out her dream, if she'd graduated with that degree and then taken the decent job that would surely have followed, she would have been set up for life. But no—Chris had put paid to that. One minute life had been good, and the next it had been over. Her parents had barely spoken to her since—she'd made her bed, literally, and must lie on it, was their attitude. Her friends had turned their backs on her too. She'd had nothing and no one. Yes, Chris owed her big time.

She meant what she said though. As soon as he gave

her the million, she'd be gone from his life. She'd leave England, and Bill, and settle in a warm country where she could enjoy a simple life by the sea beneath a hot sun.

Chris was stalling, saying he didn't have that sort of money, but she was still confident he'd pay up. Finding out he was gay, thanks to Simple Stevie and that camera of his, had been a godsend. It was only when she'd seen the desperation and the sheer, undiluted panic on Chris's face she'd realised that, to him, and to any footballer she supposed, it was a big deal. She'd thought no one cared about a person's sexuality these days, but seeing Chris's reaction, and then reading up on homophobia in football, she soon discovered how wrong she'd been about that.

Little had Simple Stevie known that he'd set her up for life. Or he would have when Chris paid up.

Looking back, it was odd, and a little frightening, to remember how reluctant she'd been to meet Chris. She'd given birth to him, given him away for adoption and then forgotten about him. She couldn't see the sense in adopted kids trying to trace their birth parents. What was the point? Even now, she didn't know why she'd agreed to meet him. She hadn't intended to but something at the last minute had made her change her mind. Curiosity perhaps. Being at a loose end maybe. Or perhaps it had simply been an excuse to go to London for the day and see the sights.

Of course, when he'd told her about himself, how well he was doing, and how much he got paid for playing football, she soon realised she could make a few quid out of him. She was his mother, after all. So she gave him a sob story and he gave her some money. Not a lot, because she hadn't asked for a lot.

It had been Bill's idea to follow him to Dawson's Clough and, in Bill's words, "get pally with him." Chris wanted to get to know her as much as she wanted to know him though. He'd given her a couple of small amounts, but she'd never expected it to amount to much.

On arrival in the town, she soon realised he was a celebrity.

She'd asked him what would happen if word got out that she was his real mother, but he'd shrugged it off. Said it wouldn't matter. She hadn't been too sure, and she'd still been wondering about who might be interested enough in her story to pay her a decent amount when she'd heard him, Matt and Simple Stevie in the back room of the pub, or the snug as Bill called it.

When she'd grabbed Stevie's camera and looked at the photos he'd taken on that small screen, she'd known she was on to something. The idiot Stevie must have had his camera set to take a burst of rapid photos because flicking through the four he'd taken was like watching a short movie. Matt wasn't really recognisable because he had his back to the camera, but Chris was. They'd been kissing, their hands had been all over each other, and they'd been a breath away from having sex right here in the pub.

Oh yes, Chris would pay up.

"I'll see you later. Won't be long." Ruby marched out of the bar, into the cold air where snow was still swirling around in a gusting wind, and began the walk to Manchester Road.

She didn't mind the walk there, it gave her time to

think and plan what she would say to Chris, but she'd get a taxi back.

A bus trundled past and a dozen faces stared out at the gloomy day. One day soon, Ruby would leave all this behind. She'd spend her days in the sun where people smiled all the time.

She walked up to those iron gates and pressed the buzzer.

"Yes?" Chris said.

"It's me. Your mother. Ruby." She never thought of herself as his mother, but she knew it annoyed him to hear her say so. "We need to talk."

"Right. Fine. Come up to the house." His tone was clipped and snappy.

He'd probably been spoiled as a kid. Sure to have been, in fact. No one got on in life as well as he had without all the privileges of a pampered upbringing.

Ruby had never planned on keeping him, she would have had an abortion if she'd known what to do and where to go but, by the time she found out, it was too late so she'd had to go through with the birth. Though if she'd been forced to keep him, she would have shown him some discipline. He wouldn't have spoken to her in that nasty tone if he'd been brought up properly.

Chris held open the door but didn't invite her to step inside out of the snow. The boy had no manners.

"What now, Ruby?"

"I thought it was time I gave you a prod," she said. "I've made an appointment with a journalist who works for one of the nationals. Of course, I can cancel it if you'd rather. I need to know if and when you're going to pay up."

"You've already made the appointment? When for?"

"Friday," she said.

"Cancel it," he snapped. "You'll get your money. Maybe not all of it, but—"

"All of it or none." She managed a nonchalant tone despite the way her spirits soared at the knowledge that he was going to pay up.

"You think you'll get a million from a newspaper? Are you mad?"

Ruby had no idea how much she'd get. Not a lot, she suspected. Or not as much as she could get from Chris. Besides, she wasn't a vindictive woman. She didn't particularly want to ruin his future. He'd ruined hers, but she was woman enough to turn the other cheek.

"With the photos?" she asked. "Yes, I think I'll get close to a million from them."

"You'll get your money, okay? You can cancel that appointment. I just need more time to get it together. I have to take out a loan. Truly, Ruby, I don't have that sort of money."

"When will you have it?"

He hesitated. "Monday."

It was all she could do to prevent the cry of joy escaping her lips. Monday—oh, God. She could fly to Italy. Until this moment, a large part of her hadn't believed it could happen. She offered up a silent thank-you to Simple Stevie and the way he'd insisted on poking his camera in people's faces.

"Okay," she said. "I'm prepared to give you until Monday. What time? Where?"

"I'll meet you at the entrance to the park." He looked at her as if she was something unpleasant he'd accidentally stepped in. "Eight o'clock. In the evening."

"Make sure you do." She gave him a motherly smile. "I'll see you then, Chris. Take care."

She turned and took a step away, slipping on the snow when the door slammed loudly behind her.

On Monday night, she would have a million pounds. On Tuesday morning, she could fly to Italy.

She'd already packed a bag and dusted off her passport. Only one bag because she didn't want Bill to see it. Anyway, she wouldn't take much. She could buy anything she needed on arrival. It wasn't as if she'd need coats and sweaters. No, she'd wear summer dresses, sandals and sunglasses…

# THIRTY-THREE

DYLAN'S BRAIN HAD turned to mush. He could think of nothing he had that would be of value to anyone else. Nothing.

He'd tried calling the unknown number several times but no one answered. The messages he'd left had so far been ignored. No one was answering Luke's phone either.

If anyone harmed so much as a single hair on his son's head—

Killing whoever had done this with his bare hands was one thing. The truth, however, was that Dylan had, albeit unknowingly, put his son in danger. First Bev— he shouldn't have left her alone that morning—and now Luke.

"He's at Charlie's," Dylan's mother said. "What's so urgent?"

"Nothing. I just wanted to talk to him about Chris Elliott." He didn't want her worrying when he could worry enough for both of them. "Have you got Charlie's number? Give me that, will you? I'll get her to pass a message to him."

At least Charlotte answered her phone.

"He didn't get to school today." She spoke reluctantly, probably worried she'd get Luke into trouble. "There was a film on that a couple of boys bunked off to see so I assume he went with them. It's odd he didn't tell me, though. He's all right, isn't he?"

"Yes. Yes, he's fine." He'd better be all right. "If he calls you, tell him to give me a shout, will you? It's about tickets to a football match. It's urgent."

"Oh, great. Yes, of course I will."

This evil bastard must have seen Luke early this morning—

Brent!

Why the hell hadn't he thought of Brent before? He wanted those bloody photos.

He punched in Brent's number and was relieved when it was answered almost immediately by the man himself.

"Ah, Mr. Scott, what a pleasant surprise. I'm so pleased you've decided to return my calls at last."

"Don't fuck with me, Brent. Where's my son?"

"Didn't you get my message?"

"I got it. I want to speak to my son. Now."

"All in good time. I'd like those photos you have that show me going with that little whore."

"You idiot. You stupid, fucking idiot. I was bluffing. All I have is a picture that shows you on Anderson Street with a bunch of sodding flowers behind your back. I lied. I wanted to hear your side of the story so I lied."

"You expect me to believe that?"

"It's the truth, for God's sake."

"All you have is that, and yet you put two and two together and decided I'd been in that little whore's flat? You think I'm going to fall for that?"

"It's the truth. I heard that Gemma King, that little whore as you so charmingly call her, had been with a wealthy man. I also heard rumours that you went with prostitutes, and that you sometimes took them flowers.

I discovered that you'd bought flowers from Forget-me-nots that day, and yes, when I found the photo of you on Anderson Street with the flowers, I put two and two together. That's all I have, I promise you."

There was a long pause.

"Eleven o'clock tonight. Turner's Mill. Alone. No police."

"You clearly haven't done your homework. I'm a disgraced copper—no police would listen to me."

"Oh, believe me, I've done my homework. If there's anyone with you, anyone at all, you won't be seeing your son again. Turner's Mill. Eleven o'clock."

"Where the—?" The connection was dead.

Dylan was soaked and chilled, but it didn't register. All he knew was that, for the sake of getting one up on Brent, he'd put his son in danger. How could he have been so fucking irresponsible?

He hit another button on his phone and was relieved to hear the familiar voice on the other end. "Hey, Dylan. How's it going?"

"It's going fucking disastrously. I'm in trouble, Frank. Big trouble."

# THIRTY-FOUR

RUBY ALMOST RAN into the Sportsman. She'd half walked and half skipped the journey home from Chris's house on Manchester Road. Her heart was singing with excitement.

Bill and Oscar were serving behind the bar.

"I have a bit of a headache," she said, "so if you don't mind, I'm going upstairs to lie down."

"How did it go?" Bill asked.

"Very well," she said, smiling at him. "Very well indeed."

A smile curved his lips too. "Excellent news. Any dates?"

"Next Wednesday. Not too long now."

"Great stuff."

She was taking off her coat as she went up the stairs. It was old, and she'd be glad to see the back of it. She'd soon be leaving it behind.

Instead of going to her bed and lying down as she'd intended, she went to the kitchen, made herself a coffee, and carried it into the small office.

She switched on the computer and was soon gazing at a map of Italy.

It was all planned out in her head. All she'd done lately was plan her future and it made such a refreshing change to the day-to-day drudgery of the past few years.

She'd take a flight to Verona, using her own passport,

and then vanish. The passport could go in the nearest waste bin because she'd never use it again.

When she'd caught a bus to somewhere else, she'd check into a hotel, buy a few clothes, and then see about getting a new passport. Fake passports were easy enough to get hold of so long as you could afford it.

The thought made her smile to herself. There was nothing she wouldn't be able to afford.

Chris had said she might not get the full million, but that was okay. He might not know it, but she'd settle for half a million. She'd settle for anything that offered her a new life.

When she had a new identity, she'd start looking for a house to buy in a small Italian village. It would be by the coast in an unspoilt area. She didn't want to live near a beach that was invaded by tourists.

She hit a few keys and her computer was soon showing her details of the most glorious villa in Sicily. The sea and mountain views were stunning. God, she couldn't wait to leave dreary Dawson's Clough behind.

She could picture herself sitting outside with a glass of Rioja doing nothing more than watch the sea ebb and flow.

There was no way she'd be able to get to sleep tonight.

On Monday evening, she'd see Chris. Early on Tuesday morning, she'd be at Manchester Airport ready to board the first available flight to Italy.

What a gem her son had turned out to be!

Part of her worried about what Bill might do when he realised she'd gone. He'd probably make trouble for Chris, but that wasn't her problem. Other than that, what could he do? He'd call the police and they'd learn that she'd caught a plane to Italy. By then, she would have vanished.

Maybe, if she left her passport and clothes in the hotel, they'd think she'd taken off for a brief holiday and been abducted or murdered. She'd be missing, presumed dead perhaps.

She didn't care. So long as she caught that flight out of the country, she'd be fine.

Only five days to wait...

# THIRTY-FIVE

TURNER'S MILL HAD a long and proud history but, when the cotton industry died, the old mill had been abandoned and forced to take its chance with the elements. It hadn't fared well over the years. Wind and rain whistled through its smashed windows, and grass clung to gaps in the brickwork high up on the tall chimney.

The mill was on the edge of town, three of its sides surrounded by a high fence topped with barbed wire to keep out intruders. A couple of large notices pinned to the fence warned people not to enter as the building was unsafe. At the front, however, were several gaps in the fencing, one of which was easily large enough to drive through. Dylan parked the Morgan close to the building's double doors. Glass panels in both doors had been smashed.

Once a car park, the concreted area was now a dumping ground. Bags of rubbish had been tossed in a corner, along with an old mattress and two sofas. Polystyrene containers from various fast-food outlets blew around in the wind.

The mill was a good distance away from any main roads. Dylan sat in the Morgan for a full five minutes and saw only two cars drive past. No pedestrians came along here. There was no point.

A large moon had been shining earlier, but even that had decided to hide behind a bank of thick cloud. If not for a lone streetlight twenty yards away, the darkness would have been complete.

Brent had chosen his location well. He'd obviously known there would be no one around to hear any cries for help. No one to hear any gunshots. Bastard.

Dylan grabbed the brown envelope from the front seat and abandoned the Morgan's warmth. He stood in front of those double doors, his heart racing with a mix of fury and fear. Mainly fear, if he were honest. Dylan's sole purpose in life was to protect his family and he'd messed up big style. Luke was in danger and he knew he'd never live with himself if anything happened to him—

A small dark vehicle, not Brent's usual mode of transport, drove slowly along the street and turned through the same gap in the fencing that Dylan had used. The headlights died before the car came to a stop.

There were possibly four occupants—a driver, what looked like two men in the back and Brent. There was no sign of Luke. It was Brent who emerged from the passenger's door and walked slowly toward Dylan. He was carrying a small torch which gave out precious little light.

"Where's my son?" Dylan demanded.

"As I said, Mr. Scott, all in good time."

Dylan lunged at him. "Where is he, you bastard?"

"Where are my photos?" Brent reached out for the envelope, but Dylan put it beyond his grasp.

"You give me my son, I give you the photos. Isn't that the way this works?"

The moon emerged from behind the clouds just as Brent's face took on a sinister sneer. "The photos first."

"My son. I want to know he's safe."

At a signal from Brent, two car doors slammed and two men, huge men, strode across to them. One snatched the envelope from Dylan's grasp. Dylan caught a glimpse of the gun hidden beneath his jacket. The other man delivered a blow to Dylan's head that sent him crashing into the wall. Everything went dark for a moment or two, and it took a few seconds for his knees to handle such a mundane task as bearing his weight.

The man who'd taken the envelope and handed it to Brent searched Dylan. Shirt buttons were sent flying across the concrete as he checked Dylan for a body wire.

"I'm not carrying anything and I'm not wired," he said, but the brute wasn't taking his word for it.

Dylan rubbed at his cheekbone. He didn't think anything was broken, but it was already swollen.

"This is it?" Brent waved the enlarged photos in Dylan's face.

"That's it. I told you, I was bluffing." His knees still felt as if they would buckle at any moment. "I'm looking into the murder of Stevie Greenwood, and I heard about Gemma King. I wondered if there was a connection, that's all. I thought it possible that Stevie knew about Gemma's killer, and equally possible that her killer knew Stevie knew. If Stevie had photographic evidence to put her killer behind bars—" He shrugged and left the sentence unfinished. Odd that Brent hadn't disputed the *killer* part of his speech. After all, he was supposed to believe she'd died of an overdose. "I thought that if I told you I had pictures, you'd tell me your side of the story. That's all. And you did. You told me Gemma was dead when you arrived and that's the end of it. If I didn't return your phone calls, it was only because I didn't see the point. You were innocent, and I didn't have anything to prove otherwise."

Brent's response was a nod to the bigger of his henchmen. Henchman's response was to deliver another blow to Dylan's face. This time, Dylan's knees didn't argue. They simply gave up and crumpled.

Dylan tasted blood in his mouth.

"Look," he said, pausing to spit out blood as he knelt on the ground, "I know what happened to Gemma King, and I know it had nothing to do with Stevie's murder. We can forget all this. Just give me my son. You have children of your own. This has nothing to do with Luke. Nothing at all. Do what you want to me, but you have to let Luke go."

He managed to stand—for about thirty seconds. The next punch had him landing face first on the concrete. He was about to get up but a boot in the ribs made him change his mind.

"So what happened to the little whore?" Brent towered above him.

Dylan pulled in a breath and forced himself into a kneeling position. There was no point attempting to stand. It would give them an excuse to kick him to the ground again. "She spent the afternoon with Al, a fellow junkie. They enjoyed heroin-fuelled sex. She also popped a couple of painkillers. She threw him out because she had another more important caller due. You. She also had a bottle of vodka. So, by the time you arrived, she was away with the fairies. Heroin, codeine, vodka—it doesn't mix well. You'd already decided you'd had enough of her, and you didn't want her telling anyone what you'd been up to, or causing a scene, so you gave her a helping hand and pushed her down into the bath water. Anyone could have done it. She was so far out of it she wouldn't have known anything about it. She wouldn't have been able to put up a fight."

Brent said nothing. He simply stared down at Dylan as he tapped the envelope against his thigh.

"Am I right?" Dylan asked. "It doesn't matter to me. It doesn't matter to Gemma either. If you hadn't pushed her under, she would have drowned anyway. She'd been admitted to hospital twice before in a bad state. It was only a matter of time."

"Exactly." Brent bent low to hiss the words. "It matters to no one. If I hadn't given her a helping hand, she'd be dead anyway."

"So indulge me. Exactly why did you kill her? Was she planning to talk?"

"Who knows? She was attractive, remarkable really, and she was very obliging. But she was never in the real world so it was impossible to know what she'd do. It was a risk I wasn't willing to take."

"Right. Well, as you've seen, I can't prove any of it, and I'm not interested anyway. All I care about is my son. Where is he?"

"He's safe enough."

Dylan scrambled to his feet, dragged in a breath, and hurled himself at Brent. "Where the fuck is my son?"

"How do I know you haven't kept a copy of these photos?"

"You don't. You'll have to accept my word. Christ, what would it matter if I had? They don't prove anything, do they? You're often in Anderson Street. You walk that way to the crematorium to visit your mother's grave, don't you? Who in hell would believe that Mr. Jeremy Brent had been visiting local prostitutes? No one."

Brent looked far from convinced.

"As for Stevie Greenwood," Dylan said, "I don't think you had anything to do with—"

"Are you still talking about him? I never even knew he existed until I read about it in the fucking newspaper. Why would I waste my time on him?"

"You wouldn't," Dylan said. "Look, let's forget it, shall we? Just give me my son."

"Okay." Brent traced a circle in the concrete with an expensive leather shoe before nodding at his henchmen. "But first, Mr. Scott, you need to be taught a lesson. You also need to be warned that if you whisper a word about me to anyone, you and your son will have a lot to worry about."

Dylan managed to remain standing after the first punch. The second floored him. He didn't feel the third. When the boots went in, he lost all sense of place and time.

All that registered, and not before time, was a flashing blue light. The police car drove up to the fence and effectively blocked the exit.

"You stupid bastard, Scott," Brent yelled. "Get off him, you morons."

Brent clearly thought he was going to talk his way out of this. He was wrong.

He only managed a "Good evening, constable," before the mill's old doors burst open and six officers emerged to arrest him and his cohorts.

Frank helped Dylan to his feet and managed to prop him against the wall. "We've got Luke. He's safe."

Relief washed over Dylan. "Where?"

"He was at Brent's office. Unharmed. Quite happy."

"Coppers might not take any notice of me," Dylan yelled at Brent, wobbling on legs that remained wary of any form of cooperation, "but they still listen to ex-Detective Chief Inspector Willoughby."

An officer was reading Brent his rights.

"I hope you managed to catch all that, Frank," Dylan said.

"Loud and clear," he confirmed.

Dylan nodded with satisfaction. "A word of advice for the future, Brent. Never arrange meetings outside derelict old buildings without first checking inside, okay? And always remember that old buildings with smashed windows make it impossible to hold a private conversation."

Brent was in handcuffs, and was being led, along with his sidekicks, to the waiting police car.

"Be seeing you in court," Dylan called.

Dylan dragged in the welcome air. Every bone in his body hurt like hell, but by some miracle, he didn't think anything was broken. "Where's Luke now?"

"At the station," Frank said. "A car's on its way."

"My car—"

"Christ, man, you can hardly walk, never mind drive. Although I have to say you take a punch pretty well."

"Why, thank you. I was quite impressed myself, especially as I don't get much practice. Good of your chums to indulge me. It wouldn't have been half as much fun if they'd turned up a couple of minutes earlier."

Frank snorted with amusement. "Here's a car. Let's get you to the station."

The drive took little more than five minutes, and it gave Dylan time to regain his breath and double-check that no bones were broken. His ribs objected every time he took a deep breath but, other than that, he was okay. Whether he'd be able to move in the morning was a different matter altogether though.

Frank led the way into the station, through a busy room where people were either shouting into phones or tapping away at computer keyboards. It took Dylan back to his time on the force.

They walked along a corridor and Frank pushed open a door into a small and cluttered office. There, sitting on a chair, with a bacon sandwich in his hands as he laughed with a female police constable, was Luke.

"Dad!" He dropped the sandwich, ran to Dylan and threw his arms around him.

Dylan held him close. The relief, the guilt—he was incapable of speech. Several times he tried to speak and each time the words lodged in this throat and brought tears to his eyes.

"He said he was a friend of yours," Luke said, and he spoke defensively as if he might be in trouble for talking to strangers.

"I can imagine." Dylan's voice shook. "You okay?"

"Yeah." Luke thought about it. "Yeah, I'm good. It was a bit—"

"Scary?" Dylan suggested.

"Yeah. I suppose it was. Only a bit though."

"There was never anything to worry about," Frank told Luke. "Your dad had everything under control. You can both stay at my house tonight. In the morning, you can come back and give your statements."

"You got him then, Dad?" Luke was fine. Or he soon would be.

"Of course."

But he hadn't. Jeremy Brent had walked his way into a murder charge all on his own. He'd be kicking his stupidity all the way to his prison cell.

Brent didn't matter though. All that mattered was that Luke was safe. Dylan could have wept with relief. Never again, he vowed. Never again would he put any member of his family in danger for a single moment.

# THIRTY-SIX

As soon as they'd completed the seemingly endless paperwork at the police station, Dylan and Luke jumped in the Morgan and began the drive home.

"Your face looks awesome today, Dad. It's bright purple. Does it hurt?"

"It hurts like hell. Still, at least nothing's broken." At least, he hoped not. He wasn't fully confident about a couple of ribs. The bruising would soon go. A decent glass of whisky and a night in his own bed would help. He was still shaken though, and his stomach churned every time he thought of what might have happened to Luke. "Maybe we won't tell your grandmother what happened, eh? She'll only worry."

"Too late. I phoned her this morning."

Dylan groaned inwardly. He'd told his mum that Luke had caught the train up because there was a local football match they wanted to watch.

"What did she say?"

"She said I shouldn't exaggerate."

They both shared a chuckle at that.

"I can tell Charlie, can't I?" Luke asked.

"Why not?"

So long as Luke continued to see it all as an adventure, one in which he'd been safe enough because his dad and his dad's friend Frank had been on the case, he'd be fine. He *was* fine. He was young, and Dylan had long been fascinated by the way nothing fazed teenagers. Perhaps he'd been the same at that age.

"What will happen to him?" Luke asked.

"He'll be sent to prison for a long time." A very long time, hopefully.

"He was nice to me. Did I tell you he let me watch DVDs in his car? That was well cool."

"You did mention it." Several times.

"He said he's got two sons not much younger than me."

"So I believe."

Letting Luke watch DVDs and playing the family man didn't make up for bundling him into a car right outside the school gates, driving him all the bloody way north and tying him up in his bloody office. Bastard. Dylan hoped he got sent down for several decades.

Seeing him on a murder charge was extremely satisfying though. In a way, the fact that he'd panicked for no reason at all and talked his way into that murder charge was even more satisfying. Brent wasn't as clever as he liked to think.

Dave Edwards would enjoy splashing Brent's spectacular downfall across the pages of the *Chronicle*. Dylan would call him later. First, he needed to get Luke home. And he needed to calm down.

The journey took almost an hour longer than usual, but Dylan finally turned the Morgan onto his drive. A grotesque stone gargoyle thing that he'd never seen before sat by the front door. If his mother had put it there to ward off intruders, she'd probably chosen well. The trouble was, it would deter guests too.

"That's Geoffrey," Luke said.

"Sorry?"

"That stone thing. Gran—Vicky calls it Geoffrey. She thinks he's cute."

"Cute?" Dylan shook his head in despair. "With any luck, the bin men will cart it away with the rubbish."

Luke grinned. "That's what I told her."

They walked through the front door and the usual, wonderful, familiar bedlam ensued. Dylan loved the chaos of it all.

Bozo grabbed the spotlight. The dog was so excited to be reunited with his beloved Luke that he bounced on the spot as if he were on a trampoline. Dylan thought he'd bang his head on the ceiling if he kept it up.

Freya was knocked over by Bozo, gave the matter no thought whatsoever, probably because she was used to it, and put her arms out so that Dylan could lift her.

"Hey, gorgeous. What's new with you?" He covered her face in noisy kisses that made her shriek with laughter.

She chattered her usual gibberish, each word punctuated with a pinch of his face that hurt like the devil. He didn't care though. His family was safe, Brent was behind bars awaiting trial—all was well.

His mother even made him a coffee when everything had calmed down a little.

"I've been introduced to Geoffrey," he told her.

"Isn't he adorable? I couldn't resist him when I saw him on the market stall. Bozo loves him too. He was wary at first, and kept barking at him, but now he drops a ball in front of him and waits for Geoffrey to throw it."

"Yeah? It's no wonder that dogs fits in so well here."

She smiled. "So how are you, love? Your face tells a good story. Looks like you came off worst."

"You should see the other bloke."

"There was only one?"

"Actually, there were three of them. Well, two and a half." Brent wasn't likely to throw any punches.

"I'm suitably impressed."

She said no more about it, but he knew she would later.

Meanwhile, he picked up his phone and had a long chat with Dave Edwards about Brent. Edwards was too excited by the news to make a lot of sense, but Dylan didn't care. He could print what he liked. Brent was spending another night in a police cell and that was good enough for Dylan.

When the kids were in bed, Dylan's mother went outside to smoke a joint, then came back inside cradling a mug filled with one of her obnoxious herbal concoctions.

"Luke seems okay," she said.

"I think so." He nodded.

"Does he realise how much danger he was in?"

"He wasn't in any real danger." Dylan shuddered at the lie.

"Hmm." She wasn't convinced, but at least she didn't intend to argue. "He says you're driving him to school in the morning."

"Yes. He's got an exam so he has to be there. I'll go straight to the office after I've dropped him off. There's sure to be a ton of stuff I need to deal with."

"Let's hope so. It would be terrible if you turned out to be as dispensable as the rest of us." She was still cackling with laughter as she took herself and her drink to bed.

WHEN HE ARRIVED at his office the following morning, the receptionist he shared with others in the building handed him a couple of messages. "Bobby's out," she said. "She was in early, but you've missed her."

Dylan thanked her, climbed the stairs to his office and groaned when he saw the number of sticky notes covering his desk and computer screen. The damn things were everywhere and they came in all shapes and sizes. Bobby was obsessed with them. A heart-shaped yellow note read *Mail received in second drawer on left. All dealt with.* If she'd dealt with it, there was no need to mention it. Was there? Another note read: *Don't forget your mum's birthday.*

Okay, so that was one reminder he'd asked for. They'd had a long argument about why setting an alert on his phone wasn't the answer—the alarm would sound at an inconvenient time and he'd still forget—that had ended with Bobby demanding to know if he'd always been so hopelessly inefficient and him asking if she'd been born anally retentive.

He was smiling at the memory as he picked up the phone to call the florist.

To pass time, he worked his way through every sticky note until his desk and screen were clear.

When lunchtime finally rolled round, he called Luke. "How was the exam?"

"Awful. I'll tell you about it later. Can't stop now because I'm late for football practice."

The afternoon dragged because he couldn't concentrate on anything. He was glad to leave the office.

He arrived at Luke's school half an hour before the last lesson finished. Minutes ticked by and he found himself growing more and more angry as he imagined Brent sitting in *his* car to wait for Luke. Bastard. Brent could rot in that damn cell.

Luke walked out of the school's gates surrounded by several boys. They were all chatting and laughing, heavy bags slung over their shoulders, and Luke was so engrossed in whatever they were discussing, he walked straight past the Morgan.

Dylan jumped out and called him.

Luke turned back, a frown on his face. He said something to his friends, and wandered back to Dylan. "What are you doing here?"

"What? Well, I said I'd drive you home."

"You didn't."

"Of course I did."

"I didn't hear you." Luke looked along the road, but his pals were already out of sight. "I don't want a lift home. We're stopping off—" He took a quick step back. "Oh, no. Freya's the one who needs a babysitter, not me. I'm not being driven to school and back every day like a five-year-old. I'd never live it down."

"I'm not babysitting—"

"Yes, you are. God, this is so embarrassing." He gripped his schoolbag even tighter. "I appreciate the sentiment, Dad, but I'm not a baby."

"Luke—"

"No. I'll be home in an hour or so." He raced off, shouting over his shoulder, "Catch you later, Dad."

THE HOUSE ALWAYS seemed too quiet when Luke and Freya were in bed. As Bozo elected to sleep on Luke's bed, Dylan couldn't even throw a ball for the dog.

"You're pacing," his mother said.

He couldn't relax. Couldn't sit still for more than five minutes.

"You can't fit an electronic tag on Luke," she said,

"so you may as well accept that he doesn't want or need watching 24/7. You were just the same with Bev. I remember she had to lie just to get a day to herself."

"That was different."

"No. Luke values his independence far too highly to tolerate any interference in his life. Just as Bev did. Just as most people do."

She was right, of course. Life went on. "I know that. I'm going back to Dawson's Clough tomorrow."

"Really?"

"Yes. I need to find out who killed Stevie."

"Do you have any suspects?"

"Yep. Ruby Wilson, for one. She's currently blackmailing a footballer. It's a long story, but she thinks she'll get a million quid out of him. If Stevie had talked, which is about as likely as me getting elected as pope, she would have needed to change her plans. I think she'd find a million pounds worth killing for."

"Why is she blackmailing him? What does she have on him?"

"He's a footballer, and she knows he's gay. She's also his mother, as bizarre as that sounds."

"That's nice. I wish I had a gay son to blackmail."

Dylan laughed at that. "And what would you do with all that money? We'd be up to our blasted eyes in beads and gargoyles."

"You're lucky I have simple tastes."

Dylan *was* lucky. She might be crazy, and she might be turning his home into some sort of weird otherworld place, but she'd always been there for him, and she'd always been there for Bev and the kids.

"Or her husband," he said. "Bill Wilson. Outwardly, he's a charming, jovial man who'd do anything to help anyone, but I'm not convinced. They own a pub in the Clough, and I'm planning to break in and have a look round."

"Great idea. I enjoyed prison visiting the last time you ended up there."

"It'll be fine."

She ignored that. "Or as you're so keen to take all these beatings, perhaps I'll bring grapes to your hospital bedside."

"I've only taken one beating, and that's the first I've had in years. No, it'll be fine."

Even to Dylan's ears that had an ominous famous-last-words ring to it.

# THIRTY-SEVEN

DYLAN PUSHED OPEN the door to the Pennine Hotel and stepped inside the warm, plush interior.

"Someone's left something for you, Mr. Scott." The receptionist did a double take as she saw his swollen cheekbone and black eye. "Wow. Are you all right?"

"Fine, thanks. Just a bit of a disagreement with two blokes who were bigger than me. So who's left something for me?" He'd never been keen on surprises.

"Here it is."

She reached beneath the curving desk and handed him a gift bag in which was a bottle of whisky. Dylan read the small tag that hung down: *Thank you! Rachel.*

He felt an even bigger fraud now because he'd done nothing to solve the mystery of her sister's death. He'd been born with a suspicious mind, and he'd got lucky with the photo and the girl at Forget-me-nots who remembered Brent buying flowers that day, and that was all. Brent had walked right into the role of killer. All Dylan had managed was to put his own son in danger, and he'd never forgive himself for that.

"Thanks. It's nice to know I have friends. By the way, do you have a copy of the local paper I can see?"

"Of course." She took one from behind the desk and handed it over. "You can keep it."

"Thanks."

He took his bag, the bottle and the newspaper up to his room and threw them on the bed.

Returning the bottle to Rachel would be rude, but he'd have to see her and explain that he'd had very little to do with it.

Meanwhile, he glanced through the pages of the *Chronicle* that contained little other than Brent's arrest. He'd seen the story break nationally, but he'd been curious as to what slant Dave Edwards had put on it. It was quite restrained. And factual. There were several mentions of Brent's dubious past though, and a lot of photos—including the blown-up version of the one Stevie had taken.

His phone rang and the display lit up to tell him Bobby was calling.

"Hi," he said. "Everything okay?"

"Better than that. I got Heather's stalker."

"Really? So it wasn't wishful thinking on her part after all."

"It wasn't. He was following her everywhere. I handed him over to the police last night and when they checked out his background, they soon got a warrant to search his house." Bobby's Liverpudlian accent became more pronounced as her excitement increased. "The walls were covered with pictures of her. He'd been writing her letters, talking of all the kinky things he wanted to do to her. He hadn't sent any, but he's been in trouble with the law before so he's currently banged up. Good work, yes?"

"Excellent work. Congratulations."

"It was disappointingly easy, actually," she said, "but he's a seriously warped bloke. The police described him as dangerous. She's a lot safer now he's in custody."

"Well done."

"I thought so. Um, does that mean I can pay myself for this month?"

"Oh, hell. Sorry. Is it very late?"

"No. It's not due till next week, but I'm skint."

"Then pay yourself," he said. "And take that boyfriend of yours out for a slap-up meal. Put it on expenses."

"Yeah? Wow. Thanks, Dylan."

"Everything else okay?" he asked.

"Yes, it's ticking along. There's nothing that can't wait until you get back, but I'll give you a shout if anything crops up."

As he ended the call, it was with his usual sense of shock that not only had he employed a woman in the first place, but that she was so damn good. Bobby was a godsend.

He pulled on his thick jacket and ventured out into the cold. An angry wind blew icy snowflakes in his face, but for once, the cold was welcome on his bruised cheekbone.

He walked through the town, stopped at a coffee bar for a hot drink, then carried on to the station. It was so cold he thought Rachel might have stayed at home, that was if she was still selling the magazine and hadn't returned to working the streets, but she was standing outside the station wearing her official bib and holding just one magazine.

"Hey," she said, and her face lit up briefly before she frowned. "What the hell happened to you?"

"A disagreement with Jeremy Brent and his chums."

She winced. "Jesus."

"It looks worse than it is. Anyway, I came along to

thank you for the bottle of whisky. You shouldn't have, though. I did nothing really. It's a long story, but Brent thought I had proof that he'd killed Gemma. I had nothing of the sort. He confessed to me when I was lucky enough to have the police within earshot."

She shook her head. "No, it was all down to you. You were the only person who bothered to think about that receipt for those flowers. The only person who cared."

"I hate to say this, but she would probably have died anyway."

"I know." She chewed on her bottom lip for a moment. "Gemma was always—different, I suppose. She never seemed to cope very well with anything. On the surface, she was a great laugh. The life and soul of every party. But underneath, there was always something missing."

She painted a sad picture of her sister.

"At least you're doing okay," he said. "I'd better buy that magazine."

She laughed. "You don't have to."

"No, but I'd like to. Is it the last one?"

"Yes. I've done well this morning."

He gave her a five-pound note and told her to keep the change.

"Do you fancy lunch?" he asked. "I'm starving, and I was going to try that Italian place. It used to be good, but it's changed hands and I haven't been there for a year or more."

She tugged at her bib and pulled a face. "I'm not dressed for it."

"I suggested the Italian place, not the Ritz. You're fine."

"Is it pricey?" she asked, doubts in her eyes.

"I don't know, but it's my treat so it doesn't matter, does it?"

"Really?" She still seemed doubtful.

"Yes, really. I hate eating alone. You'll be doing me a favour." He actually enjoyed eating alone. Preferred it to eating in company. It gave him chance to think, and watch people. It also meant he didn't have to suffer small talk.

"Okay, then. Thanks. I warn you now though, I could eat a horse. It's this cold weather."

They set off toward Market Street and the temperature seemed to drop with every step. The wind cut through bones like a knife, and Dylan was pleased when they reached Marco's.

Rachel appeared to relax when she realised that the other diners, without exception, were dressed casually. No one bothered to dress up for lunch these days. Certainly no one in Dawson's Clough bothered.

She relaxed even more when she saw the menu. "It's a good job they print it in English."

"It helps." He doubted there were many Italian speakers in the town.

"God, I'm ravenous." She studied the menu carefully, running a finger slowly down the choices. "I love pasta, but I can have that at home. Not this good, obviously, because it's only the packet stuff, but even so."

Just when Dylan thought she'd never be able to choose, she settled on Pollo Panna. Or, as Dylan preferred to call it, chicken that had been dunked in a creamy sauce.

Dylan ordered his usual—Bistecca Pepe Verde.

"What's that?" she asked, peering closely at a menu he thought she'd memorised. "Found it. Sirloin steak cooked in green and black peppercorns, flambéed in brandy. Sounds nice."

"I'm hoping so. What about wine? Red or white?"

"Red, please."

"Rioja?"

She nodded. "Thanks."

They made small talk. Rachel was fascinated by the red leather seats, matching red napkins and the small flower arrangements on every table.

"Have you ever been to Italy?" she asked.

"Several times." He guessed at her next question. "It's a beautiful country full of beautiful people. So much style on show—the people, the buildings, the cars. And the sun's always shone when I've been there."

"Did you go with your wife?"

"Yes."

"Do you miss her?"

"Yes."

"It's hard, isn't it?" she said. "I wake up every morning, suddenly remember that Gemma's not here, and know that my day will be sadder than it should be."

That was exactly it. That moment between sleeping and waking was great, but it was only a split second before reality hit. The rest of the time was bloody hard.

Their food was brought to the table and Dylan was grateful to concentrate on his steak. It was as good as he'd hoped.

"Have you found out anything about Stevie Greenwood's killer?" she asked.

"Not a lot. I don't suppose you've heard anything?"

"Nothing."

"Do you ever go in the Sportsman?"

"I've been in a few times. Not often though. It's

cheaper to buy booze from the supermarket and drink it at home."

Dylan nodded at the truth of that. "Do you know the landlord and his wife? Bill and Ruby Wilson?"

"Not to speak to," she said. "He seems all right, but she's a miserable cow. One night, she was walking down Canal Street. It was late, about midnight, and me and another girl were having a smoke. She gave us a look and said, 'You young whores deserve all you get.' Cheeky bitch. We told her to fuck off."

"What was she doing on Canal Street?"

"Walking back to the pub, I suppose. I don't know."

"When was this?"

"A month or so ago." She took a drink of wine. "Her husband's having an affair, did you know that? With the woman who runs the post office on Burnley Road. She's a quiet, mousy thing. Looks quite prim and proper. Her husband died a couple of years ago. But yeah, he often visits her. She lives next door to the post office. Mind you, if I was married to that miserable cow, I'd have an affair too." She ate for a few moments, savouring every mouthful. "What makes you ask about them?"

"Oh, just curious really. Stevie used to drink in the Sportsman and Ruby got annoyed because he poked his camera in people's faces."

She smiled. "He did. Some people used to pose for him, it was just a laugh and Stevie meant no harm, but other people got angry with him. I don't think he ever understood that people didn't like being snapped all the time."

"I don't suppose he did." Stevie hadn't been a people person. "The footballers occasionally drink in the Sportsman, don't they? Chris Elliott sometimes stops there before going to Catch-22. What do you know about him?"

"I know he's just got engaged. A pity that. He could have whisked me off to Italy any time. But I only know what I read in the papers. Me and him don't exactly mix in the same circles. I've been known to wander up Manchester Road and see how the other half live, but that's as close as I get to our superstars."

"The woman who runs the post office, the one Bill Wilson is having an affair with, what's her name?" Dylan asked.

"Sharon something-or-other. I don't know her, but I've heard people call her Sharon."

"How long has Bill been seeing her?"

"A couple of months, maybe more. Why do you ask?"

"Just curious. Nosy, I suppose."

She began chatting about the dramas taking place in the TV soaps she watched. Dylan had no knowledge of them whatsoever, but he didn't mind listening to her. She was good company. The food was excellent, as was the wine, so all in all, it was an enjoyable way to spend an hour or so.

When he'd paid the bill, they left Marco's and went their separate ways. Rachel was going to her flat, and Dylan was returning to his hotel room. He wanted to catch up with Frank and hear the latest on Brent. He also needed to prepare for the night ahead.

He took the long route, thinking and planning, and was almost level with the Sportsman when he spotted two familiar faces. Familiar heads at least. It was impossible to mistake Jo's mass of dark hair. She and Paige were about ten yards ahead of him, and they were having an earnest conversation. He'd go further and say they were arguing.

He quickened his pace until he was behind them.

"It's all Chris, Chris, Chris!" Paige was furious, her voice a hiss. "What about me? I stand to lose everything if this gets out. My job, my reputation, my future—"

"Hey, you're forgetting the money." Jo's words were heavy with sarcasm.

Something must have alerted Jo to his presence because she spun round. "Oh—"

"Hello, Jo. Paige." They both looked startled. And caught out.

Jo was wearing a grey woollen coat and jeans. A blue scarf was wrapped around her neck. A large leather bag was slung over her shoulder and gripped between her arm and waist. Paige wore a black coat, black trousers, black boots and black gloves. She looked as if she were going to a funeral.

"What brings you two here?" he asked. "Chris, I assume?"

"Yes." Jo managed a smile. "Mum wanted to see him so, as I've got a couple of free days, I begged a ride. And Paige can't keep away."

"That's nice."

"It would be," Jo said, "but Chris is on some hospital visit with the rest of the players so we're bored."

They hadn't looked bored.

"In that case, let's have a coffee to pass the time." He'd only just had some to wash down the wine.

"Oh. Okay." Jo gave Paige a helpless look. "Yes, that would be good."

"I don't think there's a coffee bar round here," Paige said.

"I know just the place," Dylan said. "Come on."

"I can't," Paige said. "I have things to do." She glared at Jo as if daring her to argue.

"Are you sure?" Dylan asked.

"Yes. I'll catch you another time." Paige strode off, fury in every step.

"Perhaps it was something I said," Dylan said lightly. "Come on. Let's get that coffee."

He led the way past Catch-22 and to the trendy coffee bar that served drinks in mugs the size of thimbles. It was good coffee though.

They sat on high red-leather stools by the window.

"So what's your mother finding to do if Chris isn't around?" he asked.

"I don't know. She went straight out. I didn't ask where she was going." She looked pale and nervous.

"Chris told me about Ruby," he said. "And about the fake engagement."

"Yes, I know." Jo smiled suddenly, and it was like a light being switched on. From darkness to light in an instant. "Ruby's such a bitch. She won't get away with it."

"Blackmailers rarely prosper," Dylan said.

"Poor Chris." Jo cradled her coffee cup in her hands. "It must be awful for him to have a mother like that, mustn't it? When he first thought of tracing her, we were all for it. Paige and I encouraged him even. I suppose we were as curious as he was. God, what a mistake that was."

"Hindsight is a wonderful thing."

"Yes." She kept fiddling with the strap of the bag that was still slung over her shoulder. "Another ten years and Chris's career will be as good as over. It might even be over sooner. You never know, do you? A bad injury can end a footballer's career just like that." She clicked her fingers. "It won't matter then, will it? No one will care so no one will be able to hurt him."

"It shouldn't matter now."

"I know. I don't think it does outside football."

"Perhaps other sports are the same."

"Maybe," she said. "I don't know."

Dylan didn't either. He'd only recently come to re-alise that being gay was a big no-no if you were a foot-baller.

"Chris is very sensitive," she said. "He always has been. So easily hurt. It's not fair, is it?"

Dylan didn't know how to respond to that. It was easy for him, he was a lot older and possibly wiser, certainly more cynical, but he really couldn't see that it was such a big deal.

"Is it?" she said again.

"Life isn't fair, Jo."

"No. I don't suppose it is." She sighed. "Matt's nice. At least, I think so. And Chris does, obviously. He can be a bit—wild, but his heart's in the right place. He won't hurt Chris."

"I only met him briefly, but he seems nice enough."

"Yes. Yes, he is."

"How does Paige feel about it all?" He was curious about the argument he'd overheard. "I suppose she'll look a bit silly if it all comes out."

"Yes." Jo sighed. "She and Chris discussed this en-gagement ages ago, before Ruby started interfering. I always said it was a stupid idea. But Chris wanted a fi-ancée and Paige was willing to help out." She sighed again. "Paige has always dreamed of starting her own magazine and Chris said he'd help finance it if she agreed to pose as his fiancée. If this gets out—"

"It'll be the end of her dream," Dylan guessed.

Jo nodded. "It's not just that though. She believes that

no one will take her work seriously. Perhaps she's right. Having made such a big thing of the engagement, she thinks she'll lose all credibility when people realise it was a pack of lies. She's convinced she'll never work as a journalist again."

She was probably right.

"Anyway, enough about my moans and groans." Jo dragged up a smile. "How are you enjoying life up north? Do you think there's anywhere in the country colder than Dawson's Clough?"

"No."

"It's funny, but I quite like it. I'm not sure why, there's just something about the place."

Dylan knew exactly what she meant. It would be so easy to hate the old mill town that was surrounded by those bleak, forbidding moors, but it had a magic all its own.

"So do I."

They finished their coffees and exchanged the warmth for the cold. At least it had stopped snowing.

"I'll go and see if Chris is home yet," Jo said. "It's been nice bumping into you again though."

"You, too, Jo. Take care."

She strode off with her dark hair being whipped around in the wind and her bag clutched tight against her side.

# THIRTY-EIGHT

RUBY WASN'T HAPPY about this, but what could she do? When Daphne Elliott had phoned the Sportsman, Ruby had been so relieved she'd been the one to answer, and so worried that Bill would overhear, she'd agreed to Daphne's request that they meet at Dawson Manor Gardens of all places.

"Three o'clock. The greenhouse," Daphne had snapped.

When Ruby had first moved to Dawson's Clough, she'd paid the gardens a visit. It had been busy that day. People had thrown coins into the pond, stretched out on the terraced lawns to enjoy the sunshine, or hired the tennis court for an hour or two. Today it was deserted apart from a couple of women with young children who walked round the petting area, where a couple of sheep and a few rabbits were available to feed and stroke. Half a dozen silver-speckled chickens followed in their wake.

Who in their right mind would meet at a greenhouse?

Ruby hadn't returned to the gardens after that first visit and she had to refresh her memory. She remembered the kiosk that sold hot and cold drinks and snacks, and she stopped there to ask for directions to the greenhouse.

"It's the best place to be on a day like today," the woman serving the tea told her.

Ruby followed her directions and found it easily

enough. It was half-hidden by tall chestnut trees, but it was huge.

When she stepped inside, the hot, humid atmosphere took her breath away. She obeyed the many instructions to close the sliding door behind her. She was alone.

The greenhouse was filled with tall, sweeping palms and dozens of exotic plants that she'd never seen before. She walked the long length of it, but she wasn't interested in the small signs that explained the plants' origins.

The door slid open, startling her. A woman—tall, slim, elegant and blonde—came in.

This wasn't Daphne Elliott, was it? In the one and only photo Ruby had seen, she'd been dark-haired. Perhaps she was wearing a wig. It was difficult to tell because a black hat and dark glasses completed the woman's outfit.

It was her. Oblivious to the humidity that was making Ruby melt, she sat on a wooden bench and patted the space beside her.

Ruby strolled over, sat and nodded a half-greeting. There was no response.

Everything about Daphne, from her leather shoes to her woollen coat, shouted money. And why wouldn't it? She was a barrister and her husband was an architect so they'd be rolling in the stuff. Her life would be an easy one. She'd know nothing of the long hours and hard work involved in trying to run a profitable pub.

"So we meet at last," Daphne said.

Ruby didn't know what to say to that. She felt awkward, out of place.

"You know blackmail is a criminal offence, I assume?" Daphne's tone was haughty and superior. She could damn well go to hell.

"I'm blackmailing no one," Ruby said, some confidence returning.

"Really? And how do you reach that conclusion?"

Perspiration broke out on Ruby's top lip. It was another bitterly cold day with a raw wind that clawed at your bones, and she'd dressed appropriately in fur-lined boots and padded coat. Now she was sweating.

"I have photos the newspapers will be interested in seeing," Ruby said, "and I merely gave Chris the chance to buy them."

Daphne smiled, a cold, calculating smile. She was definitely wearing a wig. Chanel No.5 perfume too. Ruby had treated herself to some once, when she'd been abroad and had been able to buy a duty-free bottle at the airport. It had been her favourite ever since, but she couldn't afford it. Daphne would be able to wash the dishes in it if she chose. Ruby doubted she ever washed dishes though. She'd have a dishwasher or someone to wash them for her. Probably both.

"Chris won't pay you," Daphne said.

"Fine. That's his choice."

Daphne gave her a long, slow appraising look. Ruby could see her taking in the scuffed boots and last year's coat with its worn cuffs.

"When Chris was young," Daphne said, "I told him how his mother, such a lovely woman, had been heartbroken when she was forced to give him up for adoption. I gave him the saccharine version of events in the hope that he'd grow up to know that he was loved by all. In hindsight, I should have told him of the evil person you really are. That way, he would never have been foolish enough to track you down."

Ruby shrugged. It mattered not a jot to her what tales Daphne had spun the boy.

"What pleasure do you get from attempting to ruin his future?" Daphne asked.

"I get a life for myself," Ruby said. "The sort of life I would have had if he hadn't come along and spoilt everything."

"You foolish, foolish woman. You spoilt your own life. Can't you see that? Most of us had more sense than to lie on our backs for a few minutes' fun with a man. Surely you were intelligent enough to realise the possible consequences."

Ruby felt the hot colour flooding her face. She'd been too naive to give the consequences a second thought. Not for a moment had she imagined that she might get pregnant. "What's done is done."

"Yes." Daphne crossed slim legs. "Do you know that the maximum sentence for blackmail is fourteen years in prison?"

"Like I said, I'm not blackmailing anyone." Ruby hadn't known the precise length of the sentence, but she wasn't a fancy barrister like the woman sitting next to her. "I merely gave Chris first refusal on photographs I have in my possession. If he doesn't want them, that's fine. All he has to do is say so."

"Photographs that you stole," Daphne said. "You do realise that theft is a criminal offence too, don't you?"

"I didn't steal—"

"Ah, but you did. You took a young man's camera without his permission. That's theft. You then stole photographs that he'd taken. All in all, you're looking at a very lengthy prison sentence. I'd be very surprised if you were released within fifteen years."

An involuntary shiver ran the length of Ruby's sweat-soaked spine.

She wondered if Chris had told his mother about the meeting they'd arranged for Monday night. He was going to pay up, she knew it. Perhaps he hadn't mentioned it to her. Ruby wouldn't if she were in his shoes.

"The thing is," Daphne said, "I don't really want the world to know that Chris's birth mother is in jail. It will be very unpleasant for Chris and the tabloids will make a lot of it. You're good tabloid material."

Ruby had no idea what she meant by that. Good tabloid material? Whatever she meant, Ruby knew it wasn't a compliment.

"Because of that, I'm willing to offer you a chance of freedom. You remove yourself from Chris's life completely. You destroy the photos. You forget you ever saw them. In return, I won't bring charges against you." She brushed an imaginary speck of dust from her coat's sleeve. "If, on the other hand, you so much as whisper Chris's name to anyone, I will make sure you spend the next fifteen years behind bars. Do I make myself clear?"

Ruby wasn't sure how it worked, but she was reasonably confident that Daphne couldn't have her put in prison. People sold photos to the newspapers all the time. There was nothing wrong with that. Maybe she had blackmailed Chris, but really, that depended on how you looked at it. Any judge would have to believe her when she said she'd merely asked if he wanted to buy them.

Either way, even if Daphne did take her to court, the result would be the same. Her son would still be the gay footballer that the newspapers and fans would hound for the rest of his career.

No, Daphne was bluffing.

"You must do what you must do," she said, rising to her feet. As far as Ruby was concerned, this conversation was over.

Daphne jumped up, bristling with anger. "So what do you intend to do?"

Ruby guessed that Daphne was used to people obeying her every whim. "I intend to go home. You've said what you came to say, haven't you? If I'd known that you simply wanted to make threats—"

"I've made no threats."

"No? I'd say that telling a mother to keep out of her son's life—"

Daphne's hand flew up with lightning speed to deliver a stinging blow to Ruby's right cheek. "You're not his mother. You're not fit to be anyone's mother."

"I'm sure you'll know far more about this than I do," Ruby said, rubbing her cheek, "but I think you just assaulted me. Now, I don't know about you, but I have things to do. Goodbye."

Ruby walked toward the door, her head held high and her heart racing.

"You've been warned!" Daphne's voice was a high-pitched shriek. "Don't say I haven't warned you!"

Ruby closed the greenhouse door behind her and let out a cry when a hooded figure leapt out of the greenery and ran off in the direction of the woods. She put a hand to her chest to steady her racing heartbeat and took three long, deep breaths before carrying on her way.

She was out of the gardens, walking along the road, when she saw him again. It had to be the same man.

Tall, thin and menacing. He was walking toward her, his hood so large it covered most of his face as well as his head.

He stopped in front of her, barring her way. She tried to sidestep him, but he simply jumped in front of her. "I know you," he said.

"I don't know you." She didn't want to know him either. Again she stepped to the side, and again, he did likewise.

"You barred me from that dump you call a pub."

She'd barred several people. No way was she serving the town's dregs and this man was scum. One only had to look at him to know that. "I'm sure you deserved it. Are you going to move out of my way or—?"

"Back there—" He nodded in the direction of the gardens. "Back there, it sounded to me like you were expecting a windfall."

"If you were eavesdropping—"

"Me? Nah. Sometimes, if I've got a drink, I go to the greenhouse." He waved an empty vodka bottle in her face. "It's warm in there. Quiet too. Better than that shit-hole you call a pub. I was going there just now until I re-alised it was—busy." He swayed in front of her. "What have you got then? How much are you going to make? How much are you going to give me to keep quiet?"

"I'm giving you nothing. You know nothing. You have no idea what you're talking about." She was quicker this time and managed to get past him.

She ran, and heard his laughter following her.

"My mates will make you talk," he called after her. "When someone tells you Al sent them, you'd be wise to talk. It would be good for your health…"

# THIRTY-NINE

THE SPORTSMAN WAS heaving when Dylan arrived. The pub's darts team and pool team had been playing and there was barely room to move. Dylan couldn't decide if this was a good thing or not.

There was almost an hour to go until last orders were called so the crowd was sure to thin out soon.

Despite the hours he'd spent thinking about this, he still didn't have what any sane person would call a feasible plan. He'd checked out the small window that led to the toilets. It was a tight squeeze, but he could just get through. He kept dismissing the idea in favour of not having to break in though. If he hid in the cleaner's cupboard for a couple of hours, he should be fine.

As he'd had wine at lunchtime, and as he wanted a clear head for the night, he had to make his single pint of beer last and that went against his nature.

Finally, Bill rang a small brass bell that sat on the bar. "Last orders, everyone!"

A larger than usual crowd rushed to the bar before it closed. When Bill and Oscar had served them, Dylan finished his drink and put the glass on the bar.

"Are you having another?" Bill asked.

"No, thanks. I'm off now. I'll probably see you tomorrow night. Goodnight. Goodnight, Oscar."

He left through the main door, went around the side of the building to the back door, made sure no one was around in the corridor between bar and toilets, and headed for that broom cupboard. It was unlocked, as it had been since Dylan had first thought up this idea. He got inside easily enough and pulled the door closed after him. It would serve him right if Bill or Ruby decided it needed a padlock tonight.

It was floor-to-ceiling height, about six feet wide by three feet deep, and it housed several brooms, mops, buckets and cleaning solutions. The lack of space was easy enough to cope with, but the smell was vile. Chemicals, perhaps, although it smelled as if something had died in here.

There was a little ventilation through gaps round the door, but nowhere near enough.

What he'd do if someone needed to use a mop, he had no idea. He'd have to pretend he was so drunk that he'd mistaken the broom cupboard for the toilets and then fallen asleep. He'd been drunk enough to do that in the past. Many times.

Either side of him, doors kept opening and closing. He could hear every trickle from the gents' toilets, but he couldn't hear what was happening in the bar.

He waited. And waited. Finally, when a quick look at his phone told him it was after midnight, he heard Bill muttering to himself as he turned locks and slid bolts across the back doors.

He'd give it two hours, he decided. At two o'clock, he'd leave his cupboard, walk through the bar and then go upstairs to the private accommodation.

If he could survive the smell for that long.

His back was soon protesting at his cramped position. He'd already shoved the brooms, mops and buckets as far as he could to the other side so he'd have to suffer it for a while.

There was nothing to do other than stand in the darkness, try not to inhale too deeply, and think.

Finding proof that Ruby was blackmailing Elliott was one thing. Outing her as Stevie's killer was another matter altogether. That was about as likely as Stevie rising from the ashes to take a snap of her.

She had motive, yes. With Stevie effectively silenced, any monies from her little blackmailing scheme would be safe. Opportunity? She didn't live far away, she could easily have slipped out of the pub, walked to Stevie's flat, knocked on his door—

He would have let her in without argument. He'd let anyone in. She'd catch him unawares, putting a knife in his chest before he had a chance to realise what was happening. He'd have been too shocked, and in too much pain to fight back.

Maybe.

Possibly.

There was Elliott to consider too, of course. He was far stronger and fitter than Ruby. Fitter than most people. It would have been easy enough for him to go to Stevie's flat and commit murder.

Dylan tried to check his phone, but his fingers were too big in gloves and the touchscreen was temperamental. He took off a glove and checked the time. When ten more minutes had passed, he'd leave this cupboard. He put his glove back on.

He froze as he heard a sound. A footstep? If it was, it was a very light one. A thin beam of light was visible beneath the door for a second.

It must be Bill. He must have decided to pay his

mistress a visit. Why else would anyone be creeping around in the middle of the night? *Shit*. He could be gone for hours.

Now what?

He'd give it another couple of hours and review the situation. If Bill returned in the early hours, which he'd have to if he didn't want Ruby alerted, Dylan would look pretty bloody silly poking around in their private accommodation. He'd passed himself off as a drunk countless times but there were limits to his acting skills.

At two-twenty, he saw that beam of light beneath the door again. It was unlikely to have been Bill visiting his mistress as he would have struggled to get to the post office and back in half an hour. There was nothing to say he was meeting her at her home though. Perhaps she'd been outside the pub. He'd heard no sounds and it was difficult to imagine Bill being so light on his feet. Perhaps Ruby had been prowling. She wasn't exactly nimble footed though. These nocturnal goings-on were unnerving. Dylan had expected to have been in and out by now.

He decided to give it another hour, hope whichever of them had been creeping around with a torch had finally gone to sleep, and then escape his cupboard. If the worst came to the worst, and he had a horrible feeling that it might, he'd either feign a quick heart attack or be too drunk to do anything but pass out in front of whoever caught him.

The next hour went by without incident. No sound. No lights. Nothing.

Time to go for it.

He almost did give himself a heart attack when he tried to squeeze his way out of the cupboard and managed to send a broom clattering into a metal bucket. He held his breath, but no one ran to see what all the noise was. No lights came on. It seemed he'd got away with that one.

With only the torch app on his phone for company, he walked, oh so quietly, into the bar. All was silent. He had a quick look behind the bar, but there was nothing of interest. A small safe sat there, but he'd been offered a good look at that last week when Bill had opened it to exchange notes for coins. There had been nothing inside other than cash. He'd seen Oscar open it too. Ruby wouldn't hide anything there.

He eased open a wonderfully well-oiled door that led to the stairs. What was the betting that every step creaked?

He inched his way up, step by step, hardly daring to breathe. So far so good.

Pipes creaked and groaned, but they often did in these old buildings. The layout of the accommodation was unknown, but when Bill had been talking about it once, Dylan had gathered that it was on two floors, with the bedrooms and a bathroom above.

He could smell something familiar. Soap, air freshener, Ruby's perfume or Bill's cologne perhaps?

He tiptoed into the room to his left and was delighted to see a study of sorts. Desk, chair, filing cabinet—but no computer. There was a lead dangling where a laptop might have lived.

Ruby probably took the damn thing to bed with her.

He eased open the filing cabinet. Receipts from breweries had been thrown in with a bill for painting the exterior woodwork. Filing clearly wasn't Ruby's or Bill's forte.

He moved on to the kitchen—small, cluttered, not particularly clean and devoid of laptops. Plates sat in a large white sink waiting to be washed. A circle of breadcrumbs surrounded a greasy toaster. A dirty teaspoon had been discarded on the small round wooden table. The next time food was on offer in the bar, Dylan decided he'd pass.

A sitting room housed two leather sofas, wooden armchair, coffee tables, books and magazines but no laptop. To give himself more light, and to save his phone's battery, he switched on a table lamp. Dust clung thickly so it wasn't much better than his phone. Dylan wasn't averse to clutter—the many and varied contents of his own house always looked as if they'd been dropped from a great height—but this was filthy. Dust was thick and even in the dim light he could see cobwebs. He still couldn't see a laptop though.

Maybe Ruby *had* taken it to bed with her.

There was a cupboard on the landing built under the stairs. The door was probably alarmed, and the hinges were sure to squeal at forty decibels, but he had to open it.

He carefully eased it open. It didn't make a sound. He shone his phone-cum-torch into the cramped interior and saw an old vacuum cleaner, a chain saw—what the hell?—and three black bin bags.

If there was a book on how to open a polythene bag without making a sound, Dylan hadn't read it. He unfastened the knot on the first one and peered inside. It had been filled with old shoes, some ladies' and some men's.

The second bag held more old clothes. He pulled out a coat, hoping to find a laptop hidden beneath it. There was no laptop, but there were a couple of dark stains on the coat. Blood? It was impossible to tell, but his heart began to sing with a burst of wild, glorious hope. Given the general filthy state of the house, it could be anything. But it could be blood.

The final bag wasn't hiding a laptop either. It was filled with old plates and mugs that rattled enough to wake the dead in the next county.

He left the bags as he'd found them—except the one containing that stained coat which he placed on the landing to steal later.

He was going to have to venture up the next staircase and look in the bedrooms. While the occupants slept. Sometimes, it was fun to take a breath and mentally tot up the number of crimes he was committing. Now wasn't one of those times.

That smell was there again. It wasn't unpleasant, far from it.

The stairs to the top floor were thickly carpeted and his footsteps were silent. This was all going fairly well and he gave himself a mental pat on the back.

The door to his left was open and he peered inside. He held his breath as he saw a sleeping figure in a king-size bed. Just one figure. There was no sound, no movement. No movement at all. No snoring. No deep breathing that he'd associate with sleep.

He took a step inside the room. The smell was different here. It was more metallic.

He lifted his phone as high as he dared and let the torch light up the bed.

What the—?

The light was crap and he had to take a step closer to see what was lying on the floor.

He turned his attention to the sleeping figure. Except it wasn't sleeping. Few people chose to sleep with a pillow covering their face.

He removed the pillow and shone his torch straight onto Bill's face. Bill's eyes were open. They stared but saw nothing. Above his eyes and slightly to the right was a gaping hole where a bullet had entered.

Ruby lay on the floor beside the bed. Her face was a grotesque mask of surprise punctuated by a single bullet hole.

Dylan checked for a pulse, but he was the only person breathing at the Sportsman.

# FORTY

"This," Frank said, "has to be your best yet. What in hell's name were you thinking, Dylan?"

"I was thinking that, at worst, I could find the photos that Ruby was using to blackmail Elliott."

They were sitting at a table that was as private as was possible in the Dog and Fox. Snow was falling steadily outside, as it had been all day, but the pub was a haven of cosy warmth. It was far removed from the Sportsman. Lights reflected off dark polished wood, and log fires crackled cheerily. Every time Dylan enjoyed the Dog and Fox, he wished it were at the end of his street.

An elderly man sat in a high-backed wooden chair next to one of the fires and his equally elderly dog snoozed in front of it.

"What did you do after you found the bodies?" Frank asked.

"I did the only thing possible. I legged it. Or rather, I spent another half hour looking for that computer, and *then* I legged it. I could hardly call 999 and say I'd found a couple of corpses, could I? That would have stretched even my talent for talking bullshit."

He felt guilty about leaving the gruesome discovery for the cleaner, but he'd had no choice.

"You always were the master of the understatement," Frank said. "And when they learn you were in the building? What then?"

"They won't. I wore gloves. I was careful."

"What about the clothes you found? Where are they?"

"I've sent them to a lab I use. They're great, and have a really fast turnaround. Much faster than the boys in blue will get."

"Bloody hell, Dylan, you can't steal stuff from a sodding crime scene."

"In my defence, I didn't know it was a crime scene when I decided to steal it. If the lab can tell me it's blood, then I'll hand it over to the authorities. I'll claim I found the bag in a bin or a park or somewhere. Knowing lazy-arse coppers, they'd have missed it anyway."

"Bloody hell."

"I'm sure that coat has blood on it. There was a pair of black trousers, too, and I reckon they're the same. I'll bet that blood belonged to Stevie. Whoever killed Stevie made a right mess of it. A small knife. They hacked away and let him bleed to death. It was a rushed, amateurish job, and whoever did it would have struggled to leave that flat without getting blood on themselves."

"Okay, so let's say they are bloodstained. You won't be able to tell if it's Stevie's blood unless you hand it over to the police. Unless, of course, you just happen to have something with his DNA on it."

"Funny you should say that, Frank."

Frank rolled his eyes in a despairing way.

"The day I arrived," Dylan said, "I borrowed Stevie's toothbrush when I broke into his flat. Hopefully, they'll be able to get something from that."

"Dear God, this gets better and better. You must have really enjoyed your spell behind bars since you're so keen to go back."

Dylan shuddered at the memory. "Not particularly."

Frank tutted his disapproval, sighed and took a swallow of beer. "So what else do you know?"

"Not a lot." Dylan thought for a moment. "I know that whoever killed Bill and Ruby arrived at the pub at ten to two and left at twenty past. And I know that person was light on their feet. Mind you, if I was breaking in to kill someone, I'd move pretty carefully too. I know they carried a torch—not a particularly bright one. I'm assuming they got in through a small window in the toilets. It's always left open a fraction and is easy enough to knock off the catch. I thought of getting in that way myself but it's a tight squeeze. I'd say the killer is slimmer than me." He shrugged. "That's all I know. What about you?"

Frank drank some beer. "Fortunately, the senior investigating officer is a friend of mine—one of the few I have left on the force—so I managed to have a chat with him. It's too soon to know much though. They're assuming, like you, that the killer got in through that window. The time of death they've estimated as between midnight and four o'clock—they can't be quite as accurate as you yet," he added with heavy sarcasm. "Oh, and the back door wasn't bolted so they assume the killer left that way."

Dylan shook his head. "The killer left by that window. I left by the back door."

"Bloody hell, Dylan."

"What else do they have?"

"Not a lot. I overheard someone saying they thought the gun used was a 9 mm, maybe a Glock, but that's not gospel."

"Whatever it was, it had a bloody good silencer on

it. I know I was at the back of the pub, and not in the main building, and it happened two floors above me, but even so, I'm not so deaf I wouldn't hear two gunshots." He tapped a beermat against the table. "Presumably, Ruby woke at the sound of the shot, or even before, and tried to escape."

She hadn't got far. Dylan wondered if she'd had time to say anything to her killer. "Do they have any suspects?" he asked. "Any ideas at all?"

"None. But why would they? They have no idea she was blackmailing Elliott—"

"Allegedly."

"I think it's time you had a chat with them, Dylan."

No way. "Did they find a computer by any chance?"

"Not that I know of. Why?"

"I think there was a laptop sitting on a desk, and I think whoever killed them took it away with them."

"For the photos?"

"Yes."

"And your chief suspect is?"

Two young men walked into the pub, shaking snow from their coats as they did so. The old dog lifted its head, decided they weren't a threat, and stretched out to enjoy the warmth.

"I really hope I'm wrong," Dylan said, "but Chris Elliott is at the top of my list."

"You hope you're wrong?"

"God, yes. He's got far too much talent to wind up behind bars. He'll be winning us the World Cup in a few years."

It wasn't only that though. He liked Elliott. Surely, the young man who'd written a personal message on the photo he'd signed for Luke couldn't kill a couple in cold blood. Despite the anger and bitterness he must have felt toward Ruby, killing one's own flesh and blood was a step too far.

"It all adds up though," he said. "If his story about the night in the pub is true, and I've only heard his version, the only people who knew he was gay—or could prove it—and who might have informed the media, apart from close family members and me, were Stevie and Ruby. With them out of the way, he's home and dry, isn't he? He can carry on being the fans' favourite, be the darling of the terraces, play for England, do whatever he chooses."

"It's a theory," Frank agreed.

A depressing one.

"He was training with the rest of the team this morning," Dylan said. "I considered going to have a word with him, but I thought I'd wait until I'd seen you."

He'd really hoped Frank had learned something—anything—that might offer up another suspect.

"There's Elliott's fiancée too," Dylan said. "She was in the Clough yesterday. I saw her arguing with Elliott's sister. She was furious because she stood to lose everything if Ruby sold her story to the press. Money, reputation, career—all down the pan if the truth about the fake engagement came out."

Paige had been angry, but angry enough to commit murder? He didn't know her well enough to make a judgement on that. She was certainly slim enough to get through that window. Agile, too, and extremely light on her feet—

"I also learned yesterday that Bill was having an affair. Sharon, I think her name is. Runs the post office on Burnley Road and lives next door to it. Her husband died a couple of years ago, I gather. I was hoping for a word with her, but it's only a small sub-post office and it was closed for the day. There was no sign of life at her home."

"The name means nothing to me," Frank said. "I'll check her out."

"What about CCTV near the Sportsman?" Dylan had looked, of course, because it paid to when you planned to do a spot of breaking and entering, but he hadn't seen any cameras in the vicinity.

"There's a camera in the pub's car park, but it doesn't catch the back of the building."

Dylan had checked it out. "It doesn't work anyway."

"You'd know more about that than me. Apart from that, the nearest cameras are outside Catch-22. There are four along that road and I'm sure officers are checking them as we speak, but it's a long shot."

Dylan had walked past the Sportsman on his way here. The forensics team had been busy so it was possible they might find something by morning.

"I'll have a chat with Elliott tomorrow. Meanwhile, will you let me know if you hear anything, Frank?"

"Of course. I still say you need to have a word with the senior investigating officer and tell him all you know."

"I will. When the time's right."

"And if anyone asks," Frank muttered, "we never had this little chat."

"You worry too much." Smiling, Dylan got to his feet. "We need refills."

# FORTY-ONE

As ELLIOTT WAS TRAINING, Dylan decided to pay the post office on Burnley Road a visit. He'd listened to the news reports about Bill and Ruby but, so far, nothing new had come to light. At least, nothing new had been released to the media. Dylan hoped to God he'd left no trace of his own visit.

The post office was open for business this morning. It was small, but managed to cram in greetings cards, cheap children's toys, stationery and a selection of groceries.

A woman, probably in her forties, emerged from a small back room where Dylan glimpsed a sink and a kettle.

"Hi," he said. "I'm looking for Sharon Strong."

"That's me. What can I do for you?"

She didn't look like the quiet, mousy, prim and proper woman Rachel had described. Makeup and blond hair were immaculate. Fingernails were long and pink. She was wearing a blue woollen dress. Dylan would have described her as smart and attractive. He would also have said she was slim enough to get through that small window at the Sportsman.

What he wouldn't have described her as was a grieving mistress.

"Dylan Scott. I'm a private investigator."

"An investigator? Well—what do you want with me?"

"It's a little delicate. I'm looking into the murder of Stevie Greenwood. You knew him, yes?"

"No." The denial came almost before he'd finished speaking. "I read about it. That's all. I don't know anything about that."

"I see. Let me explain then. My inquiries have led me to Bill and Ruby Wilson. You knew them, I understand. Bill, at least."

Her eyes narrowed to suspicious slits. "Who's said I did?"

Before he could answer, a bell buzzed to announce the arrival of an elderly man. Dylan stood back. "Carry on," he told Sharon. "I'm in no rush."

"Hello, Arthur." Sharon stood behind the glass screen at the counter. "How are you today?"

"Mustn't grumble, Sharon." He fished in his pocket and brought out two dog-eared envelopes. "Two. First-class, please."

Sharon took two postage stamps from a drawer and put them on the counter. Arthur was counting through loose change to pay her when he knocked a passport to the floor.

Dylan bent to retrieve it. He flicked it open, saw Sharon's face gazing back at him, and handed it to her.

She might have muttered a thank-you. It was difficult to tell.

Arthur stuck the stamps on his envelopes and left the post office.

Sharon, her face flushed, moved from behind the counter and stood before Dylan, the passport clutched to her chest. "I didn't know Ruby at all, and I hardly knew Bill. I can't help you. I'm sorry. Now, if there's nothing else—"

"You were having an affair with Bill. You must have known him quite well."

"Who says I was?"

"A couple of people have mentioned it to me."

"I knew Bill wouldn't be able to keep his big mouth shut. Idiot." She scowled. "I was good for his ego, that's all. Half of him wanted to keep our affair a secret, but the other half couldn't helping boasting about his ability to attract women. To hear him talk, you'd think he was Brad Pitt."

"Did you want your affair to remain secret?"

"I didn't want people knowing I was involved with a married man. I've never sunk that low before. He was full of talk about how he was planning to leave Ruby, but that's all it was. Talk. He was big on talk and small on action. Not that it's any of your business. Now, if there's nothing else—"

"Are you going away?"

"Sorry?"

"Your passport." He nodded at the item still held tight against her chest. "I wondered if you were taking a holiday."

"No. I'd got it out to check when it expired."

"Ah. I see." He didn't believe her. "I'm sorry about Bill. It must be very upsetting for you. Such a shock."

"Yes. Of course. It was over between us though. I'd broken things off."

"Oh? When was that?"

"A week ago. I told him I was sick of his talk. It was either Ruby or me. His choice."

"And he chose Ruby?"

"Yes."

"I'm sorry."

"It's all for the best. And now I must ask you to leave."

"Do you have any idea who might have done such a thing?"

"Me? No, of course not. Why would I know anything?"

"When did you last speak to Bill?"

"I told you. A week ago."

"When you gave him the ultimatum? Surely he spoke to you after that to tell you he'd chosen Ruby."

She sighed her impatience. "He sent me a text message."

"Do you still have it?"

"No. And even if I did, I wouldn't be showing it to all and sundry." She bristled with indignation.

"How well do you know Chris Elliott?" he asked.

She looked blank. And confused. "The footballer? I don't know him at all."

"Bill and Ruby knew him well. Very well."

"Did they? That's news to me. Now, as I said, I have a business to run. Goodbye, Mr. Scott." This time, she vanished into the back room, presumably trusting him not to steal the stock.

He wasn't going to learn anything from her. She was too tight-lipped, too controlled and far too careful with her answers.

"Goodbye," he called after her. "Thanks for your time. I appreciate it."

He returned to his car, wondering who in hell's name heard that a loved one, either ex—or otherwise, had been murdered in his bed and decided to check when their passport was up for renewal. No one was the only answer that sprang to mind.

Also, who in their right mind would choose Ruby over Sharon Strong?

And how the hell did a bloke like Bill pull a looker like Sharon in the first place?

Dylan drove off, had lunch, then went out to Manchester Road, but there was no sign of Elliott.

A coffee in a depressing little bar with windows made opaque by condensation passed half an hour, and a walk through slush passed another half an hour. Bored and cold, Dylan sat in his car and waited.

At a little after four o'clock, with darkness descending, Elliott's car approached the tall iron gates. Dylan jumped out of the Morgan and ran as fast as he dared on the slush to catch him.

Elliott hit a button and the driver's window silently opened. "I thought you might be paying me a visit. I don't have anything to tell you, but you might as well come up to the house."

"Thanks."

The Audi drove up the slippery incline effortlessly. Dylan almost fell flat on his face twice. He hoped he was invited inside and he hoped the heating was on. His bones were chilled.

Elliott grabbed a large sports bag from the passenger seat, slung it over his shoulder, and walked up to the front door with Dylan. When he opened the door, the warmth came out to meet them.

Elliott dropped the bag in the hallway, took off his jacket and dropped that on top, and walked into the kitchen. Dylan followed.

"So," Elliott said.

"So," Dylan replied.

"I suppose I'm supposed to be grief-stricken." Elliott filled the kettle and hit the switch. "I'm not going to pretend to be that."

"I wouldn't expect you to."

*Edgy* didn't even begin to describe Elliott. Shaking hands went from the belt loops on his jeans, to his pockets, to the set of keys he'd thrown down on the counter. Even his voice sounded higher pitched than usual.

"I'm having tea," he said. "Do you want one? Or a coffee?"

"Tea would be good. Thanks. Milk. No sugar."

Elliott was clearly glad to be able to do something with his hands. They weren't working too well though and he slopped milk all over the counter. He cursed beneath his breath, reached into a cupboard for a paper towel and mopped it up.

"Where were you—?"

"I knew it. I knew you'd think I'd done it. Well, I didn't." He poured boiling water into a couple of mugs. "The police say they were killed sometime after midnight and before four. No one can vouch for me because when they were being killed, I was on my own."

"Doing what? Sleeping?"

"I was driving around."

"Where?"

"Up on the hills around Todmorden and Burnley."

"At two in the morning?"

"Yes."

"Why?"

"Because I couldn't sleep and I wanted to get out of the house. My mother was staying here, as were Jo and Paige, but they were in bed, and the house was too quiet."

He pulled a couple of stools from beneath a bar and sat on one. Dylan sat on the other.

Luke would be so impressed if he could see his dad sitting next to Elliott, in Elliott's fancy kitchen, drinking tea. The irony was that Dylan wished he could be anywhere else right now.

For Elliott to say he'd been out driving around was foolish, to put it mildly. He'd had three guests in the house at the time and Dylan was sure that any of them would have been more than happy to provide an alibi.

"Where exactly did you go?" he asked. "You must have passed some cameras that can prove where you were. Did you drive through town or go on the motorway? If you only did a couple of miles on the motorway, you're sure to have been captured on camera."

"I told you, I went up in the hills." Elliott's voice was filled with despair. "I didn't go anywhere near civilisation. Unless there are cameras on those narrow roads, which I doubt, I can't prove I wasn't at the pub killing Ruby and her husband."

"Draw a map," Dylan suggested. "Think back and draw a map of the exact route you took. I'll check it out for cameras."

"You believe me?"

Dylan didn't want to extinguish Elliott's small spark of hope, but he didn't want to lie, either. "I'd like to."

"That's something, I suppose." He took a pen and a couple of envelopes from a drawer, returned to his stool and began to draw his map. After a few moments, he stopped and threw down the pen. "I can't do it. Once I got out on the hills, I just turned down any road that looked peaceful. I parked up for a while and sat in the car listening to the radio."

This wasn't going well. Dylan had a suspect with no alibi.

Still, that wasn't the end of the world. Killers, and Dylan had met a few in his time, usually made sure they had watertight alibis. Watertight alibis that it took days or weeks of probing to find a leak.

Elliott pushed pen and envelope away. "Every time the phone rings, I expect it to be the police."

"Why would the police want to see you?"

"Have you told them Ruby was blackmailing me?"

"I haven't spoken to them. Yet."

"But you will?"

Dylan shrugged. "You've seen more of Ruby than I have. Was she blackmailing anyone else?"

Elliott's eyes shone as if Dylan had handed him a lifeline. "Hell, I hadn't thought of that. I bet she was. She was vicious and vindictive enough. This could have nothing to do with me after all."

"It's possible." Dylan took a sip of his tea. It was too hot. "But that wouldn't explain why Stevie was murdered, would it?"

"No." Elliott began chewing on a fingernail. He was as edgy as hell.

"So you have no ideas at all?"

"No."

Dylan was convinced he was lying. He knew something. Either he'd killed them, or he knew who had.

"Where was Matt at the time?" he asked.

"Oh, no. Matt had nothing to do with it. Why would he? Of course he wouldn't. That's insane."

"Didn't he say he'd do anything to help you?"

"Well, yes, but not that. It's only a figure of speech, isn't it? For fuck's sake, I hated Ruby. Matt hated her too. Everyone I know hated the damn woman. But no one goes out and kills someone just because they hate them, do they?"

"Actually, yes. They do. So where was Matt?"

"In London. Working."

"In the middle of the night? Come on, Chris, you can do better than that."

"It's true. He's raising interest in a film he's hoping to make and as little's been forthcoming from the U.K., he's trying to break into America. Half a dozen people, Matt included, were in a TV studio in London, discussing all sorts of stuff that was being broadcast live on a late-night chat show in the States."

"That's an impressive alibi."

"It's also the truth. If he'd been here, I wouldn't have been driving around the bloody hills, would I? I've told him what's happened, obviously, and he's coming up tomorrow. He had nothing to do with it, I can promise you that."

Dylan didn't trust alibis connected to any sort of technology. Cameras *did* lie. What appeared to be live could have been filmed days or weeks beforehand.

The drive from London could be done in three hours at a push. Dylan knew that from experience. Anyone leaving London at ten o'clock would have reasonably clear roads and would be in Dawson's Clough by one o'clock. That person could then do the dreaded deed and be back in London for six.

Unless he'd hired a car under a false identity, that would be easy enough to check. There were plenty of cameras on the motorways, too many of the damn things when you were in a hurry as Dylan often was.

"Will the police want to speak to me?" Elliott asked.

"That depends. If you were at the Sportsman and you left any trace behind, then yes."

"I told you, I was nowhere near the place."

"Then, no. I don't suppose they will."

"What sort of trace?"

"Anything. A fingerprint, a footprint, fibres from clothes, blood, saliva, hair—anything."

"I was nowhere near the place." He took a swallow of his tea and pulled a face. "What about the photos Ruby had? What do you think will happen to those? Will the police find them?"

Was that interesting or not? Dylan couldn't decide. He'd firmly believed that whoever had killed Bill and Ruby—and Elliott was still topping his list of suspects—had taken the computer with them. Maybe they hadn't. Perhaps Ruby had put it somewhere safe. After all, she'd thought it was her million-pound lottery ticket.

"I don't know."

Dylan's tea was cold now, and too milky for his taste, but he drank it anyway. "Did you know Bill was having an affair?"

"Was he? Did Ruby know?"

"I don't know. Apparently he was seeing Sharon Strong, she owns the sub-post office on Burnley Road."

Elliott shook his head. "I don't know her. Perhaps Ruby *did* know about it though. She was planning to leave Bill. At least, that's what she told me."

"Perhaps she did know." Dylan jumped off the stool. "Okay, I'll be off now."

"That's it?" Elliott sounded surprised.

"Yes."

"But what will happen now?"

"I don't know. There's nothing you can tell me, though, so I won't waste any more of your time."

Elliott seemed almost reluctant to let him go. And that *was* odd.

"Will you let me know if you hear anything?" he asked.

"Yes. And if you think of anything, or anyone apart

from yourself who might want Bill and Ruby dead, give me a call, will you?"

"Of course." Elliott threw his unfinished tea in the sink and showed Dylan out.

Dylan had taken two steps away from the door when Elliott suddenly shouted, "Wait!"

Dylan turned around.

"I stopped for fuel," Elliott said. "I'd forgotten that. They might have had cameras at the filling station."

"More than likely."

Unless he'd stopped at some place in the sticks. But they wouldn't have been open at that time in the morning. The all-night fuel stations would have cameras and probably an automatic registration plate recognition system to make sure people didn't drive off without paying.

"I paid with my credit card." Elliott left the front door open and strode back inside. Dylan followed.

"Where's my wallet?" Elliott looked all round the kitchen then returned to the hallway to the jacket that he'd slung on top of that large sports bag. "Here."

He was so stressed, he could barely open his wallet. There were several notes and several scraps of paper inside. He pulled them all out, tossing stuff on the floor.

"Here." Relief had him leaning back as if he needed the wall to support him.

Dylan took the receipt from him. He'd spent fifty pounds on fuel at 2:07 a.m.

"I don't know exactly when they were killed," he said. "Between midnight and four the police say, but at least this proves that I was driving around, and that I bought fuel in the middle of the night."

Dylan knew exactly when they'd been killed—the same time that Elliott had been filling his car with petrol.

"No," he said. "It proves that someone using your credit card filled up with fuel at 2:07 a.m."

Elliott's face crumpled.

"But they'll have cameras," Dylan added, "so it will be easy enough to check that it was you."

Elliott was still leaning against the wall as if he doubted his legs would support him. His eyes were closed.

"It's easy enough to check credit cards and CCTV but, if I were you," Dylan said, "I'd hang on to that receipt."

"Okay. Yes, I will."

"Right, I'll be off then. Have a good evening."

As he walked down the driveway, almost falling on slush that was now freezing hard, Dylan wondered if Elliott was cleverer—and a better actor—than he appeared.

Elliott had already gone to ridiculous lengths to make himself out to be the blokey sort of footballer that everyone loved, including showing off a brand-new fiancée to the world.

He and Matt could easily have been in on it together. Matt could have killed Bill and Ruby—a few hundred quid in a dodgy bar in London would buy a handgun— while Elliott drove around providing himself with a convenient alibi.

Or maybe he was on the wrong track completely. Perhaps Sharon had been telling the truth in that Bill had chosen Ruby over her. Perhaps murder was the price he'd paid for that choice…

# FORTY-TWO

Thanks to one of Frank's friends, Dylan had CCTV from the filling station where Elliott bought his fuel.

Dylan was sitting on his hotel bed, and had already checked the images for 2:07 a.m. Elliott was easily recognisable. He'd filled his car with petrol, strolled to the window to pay, bought himself a chocolate bar, stopped at the ATM for cash, unwrapped his chocolate bar and taken a bite, returned to his car and driven off. It was definitely Elliott.

That meant nothing though. It certainly didn't mean Matt hadn't been at the Sportsman shooting the landlord and his wife.

Dylan hoped the police were making more progress because he didn't know where to start or even what to do.

He had twenty-four hours' worth of video footage so he started looking through that. It was probably hoping for too much to see Matt stopping for fuel at the same place.

He made a coffee, drank that, and watched countless people buying fuel. Maybe there was something more boring he could be doing. Counting snowflakes perhaps. Or watching daytime TV.

His mind flitted from one thing to the other and kept settling on Sharon Strong. Assuming she'd been lying about checking the expiry date on her passport, what exactly was she up to? Where was she going?

If Bill had promised her they'd sail into the sunset as soon as Elliott paid up, she might have needed her passport. But if that were the case, she wouldn't have killed him and his wife. Not yet. If he'd promised her they'd sail into the sunset when Elliott paid up and then changed his mind—that would have pissed her off considerably. Unrequited love was a bugger. As was a lost fortune...

Hunger pangs reminded him it was past his lunchtime and he was about to head to the dining room when Frank phoned.

"I've just heard," Frank said, and he sounded a little breathless, "that Chris Elliott has been invited to talk to the police."

"You're kidding me. What sparked an interest in him?"

"They found a letter at the Sportsman, one he wrote to Ruby when he found out that she was his birth mother."

"Do they have anything else?"

"Not as far as I know."

"Are they talking to him now?"

"They soon will be. He's said he won't talk to them unless his lawyer is present."

"Wise young man. Makes him sound guilty as hell, of course."

"It does. And they only want a chat."

"He's young and naive. He'll be safer with his lawyer present. On his own, it would all come out—how Stevie took his photo, and how Ruby was blackmailing him."

"Do you think he's guilty?" Frank asked.

"I don't think he did the job himself. He couldn't have because he was buying fuel at the time. However, he's a very wealthy young man. His choice was either pay Ruby a million quid in the knowledge that she might talk to the press anyway and might be back for more, or pay someone a couple of hundred grand to get rid of her once and for all. I know which option most people would choose."

"It's not looking good for him, is it?"

"It could be better."

"There's something else too, although probably not of any great interest. Ruby went out in the afternoon. They think, although they're not sure, that she might have visited the Manor Gardens around three o'clock."

"What would she be doing there? It was snowing. Who the hell would go to enjoy gardens in the snow?"

"I don't know. They can't say for certain if she went there or not, but there's nowhere else up that road. They spoke to staff there early this morning but no one remembers seeing her.".

"Surely they have cameras? Have they been checked?"

"I don't know."

"Who stands to benefit financially from their deaths, Frank? Do we know?"

"No. Ruby had left everything to Bill, and he'd left everything to her. Solicitors are trying to contact relatives."

"Okay. Thanks for that."

When Dylan ended the call, he carried on watching people buy fuel for another twenty minutes. Then, when he could stand it no more, he headed for the dining room and lunch.

A hot beef sandwich later, he jumped in the Morgan and drove to Manor Gardens. It was bitterly cold and, apart from falling snow, there was nothing to see. Everything looked dead. What would be beautiful flowering shrubs in a few months looked like lifeless twigs. Apart from a few snowdrops and crocuses, and some fairly large patches of purple and white heather, there was nothing to see. Even if there had been, Dylan couldn't imagine Ruby being the type to admire anything of beauty.

A small kiosk sold hot and cold drinks and snacks, and Dylan wandered over.

"Hi," he said to the young girl who was ready to pour him a coffee. "Adam Smith, CID. My colleagues were here earlier—"

"Yes," she said, eyes alight in readiness for a tasty snippet of gossip. "I spoke to them. Was there something else you wanted?"

"I was wondering if you had surveillance cameras on site."

"I told them. There's only one and it's over by the greenhouse." She pointed in the vague direction. "It's to keep an eye on the barn where all the equipment's kept, and when I told your people about it, they said it didn't matter. If you go over there, Stan, the groundsman, will be able to show you. I know he's in the barn because he's just been here to get his cup of tea."

"Thanks." Dylan gave her his broadest smile. "You've been very helpful."

"It's to do with this murder, isn't it?" she said with relish.

"We're following up on a couple of leads. Thanks. Sorry, what was your name?"

"Sophie."

"Thanks, Sophie. I'll probably see you again."

And now he was impersonating a police officer. Was there no end to the crimes he was committing this week? No point simply asking to see cameras, though, because someone would start talking about the Data Protection Act and he'd get nowhere. Members of the force could ask for anything and get it.

A man was sitting on a wooden box in the barn, a huge mug of tea cradled in his hands.

"Hi, are you Stan?"

"I am. And you'd be?"

"Adam Smith, CID. I've spoken to Sophie and she said I'd find you here. I gather you're in charge of the surveillance camera."

"What? Well, yes, I am. It only keeps an eye on this track past the barn though. We had a few break-ins but this has stopped them." He scowled at Dylan. "Your lot couldn't catch the buggers."

"Ah. Sorry about that. So could I have a look at the system?"

"It's in the office." He ambled off, limping a little, to a small, untidy and extremely cold room. A single light bulb dangled from the ceiling. "This is it. You have to plug it in to a computer."

"You don't have a computer?"

"Nope. Don't need one. All we wanted was something to stop the buggers breaking in. They see the camera and they know to keep away. This—" he pointed a disdainful finger at the small black box, "—records everything automatically. When it's full, it deletes the old stuff and shuffles it all along. I dunno. Don't really understand it, but that's what the bloke said. You plug it into a computer with one of those connector things, he said."

It was basically an external hard drive.

"Here." He hunted in a drawer in a tatty old desk and pulled out a short cable. "This goes with it."

"Okay, thanks. I'll need to keep it for a few hours. Is that okay?"

"I suppose it'll have to be."

"I'll have one of my men get it back to you as soon as possible."

"It'll be before nighttime, I hope. That's when the buggers try to break in. They're after mowers, leaf blowers, stuff like that."

"I'll make sure it's back before then. Thanks."

Dylan pocketed it before Grumpy Stan changed his mind.

He explored the gardens. It was like a rabbit warren. Paths, used mainly by dog walkers by the look of it, led off in all directions. A well-used path went from the greenhouse to the small wood. Dylan walked through it, met two people walking dogs, and was about to emerge onto the road when he saw a familiar figure shuffling away from him.

He caught up and grabbed Al's shoulder.

"Aw, fuck. It's you again." Al was drunk. "Now what?"

"What are you doing here?"

"None of your fucking business."

"Let's go tell the police then, shall we?"

"What? I'm breaking no fucking law. I've been in the greenhouse enjoying a drink. That's not a crime. It's open to everyone."

"Why go there?"

"Because it saves me putting a fucking quid in the gas meter. It's warm, right? Fucking hell."

"Do you come around here often? Have you seen anyone else here? How about the woman who runs the Sportsman pub? Have you ever seen her here?"

"Should I have?"

"Have you?"

"What do you know about her?" Al rubbed a grubby sleeve across his face.

"What do *you* know?"

Al thought for a minute. "I know she's dead. It was on the front page of the paper. I never knew her. Never seen her here. So can I go or what? Fuck me, it's supposed to be a free country."

"You can go," Dylan said.

Al swayed toward the road. He was drunk enough to walk into an oncoming car. Drunk enough not to feel the impact too.

Dylan was grateful to return to the warmth and comfort of his hotel room. With a cup of coffee to hand, he plugged in the drive and hoped his computer could deal with this particular piece of hardware.

It could, and he was impressed. Very impressed. Manor Gardens was council owned so presumably they'd paid for the system. It was excellent.

The camera had been big enough to deter would-be burglars, but it hadn't looked anything special. The footage, however, was crystal clear. Even at night, when only a couple of security lights from the barn and one from the nearby greenhouse lit the track, Stan could be clearly seen limping around.

It was super easy to fast forward too. Brilliant.

He soon spotted Ruby. She was only on film for four seconds as she walked on the track past the barn, but it was enough. She had to be meeting someone, there could be no other reason for her to be there, and his money would be on Elliott.

During the next hour, only three people walked along

the track. One was Stan, the other was Sophie hurrying to her kiosk, and the third was a woman he didn't recognise. Fairly tall, slim, blond hair under a hat and dark glasses.

Disappointingly, there was no sign of Elliott. Perhaps he'd entered the gardens from a different direction. There was a wooded section used mostly by dog walkers and, if he'd walked through that, he could have met Ruby without passing the camera.

He saw Ruby leaving the gardens. A minute later, the blond-haired, hat-wearing woman walked past the camera.

He saved the eight seconds of footage that showed the mysterious woman coming and going. Maybe Ruby had met her. It was feasible that she was another of Ruby's blackmail victims.

Or could it be Sharon Strong? It was difficult to tell because of the hat and the dark glasses. Blond hair.

Maybe, just maybe, Ruby had met up with her husband's mistress…

# FORTY-THREE

DYLAN WISHED HE could have stayed away from Stevie's funeral, but he couldn't think up an excuse good enough to ease his conscience. He hated funerals. He'd always hated them, but this was the first he'd attended since Bev's and he didn't feel able to face it.

However, when he joined the pathetically small group at the church, he was glad he'd turned up. His presence boosted the total number of mourners to nine.

This would be nothing like Bev's funeral. Dozens of people that Dylan didn't even recognise had turned up for that. Bev had left instructions that everyone must wear colourful clothes and some had looked a little absurd in their bright outfits with tears running down their faces. As awful as that day had been, however, it hadn't been so sad and dismal as this forlorn affair.

He spotted Rachel and Lizzie enter, and he went to join them at the back of the church. Minutes later, realising they made up thirty percent of the mourners, they reluctantly moved to the front row.

A female police officer who looked as if she'd drawn the short straw was present, as was a social worker, and four people Dylan didn't know.

Stevie's sad coffin was bare of flowers, and the vicar stood beside it and told the small gathering that they were here to celebrate Stevie's life. Dylan disliked the man immediately, and disliked him even more intensely when, halfway through his speech, he mistakenly referred to Stevie as Simon.

As far as Dylan could see, there was nothing about Stevie's life *to* celebrate. Perhaps it had gone well for him until he was five years old. In a few tragic seconds, however, he'd lost his mother and spent months in hospital. He'd been handed to grandparents then placed into care. He'd had no real education, met a series of social workers who'd done nothing for him, stumbled through life, been moved out of his home and into another, and had then been murdered in cold blood.

Dylan and the vicar clearly weren't on the same wavelength because Dylan could see sod all to celebrate about that.

They sang "Abide with Me," or tried to. The vicar did his valiant best but, unfortunately, he couldn't sing in tune.

Snow was falling as they stood beside the grave and watched the coffin being lowered into the cold ground. Maybe, Stevie would have a better time in the next life. Dylan didn't believe in any sort of afterlife, but he'd like to for Stevie's sake.

The vicar shook hands with them when the ordeal was over. "Friends of Stephen's?" he asked.

"Yes," they replied as one.

They hadn't been friends though. On the few occasions he'd spent time with Stevie, Dylan had mentally cursed him for his aversion to talking. He'd struggled to keep his patience. Stevie had been kind to Lizzie and Rachel, but Dylan doubted they'd repaid that kindness.

The snow turned to sleet and capped what had been a thoroughly depressing experience.

As he walked out of the cemetery with Rachel and

Lizzie, he switched his phone back on and saw that he had two missed calls from Glyn at the lab. He tried calling him back, but it went straight to voicemail and he didn't bother leaving a message.

"I don't know about you two," he said, "but I'm going to the nearest pub. Fancy coming along?"

"Yeah. I could do with a drink after that," Lizzie said.

"Me too." Rachel wrapped her arms around herself. "Didn't that vicar talk some fucking crap?"

"I hated the way he kept calling him Stephen," Lizzie said. "No one called him that, did they? It was like he was talking about a stranger."

"He could hardly call him Simple Stevie, could he?" Rachel said, and she managed to raise small smiles.

"We'll give him a good send-off," Dylan said.

The nearest pub was the Queen Victoria which, according to a plaque in the entrance, had been serving drinks to the public since 1876. On stepping inside, Dylan decided the barmaid had probably been pouring those drinks. She had thin grey hair, no more than three teeth, and her creased skin was in need of an iron.

If she wasn't the youngest, most attractive barmaid he'd ever seen, it wasn't the best pub, either. It wasn't the worst though. Far from it.

As he ordered their drinks, he realised it was going to be an expensive session. He hadn't done any paid work for weeks, and he had a family that needed feeding, but if he couldn't afford it, neither could the cut-price whore or the *Big Issue in the North* seller.

Still, it was only money and, as his mother was fond of telling him, there was no pocket in a shroud.

"It's getting a bit bloody creepy in the Clough," Rachel said. "First Stevie's done in, then that grumpy old bitch from the Sportsman and her old man. She was hateful to Stevie but I bet she'd have gone to his funeral if someone hadn't got to her first. She enjoyed a good funeral."

"Was she? Hateful to him?" Dylan asked.

"Oh, yeah. Always had it in for him. She had a right go at him one night when all he was doing was having a drink and minding his own business. Mind, it was funny. While she was laying into him, some drunk walked over to her and had a good go at her. In the midst of it, the drunk managed to spill most of a pint of beer over her. She went bloody mental."

"The best though," Lizzie said, "was when someone—can't remember who—put a bag of shopping on the stairs, right in front of the door that leads off the bar. She walks downstairs, opens the door to come into the bar, and doesn't see the shopping. There were tins in the bag. She put her foot on one and her feet went from under her. God, it was funny. Her legs went every way possible."

Rachel was chuckling at the memory. "It must have hurt like hell because she was black and blue for days afterward. Serves her right."

"And what about the time she put that bag of shopping on her coat?" Lizzie asked, and the two women were laughing so hard it was several long moments before Lizzie could tell the story.

"She came into the pub one night. I think it was after last orders. Anyway, she'd called at the late shop and bought some meat. If they haven't sold it during the day, they sell it off cheap at night so she'd gone along to get herself a bargain. Anyway, she walks in, puts her coat on the chair and the carrier bag on top of it." Lizzie stopped to wipe the laughter tears from her face. "She had a moan about Oscar not serving quickly enough, told everyone it was time they drank up and went home, then picked up her shopping bag. Well, the bag had a hole in it and all the blood from the meat had run onto her coat. God, it was funny."

"It was the same day Stevie was killed," Rachel said, and both girls stopped smiling. "It doesn't seem quite so funny after that, does it? God, I hate this. I can't stop wondering who'll be next."

Dylan experienced a sinking feeling, which wasn't easy when you felt about as low as it was possible to be. "What colour was her coat? The one she put the bag of meat on."

"What?" Lizzie looked at him as if he'd gone mad. Perhaps he had. She looked to Rachel. "I don't know. Grey, I think, but I can't really remember. Why?"

"Oh, just curious." Sod's Law said it was the same grey coat he'd sent to the lab. No doubt Glyn and his colleagues were having a good laugh about it.

"Who do you reckon's doing all this?" Lizzie asked. "It must be a serial killer, mustn't it? Gives me the bloody creeps, I know that."

"I'm sure there's nothing to worry about. It's a pretty safe bet that the murders are connected."

"The police say it's not the same killer," Lizzie said, "because Stevie was stabbed and the other two were shot. But perhaps they're wrong. Maybe there's a madman on the loose."

"I don't think so." As they all had empty glasses in front of them, Dylan ordered another round.

The second drink managed to lighten their moods a

little. Midway through the third drink, they were laughing again.

Lizzie bought the fourth round and Dylan was about to take a sip when his phone rang and he saw that it was Glyn.

"We've got the results you wanted," Glyn said.

"And you're going to tell me it was remnants of a sirloin steak, aren't you?"

He could hear the smile in Glyn's voice. "Much of it was cow's blood, yes. Not all, though."

"Oh?"

"There are several small spots of human blood on the sleeves of the coat, and on the trousers. Unfortunately, we can only get a partial DNA from the toothbrush."

"But is it possible that the two come from the same person?"

"Yes. There's a potential match."

"You're kidding me."

"No."

"How confident are you that the two match?"

Glyn wasn't a betting man, but he thought for a moment. "Reasonably."

"Brilliant. Thanks!"

"I assume from the instructions you gave us that the items weren't obtained legally?"

"There might have been a technical infringement of the law," Dylan admitted. "If you can return everything to me at the Pennine Hotel, with no signs of it having been anywhere near a lab for testing, I can make sure they're obtained legally the second time around."

Glyn chuckled. "They're on their way."

The force would have Stevie's DNA on record so all Dylan needed to do was "find" those clothes in a convenient location. That location would need to be near the Sportsman to put them on the right track, and given that police had searched the area thoroughly, it wouldn't be as easy as it sounded.

Did it matter, though? It seemed fitting that, on the day of Stevie's funeral, Dylan was *reasonably* sure he'd found his killer. The fact that his killer had met her own end would have to be justice enough.

Another round of drinks was in order and Dylan was about to organise that when Frank's name flashed up on his phone.

"Does that thing ever stopping ringing?" Lizzie asked.

"I'll switch it off when I've taken this," he told her as he answered it.

"I don't have any details," Frank said, "but I thought you'd like to know that Elliott has been arrested on suspicion of murder."

# FORTY-FOUR

DAPHNE STOOD BEFORE the full-length mirror in her bedroom and, as she did every morning, she inspected her appearance for flaws. She'd lost weight recently, but apart from making her face look a little haggard, that probably wasn't a bad thing. It meant that her light grey suit was a better fit. The skirt touched her knees, and the jacket hugged her narrow waist. Black leather bag and matching shoes had been chosen with the gravity of the occasion in mind. Jewellery consisted of small pearl earrings, a simple gold chain around her neck, and an expensive but understated wristwatch that peeped out from beneath her cuff. Her makeup received another mental tick. It was fine. The pale pink lipstick added enough colour to her face without any hint of frivolity.

The house was silent, but it often was these days. Trevor had left for his office, as Daphne would have if it had been a normal day. There was nothing normal about today though.

She was about to pick up the phone, but her nerve failed.

She kicked off her shoes, lay down on the bed and closed her eyes. A series of deep, slow breaths had her feeling more in control. She could allow herself another hour.

Age was a strange thing. Twenty years ago, she'd done nothing but look to a future that had seemed so bright. These days, she lived in the past. She also lived with a constant feeling of anger, yet couldn't decide where to place the blame for the situation. Ruby, certainly. If not for Ruby, everything would be fine.

She'd wanted to blame Matt, but couldn't. As much as she hated the idea of her son being in love with Matt, she knew that if it hadn't been him, it would have been some other attractive young man. Over and over, she'd questioned her own actions. She knew, on a rational level, that there was nothing terrible about raising a son who was gay. It was on a personal level that she struggled to grasp it. She couldn't help wondering if it was her fault. Maybe if she'd raised him differently, loved him less perhaps, he would have been—she didn't like to use the word *normal* because she knew he wasn't abnormal, but it was how she felt. All the pride she felt was tarnished.

Jo, and Daphne always hated to admit this, had been loved less and had perhaps turned out more mature. More sensible. Daphne couldn't say for sure because she didn't know Jo as well as Chris, or even as well as a mother should.

After years and years of waiting, she'd held Chris in her arms for the very first time and had never, ever wanted to let him go. She'd wanted to watch his every breath, hear every word he uttered, inhale his scent and gaze at his perfect form. To discover she was pregnant had infuriated her. She'd wanted nothing to take her away from Chris—even her own child.

Jo had known discipline whereas Chris hadn't. Daphne hadn't thought he'd needed it. Jo had been smacked as a child. She'd been a defiant little thing who had been rebelling ever since.

The fact that Daphne had been jealous of her daughter hadn't helped. Some nights she'd climbed into bed and cried at the knowledge that Chris loved his sister more than his mother. It was mutual too. Jo loved her big brother more than anyone or anything in the world. They shared a bond that didn't allow room for Daphne.

When Chris told her he'd traced his birth mother, Daphne had been beside herself with jealousy and rage. She'd wanted to hit him, to give him the slap in the face that he'd given her. Her life had been devoted to him, and yet he'd been busy behind her back, finding the woman who'd given him up. Daphne would have died rather than give up her son.

She took another long, deep breath. None of it mattered now. It was all over.

It was time to face the music. Time to pay for her sins.

She picked up the phone and called the taxi firm.

"He'll be there in five minutes," she was told.

Five minutes or five hours, it no longer mattered. "Thank you."

She walked down the stairs, took a long look at her home, then stood at the window looking across the garden to the road outside. She wondered if the roses would have a good year, then smiled at herself. It didn't matter. Nothing mattered.

The taxi pulled up, and the driver gave a honk on the horn.

Daphne picked up her bag, walked out and locked the door behind her.

The taxi smelt of disinfectant. She'd bet someone had been sick in it last night, and the idea made her feel like vomiting.

It didn't matter. There would be worse ahead, she was sure of that.

She paid the driver, thanked him and climbed out. It was a few yards and half a dozen steps into the entrance of the police station.

Head held high, she walked up to the desk.

"Can I help you?" a young man asked.

"Yes," Daphne said. "I'd like to confess to a murder. Two murders."

# FORTY-FIVE

"So it's case solved?"

"Yes." Dylan sat back on his sofa and put his feet on the coffee table. It was good to be home. It meant he could prevent his mother from filling his house with any more candles, dream catchers, stone pixies or other assorted crap.

"You don't need to go back up north?" his mother asked.

"No. It's all finished."

"So why are you frowning?"

"Am I? I didn't realise."

She looked at him long and hard. "You don't have your usual smug sense of satisfaction at a job well done."

"I'm just tired." The kids were in bed and Dylan would soon be following them. The drive home from Dawson's Clough had taken five long hours. "And anyway, it wasn't a job done particularly well. Everyone's favourite Tory, Jeremy Brent, talked himself into criminal charges. I wasn't even sure Gemma had been murdered until he said he'd given her a helping hand."

"But you were the one who got him talking, right?"

"Only because the bastard took Luke." Dylan would never forgive himself for allowing that to happen. Rotting in a prison cell was too good for Brent. "Then Daphne Elliott walked into a police station and confessed to Bill's and Ruby's murders. I should have known—I *did* know she'd do anything to protect her precious son's reputation, but I didn't think she'd walked past me as I hid in the bloody cupboard. I knew it wasn't Elliott, but she wasn't at the top of my list of suspects either."

It explained a lot though. The blonde woman in the video Dylan had seen from Manor Gardens had been Daphne. She'd met Ruby at the greenhouse, she'd claimed in her confession, to try to reason with her. As Ruby hadn't been prepared to listen, Daphne had killed her and her husband.

She said she'd bought the gun years ago when on holiday in the States. There had been intruders in a couple of nearby properties and she'd wanted to be able to protect herself. Possibly true, possibly not.

"It feels wrong," he said, "because she's claiming, and I know this is bullshit, that the back door to the Sportsman was open and she got in that way. It was locked and bolted. She's saying she knocked on the door, intending to try to reason with Ruby again, but got no answer. She then tried the door and it was open. When she saw them sleeping, she lost it. It has to be bullshit. The only way for her to get in was through a very small window that opened into the toilets."

"Could she have got through that?"

She was ten years older than Dylan, and almost as tall, but she was very slim and very elegant. He wouldn't have been surprised to learn she'd been a dancer or perhaps a gymnast in her youth.

"Yes, she could."

"Well, I'd look smug if I were you," his mother said.

"All you went up north for was to find Stevie's killer. You did that."

"I did, yes." At least he'd got that right.

He'd carried the clothes into the local police station and said he'd found them in an alley off Anderson Street.

"There was a skip there," he'd told the officer, "and I can only assume this bag had been thrown on the top and then fallen off. That's why it wasn't taken away with the rubbish. Anyway, when I saw a sleeve sticking out with what looked to be blood on it, I thought I should bring it to you. You've got three murders on your books—you never know, do you?"

He'd left them to it, more in hope than expectation, and they'd been surprisingly quick to check the contents and, more important, the DNA on each. Ruby, had she not ended up with a bullet between the eyes, would have been charged and subsequently locked up for the murder of Stevie Greenwood.

At least the file could be closed and Stevie could rest in peace.

"So why aren't you looking smug?" his mother asked. "You usually do that so well."

He smiled at her sarcasm. "It all feels wrong."

"In what way?"

"It's the way Daphne claims she broke in. Either she's lying, and I can't imagine why she would, or she doesn't know how the killer got in."

"What? Are you telling me you don't think she did it?"

"I don't know. It just doesn't feel right." That was probably simply gut instinct letting him down. It wouldn't be the first time, and it wouldn't be the last. "Still, at least

I'm home now. I need to catch up on work stuff, and I need to spend time with the kids. I've missed them. I've missed my home too. We'll go out somewhere tomorrow and do nothing but enjoy the day."

"That sounds like a plan."

"Yeah. And pouring myself a celebratory whisky sounds like another. After all, I did find Stevie's killer."

# FORTY-SIX

---

*It's snowing today. Not proper snowflakes, not the big white fluffy ones. This is wet, slushy snow, the sort that soaks you through and gets grubby as soon as it hits the road. It's being blown against the window and soon I won't be able to see anything.*

*I suppose I should be talking about regret. It's so easy to question our actions, isn't it? So fruitless too. We often have to make decisions in an instant and don't realise that we could regret those actions for a lifetime.*

*Me? I don't regret anything. If I had to do it all again, I would.*

*Don't think I reached the decision for this final act in an instant. I didn't. I thought about it long and hard, and decided it's what I want.*

DAPHNE WONDERED IF this was a letter she needed to write. She couldn't say much because prison authorities would check, but she had to tell Chris, one last time, that she loved him more than life itself.

Without saying the words, she had to let him know that she didn't blame him for what he'd done. Deep down, a small part of her admired him for it. Killing Ruby and that husband of hers would have seemed like his only option.

Daphne couldn't allow him to suffer for his crime. It had been bad enough for him when the press had learned that he was in custody, and they'd had a field day when news of Ruby's blackmailing her birth son came to light. He had his future ahead of him. If they'd imprisoned him for murder, Daphne would have had no life so the end result would have been the same. She willingly gave her life for his.

*I can't clearly remember what my life was like before you came into it, but I know it was lacking. You've been everything to me. All I ever wanted and more. I hope you'll have a good life. I hope you'll be as happy as you deserve to be. I know things will be difficult for you now that everything's come out, but you're strong enough to deal with it. Be an openly gay footballer and be proud, stand up for yourself and for the rights of others. Set an example. Above all, be happy, Chris.*

*Don't be sad when they tell you the news and give you this letter. That's the last thing I want. I can't spend years of my life in this prison cell so I'm taking the coward's way out.*

*Give my love to*

A tear dropped onto the paper and was quickly followed by several more. Daphne wiped her face with an impatient hand.

*Jo. Tell her I'm sorry. For everything.*

She folded the sheet of paper and left it in the centre of the table.

There was another hour to go before the noise died down and the lights were extinguished.

Daphne lay on the narrow, uncomfortable bed and waited.

Trevor would be shocked, but he'd get over it. Their marriage hadn't been anything special for years, since before Chris even. He'd take good care of Jo, and he'd help Chris—they'd be fine.

The lights went out, and Daphne's heartbeat took off at an alarming rate. There was no time to think. No regrets, she reminded herself.

She slipped her hand under the mattress and pulled out the razor blade that she'd stolen from the shower room a couple of days ago. It wasn't as sharp as it could be, but it would suffice.

She pulled in a breath. This job needed to be done now so there was no hope of finding her before she'd bled out completely.

A cut lengthways into her artery—

Her last thought would be of Chris, and of the way the world had looked like a giant snow globe and full of promise on the first day she saw him.

# FORTY-SEVEN

As DYLAN DROVE across the hills that watched over Dawson's Clough, he had the feeling it would be for the last time. He needed to be home for his children, and he needed to earn a decent living. Gone were the days when he could take off for the north and leave Luke and Freya in Bev's capable hands. He was needed.

He wasn't really sure why he'd come back today. Twice during the journey he'd almost turned around and gone home. Everything was neat and tidy in Dawson's Clough. Brent was awaiting trial, Stevie's killer was dead, and Daphne had committed suicide.

Perhaps he'd come because it was *too* neat and tidy.

The more he thought about it, and he struggled not to think about it, the more convinced he became that Daphne had been innocent. And he'd bet she'd confessed to save her son from a life sentence.

Elliott couldn't have murdered Bill and Ruby because he'd been buying fuel ten miles away at the time, but he could have instigated it. He could easily have paid someone to do the deed for him.

On the surface everything was tied up. In reality, there were too many loose ends. Nothing made sense. The way Daphne had lied about breaking in to the Sportsman, the fact that she couldn't remember the actual shooting—whether Bill and Ruby were both in bed, whether she'd shot them in the heart or head—it simply didn't add up.

So if Daphne hadn't killed them, and Dylan would bet his life that she hadn't, who the hell had?

Dylan had booked a room at the Pennine Hotel for the night, but he didn't know if he was staying or not. Either way, he drove past the building and on to Frank's house.

"You can't keep away, can you?" Frank shook Dylan's hand and ushered him along the hallway, through the kitchen and into a conservatory that looked out at the hills. "Do you want a drink?"

"No, thanks. I'm driving."

Frank glanced at his watch. "I was only offering tea or coffee. It's a bit early, even for me, to hit the bottle."

"In that case, I'll have a coffee. Thanks."

While Frank clattered kettle and cups in the kitchen, Dylan stared out at the hills. It was bitterly cold, and a stiff wind gnawed into your bones, but the sky was an almost unbroken blue and the sun was shining, something of a rarity in this corner of east Lancashire.

"If Daphne Elliott *did* kill them to protect her son's reputation," Frank called from the kitchen, "she failed miserably. His face has been on every TV channel and every newspaper. The tabloids especially love a gay footballer, it seems. They've really gone overboard."

"I know. Let's hope he can cope with it."

"He should have thought of that before he spilled everything," Frank said. "One minute he was refusing to talk to coppers until his lawyer arrived, the next he was telling them how Ruby had been blackmailing him because he was gay."

"He got scared, I suppose." Being stuck in a police

interview room opposite two seasoned detectives would frighten a lot of people.

"He's lost that big sponsorship deal." Frank brought in two cups of coffee and a plate piled high with biscuits, and set them on the table.

Dylan grabbed a cup. "Thanks. Yes, so I heard. It seems that gay men can't advertise energy drinks. Bloody ridiculous."

"He was dropped from the team for yesterday's game too."

"Really?"

"Some say he's coming to terms with the death of his mother, which makes sense, some say he picked up a knock during the last match, and some are saying the club are making sure he keeps a low profile until the fuss dies down."

"I expect it's the former." Dylan helped himself to a handful of biscuits. "No one's going to be at their best when their mother's just slashed her wrists in a custody cell."

"Quite."

"I'm planning to see if he's at home," Dylan said between mouthfuls. "I can't think what he might be able to tell me, or rather what he'd be *willing* to tell me, but I'm sure there's something. And I'm sure that if I listen long enough, it'll come out."

"Like what?"

Dylan smiled. "If I knew that, I'd be down in the civilised south."

"He's definitely at home. Or he was. Every reporter in the country is camped outside his gates."

Dylan took another handful of biscuits. "There's no way Daphne murdered Bill and Ruby. No way."

"I'm inclined to agree. There were a few holes in her story, to put it mildly. But if she didn't—"

"There's the boyfriend. Matt's always said he'd do anything for Elliott."

Frank shook his head. "When news broke that Elliott was gay, Matt was questioned. He has a rock-solid alibi. He was being interviewed on some American TV show about a film he's hoping to make. He was in a studio in London and it's all on camera."

"So Elliott told me. That's convenient. A little too convenient for my liking."

"Sounds it, I agree, but it had been booked months ago. When that finished, he raced across London to appear on a breakfast show here in the U.K. That went out live too."

"So Elliott and his boyfriend have perfect alibis," Dylan said.

"People tend to if they're innocent."

"Hmm." Dylan wasn't sure they *were* innocent. "I'll bet they arranged it between them. Elliott could afford to hire a killer. Hell, he could afford to hire a whole sodding army."

It wasn't a good thought. The photo Elliott had signed had been framed and given pride of place in Luke's bedroom. It would be nowhere near as special if Elliott was found to be a killer.

"There's Paige too," Dylan murmured. "She had motive, a bloody shedload of motive, and she'd fit through that window. Daphne might confess to protect her."

Frank nodded. "It would be her way of protecting Elliott."

"Quite. But she wouldn't have needed to take such drastic measures. By all accounts, Paige was at Elliott's house that night along with Jo and Daphne." He munched his way through a chocolate chip cookie. "If I could just find—something. Anything."

"What? Like a shred of evidence, you mean?"

"That would be useful." But there was no evidence. Or none that Dylan could find. Suspects, yes. Evidence, no. "At least our lovely postmistress is in the clear. Daphne wouldn't confess to a murder that Sharon committed."

"Damn it. I almost forgot." Frank strode off to the kitchen and returned brandishing a magazine. He flicked through pages until he found what he wanted. A six-page spread of photos from the fundraiser at the Town Hall. "I picked this up yesterday. Here."

Dylan glanced through the photos of the town's finest in their best clothes. A few photos showed the speeches being made, others highlighted the grand surroundings, and more seemed random pictures of guests chatting.

Frank prodded one with his finger. It showed Elliott signing photos and there, in the background, was his mother Daphne. She was in conversation with Sharon Strong.

"Well, well, well. When I spoke to Sharon, she denied all knowledge of Elliott. I'll see what she has to say about this."

Another coffee, and another plate of biscuits later, Dylan stood to leave.

"May I borrow this magazine, Frank?"

"Of course. I don't know why I bought it. Apart from the photos of our local celebrities, it's full of houses for sale, none that the likes of us could afford, and ads for exotic holidays. A waste of money."

"Thanks." Dylan rolled up the glossy magazine. "I'll have a chat with Sharon Strong, then see what Elliott has to say, and then—" he shrugged, "—I suppose I'll have to leave it and get back to some real work. Work that pays bills."

"I think so," Frank agreed.

"Come and visit us sometime soon, okay?"

Frank smiled. "I thought you'd never ask."

"Yes, well, after Bev—"

"I know. And now?"

"Now it's okay. Everything's different, but it's okay. We're doing well between us."

Frank nodded. "I'm glad. I will come down. You can take me on a pub crawl."

"It's a deal." They shook hands and Dylan walked back to the Morgan.

If he had the brains he'd been born with, he'd go straight home right now. Coming here on a whim had been a ridiculous idea. He had no evidence of anything and was unlikely to find any. Thanks to his suspicious mind, he had plenty of suspects, but no evidence. All he knew was that Daphne hadn't killed Bill and Ruby.

Really, though, what the hell did it matter? He'd come to Dawson's Clough to find Stevie's killer, and he'd done that.

Sod it. It *did* matter because he wouldn't rest until he unearthed the truth.

His first stop was the post office on Burnley Road. Today, three people stood at the counter waiting to be served by Sharon. She glanced up as he entered, and the welcome smile turned to a scowl in a nanosecond. Mr. Popular, he most definitely wasn't. He didn't care. All he wanted was to learn the truth.

As she served the three customers, her mood worsened. She was positively snappy with the elderly woman who'd lost her pension details.

Finally, the shop was empty. Sharon stood, arms folded, behind the counter with the glass barrier between them.

"What do you want?" she asked.

"How well do you know Daphne and Chris Elliott?"

"What? I already told you, didn't I? I don't know either of them."

Dylan opened Frank's magazine and found the photo in question. He pushed it under the glass barrier for her to see. "You look friendly in that picture."

She frowned at the photo, then shook her head and pushed it back to him. "I don't know them. I spoke to many people, most of them strangers, at that fundraiser. I don't recall talking to that woman, but, as I said, I spoke to a lot of people."

"So you don't know Daphne Elliott?"

"Of course not."

"And you have no idea what you were talking to her about?"

"None whatsoever. The weather perhaps. The money being raised for the hospice. I have no idea."

A customer entered carrying a huge parcel.

"Thanks for your time." Dylan took the magazine and left.

He wasn't sure if he believed her or not. Her story was feasible, he supposed. He, too, had spoken to several strangers at the fundraiser.

He jumped in the Morgan and drove out to Manchester Road with sunshine blinding him. That had to be a first.

Frank had been right. Dozens of journalists and cameramen were camped outside Elliott's house hoping for a glimpse of the footballer. A lone police constable stood at the gates.

Dylan had to park some distance away. He walked through the throng of reporters, all of whom wanted to know who he was and what he was doing there. Head down, not speaking or making eye contact, he walked on.

"I'm a friend," he told the constable, and he rang the buzzer.

The intercom clicked into life but no one spoke.

"Hi, it's Dylan. Can I come up?"

The gates opened a fraction, the constable stood his ground, although Dylan had no idea how one copper would stop such a crowd if they decided to breach the gates, and Dylan slipped inside.

The front door opened, but no one appeared. Dylan stepped into the hall.

Elliott peered out from behind the sitting-room door. "Hi, come in."

"Thanks."

He followed Elliott into the sitting room. Elliott threw himself down on a sofa and hoisted his legs onto the coffee table. He was wearing shorts and had an ice pack strapped to his knee.

His sister was pacing.

They both looked like the walking dead.

"You're quite safe," Jo said, trying to smile. "I don't have a drink to throw over you today."

Dylan tried to return the smile and failed as spectacularly as Jo had. "I wanted to offer my condolences. I'm so sorry for your loss."

"Thank you." She'd looked too slim when Dylan had

first met her, but this afternoon she looked emaciated. Her face was a sickly shade of puce. Eyes were surrounded by dark circles.

"It's good of you to call," Elliott said.

Dylan nodded in the direction of the crowd outside. "They'll soon get bored, you know. Some other celebrity will be caught speeding and they'll go and hound them instead."

"I hope so." Elliott spoke with feeling. "They can be very cruel."

No one suggested it, but Dylan sat. He hoped it would stop Jo pacing. He could feel her tension, and it wasn't pleasant.

"Good manners don't get them stories," Dylan said. "Don't take it personally."

"What are you doing here?" Jo asked. "According to the local paper, the police have proof that Ruby killed your friend, Stephen Greenwood. Isn't your work finished?"

"It is, yes. I always struggle to let things go though. I would have liked to see Ruby on a murder charge. Instead, I'm curious as to who got to her."

Two pairs of eyes fixed on him.

"What do you mean?" Elliott asked.

"I know, and you do too, that your mother didn't kill Bill and Ruby. I'm intrigued, that's all. I'd like to know who *did* kill them."

"Are you crazy?" Elliott said. "Our mother is—was a barrister. She wasn't the type to walk into a police station and confess to a murder she didn't commit, was she?"

"I bet she was if it meant saving your skin."

"That's ridiculous," Jo said. "Of course she did it. As

you say, she'd have done anything to protect Chris. If she hadn't killed them, Ruby would have talked. Blackmailers always do. It would have been on the front page of every newspaper."

"It *is* on the front page of every newspaper," Dylan reminded her.

"We hardly need reminding of that. It's not her fault though, is it?"

The tension in the room was palpable. Dylan had expected grief and sadness, but he hadn't expected such anxiety. Jo couldn't sit still. Elliott was sitting, presumably resting his knee, but his hands were shaking and he kept fidgeting with his fingernails. His chest was rising and falling rapidly.

"Our mother killed them," Elliott said, "and that's that. It's all over bar the shouting. And the funeral, of course."

Jo let out a choked sob that she tried to disguise as a cough. Of the two, she looked the most disturbed by it all. That was odd given that she'd never really got along with her mother.

"How's Paige taking it?" Dylan asked.

"Badly," Elliott said. "She can be a bit of a drama queen—"

"That's an understatement," Jo muttered.

"She'll be fine when she's calmed down," Elliott said. "I've told her I'll help finance her magazine. She's a good journalist. People will still take her seriously."

It was difficult to tell if Elliott was trying to convince Dylan or himself.

"What will you do now?" Dylan asked.

Elliott tapped the ice pack. "I'm resting my knee. It's only a silly knock I picked up in training. In another week or so, I'll be back running. A couple of weeks after that, I'll be playing again. Assuming the fuss has died down by then, of course. Assuming I'm picked for the team."

"I don't see why you shouldn't be."

"We'll see. Gay footballers are rarer than rocking-horse shit."

"So is talent like yours in England."

He smiled. "Thanks."

"What about you, Jo?" Dylan asked. "What are your plans?"

"I'll help Dad arrange the funeral, I suppose. When they release the body, that is. He's gone to pieces. All he can do is wallow in his grief—"

"Jo!"

"It's true, Chris. He's falling apart just when we need him to be strong." She looked at Dylan and shrugged. "I'll go back to uni. Life will go on."

She pulled back the blinds a fraction and peeped out. "They're still there." For Dylan's benefit, she added, "I want to get the train back to London, but Chris can't drive me to the station so it means getting a cab. Which means walking out through that mob."

"I can drive you to the station," Dylan said. "Hell, I can do better than that. I can drive you back to London, if you like. That's where I'm heading."

There was nothing for him here. Elliott was sticking to his story. Dylan didn't believe that story, but he had no evidence to disprove it. He might as well go home. God knows what madness had made him come back anyway. He'd go home, spend time with his kids and get back to real work.

"Really?"

"Of course."

"When are you leaving?" she asked.

"I was planning to set off from here, but an hour or so won't make any difference."

"Thanks." She seemed pleased to have reached a decision. "I'll pack a bag and be ready in five."

She ran from the room, leaving a difficult silence in her wake.

"I know you didn't kill Bill and Ruby," Dylan said.

"That's a relief." Elliott tried to joke. It didn't work.

"But I believe you know who did."

Elliott didn't look surprised. He simply shook his head. "As far as I'm concerned, my mother did it. She'd tried to talk to Ruby and, when Ruby wouldn't listen, she did the only thing she could to protect my reputation and my future."

"She didn't." Dylan sighed. "But I don't suppose it matters too much. They're dead, and nothing can change that."

"Indeed." Elliott looked relieved at Dylan's acceptance. "By the way, I've got something for you. Hang on a minute."

He walked out of the room, not limping at all, and came back a minute or so later with a pair of football boots and a large black marker pen in his hand. He wrote on the boots and handed them to Dylan. "For Luke."

"Wow. You're sure?"

"Of course. It's my pleasure."

On one boot, Elliott had signed his name. On the other, he'd written, For Luke.

"Luke will be so thrilled. Really. Thanks so much, Chris. You're a very generous young man. Thoughtful too." He wanted to add "for someone involved in murder," but he left that unsaid. It didn't matter. It was time he went home and left Dawson's Clough to keep its own secrets.

"You're welcome."

Jo returned with a small overnight case and a huge handbag. She dropped them both on the floor and hugged her brother tight. "You'll call me, won't you?"

"Don't I always?"

She pulled back, nodded, then hugged him as if her life depended on him. When she let him go, she looked bereft.

"Will you help me walk past those cameras?" she asked Dylan.

"Of course. Hold my arm and keep going. Don't pause, don't look at them. Keep your head down and keep going. Okay?"

She nodded, but she looked like a frightened five-year-old.

"Here." Elliott produced a canvas bag and put the football boots inside. "Easier to carry."

"Thanks." Dylan shook his hand. "Take care, Chris, and don't let the bastards grind you down."

"I'll try."

Cameras snapped when they appeared in the doorway. Dylan was carrying Jo's bag and the football boots. She gripped her handbag and Dylan's arm.

"Keep walking," Dylan said, and they strode down to the gates.

A barrage of microphones was stuck in their faces. "How's Chris?" "Does he believe there's a place for gay footballers in the England team?" "How have the fans reacted to the news that he's gay?" On and on it went. There were no questions about Daphne's crime or suicide, or the horrors that Elliott and Jo were going through. All they cared about was Elliott's sexuality.

"Almost there," Dylan murmured.

He threw the bags in the Morgan and bundled Jo inside. The few journalists who'd followed them realised they weren't going to get any juicy tidbits and returned to their station at the gates.

Dylan fired the Morgan's engine and drove off.

He was in the middle of town when a thought came to him that shocked him so much he missed a gear. The Morgan grumbled in protest.

"I need to stop for fuel," he said.

"No rush. I'm really grateful for the ride. This is a beautiful car too. I love the colour."

Women always commented on the colour. The Morgan's Daytona Yellow paintwork had been called *pretty* many times. They couldn't see past the colour to admire English design and engineering at its best. When summer came, he'd think about having it sprayed black.

"Thanks."

He pulled into the nearest filling station and climbed out. The Morgan's tank was almost full, but he put in a few more litres and went inside the building to pay. Having done that, he went to the toilets and did the necessary.

Jo was checking her phone for messages when he returned to the car, but she dropped it in her bag and settled down for the journey.

Dylan drove through the town but, instead of taking the motorway, took a left turn and pulled in to the nearest parking spot.

"Get out of the car a minute," he said.

"What? Why?" She laughed. "What are you doing?"

"Just do it."

She did as he asked. He got out and walked around the car until he was standing in front of her. He pushed her back against the bodywork, ignored her cry of surprise, and searched her. No way was he sitting in a car with someone who could be armed and bloody dangerous.

"What did you do with the gun?" he asked.

She laughed again, a nervous shaky sound. "What on earth are you talking about?"

"The gun you used to kill Bill and Ruby. Where is it?"

"Dylan, I really don't know—"

"I was there, Jo. I was at the Sportsman when you broke in through that small window into the toilets."

Shock rendered her speechless for a moment, then she gave a groan. A solitary tear ran down her cheek. She pulled in a breath, which only served to have several more tears following.

"Why?" she asked. "Why didn't you say something before now?"

He shrugged. He hadn't said anything because he hadn't known until now. Until he'd sat next to her in the confines of his car and let her perfume fill the air. Beautiful, unmistakable perfume.

"Why the hell did you do it?" he asked. "How could you be so fucking stupid?"

She brushed the tears aside with an impatient hand. "Why? Because I've always looked out for Chris, that's why. Always. I always have and I always will. He's all I have in my life."

Dylan shook his head as despair washed over him. "So your mother confessed to save you from a prison sentence?"

"God, no. Is that likely?" Her tone was scoffing. "She

confessed because, no matter how many times Chris told her he didn't do it, she didn't believe him. When the police arrested him, that was it. She knew that if she walked into a police station, her precious son would walk out of one."

That was feasible. "She did see Ruby that day though."

"Yes, she met her at some gardens or other. If she'd left well alone—" Frowning, she shook her head. "I had everything under control. I'd sorted it. There was no need for her to get involved."

Dylan felt a little sick. There was no regret or remorse for what she'd done. All that came through was anger toward her mother for interfering.

"So where's the gun? Where did you get it?"

"I stole it from my mother. That part of her story was true. She really did buy it in America because there had been a few break-ins locally."

"Where is it?"

"There was a skip full of builders' rubble on Anderson Street. I threw it in there. It will be long gone."

The police would be able to find it. They'd know where the skip had been emptied.

"Did you steal a computer from the Sportsman?"

She nodded and looked quite proud. "Yes."

"What happened to that?"

"I smashed it to pieces, put it in a rubbish sack and took it to the recycling centre. It's gone."

Dylan wouldn't count on that. He'd bet it could be found.

"Anyway," she said, "it doesn't matter now. The police are happy. Everyone's happy. Well, except Chris.

And there's the irony. I was supposed to protect him and everything's gone horribly wrong."

Traffic raced past them, heading for the motorway. "Get in the car."

Silence settled around them as they sat in the Morgan. Dylan made no attempt to fire the engine.

"Are we going then?" She might have been discussing the weather, or asking if they should stop for a coffee.

"Going where? To London? To pretend that nothing's happened?"

"What else is there to do?"

Dylan couldn't answer.

He could so easily drive her back to London. The police had their man—or woman—and, as far as they were concerned, the case was closed. No one was looking for a killer. Jo could return to university, follow her dream and become a great doctor. Chris had lost his mother, and the world was taking an unhealthy interest in his sexuality, but he'd cope. Possibly. He'd cope a hell of a lot better if he had his sister to lean on.

If Dylan turned her in to the police, he'd ruin her life. Her brother's too. He'd also have to explain what the hell he was doing at the Sportsman in the early hours of the morning.

He fired the engine and pointed the Morgan in the direction of the motorway.

Jo settled down for the long journey home.

His foot pressed harder on the accelerator, but it was no use. After ten miles or so, he took the exit and turned the car around.

"Where are we going?" she asked.

"I need to see someone."

They were soon back in Dawson's Clough.

When he drove into the car park, Jo spotted the police station and threw out a panicked hand at the door.

"It's locked," he said.

"What the hell are you doing? I thought you were my friend."

Dylan killed the engine. "I am your friend. I'm sorry, Jo, but you need help. You want to be a doctor, yet you've killed a couple in cold blood. You can't vow to protect life one minute, and kill the next. Like it or not, Chris will be beneath the media spotlight for years to come and, consequently, will attract lots of nutters. What will you do? Kill them all? I'm sorry, really sorry, but I'm turning you in. You'll get the help you need."

"Are you mad?" She laughed, a bitter, angry, crazy sound. "Do you think they'll believe you? It will be your word against mine. They'll think you're insane."

"They probably would have if I hadn't switched on this recorder when I stopped for fuel." He touched his key fob, pulled off the cover and revealed the USB.

She tried the door handle again, as if it might have magically unlocked. It hadn't. She lashed out in a fit of blind fury, and she was a hell of a lot stronger than she looked.

It took him fifteen minutes to manhandle her into the station.

## FORTY-EIGHT

DYLAN WAS PLEASED he'd booked a room at the hotel. He'd spent hours at the station talking to police yesterday. His own story had been relatively easy—he'd had too much to drink, passed out in the toilets and had been trying to make his escape when he'd smelled the intruder. Why hadn't he reported it? He'd been going to, but then police had taken Chris in for questioning, then Daphne had confessed, so it hadn't seemed important.

Sometimes it bothered him that he could lie so easily and convincingly. Of course, being able to claim the hero of the nick, one ex-Detective Chief Inspector Frank Willoughby, as a friend always helped.

After a few hours' sleep at the Pennine Hotel, he'd been back to the station to answer yet more questions and sign a statement.

Now, he was in Elliott's kitchen trying to apologise.

"I couldn't believe it when she told me what she'd done," Elliott said, wiping tears from his face. It did no good as fresh ones fell. "She's always been overprotective of me. God knows why. But this." He shook his head. "Never in a million years would I have believed her capable of—" He seemed unable to utter the word.

"No one should get away with murder," Dylan said.

"I know. Yes, I know."

"She'll get the help she needs." At least, Dylan hoped

she would. "Psychiatrists will get involved. She'll be fine."

Elliott nodded.

"She might have taken someone else's life," Dylan said, still feeling the need to defend his decision. "If someone had made life difficult for you—"

"I know." Elliott wiped more tears away, then shoved his hands in the back pockets of his jeans. "Not that anyone will make life difficult for me again. I'm giving up football."

"What?" Dylan was horrified. "You can't do that."

"I can. All it's brought me is tragedy. Money, yes. Fame, certainly. It's not what I want though. I can get as much pleasure playing in a five-a-side village team. Matt and I are thinking of moving abroad. Matt will still be able to run his business. Maybe I'll coach young kids. Who knows?"

"But you could be playing for England in a couple of years."

Elliott managed a wry smile at that. "I doubt it. It would be too—awkward. I'm sure the manager would find some reason to overlook me."

"It would be a sin to waste that talent."

"Not really. I can teach youngsters. I'll visit Jo, of course. Wherever I end up, I'll still see Jo. It'll be fine."

When Dylan walked back down the drive and climbed in the Morgan, it was with a heavy heart. So much tragedy—and why? Because Elliott was gay. It was the twenty-first century, not the dark ages. It was ridiculous that so much pain and loss could stem from something so trivial.

Perhaps Elliott was right. Maybe, after all, he'd share

his talent with young kids and be happy doing it. Dylan wasn't so sure.

But if Elliott's mind was made up, there was nothing he could do to change it.

It was over. It was time to go home.

As he drove into the town, he tried to push it all from his mind, but couldn't. One unimportant, trivial event had ended in tragedy for so many. If Stevie hadn't taken those photos on that fateful night in the Sportsman, none of this would have happened. Stevie wouldn't have been stabbed in his own home, and Dylan wouldn't have returned to Dawson's Clough. If he'd stayed in London, he wouldn't have heard about Gemma. Jeremy Brent would be standing for election to government rather than rotting in a custody cell awaiting trial. Thinking about it though, that probably wasn't such a bad thing. But Ruby wouldn't have blackmailed Elliott over those photos and Jo wouldn't have felt the need to protect her brother.

If only Stevie had gone to a different pub that night. If only he'd left his camera at home…

Dylan glanced in the rear-view mirror and saw the hills surrounding Dawson's Clough receding. He wondered if he'd ever see those hills again.

It didn't matter. It was time to go home.

\* \* \* \* \*

## About the Author

Shirley was born and raised in the Cotswolds, where her headmaster wrote on her school report—*Shirley is content to dream her life away.*

Years later—as an adult living in Cyprus—it dawned on her that this wasn't necessarily a bad thing and that fellow dreamers, in the guise of fiction writers, had been getting away with it for centuries.

A move to the Orkney island of Hoy followed and, during the twelve years she spent there, she wrote short stories as well as full-length romantic fiction for UK women's magazines.

She's now settled in Lancashire, where the Pennines provide the inspiration and setting for her popular mystery novels. She and her husband share their home with an ever-changing selection of deranged pets, who often insist on cameo roles in Shirley's novels.

When she isn't writing, Shirley loves reading (anything and everything), listening to live music, watching TV, eating chocolate and drinking whisky—though not necessarily at the same time. She's also a season ticket holder at Burnley Football Club and can often be seen in the biting wind and pouring rain cheering on her favourite team.

And she's still content to dream her life away.